Book One | F

THE NIGHT THE STARS FELL

AMBER D. LEWIS

Thank you &
Happy Reading!

Amber D Lewis

Copyright © 2021 by Amber D. Lewis

All rights reserved.

No part of this book may be reproduced in any form or by any electronic or mechanical means, including information storage and retrieval systems, without written permission from the author, except for the use of brief quotations in a book review.

This book is a work of fiction. All persons, places, events, and names are creations of the author's imagination and any resemblance to real people, living or dead, or existing situations is coincidental.

Editor: Andi L. Gregory

Back Cover Art and Map Design: Ben Lewis

ISBN 978-1-7370541-0-8 (Print Paperback)

ISBN 978-1-7370541-1-5 (ebook)

For Business Inquires visit www.amberdlewis.com or write to 4359 Wade Hampton Blvd, #282, Taylors, SC 29687

❀ Created with Vellum

CONTENT WARNING

**This book contains mentions of suicide and abuse. For more detailed information, please see the Content Warning Information page at the end of the book following the acknowledgments or visit https://www.amberdlewis.com/content-warnings.

Dedicated to my dad. I miss you and I know you would have been proud.

Ascaria

Embervein

Athiedor

Hollowcreek

rineshore

Oyrain

Gleddon

Character
Pronunciation Guide

Aine:	än-yā (Awn-yay)
Alak:	æl-ik (Al-ick)
Arcanis:	ar-kā-nis (Ar-kay-nis)
Astra:	æs-truh (Ash-truh)
Betron:	be-tron (Beh-tron)
Bram:	bræm (Bram)
Cadewynn:	kad-u-win (Kad-uh-win)
Caitlyn:	kāt-lin (Kate-lin)
Cal:	kæl (Kal)
Ehren:	eh-ruhn (Air-un)
Felixe:	fē-liks (Fee-licks)
Fionn:	fin (Fin)
Ian:	ē-uhn (Ee-un)
Kato:	kā-tō (Kay-toe)
Kayleigh:	kā-lē (Kay-lee)
Makin:	Māk-in (Make-in)
Mara:	mär-uh (Mar-uh)
Niall:	nī-el (Nile)
Pax:	pæks (Paks)

Kingdom
Pronunciation Guide

Ascaria: æs-kâr-rē-u
     (Ass-scare-ree-uh)

Athiedor: æ-thē-u-dōr
     (A-thee-uh-door)

Callenia: ku-lin-ē-u
     (Kuh-len-ee-uh)

Gleador: glē-u-dōr
     (Glee-uh-door)

Hundan: hun-dun
     (Hun-done)

Naskein: næs-kēn
     (Nas-keen)

Portia: pōr-šu
     (Pour-shuh)

PROLOGUE

*M*y name is Astra Downs, and in three days I may destroy the world.

I'm a twin, which might seem insignificant, but, in reality, very little about my existence is insignificant. After all, my brother Kato and I are the only twins ever born in our kingdom. Some say we're blessed while others claim we're cursed. I believe we are both.

The night we were born quite literally shook the foundations of Timberborn, the village we call home. But the earthquake was only one thing that marked that night as unique. Not only was it the final night of celebration for the annual Kriloa festival, but also the night the stars poured down, streaking across the night sky. That night set everything into motion, fulfilling prophecies we never even knew existed. The plans of the gods were at play.

Now, Kato and I alone bear the secret of a power prowling beneath our skin. It's volatile and growing in strength. When we turn eighteen I have no doubt this power will break free, bringing with it destruction.

Perhaps I'm overreacting, overthinking. After all, magic has been dead for centuries. How can I possibly know that some power dwells inside me? The truth is I don't know anything for sure, but I know *something* isn't right. I am a scholar, and I've studied everything given to me in search of an answer. Of course, my village is small and my resources limited, but I know that my brother and I are different from everyone else.

From the moment we were able to form coherent thoughts, we could communicate with one another, no matter the distance between us. Through Kato's eyes I could sense the strength he had when training to become a village soldier, and I begged him to teach me. In return, he wanted to learn more about reading and writing than the basics offered to boys with his skill. In secret, he trained me in the art of weapons best suited for my small form, and I shared with him all I learned. In many ways, it felt like we were one mind and soul with two hearts.

At a glance, we look very different. Kato is gifted with dark hair, black and shiny as raven wings, that spills off his head in loose, uncontrollable, shoulder-length curls. He has broad shoulders and naturally tan skin like our father and strong, handsome features that most envy. Even as a small child he towered over most our age and now stands a full head taller than many full-grown men. I, on the other hand, am the stark opposite—small and dainty to the point of looking almost frail with pale, porcelain skin and sharp yet feminine features. It doesn't help that my hair is whiter than freshly fallen snow. And, while I am not uncommonly short, I am shorter than the majority of the other village girls my age. The only thing Kato and I have in common when it comes to appearance is our eyes —a perfect shade of amethyst.

From a very young age we felt a keen restlessness, more so than other children in Timberborn. It couldn't be satiated with sword drills or tomes. Whenever we felt traces of our power, we spoke of them to only each other and never aloud, only ever speaking in our minds, communicating in the way that only we could. It was far beyond our understanding and knowledge, so we chose to bury it. Hide it. Ignore it. All in the hopes we were imagining it and it would someday fade.

In three days we turn eighteen. Our power has been growing inside us, biding time. It's getting stronger, making it harder to ignore, to push down. While I have no proof, no precedent, I know that in three days, it will finally be revealed. Once we turn eighteen, there will be no going back. There will be no more hiding. I just hope we, along with everyone we love, make it out alive.

Part One:

Kriloa

CHAPTER ONE

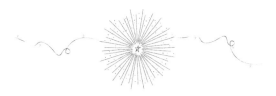

The streets already buzz with merchants selling their wares for Kriloa, even though the festival doesn't officially begin until sundown. Kriloa is considered a celebration of life and being; therefore, everyone wants to be a part. From where the festival originates, no one knows for sure. It is one of those things that is simply ingrained in our culture and has always been celebrated for as long as anyone can remember. The festival starts on the first night of the spring solstice, ending three nights later when the night finally gives way to dawn.

Workers gather in the center of town, preparing the large bonfire that will burn all three nights as the center of most of the activity. Smaller fires will burn throughout the village and along the outskirts with more personal gatherings, but any fire will be welcome to anyone.

The first night is marked with performances galore. Some of the performers are practiced and planned while others are impromptu. I glance toward an array of brightly colored carnival carts not far from the bonfire and wonder who waits inside, ready to perform in the hopes of gathering coins from those drinking more heavily than usual. A voice calls my name from behind and I turn to see a girl my age with wavy brown hair and bright hazel eyes rushing toward me.

"Astra," she calls. "Please tell me you've gotten your nose out of your books enough to have heard the latest news!" She rushes up to me almost breathless, her eyes shining.

"Heard what, Mara? Were you spying on your father's business again? Do we have a new export? Something fun?" I ask with enthusiasm.

Mara rolls her eyes. "I don't spy on my father. Sometimes I just accidentally overhear things."

"Or, perhaps, you've found an amazing present for my birthday? Is my present the new, fun export? Have you finally gotten me a pony?"

"When have I ever *not* given you the best present? But no. The prince is coming to one of the festival nights!" She links her arm through mine, guiding me toward the center of the square to examine the tents and carts.

"What prince?" I ask, scowling.

Timberborn is a wonderful place to live, but we are little more than a small village that serves as a stopping point for occasional merchants traveling throughout the kingdom. We have nothing of real interest to attract a prince or any other sort of nobility. We barely attract these merchants.

"*The* prince, of course! Prince Ehren? The crown prince of Callenia? Surely you know what prince." Her whole face glows. "Anyway, he was on an official mission in Bugharion and won't be able to make it back to the capital for the royal Kriloa festival."

"So he's coming here? To Timberborn?" Mara nods and my scowl deepens. "But why? There are dozens of cities more suitable along the border between us and Bugharion. Why would he come here?"

Mara shrugs. "I'm not entirely sure and, quite frankly, I don't care if it means I might get to meet the prince. All I know is that my father received word to prepare for the arrival of Prince Ehren and his entourage of guards. Oh! What do you suppose is in that tent?" She breaks off from me and wanders toward a bright red tent with a rainbow of ribbons above the door.

I follow her and send a quick message to my brother through our twin bond. *Kato, have you heard news about the crown prince coming?*

A few moments of silence pass before his voice echoes through my head. *Yes. We just received word to prepare extra sentries and guards for the festivities once he arrives.*

Why didn't you tell me?

Commander Jetson literally just informed me. Besides, when did you care about the movements of royalty? Do you even know the prince's name?

Yes. Of course I know his name. I don't live in a cave, Kato.

Fine. What's his name?

Ehren.

A pause. *Mara told you. I was going to ask how you knew the prince was coming, but that would explain everything.*

"Astra?" Mara's voice breaks into the conversation. "Are you all right? You look distant."

I force a smile and nod. Even as close as Mara and I are, I've never told her of my twin bond with Kato. It's too personal. Kato, likewise, has never told anyone either, including his closest friend, Pax. Yet talking to him in my head seems so normal I often forget my surroundings.

"I was just looking at that cart over there," I cover, pointing randomly, my finger inadvertently landing on a worn, wooden cart with blue chipping paint. "Is that the man who performed the fire dances last year?"

Mara squints. "I don't remember what his cart looked like but he was one of the most talented fire dancers. I hope he's back this year."

We turn and weave our way through the carts. I see my youngest brother, Broderick, weaving through the carts opposite me, heading my direction. His face is red and his hair is sweaty, as if he ran all the way from the house.

"Astra!" he yells, breathing hard as he approaches. "I've been looking for you everywhere!"

"Why? What is it?" I scan his face, worried. "Is something wrong?"

"Father's home."

Despite the warmth of the day, a chill rushes down my spine. Our father is a merchant who deals in forbidden or questionable goods and rarely makes it home due to his constant traveling. When he is home, he often stays drunk which, in turn, makes him cruel. He hates the fact that I was born before my brother, making his eldest child a girl. If there hadn't been so many witnesses to our twin birth, it's more than likely he would have just gotten rid of me shortly after birth and claimed my brother as the only child born that night. I avoid him as much as possible.

"What does he want?"

Broderick opens his mouth to answer, but closes it again, shaking his head. "I don't think I'm supposed to say. He just wants you home as soon as possible."

I turn back to Mara, but I don't need to say anything. Sad understanding shines in her eyes. "Go. I'll see you later tonight?"

I nod and force a smile. "I'd never miss a night of the festival."

I turn and quickly follow Broderick as he weaves back through the gathering crowd toward our home at the opposite end of the village. I try to push down my concern and panic as I reach out to Kato.

Father's home.

What? I thought he was supposed to be gone for several more weeks. A month at least.

Broderick disappears behind a wagon, no doubt taking some shortcut to get home as quickly as possible. I try to follow him, unwilling to give Father any excuse to take out his frustrations on me.

Well, regardless, he's home now. Rick found me in the square with Mara and told me I'd been ordered home.

I don't like that he's home so early. I'll wrap up what I'm doing and get home immediately.

You don't have to leave training on account of me. Don't get yourself in trouble.

I won't leave you alone to deal with him, Ash. We're basically done for the day, anyway. It is a holiday, you know.

Thank you.

I'm about to add more, but a nearby worker slips from his unsteady stool, the banner in his hand flying toward me. I duck out of the way in time to avoid injury, but stumble hard into a bystander, pulling him down with me as I fall.

"Oh! I'm so sorry," I say, scrambling up. "I wasn't paying enough attention to my surroundings."

I turn to the man I just knocked to the ground. He stands, brushing himself off, scowling. He's a little older than me with dark brown hair and eyes. His face is marred only by a small, almost imperceptible scar on his left cheekbone. His clothes, despite being a simple white shirt and dark blue pants, look slightly nicer than what the average villager might wear, indicating he has a specific reason for visiting our town.

"It is quite all right," he mumbles, glaring down at the dirt now smeared across the front of his white shirt. "I don't believe it was entirely your fault." He looks up me and forces a smile. "I suppose if one must be knocked into the dirt, a lovely girl is not the worst way to go down."

Heat rises in my cheeks, but I manage a smile. "Most people prefer not to be knocked down at all."

"I suppose." He grins. "Are you from this village?"

I nod. "I am, but I take it from your question that you aren't? Are you one of the performers?"

His eyebrows shoot up. "Do I look like a performer?"

My cheeks grow redder. "I don't suppose so, but is there any one look for a performer?" I gesture to the many people shuffling around us.

He shrugs, his smile genuine. "I suppose not. But, no, I am not one of the performers. Just someone passing through. I am from another village, much like this one, and I thought it might be fun to enjoy the festival before continuing on my way. I am hoping to get a room at the inn, if your town has one."

It's only then I notice the bag at his feet.

"We have a couple of inns, just down that way," I reply, pointing in the opposite direction. "I would show you the way, but I'm afraid I'm expected at home. You can't miss them, though. They're right off the main road. The Briar Hog is the better of the two, if you can get a room there."

"Thank you. I appreciate your help." He reaches down and grabs his bag as I turn to resume my path home.

"Will I see you tonight around the bonfire?" he calls out to me.

I glance over my shoulder but keep walking. "Perhaps."

He smiles and I can feel his eyes on my back as I turn my focus ahead. If I didn't have other concerns weighing on my mind, I would smile.

Our little house is nestled among others toward the end of town opposite from most places of business. It's a simple dwelling made mostly from split logs. The doorway and windows are open, save for a large cloth serving as a door and some basic curtains over the windows. Today, it's warm enough that those cloths have been tied back to let air circulate through the house.

Despite running the last few yards to our house, Broderick beat me home by several minutes. He sits outside with my younger sister Tabitha drawing in the dirt with a stick. They both pause in their play and look up at me as I approach, their faces etched with worry too deep for their young faces. I give them a weak smile before ducking through the doorway into the house.

The small main room of the house is filled with the smell of cooking spices, bread, and meat. Most people will eat small dinners tonight and then eat specially prepared treats and breads around the bonfire, but Father must have insisted on a full meal. My mother and eleven-year-old sister, Beka, are busy in the corner of the room cooking that dinner. My father sits at the table in the center of the room with a man I've never seen before. I force myself to focus on my father as he rises from the table, an unsettling grin on his face.

"My beloved daughter, Astra!" he says, placing his hands on my shoulders and kissing my cheek with forced affection. My initial reaction is to jerk away, but I smell mead on his breath and know better than to fight against him. "Come! Meet our guest!"

He ushers me toward the table and gestures to the strange man. The man is younger than my father but older than me by at least ten years. He isn't what most people would consider handsome, but he's not entirely horrible to look at. He has rough, hewn features with dark, curly hair and a matching beard. His thick eyebrows knit into a scowl as his dark eyes scrutinize me.

"This is Marco," my father says proudly.

I manage a small nod and force a smile. "Pleased to meet you, Marco. Welcome to our home."

He grunts in response and then looks at my father. "This is your eldest daughter?" There's something akin to disgust in his voice. "She's a waif! And it looks as if her skin's never seen sunlight."

"Now, now," my father counters, taking his seat next to Marco at the table. "She may be on the more . . . petite side and a bit pale, but she is hardy and has enough skills to make you a decent wife. I swear by it. She does carry my blood, after all." He chuckles to himself.

"Wife?" I choke out, the color draining from my face.

My father glares over his shoulder at me, narrowing his eyes, daring me to defy him.

"Yes. Wife. Marco needs a wife, and you'll be of marrying age in just three days. It's a perfect match."

He follows his declaration by gulping mead from his nearby mug. I swallow hard and fight the urge to run or cry. I'm determined not to let him see my fear. I glance toward my mother, but she purposely has her back turned as she prepares dinner.

"But, Father—"

"Now is not the time for discussion," my father cuts me off with a dismissive wave, not even bothering to face me. "Go help your mother and sister finish dinner. Prove to my good friend that you do indeed have some worth."

Fighting tears, I make my way to the corner of the room. My mother avoids eye contact as she hands me vegetables to chop and then turns away to go back to whatever she was doing. My sister, at least, is kind enough to shoot me an occasional glance of sympathy. For a few minutes we work in silence while Father and Marco talk in low voices at the table, gulping mead from their cups.

"I'm home!"

I spin to see Kato waltzing through the door, a smile on his face and his arms spread wide.

"Father! You're back!" he says, acting perfectly surprised. "I didn't think we were to expect you for some time yet!"

Father rises and pulls Kato into a back-slapping hug. "Ah, the Southern winds carried me home early! Come, come! Meet our guest!"

Kato eyes Marco, who stands and reaches out his hand to shake Kato's. Kato is a good head taller than Marco with a more muscular build. I'm pleased to see how noticeably uncomfortable Kato makes him.

"And who's this?" he asks as he firmly grips Marco's hand.

My husband-to-be.

Kato's eyes widen and the shock registers on his face for a fraction of a second before he schools his features, looking to our father for his response.

"Marco is an exporter based out of . . . well, I best not say. Security reasons, you understand." Father chuckles like he's just told a masterful joke. "But he does well for himself. He will make an excellent match for your sister. He plans to marry her once she turns eighteen."

Kato surveys Marco with a cold stare that would make a wiser man shrink away in fear. Out loud to Marco he says, "Well, I'll need to get to know you better then, I suppose!" To me he says, *No way in hell, Ash. I'll talk to Father. I'll find a way out.*

I release a sigh and go back to the dinner preparations. Within the hour we're seated around the table, eating our meal. Father and Marco entertain us with stories from the road, the majority of which are laced with illegal activities, loose women, alcohol, and a lot of swearing. Father makes it clear throughout the meal that I'm expected to keep both his and Marco's cups full of mead and I do my best. The more Marco speaks the more I grow to hate him.

CHAPTER TWO

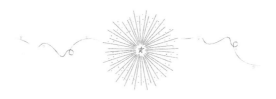

*B*y the time dinner ends, darkness has started to fall. Kato glances out the nearest window and grins as he pushes up from the table.

"Well, now, if you would be so kind as to excuse us, Astra and I need to attend Kriloa."

My father scowls. "Don't you think Astra should stay and get to know our guest some more?"

I shudder. His words are more a challenge than a question. One, that if answered incorrectly, could mean consequences.

Kato forces one of his most charming smiles. "Come, Father, we always celebrate Kriloa together. If Astra is married off, next year I may not see her. Consider this a birthday present. After all, we'll only turn eighteen together once."

Marco glances from Kato to me and to my father, a confused scowl on his face. Suddenly, his eyes grow wide and he shoots to his feet. "What? Twins? You didn't tell me she was the twin!" He shakes his fist at my father. "You have tried to trick me, Baffa!"

I wince. All my life I've been treated as an oddity. While I have drawn a few glances from the village boys, most see me as little more than a curiosity to be explored.

"Now, now," my father says, rising and holding up his hands defensively. "She is a twin but she'll still make a fine wife."

"Everyone knows that twins are cursed! That's why the gods have forbidden them to be born! They have put a curse upon your family!" He makes a religious sign with his hands that seems oddly out of place for his character.

Come, Astra. While they're distracted.

I glance back at my brother. His worried eyes lock with mine and he motions his head ever so slightly toward the door.

Come.

I nod and quietly slide away from the table as my father flies into a full argument with Marco. Kato grabs my hand and pulls me out the door into the night before they can notice I've risen from the table. We hurry along the street, drawn toward the main square by the glow of the bonfire, the smells of festival food, and the cacophony of joyous sounds. Neither of us speak until we are safely away from the house, nearing the throngs of celebrating people.

"Never. I will never let that man marry you and take you away," Kato says, stopping to look down at me.

I look up at him and let the tears I've been holding in for the last hour break free. "It seems the deal has already been struck."

My brother's lips tighten into a firm line, and he shakes his head with determination as he takes both my hands in his own, pulling me to face him. "No, Astra. I don't care what bargain father has made or, more likely, what debt he's trying to get out of, but I won't let some stranger with no regard for the law whisk you away. I will kill him with my bare hands if I need to. Do you understand?"

I smile weakly and nod, wiping away my tears with the back of my hand.

"Good." He pulls me to his side in a quick hug. "Now, let's get to this festival. What are the chances a few girls have had enough mead to find me charming and be willing to sneak off for a few kisses?"

I laugh. Truth be told, most girls in our village have their eye on Kato, mead or no mead. "You mean, you wonder if Mara has had enough."

Kato chuckles. "One day she will see my charms!"

"Speaking of charms, what do you know about the visit from the prince?"

"Not much. Just that he's arriving sometime tomorrow, and we're to be on alert and ready to aid as needed."

"But why is he coming? It doesn't make sense. He's never bothered with our village before. Why now? Surely he could find much better celebrations elsewhere."

Kato shrugs. "No idea. Pax heard that the prince is looking for a commoner wife."

"What? Why? Daughters of nobles can't be that bad to look at."

Kato laughs. "I hardly doubt that's the true cause. However, if it's even remotely true, I'm sure the prince has his reasons for wanting a commoner wife. Pax isn't necessarily the most reliable when it comes to information."

We reach the edge of the main celebration, and Kato pauses to scan the crowd.

"What do you want to see first?"

I shrug and grin. "All of it. Let's just make our way through."

Kato nods and we wend our way through the people, watching the performances. Little pockets of performers are woven throughout the crowd, each with their own audience.

Kato seems particularly enthralled with a small group of scantily clad belly dancers and wants to linger longer than I do.

"I'm going to go find some fried snacks," I yell to him over the crowd. He nods but keeps his focus on the dancers. I roll my eyes and follow my nose to a small booth selling an assortment of delicious fried doughs covered in a variety of spices and sugars. I've just settled on a delectable piece covered in pink sugar and twisted into the shape of a heart when a hand reaches in front of me and plops coins down for the vendor.

"Allow me," says a smooth voice. I turn to find the man from earlier standing behind me. "And I will take one as well."

The vendor nods, handing us each our treats and slipping the money in a little pouch. We step out of the way for the next customer.

"You didn't need to do that," I protest before taking a bite of my heart.

"Perhaps. But you did guide me to the best inn in town, so, then again, perhaps I owe you." He offers me a soft smile. "I never got your name."

I swallow my food quickly and answer. "Astra."

"Astra," he muses. My name sounds different on his lips. Different in a way that makes my cheeks feel suddenly warm. "A lovely name."

"And your name? Is it lovely as well?" I say before I can think of a better response. I immediately regret my words, but he chuckles, putting me at ease.

"Not quite as lovely as yours. You may call me Bram."

"Bram," I mumble. "I like it."

"I am glad my name pleases you," he says, grinning as he takes a bite of his heart. "Mmm. This is quite excellent."

"Mm hm," I agree, taking a bite of my own. "The food is one of my favorite things about festivals."

He nods his agreement as we stop to watch a performer

juggling with fire. We both watch in silence for a few moments as we finish our fried dough hearts. When we're done, he looks down at me as I lick sugar from my fingers in a very unladylike manner.

"Perhaps you could show me where to go for the best drinks."

"Um, sure." I stand on my tiptoes and look through the crowd, but it does little good. It's times like these when I hate being so short. "The Mastons make the best honey mead, if you like that sort of thing. They usually have booth set up in the northwest corner."

"Excellent. You have yet to lead me astray. Show me the way," he says, gesturing with his hand for me to take the lead.

We begin once again weaving through the crowd toward the Mastons' small booth near the edge of the main crowd. We get distracted several times by various performers along the way. As we finally near the booth, Mara cuts us off.

"There you are! I've been looking for you for a good thirty minutes! I heard that—" She stops suddenly, realizing I'm not alone. She eyes Bram and arches an eyebrow as if to ask, *And who is this?*

"Oh, uh, Mara this is Bram," I say, with an awkward motion to the man at my side. "And Bram, this is Mara."

Bram inclines his head toward her. "It is a pleasure to meet you, Mara."

"What brings you to Timberborn?" she asks with a smile bordering on flirtatious.

"Business, mostly."

"Oh! How nice that business brought you here during Kriloa! Our town may be small, but we can celebrate with the best of them. I don't know how exactly they celebrate in the big cities but I can't imagine them outshining us by much! Are you from a village like ours or from one of the larger cities?"

Sometimes I envy how easygoing Mara can be with people, especially complete strangers. She always seems to know what to say. I can barely string together coherent thoughts half the time, let alone make pleasant conversation.

"I am from a small village much like this one further north, but business has brought me into more cities in recent years," Bram replies with an offhand shrug.

"The best of both worlds!" Mara laughs.

"I was just about to introduce him to the Mastons' honey mead," I cut in, selfishly wanting to draw Bram's attention back to me.

"Oh, yes! You must try their mead! My father is the head of the merchant guild here in our village. Really, he oversees everything, and their honey mead is one of our most sought-after exports!"

She begins leading the way toward the booth, linking her arm with mine.

Where are you? Kato's voice echoes in my head as Mara rambles on about exports, imports, and mead.

Done with the half-naked girls, are you?

For now. I can hear the smile in his voice. *But I may need to check on them again later.*

I'm sure you do. I'm getting honey mead with Mara and . . . um, at the Mastons' booth.

Who's "um"?

No one.

Astra, are you trying to seduce one of the performers? A juggler perhaps? Don't settle for anyone less than a fire juggler.

Gods, no. Just—just come meet us. I roll my eyes.

Fine. Be there in a minute.

I sigh and focus on what Mara's saying as we take our place in line.

"Of course, he's been busy of late in preparations for the visit from the crown prince."

Bram, who's been casually listening at best, suddenly sharpens his gaze on Mara. "The crown prince? What is this about a possible visit? What have you heard?" His voice is harsh and sharp. Mara seems unusually rattled.

"Um, not much. Honestly. My father just received word he was to visit."

"When?" Bram's gaze is intense and the air around us suddenly feels thin.

Mara backs away a half-step. "I—I don't know. Not really."

"You know nothing of when he is to arrive or leave or where he will be staying?"

"No," Mara gulps.

"And even if she did, why would she tell you?" Bram's gaze snaps to me, the intensity slowly leaving his eyes as I add, "She did only meet you a few seconds ago."

Bram lets out a long sigh and nods, running a hand though his hair. "You are right. I am quite sorry. I did not mean . . . I am sorry if I sounded rude." The line moves forward, making it our turn to order.

"What can I get for you tonight?" a bubbly, pink-cheeked Mrs. Maston asks.

Bram turns to face her, a winning smile replacing his scowl. "Three honey meads, if you please."

"Better make it four," I add. "My brother will join us soon."

Bram's smile widens as he gives me a wink. "Four then."

Mrs. Maston nods and busies herself filling four tankards with mead. Bram turns back to Mara, his expression much softer.

"I sincerely apologize if I seemed . . . intense. I am afraid it has always been one of my shortcomings. Growing up, my siblings never ceased to let me forget it."

Mara offers him a small smile, but I can tell she's still a little flustered. "It's all right. We all have our faults. I tend to babble endlessly sometimes."

Mrs. Maston places the four full tankards on the counter of the booth and Bram pays her. I grab up one for me and one for Kato while Bram and Mara grab theirs. Bram takes a sip as we step out of line.

"This is quite excellent." He glances at Mara. "I can indeed see why it would be one of your main exports."

Mara begins to respond but is distracted by Kato emerging from the crowd. I wave him over. He smiles shyly at Mara before sliding his eyes to Bram. I'm used to Kato being the tallest in the crowd and am surprised that Kato and Bram are almost perfectly eye to eye.

"Bram, this is my brother, Kato."

Bram offers his hand and Kato gives it a hearty shake. "Pleased to meet you, Kato."

"And you. How do you know my sister, if I may be so bold to ask?"

Kato!

Tall handsome strangers get vetted by twin brothers. I don't make the rules, Ash. I just follow them.

You most certainly do *make the rules.*

I roll my eyes while Kato continues grinning. Bram, however, doesn't seem startled or put off by Kato's somewhat rude question.

"We met earlier when she knocked me over."

Bram glances toward me, eyes twinkling, and I feel slightly mortified.

"Yes, that sounds like my sister," Kato laughs, earning a glare from me. "And, now, I suppose she's indebted to you and must show you around to make up for her clumsiness?"

"On the contrary. She directed me to a pleasant little inn,

and I have found her judgment to be quite excellent. I am actually quite lucky she has agreed to put up with me."

Kato laughs again. "If you say so! However, if you'll trust *my* judgment, I saw a performance on the way over here that seems worth checking out."

"Oh! What is it?" Mara asks, eagerly.

"He's a magician, but not the boring kind with predictable tricks. I'm pretty sure this guy is using actual magic."

"Magic died out over a century ago, Kato," I mutter, rolling my eyes.

Kato shrugs. "Believe what you will, but you really should check him out with me." He glances between the three of us. "What do you say?"

Kato has the energetic eagerness of a puppy, making it hard to say no. As we sip our mead, he leads the way to the bright red tent with rainbow ribbons that attracted my attention earlier. Standing just outside the tent is a handsome young man with high cheekbones, shocking emerald green eyes, and almost unnatural red hair pulled back with a thick black leather strap. He's dressed in a pair of black pants striped with silver, with a matching jacket over a slate blue shirt. A couple yards away, Bram freezes, his jaw set and his eyes cold. His eyes are locked on the performer, barely concealed rage flashing in his eyes as he clenches his fists by his sides. I furrow my brow in confusion, and his gaze falls to me. He forces a tight smile, but I can sense something has shifted.

"Actually, I think I may head back to my room at the inn for a bit of rest. I traveled most of the day, and I am afraid my journey is catching up with me," he speaks to us but his eyes drift back to the performer. After a moment, he tears his gaze away and looks down at me. "Hopefully, we will meet again tomorrow?"

I smile softly, nodding. "I would very much like that."

"Excellent! Well, a good night to you all," he says, glancing to each of us with a nod before he makes his way back toward the inn, disappearing into the crowd.

Well, he was a little odd.

I don't think so. I pause. *Was he odd?*

Kato laughs out loud. Mara doesn't even seem to notice, she's so entranced by the performance.

Well, he wasn't what I would call "normal," Ash. But he did seem like a good guy. Better than that Marco guy for sure.

My heart sinks. Somehow in the last hour or so I'd managed to forget about the horrible man sitting in my home, waiting to drag me away to gods know where to be his wife. Kato notices the shadow cross my face. He reaches an arm around me and draws me close.

Don't worry, Ash. We'll figure it out. I promise. For now, just enjoy the show. After all, it's not every day you get to witness real magic.

I laugh and Kato grins. Mara glances back at us. "What are you laughing at?"

"Nothing," we say together. She eyes us suspiciously before turning back to watch the performer.

I lean into the safety of my brother's arms and watch the magic tricks. And, I have to admit, they truly seem like real magic.

CHAPTER THREE

I stand in the center of an empty village square. It's night but not a single home or shop has a light lit. I look up at the sky and even it's pitch black and empty of stars or the moon. My pulse quickens. I spin around, searching desperately for anyone.

"Hello?" I call out, my voice echoing in the void. "Is anyone here? Kato? Mara? Anyone?"

Nothing but my own voice answers.

I reach out in my mind to Kato, but for the first time in our lives he isn't there. I panic and take off running, searching desperately. There has to be someone here. There must be a way out. But there's not. It's a village maze with no end and no help.

"Hello!" I yell. "Somebody! Anybody!"

Suddenly, there's whisper; a voice so faint that I wouldn't be able to hear it had I been surrounded by more than silence. A voice far from human. A voice that sends chills crawling across my skin.

"I am with you," it whispers. I whip around, looking for the source of the voice. The village is still empty. "I am always with you. I will never leave you alone."

I realize with a start that the voice is coming from inside me. I stare down at my chest in horror as it begins to glow. I scream as light bursts from my body and I fade into nothingness, taking everything else with me.

I wake, breathing hard, my blanket and pillow soaked with sweat. My heart still pounds in my chest. I take a deep, shuddering breath in an attempt to clear my head. It was just a dream. Another dream. The closer I get to turning eighteen, the worse the dreams are getting. It's harder to shake the feeling that these dreams aren't real experiences.

I turn over on my cot and glance across the small loft room I share with my siblings, looking to where Kato sleeps. It takes my eyes a moment to adjust to the dark, but once they do, I see Kato's cot is vacant. I don't even need to call out to him to know where he is. I slip off my own cot and sneak across the room, stepping carefully over my sleeping siblings, to the solitary window at the end of the loft. I pull myself through the window onto the roof and find Kato sitting on the edge, staring down into the quiet village below. I pick my way across the roof and settle beside him, leaning on his arm.

"Nightmare?"

I nod. He wraps his arm around me. "Me too."

What do they mean, Ash? This power, what is it? Even in the solitude of the night he doesn't dare to speak aloud. I don't either.

I don't know, but I'm terrified.

You've never read of anything like it in all your studies? We can't be the first. We can't be the only ones.

I've looked, but I haven't found anything. Nothing definitive, anyway. In the days before, when magic reigned, many people had powers, but if they had dreams beyond recorded prophecies, they didn't make note. At least not public notes. I don't know if their powers unlocked at a certain age or an event. My resources here are limited, and even with everything I have discovered, I've never found any other mention of twins.

He sighs. *I'm scared, Ash. Scared of what this power means. Scared of it consuming me. But mostly, I'm scared I'll lose you.*

I pull away from his side enough to look up into his face. The moonlight is bright enough I can see tears shimmering in his eyes, slowly falling down his cheeks. I reach up and wipe them away with my thumb.

"None of that," I whisper. "We'll have each other until the end of time."

He smiles softly and then stares straight ahead. *But what if the end of time happens in three—well two—days?*

At least we've had a great eighteen years.

He pulls me close in a tight hug and murmurs, "We should probably get some sleep."

I nod. He stands and offers me his hand. I take it and rise with a long sigh. We make our way back inside, hoping that the nightmares will stay away.

WHEN I WAKE a couple of hours later, dawn is just beginning to break. Rick, Tabitha, and Beka are still out cold but Kato, with his soldier's instinct and schedule, has already risen for the day. I creep from bed and quietly dress, braiding my hair before sneaking down the ladder to the main part of the house. Mama is busy in the kitchen already, preparing bread for the day. I hear my father's snores from their bedroom. Marco lies passed out on a cot in the corner of the room, mouth open but no snores coming out, just excessive drool. The sight of him fills me with renewed disgust, and my stomach turns. I cross over to my mother.

"Here," she says quietly, handing me a ball of dough, avoiding eye contact. "Knead."

Silently, I obey. I fall into the pleasant rhythm of kneading the bread, refusing to think about the strange man in the corner or the nightmares haunting the corners of my mind.

"I tried to talk him out of it," my mother mutters at last, breaking the heavy silence between us. "He won't budge." I concentrate on the bread. My mother continues, tears edging her voice. "Your father, he says he owes Marco a great debt. One that, if it were collected, would drive us beyond the help of the poor house." Her hands cease kneading. I don't need to look up at her to know she's crying. "I don't know what to do. I don't want you to marry that gods awful man, but, Astra, I don't think your father will leave us any other choice."

I force myself to look up into her eyes, my own brimmed with tears. "Mama, I won't marry him. I can't."

She studies me long and hard for a moment before continuing, softly but sternly. "My child, I want nothing more in life than to see you happy and well. I want that for all my children. But a marriage does not make or break you. You are strong. If you must go through with this, if we find no other way, you will survive. If I can survive my marriage, then you can survive this match."

She turns back to her bread, pounding it with her fist with more force than necessary before placing it in a bowl. I just stare at her, allowing her words to sink in. I have long suspected there is no love in my parents' marriage but a piece of me has always assumed at one point there had been. I've had to bear witness to their loveless match. I've seen firsthand how miserable it can be. I don't want that and I can't believe my mother would force it on me, given her own experience.

"I need to go into town today," I say abruptly, needing an excuse to get away before I say something I'll regret. "I made promises to Mara. I may not be back until dinner."

My mother says nothing as I walk out of the house.

THERE'S something beautiful and peaceful about walking through the village at early dawn. Most households are beginning to rise and prepare for the day, but they remain inside their houses, leaving the streets empty. With today being another holiday, many people will sleep in, especially after being up all hours of the night last night. Kato and I returned home around midnight, but the festival had still been going strong.

As I stroll into the main part of town, the ash from the smoldering bonfire drifts on the wind, mixing with the smell of bread baking and breakfast cooking. I find myself wandering toward the center of the square, looking down into the glowing embers that remain. Soon, workers will begin clearing away the ash from last night to prepare for another bonfire tonight, but, for now, the area is empty. Even many of the caravans that came to town to perform last night have already packed and left, some last night as soon as their performances were done and others early this morning. A few will remain for the entirety of Kriloa, but even those will move to the outskirts of the town within the next hour or so to make room for the celebration tonight. The second night of Kriloa centers on singing and dancing. It would be my favorite night of celebration, if my birthday didn't fall on the third night.

I wend my way through town. To anyone who sees me, I probably look like I'm wandering aimlessly, but my heart knows where I'm going perhaps even before my mind realizes it. The library calls to me. It may be a simple building a little way off the main road, but to me it's my true home.

I push open the door and step inside, breathing in the comforting scents of ink and parchment. The small main room is open, with a few tables and chairs spread around. To the left is a door leading to the classrooms—small, somewhat cramped rooms where dozens of girls usually crowd around long tables learning to read and write, memorizing histories. The classes grow smaller and smaller each year as the girls learn basic skills and move on to "more practical" educational choices. A few girls, like myself, continue on to be scholars and caretakers of the books.

At the back and center of the main room is the door that leads to the historical texts. Unlike the other doors, this one remains locked most of the time. I walk to the door, pulling the key I wear around my neck from its hiding place beneath my dress. I am one of three scholars permitted to have a key. I quietly unlock the door and slide inside. Shelves and shelves of books fill the large room. I've never seen any library beyond our own, but I know that ours is small by comparison. Most of these books are poorly made copies. The only original books these walls contain are journals kept by our village historians. I walk toward those red-bound books. Their spines are labeled with the years and seasons, but I don't need to read them to find the one I seek, the one that calls to me. I pull it from the shelf and turn to the page I've viewed a million times before.

Tonight, the third night of Kriloa commenced as usual. A great feast had been prepared and laid out for the whole village to enjoy. It was, as always, a beautiful night for celebrations. The sky was clear and the weather warm and pleasant.

I scan down the lines of text, skipping over more descriptions of the feast to the part that I'm really looking for—the words I memorized long ago.

In the midst of the celebration, Geneva Downs, wife of merchant Baffa Downs, gave birth. She had a daughter, small and weak, roughly five minutes before midnight. Becca Pavra served as midwife. As with most births, Pavra thought her work done after the daughter was born and began to clean the area. But Geneva began to cry out that she had yet another child to birth. Pavra assumed some sort of madness had set in from the trauma of a long labor and tried her best to soothe the tired mother. Then, upon the insistence of Geneva, Pavra looked between the mother's legs and was surprised to see a second child desperate to be born. Moments before the stroke of midnight, a second child was born to Geneva, this one a strong son. Then, as the baby boy's cries broke through the air, the gods looked down from the heavens and blessed the only twins born in the kingdom of Callenia by sending stars shooting across the night sky while the ground shook with mighty power. The stars did not cease until the sun drove them away. Blessed be the twins, for they shall be our salvation.

I read the passage through twice before placing the journal back on the shelf. I've asked the historian many times why she ended her entry with that line and what it meant. She would only smile and shake her head.

"I write what my soul tells me to write, Astra. If you ever become our historian, you will do the same."

It's the only answer she would ever give. And no matter how many times I ask, beg for more, she always gives me a sad smile, as if she knows I bear some great burden. Now more than ever, I feel that impending burden, fearing what it may be.

As quietly as I arrived, I leave the library, locking the book room behind me. The village is waking, more people spilling into the streets. The smell of fresh bread from the bakery calls to me and makes my stomach growl. I only have a few coins, but they should be enough for a sweet roll or two.

The bakery is mostly empty, save for the baker's teenage daughter, Esme, who sits behind the counter on a stool, leaning forward with her arms crossed on the counter. Today, she shows every mark of a girl who stayed out far too late at the celebrations the night before. She lifts her head and forces a weary smile as I approach the bakery counter.

"Good morning, Astra," she says, pushing herself up from the counter.

"Morning, Esme. Did you enjoy the festival last night?"

She nods, stifling a yawn. "I did. Unfortunately, the part of the holiday where people get to sleep in doesn't apply to baker's daughters, apparently."

She sounds bitter, and I bite back a smile.

"I was at the library myself at dawn," I reply with a knowing nod. I don't bother adding it was of my own volition.

"Well, we all do what's required of us I suppose. What can I get for you this morning?"

I glance down into the bakery case, weighing my options. There are a few basic loaves of plain bread, some crusty white rolls, poppyseed rolls drizzled with honey, sweet rolls sprinkled with sugar, and some sweet buns filled with candied fruit and topped with swirls of icing.

"I think I'll take one of the poppy rolls, if you don't mind." Esme nods and hops off her stool to reach inside the case.

"I will take one of the same," a voice booms behind me.

I jump and spin around. I didn't even notice anyone else

come into the bakery, but there Bram stands, inches away, smiling.

"Bram!" I narrow my eyes playfully. "Are you following me?"

His smile widens as he leans toward Esme. "I will take one of those sweet buns as well."

I glance to Esme, who nods, watching us with interest.

Bram turns his attention back to me.

"It is merely a happy coincidence we meet again so soon. A coincidence with which I am quite pleased."

He smiles and my heart skips a beat.

"Um, will these be paid for together or . . ." Her eyes dart curiously from me to Bram and back again.

I open my mouth to say mine will be separate, but Bram cuts me off, stepping forward with a pouch of coins.

"I'll pay for all three." He winks at me. "It is the least I can do for constantly invading your schedule."

"Bram, no. I can pay for mine," I insist, but he only smiles and ignores me, passing coins to Esme in exchange for the three rolls.

"Have a nice day," Esme says, settling back on her stool.

I give her a parting nod and follow Bram back outside. Esme watches us the entire time.

"You don't have to pay for everything every time you see me," I mutter as he hands me my roll.

"I know. But I don't often get to buy things for lovely girls, so when I see an opportunity, I take it." I feel heat rising in my cheeks. "Shall we go sit somewhere and enjoy our breakfast?"

I sigh and nod, leading the way to a small fountain not far away where we can sit. For the first few moments, we sit in silence, enjoying our food. I'm about to speak when Kato's voice flows into my mind.

How are you doing this morning?

Fine.

Have Father and that man woken up yet?

I'm not sure. I left home a while ago. I'm in town with Bram right now.

Bram? That fellow from last night? The odd one?

He's not odd, Kato!

I sense his laugh. *Whatever you say, Ash.*

Don't you have better things to do than judge the people I talk to? Where are you anyway?

Training. Commander Jetson has us all on high alert in preparation for the prince's arrival. He should be arriving at some point today and we have to be ready. Though I suspect he'll have his own small army with him.

That's likely. I guess you'll be busy most of the day.

Most likely. I'm technically busy now, but I wanted to check in with you. Make sure you're okay.

I'm okay, Kato. I promise.

All right. I love you, Ash.

I love you, too.

I assume the conversation is over but then one more whisper comes through.

And be careful with Bram, Astra. There's something I feel like he's not telling you.

I might have argued but one glance at Bram's face tells me I must have been staring off at nothing for a few moments too long.

"Are you all right?" he asks, his brows knitted in concern.

"Yes. Yes, I'm fine," I mumble, blushing. "I'm just a bit tired and distracted. I'm sorry if that makes me bad company."

He smiles softly. "On the contrary. I cannot imagine better company. I suppose you were out much later than I was, celebrating the festival last night."

I nod. "Yes, it was midnight before my brother and I got back home and I'm afraid I didn't sleep well."

"Worries weighing on your mind? I have been told I am an excellent listener if you care to share your burdens."

I look up into his deep brown eyes. They are kind and caring and there's a sweet earnestness there. I know Kato's warned me to be careful, but something in my gut tells me I can trust Bram, despite having known him for less than a day. But, as much as I ache to tell someone else about the power swirling inside me or my nightmares, mentioning it to anyone besides Kato feels like a betrayal to my twin.

"It's nothing, really," I say, glancing down to the last couple bites of my roll in my hands, my appetite fading.

Bram scowls. "It does not seem like nothing."

"I just . . ." I glance away, looking into the water of the fountain and then back up into Bram's eyes. "My father has found me a husband."

"Oh, I see. And I take it this husband is not someone you would have chosen for yourself?"

I shake my head, glancing away again. "He's too much like my father." Tears threaten to spill but I push them back.

"And when is this wedding to take place?"

I'm sure by this point in the conversation, Bram is less interested in my problems and is merely being polite. I feel I should change the subject to something more amiable, but talking about the marriage seems to relieve some of the pressure weighing on my mind.

"I'm not sure. I've been avoiding my house as much as possible since my father brought the man home. I'm assuming a day or so after I turn eighteen. My father will want the marriage done and over as soon as possible."

"When is that?" His voice is almost unnervingly steady.

"Tomorrow," I sigh, looking back at him. "We turn eighteen tomorrow."

"We?" Bram asks, his eyebrow arching.

"Kato and I. We both turn eighteen tomorrow."

I enjoy watching the surprise flood his face and hold back a laugh.

"You are the twins?"

"Ah, you've heard of us," I tease, but worry tugs at my chest as I wait for his response.

"I believe every person in this kingdom has likely heard of you, though most people assume you're a myth," Bram replies, his eyes twinkling.

I laugh. "I'm definitely not a myth. I'm very much real, as is my brother."

"Forgive me. It is just that you two don't look as much alike as I would have expected twins to look."

"Trust me. I know."

"I am sorry if that sounded rude . . . ," he begins but I cut him off, shaking my head.

"No, no. Not at all. I've heard it my entire life. And it's true. In looks we are about as opposite as we can be."

He studies me for a minute before asking, "What about in spirit? How do you compare?"

I pause, tilting my head as I consider his question. "In spirit, I think . . . we may be the same."

He nods. "Well, I have very much enjoyed your company but I am afraid I have business that requires my attention."

He rises and I stand with him. My heart sinks slightly at the thought of parting already. As awkward as most of our conversation may have been, I'm enjoying his presence. Most new acquaintances balk as soon as they discover I'm a twin. Though surprised, Bram seems to be taking the information in stride.

"Oh, will your business be taking you from town today?" I

ask, secretly hoping he'll be around for a while, though I'm not sure what good it will do me.

"On the contrary. My business actually has me in town for at least a couple more days. Hopefully, I will have the pleasure of seeing you again soon, Astra."

He smiles and looks into my eyes. My heart flutters and my cheeks warm.

"I do hope that's the case," I mumble.

"Until we meet again." He gives a parting nod and begins to walk away. After a few steps, he pauses and turns back. "Fate has intervened in your life before, Astra, when she made you a twin. Perhaps she will intervene again and save you from your impending marriage."

Then, before I can reply or even truly register what he said, he strides away, leaving me and my fluttering heart standing alone by the fountain.

CHAPTER FOUR

*E*ager to avoid going home, I spend my morning wandering around town, peering into shop windows, biding my time until I know Mara will be awake. With Mara's father one of the main men in town, her family's residence is one of the few homes in the main town area, nestled among the businesses. It's much larger than most, with actual doors and windows as opposed to cloths like many of the household dwellings. Once mid-morning arrives, I make my way to her front door and knock. Mara's mother opens the door and greets me with a smile.

"Astra!" she says, pulling me into a warm hug. "Good morning!" I return the hug and follow her inside her home. "How are you today?"

"I'm well," I reply, forcing a smile. Mara's mother has always treated me as another daughter, and she feels like a second mother to me. I have the urge to tell her about my impending marriage and see if her reaction would be different than my own mother's, but seeing the happiness on her face makes me hide the news. I don't want to dampen her mood so early in the day.

"Mara woke up not long ago. She's in her room getting ready if you want to go in."

I nod. "Thank you."

I walk down a narrow hallway to Mara's room and knock on her bedroom door.

"Mara? It's me. Is it all right if I come in?"

Mara throws the door open and jerks me inside. "Of course! I'm trying to decide what to wear today and you can help." She is still in her night clothes but has a rainbow of colorful dresses spread across her bed.

"You know I'm absolute rubbish when it comes to these things!" I moan.

Mara rolls her eyes. "You're not as bad as you think. You just need to learn to trust your natural instincts. Now, help me decide and once I'm ready I'll show you your birthday present."

"My birthday present? But my birthday isn't until tomorrow."

She grins. "I know! I know! But I need to show it to you today so it will be ready for you tomorrow." I open my mouth to protest but she shakes her head. "No arguing. Now help me decide."

Thirty minutes later Mara wears a simple pink dress, her long hair braided into a crown. Satisfied with her appearance, she leads me from her house and into town, babbling away about whatever random thoughts enter her head. Mostly, she's recounting all the things we did last night at the festival. I nod along. I learned long ago that Mara doesn't often require assistance to keep a conversation going. When she halts abruptly, I nearly crash into her.

"We're here!" she declares, turning me to face a shop. The sign hanging above the door reads "Madame Gosspick's Dress

Shop" in curling gold letters. I've only been inside this shop on a couple of occasions. Each time at the bequest of Mara, who dragged me inside to "help" her with dress fittings.

My eyebrows knit in confusion as I turn to Mara. "The dress shop?"

Mara's face glows. "Yes. I've ordered you a special dress for you to wear for your eighteenth birthday!" She claps her hands in excitement.

"Mara, I—" she cuts me off, shoving me toward the door.

"Come on. I told Madame Gosspick we would be by this morning for an official fitting."

She shoves me through the door rather unceremoniously, a tiny bell announcing our arrival. A small, ancient-looking woman pokes her head out from a back room.

"Ah! Yes! My best customer!" she grins. "I'll be right out!"

Her head disappears back into the room and I hear her shuffling things around. "Make yourselves comfortable!" she calls, her voice muffled slightly.

Mara plops gracefully onto a cushioned seat, but I wander around the room, taking everything in. Colorful paintings and dress sketches decorate the walls, and fabrics of all colors and textures are draped over the many chairs and seats scattered throughout the room. I reach out to feel a soft silk when Madam Gosspick shuffles out of the storage room, a dark green satin dress draped over her arm.

"Here, girl," she addresses me, thrusting the dress in my direction. "Take this and put it on. You can go back there if you require privacy." She thrusts her thumb at a gray curtain at the back of the room.

With a tentative glance toward Mara, who shoots me a supportive grin, I slip behind the curtain. I let my simple brown dress drop to the floor and pull the soft green material over my head. The dress slides over my body, highlighting each curve with gentle grace. I swallow and step back into the room, feeling exposed and out of place in such a lovely gown.

Mara gasps, her hands flying to her mouth, her eyes sparkling with delight. "Astra! You look beautiful!" she breathes.

Madame Gosspick nods approvingly as she surveys her work. "Not bad but it needs a few tweaks. Step up here and let me get a good look at it." She gestures to a short stool in the center of the room. I step up on the stool, careful not to step on the edges of the dress dragging the ground.

Madame Gosspick sticks several pins in her mouth and begins circling me. "Hold very still," she warns, pulling a pin from her lips and sticking it in the fabric at the waist of the dress. She sticks in another pin in the same place on the opposite side, another near my shoulders, and then several more across the bottom to bring up the hem of the dress. I'm barely breathing, afraid the slightest movement will cause one of the many pins to shift or dislodge. After several minutes she stands back, her eyes scrutinizing every inch of the dress, her face gleaming with pride.

"Yes, I think this dress is one of my best. I misjudged the length a bit, but the other measurements were mostly accurate," she says with a satisfactory nod. "Well, what do you think?"

She motions to a tall mirror in the corner of the room. I take a deep breath and turn to face it, hesitant. I gasp at the reflection staring back.

I have never cared much for dresses or fancy things, probably due in part to the fact that my family could never afford them, but seeing how the green dress looks on me takes my breath away. The color doesn't wash out my skin and compliments my hair in a way I never thought possible. I hardly recognize my reflection. The dress has capped sleeves with a modest, scooped neckline. The top clings to my body, making me look far curvier than usual. The material is cinched at the waist before falling to the floor in green waves. With the hem now pinned, it looks as if I am floating just above the ground.

"It's beautiful," I breathe, tears forming in my eyes, as I run my hands absentmindedly over the smooth material.

"Of course it is!" Madame Gosspick says. "Now, you can take it off so I can make the changes. Be careful of the pins. Blood is impossible to get out of that material." She ushers me gently toward the curtained room.

As soon as I slip off the dress and change back into my simple brown dress, I miss the way I felt in the green dress. I felt stronger, more confident. Now, I just feel like me again—a simple village girl with no prospects beyond a forced marriage to a horrible man. With a sigh, I exit the room, handing the dress back to Madame Gosspick who extends her hands expectantly.

"I'll have it ready for you in the morning."

With a smile, she disappears into the back room.

"Best present I've given you yet?" Mara asks, grinning as we exit the shop to head back to her house.

I look into her sparkling, excited eyes as I fall into step beside her. "It truly is wonderful, Mara. But I don't know if I can accept it."

She scowls, looking a bit affronted. "And why not? I know you may not have many occasions to wear it in this little town, but every girl needs a beautiful dress. You can wear it to catch a handsome suitor, if nothing else."

She waggles her eyebrows playfully, but reality crashes down on me. The tears I've been holding back all morning come rushing out. Mara's eyes grow wide as she draws me into a hug.

"I know the dress is beautiful and a surprise, but this is a little more of a reaction than I was expecting," she whispers, hugging me tightly.

"It's not just the dress," I mumble, pulling away and wiping my tears with the back of my hand.

"What's wrong, Astra?" she says, concern replacing the joy that had been there only moments ago. "You know you can tell me anything."

I nod, linking my arm in hers as we continue down the street. I tell her all about my father bringing me home a husband to fulfill some debt and fill her in on how awful Marco is. I confess I'm avoiding my home so I don't know the details on when exactly I'll be forced to marry and dragged away from all I've ever known. As the words spill out, she listens in horrified silence, nodding occasionally.

When I finish she asks quietly, "What does Kato think?"

"Kato doesn't agree with it at all."

"Well, if I know one thing in this whole wide world— besides fashion that is— " she adds with a wink, "it's that you and Kato will protect each other. If Kato isn't on board, it's not going to happen. End of story."

She says it so matter-of-factly I can't help but feel a glimmer of hope.

"I hope you're right."

"I'm always right," she says, poking my side. I laugh. "And I bet when you wear that dress to the final feast tomorrow, you'll have suitors galore lined up ready to fight to the death for your hand in marriage."

I laugh again, shaking my head at the ridiculous thought. We both know the village boys have little to no interest in me.

"If only."

I'm about to relay my encounter with Bram that morning when Kato interrupts my thoughts.

The prince is arriving any minute now. We're stationed at

*the end of town awaiting him. Just thought you might find that
information useful.*

I don't bother replying. Instead, I grab Mara's arm and pull
her quickly toward the edge of town.

"Come with me. I think I know something that'll distract us
from my troubles for a bit."

Mara doesn't question me. She only grins and follows in
eager anticipation.

As we approach the edge of town, we're clearly not the only
ones who know about the prince's impending arrival. A small
crowd is already gathering. I wonder how many people actually
know who's arriving and how many others are just there
because they saw others were gathering. Mara looks at me,
questions in her eyes until it clicks.

"The prince?" she gasps and I nods. "But how—"

But before she can finish her question, she has her answer.
A group of village soldiers dressed in their simple gray
uniforms line the street up ahead, Kato among them. With his
height and build he's always easy to pick out in the lineup. He
stands at attention next to his fellow soldiers, expressionless. I
wonder if he spotted me hidden among the gathering crowd
before he assumed his position. Despite my unusually white
hair, my height makes me much more difficult to find in a
crowd.

*Cover Mara's eyes when the prince rides in. I can't have her
falling in love with him when she's supposed to be falling in love
with me.*

I stifle a laugh. *I guess you're just going to have to step up
your game.*

*Right. Let me just go conquer a country to rule really
quickly.*

For the next several minutes, we all wait in anxious anticipation as the crowd grows larger. Finally, the prince and his

entourage are spotted. Even though I've never put much thought toward the prince, I feel oddly nervous and excited. I'm surprised to see several less people with him than anticipated. Only seven horses ride into the town, including the prince. Perhaps Kato and the other soldiers will have more to do than they thought, though I can't imagine the prince is at much risk in a village as simple as Timberborn.

The prince rides at the front of the small caravan on a brown horse. His clothes look mostly casual, or what I assume is casual for a prince, displaying the royal blue he's known for wearing with a golden crest stitched on the left corner of his tunic. As he gets closer, I'm able to make out his features. He's easily one of the most handsome men I've ever seen. He has lightly tanned skin with high cheekbones, complemented by his short, neatly cut brown hair so dark it borders on being black. His bright, sea-green eyes are taking in everything as he rides, his teeth flashing in a wide smile.

I look over at Mara, who's practically about to faint from excitement beside me. I chuckle and turn my gaze back to the prince, but my eyes fall on the man riding beside atop a dapple gray horse. It's Bram.

My heart starts racing. I blink several times, sure I've seen incorrectly, but, no, Bram sits on the horse next to the prince. The everyday clothes he wore just hours before have been replaced by a crisp maroon Guard uniform bearing the royal crest. He leans toward the prince, whispering something with a grin, making the prince burst out into rich laughter. I lock my eyes on Bram, nerves swelling, my breath caught in my throat as I wonder if he notices me among the crowd. Part of me hopes he doesn't. He probably thinks I'm a fool for thinking he was just a simple man. I feel like an idiot for not suspecting who he really was, though there was no way I could have known. I sink back into the crowd, willing myself invisible as the prince and

Bram approach. I think I'm in the clear, managing to go unnoticed as they pass directly in front of us, when Bram's voice drifts toward me, just barely audible over the noise of the crowd and horses.

"Thanks to a wonderful young woman I have procured you a room at the very best inn in town."

I feel my cheeks grow red.

"Excellent," Prince Ehren replies. "I suppose it's lucky you found someone to suggest a place so you didn't have to do the work yourself. After all, that inn in the last town was less than ideal."

"Very lucky, indeed," Bram replies. And then, I swear, just for a fraction of a second, his eyes slide from the prince's face to mine, a smile playing on his lips as he winks. But I could have imagined it. I'm sure I did.

As soon as the prince and his Guard have ridden away, the crowd begins to disperse, lively with chatter and gossip. Mara drags me back in the direction of her house, babbling on and on about how handsome and regal the prince looks. I nod along, barely able to focus on her words. My head spins and my heart won't stop racing.

Did you see who was with the prince? Kato asks.

Yes.

Did you know? Even in thought his tone is accusatory.

I had no idea, Kato. I swear it. He gave no indication.

I knew there was something he was hiding. He's Captain of the Prince's Guard.

Captain?

He had obviously been among the prince's Guard, but I hadn't realized the position he held.

Yes, his uniform is that of a captain and his position next to the prince pretty much confirmed it.

I had no idea. I pause before adding, *Are you going to be busy all day, then? It didn't look like the prince brought many soldiers with him.*

We're taking shifts patrolling the streets where the prince is staying. I'm on duty now but will be done for the festival tonight. Where are you?

I'm with Mara. We're heading back to her house to plan her royal wedding.

Um, excuse me? I'm not royalty and any wedding planning should involve me as the groom. We've gone over this.

I laugh and Mara glances at me, her eyebrows arched in question. Apparently whatever she last said wasn't something to warrant a laugh.

"Sorry, I think I'm just in shock about being so close to the prince," I mutter. I don't expect my excuse to work but Mara nods in agreement.

"I know how you feel! I'm giddy as well."

Even when we reach her house, her accolades for the prince don't cease. I focus my attention on her and surrender to her game of guessing what the prince is doing the rest of the day. That conversation quickly turns into imagining what the prince is like in real life. We go back and forth supplying guesses.

"His favorite food?" Mara asks.

"Hmmm . . . ," I muse. "I think it's roasted lamb with vegetables covered in some sort of fancy sauce."

"That sounds good but is it royal enough? Do princes eat roasted lamb?"

I shrug. "I think they must but I don't know any better than you." It's my turn to pose a question. "What about his favorite color?"

A knock at the door interrupts our game, but Mara answers me as she rises to go to the door. "That's easy. Blue. It's why he's known for wearing it."

Mara throws the door open. I can't see who it is from my seat, but the expression on her face looks surprised and extremely pleased at the same time.

"Oh! Good afternoon! How may I assist you?" Her voice is unusually high. I start to rise from my seat to see who can wield that sort of power over Mara but freeze when a familiar voice answers.

"Good afternoon. I am actually looking for Astra. Her brother told me I might find her here."

Mara's eyebrows knit in confusion and then her eyes grow wide when she recognizes Bram as the man I was with last night. She glances quickly toward me and motions for Bram to come inside.

"Yes, yes, she's in here," she says quickly as Bram steps over the threshold.

Bram stands awkwardly for a moment as Mara shuts the door. He's still wearing his captain's uniform and stands tall and straight as his eyes find me. For a moment we just stare at each other in uneasy silence until Mara swoops to my rescue.

"Please, make yourself comfortable. Have a seat. Would you like anything to eat or drink?"

"No. No, thank you," Bram says with a polite smile. "I just came to invite Astra to dine with me and the prince tonight at the inn." His eyes dart to Mara's surprised face. "You, of course, are also welcome."

"The prince? Dinner?" Mara asks, her voice going slightly higher. "We would be honored!" She glances over at me where I stand, silent. "Wouldn't we, Astra?"

I realize my mouth is gaping open and quickly clear my throat, finding my voice. "Um, yes. Dinner. That would be . . . nice."

Bram smiles and nods once. "Excellent. I will let the prince know. We will dine early so we won't have to miss any of the festivities tonight." Bram locks eyes with me. "I have also invited your brother. He has gone home to inform your family so they will not wonder where you are."

I incline my head slightly. "Thank you."

So, Kato knew Bram was coming and gave me no warning. He'll hear about this later.

"Yes, well then, I will leave you ladies to prepare and I will see you later," he says, turning toward the door.

"Yes, we look forward to it," Mara says.

Bram steps outside, turning to look at Mara before she closes the door.

"By the way, you were correct."

Mara scowls. "Correct about what?"

"His Majesty's favorite color is blue."

Mara blushes, realizing Bram overheard our conversation when he arrived.

"What's yours?" I blurt, immediately regretting my question.

Bram doesn't seem bothered, his smile going all the way to his eyes as he replies, "Perhaps I will tell you at dinner."

Once he's gone, Mara flies into a frenzy.

"We have a million things to do before dinner tonight!"

"Like what? It's not like we have to prepare the dinner," I grumble incredulously.

"Seriously, Astra?" She gapes at me in disbelief. "We have to find dresses appropriate enough for a dinner with the prince, fix our hair, and make ourselves overall acceptable for such an occasion." She sighs dramatically. "We have so much to do."

Her eyes scan me quickly, and it doesn't take much to guess that she finds my plain brown dress and simple braid less than acceptable for dinner with a prince. I don't even have to see my reflection to agree with her. But, unlike Mara, I don't have a large selection of gowns to run home and choose from. I feel woefully inadequate.

"It's a pity your birthday dress won't be ready tonight, but I'm sure we can find you something else acceptable to wear. I have plenty of gowns you can borrow," she says, linking her arm with mine and steering me toward her room.

As much as I appreciate her assistance and enthusiasm, I doubt I'll find anything of Mara's that will fit. She's a good two to three inches taller than me with a much fuller feminine figure. The more dresses Mara pulls from her closet, the more I become positive I'll just have to settle for looking like the poor village girl I am. That's fine. It is who I am after all. Why should I pretend to be someone I'm not?

Miraculously, though, after nearly an hour of being forced into dresses that fit like tents, we find one that works reasonably well. It's a simple light purple dress that falls to the floor. It isn't the fanciest of the gowns, but it fits and isn't so long I'll be tripping over it all night. Once my dress has been settled on, I'm forced to watch Mara try on every other dress in her wardrobe to find one worthy of a prince. As she spins, modeling a red dress, I reach out to Kato.

A little heads up would have been nice.

Heads up about what?

You know what.

Oh, you mean that little visit from Bram?

I can hear the insufferable grin in his voice.

I just stood there like a gawking idiot!

So you were your natural self, then.

Kato! I'm going to kill you later. I swear.

Honestly, I thought you might like the surprise. And I was a little distracted figuring out what to tell Father.

Oh, gods. Have you told him yet?

I just left the house.

What did he say?

What could he say? It's not like he could deny the crown prince. I don't think he was particularly happy, especially since you've been gone all day. He's apparently convinced Marco you're a worthy bride, despite being a "cursed" twin, but Marco is starting to feel jilted. I have a feeling he'll force you to make it up to Marco in some way but no idea how yet.

Shit.

I know. But don't worry. Let's get through tonight and we'll face tomorrow when it comes. We've got this, Ash.

I smile to myself and watch Mara examining her reflection as she smooths the folds of the pale blue dress she just slipped on.

"I think that's the one, Mara. Not too fancy for a dinner at the inn but fancy enough for a prince. Plus, Bram did say the prince's favorite color was blue."

Mara grins. "I think you're right." She turns toward me, her grin growing. "Now to find appropriate jewelry and fix our hair."

It's going to be a long day.

CHAPTER FIVE

*M*ara fills the remaining hours before dinner getting ready. She does, however, work in a few minutes for her to gush about the day's events with her father and mother who seem equally pleased and excited. Never in my life have I ever taken this long to get ready for anything, but the results are undeniable. By some miracle, Mara manages to transform a simple village girl into someone worthy of a dinner with the prince. She twists my hair into an elaborate braid at the nape of my neck and adds touches of color to my cheeks and lips. Her attempts to convince me to borrow some of her jewelry fall short, but I concede to let her put jeweled pins in my hair. She adorns her own neck with a sapphire on a gold chain with coordinating earrings, bracelets, and rings. Having a father who basically runs the town clearly has its perks.

She's slipping one final pin in her hair when someone knocks on the door. Her eyes dart nervously to mine. I offer her a nervous smile before we exit her room. As we round the corner her father's voice booms, "Ah! Good evening, Kato!"

Mara and I hurry over to where my brother stands in the doorway, dressed in his most formal uniform.

"Good evening, Sir," he replies politely. "I've come to escort Mara and Astra to dinner." He inclines his head in our direction.

"Yes! Of course! Excellent!" her father answers jovially, stepping aside so we can slip out. "Have a good night," he says with a wink, shutting the door.

We linger awkwardly for a moment before Kato offers us each an arm. "Well, shall we be off?"

We each take an arm, me on Kato's right and Mara on his left, and begin the short trek from Mara's house to the inn. Along the way, none of us speak. My head is too busy whirling, trying to make sense of what this dinner means and what may be expected of me. When we finally arrive at the inn, a small crowd hovers outside, surely waiting for the prince to emerge. Two of the prince's Guard stand outside the door along with a handful of the village guards. Kato nods to his comrades and leads us inside.

Due to Prince Ehren's presence, I expect the inn to be empty, save for the prince and his Guard, but the inn is packed nearly as much as normal. The only exception is a small area in the back corner where the prince sits with Bram at a table all their own. Three of the prince's Guard sit at the nearest table. I recognize a few other familiar faces of village guards nearby. We weave through the crowd toward the prince, who rises from his seat with Bram as we approach. Mara dips into a full curtsy and I'm trying to figure out exactly how to curtsy when the prince holds up his hand.

"Please," he grins. "There is no need for any formalities tonight. I get more than enough of that everywhere else. Tonight, you are invited here as friends. Shall we sit?"

He motions to the bench seat across from where he and

Bram have been sitting. I notice a bright twinkle in the prince's eye and feel warmed by his energy. Something in me settles slightly, but my nerves don't dissipate entirely.

I barely manage a nod in reply to the prince's suggestion but Mara replies to the prince with ease. "Yes, of course. Thank you so much for the invitation to dine."

"It is my pleasure," Ehren replies, grinning as he and Bram take their seats. "Honestly, I'm glad to be able to dine outside palaces and houses of nobility for once."

We settle into our seats. Kato slides in first, putting me directly across from Bram who meets my eyes and smiles as I take my seat. I glance away and stare down at my hands folded in my lap. Mara happily sits directly across from the prince.

"But surely the food makes those dinners worth it," Mara says smoothly.

The prince chuckles. "The food is undeniably excellent at every event. However, I do like a change of pallet every so often. I hope you won't be offended, but I've requested lamb stew tonight. I must admit, despite my proper upbringing, stew is one of my favorite dishes. It's right up there with roasted lamb."

His eyes twinkle mischievously, and I glance at Bram, who is doing a horrible job at hiding a smile. I wonder how long he listened outside the door earlier.

"Interesting. Of course, we would never be offended with any dinner you decided for us, I'm sure," Mara replies, smiling. "I must admit, stew is delicious and this inn has some of the best."

I struggle to hide a smile of disbelief as I glance toward Mara. I can't think of a single time she's eaten inside the inn, let alone eaten the stew. Whatever her flaws, Mara has been made for dinners like this one. The prince opens his mouth to reply but pauses as Jaxon, the middle-aged owner of the inn, approaches the table with a bottle of wine.

"Good evening, Your Majesty," he mutters, running his tongue across his dry lips. "Your stew will be up in just a moment, of course, if that is what you still desire. My wife is an excellent cook, and we can prepare anything—"

Prince Ehren cuts off his rambling with a wave of his hand. "The stew, I promise you, is more than adequate."

Jaxon bows his head. "Of course. Of course. I have brought some of the finest wine we have, if I may have the honor of filling your cups."

He holds the wine out with trembling hands so we can see and approve his selection.

"Much obliged," the prince replies with a pleased nod.

Jaxon pours a deep red wine into the simple goblets provided at each place. Once he is done, he skirts away like a mouse happy to escape the presence of a cat, leaving the bottle behind.

"Now then," Prince Ehren says, leaning forward, "I suppose it is best we introduce ourselves."

Mara blinks and dips her head. "Of course, we know who you are, Your Majesty."

"Let's start with that," the prince says, making a face of feigned disgust. "I insist you call me Ehren. Forget my title. And, please, none of that 'Your Majesty' stuff. Reserve that for my father." Mara nods and Ehren claps his hand on Bram's shoulder. "I believe you have already met Bram, the Captain of my Guard and my closest friend."

I meet Bram's eyes for the first time since taking a seat, words slipping from my mouth before I can stop them. "Yes, we have met. Though we had no idea who it was we were meeting."

Bram grins sheepishly, while Ehren laughs. "Please, do

forgive the deception. I sent Bram ahead to scout out the town and make sure it was secure before my arrival. He was sworn to secrecy as to why he was here. I am sure you understand."

"Of course we do!" Mara declares, throwing me an admonishing sidelong glance. "Your safety is top priority."

"I must admit, I did enjoy the anonymity. While I am proud of my position, this"—Bram gestures to his captain's uniform—"makes it difficult to blend into the crowd. And, to be candid, I am very much glad I was able to blend in so I could meet you all." His eyes lock with mine for a moment, and my heart flips. He breaks his gaze, suddenly very interested in his wine.

"I, for one, am always glad to find friends so easily when entering a new town," Ehren says, taking a sip of his own wine.

"But surely, as the crown prince, you can easily find friends whenever and wherever you please," Mara counters.

Ehren shrugs casually, but there's something sad in his eyes. "Perhaps. I can almost always find allies within the walls of my kingdom, that much is true. But being able to vet out who could actually be a friend to who I really am from those who just want to be near me for my position is often a difficult task. Bram is excellent at judging between the two, having been my friend for many years."

The prince's words, despite their cheerful delivery, are heavy, and I can sense some of the weight he carries with him every day. A shadow flickers in his eyes but is quickly replaced by years of practiced acquiescence.

Bram gives his friend a grateful nod. "It is always an honor."

Mara's head bobs along in understanding as the table falls silent for a moment before Bram speaks up, addressing Kato.

"I was speaking with your commander earlier and he

informed me that you have incredible skill. More so than any other soldier he has ever had the privilege of training."

Kato smiles. "Commander Jetson is generous and kind. Several of our village soldiers deserve recognition."

"I have no doubt, but how many of them completed the necessary training two years ahead of time with scores rivaling that of soldiers trained from childhood for the king's army?" Bram counters, and my chest swells with pride for my brother.

"Not many, I guess," Kato replies with a shrug. "I've always been determined and willing to work hard. In this village, it's the only way to get out."

"You wish to get out?" Ehren asks, his eyebrows arching slightly as my eyes widen, betraying my surprise at Kato's answer.

Kato nods as I glance at him, brow furrowed with concern. "There's little future for me here." He glances over at me. "Or for my sister. Did you know that her training as a scholar has already surpassed any other in the history of our village?"

Bram surveys me with renewed interest, and I blush under his gaze.

Ehren's eyes shift to me, intrigue flashing across his face. "I was not aware."

I swallow hard as Kato continues. "It's true. She long surpassed what they could teach her here, but she never stops searching for ways to increase her knowledge. She hopes to one day be the village historian, but I know she is meant for much more. My hard work and determination pale in comparison to hers."

Kato looks down at me and gives me an earnest smile.

"Kato," I whisper, fighting back tears.

"Interesting. I think you and my sister would get along incredibly well," Ehren says. "She has always been obsessed with our histories and reads any and every book or text she can get her hands on. I believe you two have much in common."

"I agree." Bram grins, his eyes shining. "Princess Cadewynn would never let you out of her sight if you ever entered the palace. She would trap you in the royal library with her and not let you leave until you have discussed every single prophecy and history available!"

"To be honest, that doesn't sound half bad," I say with a small laugh.

Before anyone else can reply, Jaxon and a serving maid approach our table with bowls of steaming stew and a long loaf of bread. They carefully place a bowl in front of each of us, the serving maid glancing nervously at Prince Ehren and his Captain of the Guard like they could consume her at any moment. As soon as we all have our food, she scampers away to the kitchen, but Jaxon lingers by the table, his hands clasped in front of him.

"I hope you find everything to your liking. If you need anything else, just say the word."

"Everything looks excellent. We will let you know if we require anything more."

I hide a smile as I watch Ehren thank Jaxon. Despite his proper posture and general princely demeanor, there's something earnest and kind in his smile.

Jaxon gives a quick bow before retreating. We fall silent, digging into the stew. I can't help but wonder if Jaxon or his wife added something special or extra to the stew to make it taste better than normal. After several minutes, Ehren breaks the silence.

"Am I correct in understanding that you two are the twins?" he asks, his sharp gaze darting between me and Kato. I can tell he's trying to sound as casual as possible, but there's an urgency lacing his words.

A knot twists in my stomach as my face falls. The whole dinner felt off from the start, but now I know why. Twins are apparently an oddity worthy of a dinner with a prince. My hope that the prince's offer of friendship was sincere crumbles. I wonder if Bram's attention was forced as well. I feel like I'm on display as a side-show attraction. I should have known better than to believe someone would be interested in me alone. I drop my hands to my sides, pressing my palms against the bench as I stare into my bowl of stew. I feel a strange chill gathering inside me. I can't tell if it is from the strange power I possess or just embarrassment and disappointment. Kato grabs my hand under the table, giving it a squeeze. His hand feels unusually warm.

"We are more than twins," Kato replies, his voice firm and cold. "I think our earlier conversation proves that much."

"Oh, I agree," Prince Ehren says, trying his best to backtrack as concern flickers in his eyes. "And I mean no offense. At all. I swear it. I figured it was best to be blunt about it instead of pretending I didn't know. You must understand, it is as much of an honor for me to meet you as it is for you to meet me. Perhaps more so."

I lift my eyes from my stew, meeting the prince's gaze. "What do you mean?"

"I remember the night you were born." He pauses, chuckling as he realizes how odd that sounds. "Of course, at the time, I had no idea what was happening. It was years later before I knew of your birth. What I remember are the stars falling in the sky. I wasn't quite three, but I had been allowed to stay up for the royal celebration of Kriloa. Wishing to get away from the noise, I went out into one of the palace gardens and saw the stars shooting across the night sky. My governess was with me and when I asked what was happening she told me, 'The gods are blessing the earth this night, young prince. Tonight is a night of true celebration.' It is one of my earliest memories and something I will never forget."

Prince Ehren pauses, taking a bite of his stew before continuing. "Of course, it wasn't until a couple of weeks later that news reached the palace that the first ever twins had been born. I had no idea what that meant, but everyone else at the castle seemed to suddenly lose their minds, especially the scholars. There was much talk behind closed doors of exactly what your birth meant. In the end, nothing was ever done. At least nothing of which I am aware. I forgot the matter altogether until my sister began her education years later. As I already mentioned, she was a quick study and loved her histories. She was born on the first night of Kriloa, albeit two years after you, so you can understand why she took a special interest in your story. Her interest piqued my interest. I've spent the last couple years learning all I can about you, so it was inevitable we meet."

Something inside me grows unsteady and cold. I clench my fists under the table.

"So you came all the way from your comfortable palace to gawk at us?" I snap, surprised by my own anger.

"No!" Ehren declares, shaking his head adamantly. "Not at all. I'm afraid I didn't explain very well."

The cold inside writhes and rises. My brain tells me to calm down and let the prince explain but something else, something stronger, makes me irritable and angry.

"I think you explained well enough." My heated gaze snaps to Bram, who sits watching me wide-eyed. "Was any of your friendship sincere? Or did you just want to help deliver the prize to your prince?"

"Astra, I swear I had no idea who you were the first time we met. How could I? We met at complete random in the street. I know we may have blindsided you, but I promise I never pursued a friendship with you for the sake of Ehren. I wouldn't do that."

"How do I know that?"

Bram's eyes lock with mine. I can see him shifting through his thoughts, trying to sort out what to say, how to calm me. His reaction just upsets me more.

Astra.

I ignore Kato and continue yelling at Bram. "Fine. The first time we met on accident, but what about the second time? When you met me at the festival did you know who I was then? Did you seek me out, hoping I would lead you to my twin?"

Bram takes a deep breath, closing his eyes. Ehren looks uneasy, and I can tell he's trying to find the words to deescalate the situation.

Astra!!! Kato's voice is forceful, but I go on, tears of fury and frustration burning my eyes. Mara watches me in wide-eyed horror.

"What do you get for delivering the prize of twins to your prince? Gold? Jewels? A new horse?" I spit.

"I didn't promise him anything," Ehren insists. "He was only—"

The rest of Ehren's words fade as Kato's voice breaks through, yelling in my head.

ASTRA! YOUR HANDS!

Confused, I look down at my hands hidden beneath the table. They're glowing, the silvery light seeming to come from beneath my skin. I gasp and shove my hands into the folds of my dress.

"I'm sorry, but I think my sister and I need to leave," Kato says firmly, rising from his seat, pulling me with him. "Thank you for dinner."

I keep my hands hidden in the folds of my dress as I rise.

Ehren and Bram jump from their seats as we race toward the door.

"Astra! Wait! Please!" Bram calls after us, but we don't pause.

Once we're safely hidden in the alley behind the inn, I collapse against the wall.

"What the hell was that?" Kato asks, his eyes still wide with concern.

I shake my head, tears flowing down my cheeks. "I have no idea. I think . . . I think it's what we've been dreaming about. I don't think those were just dreams. I think they were visions, Kato."

Kato shakes his head firmly. "No. No they can't be. They just . . . no." He paces the alley and runs his hand through his hair.

"But what if they are visions? What if—"

"NO!" he screams, slamming his fists against the wall, making me jump.

He takes a shaky breath to calm himself. His eyes meet mine, and I see the overwhelming fear.

"No," he whispers so quietly I'm not sure if he actually spoke or just mouthed the word.

Slowly, he sinks down beside me his back against the wall, his head bowed into his hands.

In my dreams, my nightmares, I set everything and everyone on fire. They can't be real, Astra. They just can't. I can't kill and destroy everyone and everything I love.

I scoot closer to my brother, slipping my arm around him as I rest my head on his shoulder. The glow is spreading from my hands all the way up my arm. For a moment, we just sit there, not speaking. I take a deep breath and reel in my anger and frustration. Little by little the power begins to settle until my arms and hands no longer glow.

Look, Kato. My hands are normal again.

I pull my arm from around him and hold out my hands. He lifts his head from his hands and looks up at me, desperation lingering in his eyes.

Maybe whatever this is can be controlled. Maybe we can stop it.

He releases a long sigh and tilts his head back against the wall.

How can we stop something when we don't even know what it is?

I don't know. But we can try, right?

I offer him a weak smile, and he stands, offering me his hand.

"What do you say we forget this all happened? Let's go dance around a bonfire for a few hours and avoid thinking about anything remotely unpleasant."

I place my hand in his and let him help me up. "Sounds like an excellent plan."

He drapes his arm across my shoulders as we make our way back to the main bonfire, weaving through back alleys and side streets in case Bram or Ehren decide to search for us.

"Do you think Mara will forgive us for abandoning her?" Kato asks.

My laughter echoes down an alleyway. "Are you seriously asking if Mara will forgive us for leaving her alone with a hand-some prince and his handsome Captain of the Guard? Once she gets over the shock of it, I'm sure she'll find it in her heart to forgive us."

Kato chuckles. "I guess you're right, though that does severely limit my chances of winning her over." We walk quietly for a moment and then he adds quietly, in barely more than a whisper, "At least if we destroy the world, we do it together."

CHAPTER SIX

*W*e easily lose ourselves in dancing. The bonfire's flames already reach high, and the villagers are out in full force. The large size of the crowd this early in the night is more than likely because everyone hopes to spot the prince. Kato and I, however, are more than happy to avoid seeing the prince or his captain ever again. We debate going home to change, but we'd rather avoid the dismal reality waiting for us there and lose ourselves in the drunken crowd. As night falls, we drink more, forgetting our worries.

I'm not sure how long we dance and drink before Mara finally finds us. She's still wearing the same dress she wore to dinner, making her stand out in the crowd. Her eyes flash in anger as she approaches. I consider slinking away but decide to face her ire now rather than later.

"What were you thinking?" she demands once she's close enough for me to hear her without drawing too much attention. "He's the crown prince for gods' sake!"

"Right now I'm just thinking about dancing!" I reply with a giggle.

"Me too!" Kato agrees leaning toward Mara. "Dance with me."

Kato draws Mara into his arms, the mead we've been drinking boosting his confidence. Mara stares at him, wide eyed, as he attempts to lead her in a choppy dance.

"Kato!" she cries out, twisting in his arms to look back at me. "I'm trying to talk to your sister!"

"No, you're dancing. Come on, Mara! Dance with me!" He spins her gently and she laughs.

"Fine," she concedes, her eyes sparkling. "But when we're done, I'm finishing my conversation with your sister."

Kato nods. "Yes, of course, dear. Whatever you say," he says as he whisks Mara deeper into the crowd, winking at me over her shoulder.

Go. I'll keep her distracted. I'm happy to sacrifice myself.

I wave at him, laughing as they disappear, swallowed into the revelers. For a moment, I just stand in the midst of the dancing crowd. Finally, I turn and make my way to one of the treat carts. Dinner was hours ago and I didn't even get to finish. I know firsthand the dangers of drinking too much without enough food in my stomach. I fish the last few coins out of my money pouch and purchase a caramel apple before making my way to one of the log seats set up near the bonfire. For a few blissful moments I block out the world around me, eating my apple, transfixed by the flickering flames. The festival is such a blurry haze, I don't even notice when someone sits down next to me.

"I am sorry about dinner."

I startle and look up into Bram's face, inches away from mine. I swallow and force my gaze back to the fire. "I don't want to talk about it."

"Please, I . . . we meant nothing bad. It all went wrong."

I take a deep breath but remain silent. The last thing I need is for my hands to start glowing in the middle of this crowd. I have to stay calm.

"Astra, I swear—"

"Just stop," I cut him off sharply.

"Let me explain," he pleads.

I look up at him again. His eyes seem earnest enough, but the anger starts swirling inside me.

"Fine. Let's talk. Start by answering this: did you come to Timberborn for the sole purpose of locating me and my brother for your prince?"

He holds my gaze without blinking. "In a manner of speaking, yes."

"Okay. Now, if I hadn't been who you were looking for, if I hadn't been one of the twins, would you still have wanted to get to know me?"

For a moment he stares deeply into my eyes before he whispers, "Yes."

My heart gives a little leap. I wasn't expecting that answer, and, despite everything, it's what I wanted to hear. It means it's possible Bram can actually look past me being a twin. He can see *me*.

"From the moment you knocked me into the dirt, I knew I wanted to get to know you more. It turned out to be convenient that you were who I had been sent to find, but I would have wanted to know you regardless of my mission. Gods help me if you hadn't been who I was seeking. You were far too distracting for me to concentrate on anyone else."

"Truly?" My voice is barely more than a whisper.

He laughs, reaching out to take my free hand. "Truly."

After a moment, I force myself to look away. "But why is the prince so interested in me and my brother? Did he just seek us out for the novelty of it?"

"No, not at all," Bram replies, firmly. "He will be the first to admit that the idea of twins is fascinating, but it's much more than that. His sister found some very interesting things about you buried in books long forgotten. Things no one knows. Things you and your brother need to know."

I look back up at him. "What sort of things?"

"I do not know the details, having never read them myself. Princess Cadewynn only showed Ehren the texts. I just know that they speak of a rare power held by twins. They include records and prophecies claiming you and your brother are tied up in magics believed dead."

"They mention a power?" I ask, unable to hide the urgency in my voice.

His eyebrows twitch up as he studies my face.

"Things are happening, aren't they?"

I don't say anything and focus intently on the bonfire.

"Astra," he says, inching closer so I can feel the heat of his breath on my neck, "if things are starting to happen Ehren needs to know. He can help. He can—"

"Get away from my sister!" Kato's yell roars over the crowd, snapping our attention to him, making me drop the remainder of my apple on the ground. He stands a couple yards away, his hands clenched into fists by his side. People quickly clear away from him, glancing in disgust over their shoulders. His eyes are focused on Bram, reflecting the bonfire, making them look as if they're on fire. No, it isn't a reflection, I realize with a start. Actual flames flicker in his eyes. I jump to my feet, my heart pounding.

"Kato, it's okay," I say calmly, reaching a tentative hand toward him.

He shakes his head with fervor. "No, it's not okay, Astra!" The flames in his eyes grow. "He can't just come from his cozy palace with his handsome prince to gawk at us."

His words are slightly slurred and I wonder how much he's

had to drink. Drunken outbursts are common at festivals, but people still turn to watch.

"His eyes," Bram gulps beside me. The flames have grown enough now they are obviously not just a reflection. I pray no one else notices.

"What about my eyes," Kato challenges, tightening his fists as his hands start to glow, matching the flames in his eyes.

Kato, your hands.

"What?" he asks out loud before glancing down.

His hands glow like the embers of the fire behind me. He looks back up at me, eyes wide with panic. Beside me, Bram swears. A few other bystanders have stopped to see what is causing the commotion and now watch uneasily.

"We need to get him out of here," Bram whispers to me.

"Obviously," I hiss through clenched teeth.

Kato, calm down. We need to leave before we draw too much attention. Trust me, okay?

Kato swallows and nods. I quickly close the gap between us and loop my arm around his waist, guiding him out of the crowd. Bram comes up beside me, keeping a wary distance from my brother.

My eyes are burning, Astra. I can feel them burning.

Close them and hold on to me.

"Do you have somewhere we can go?" I ask Bram quietly.

He nods. "If you will trust us, I will take you to Ehren. He can help." His eyes dart to Kato, who has his eyes shut tight. "Will he be able to make it?"

I nod, although I really have no idea. "He'll be fine." He has to be.

"Then come with me."

I follow Bram through the crowd, guiding Kato, who keeps his eyes closed tight.

Just breathe. Concentrate on calming down. It's what helped me.

I'm terrified, Astra. This is what happens in my nightmares. I can never stop it.

Heat flares in his touch, but I don't flinch away.

This isn't your dream, Kato. You have control here. Just breathe. Breathe.

He takes a deep breath as I lead him out of the heaviest part of the crowd, followed by another breath and then another. I look down, relieved to see his hands returning to normal.

It's working. Try opening your eyes. Leading you like a blind puppy isn't ideal.

I don't know, Ash.

Come on. You can do it.

I glance up at him as he slowly opens his eyes. They appear a slightly darker shade than normal, but otherwise, they're fine. I give him a reassuring nod and he releases another long breath. By the time we reach the inn, Kato is back to his normal self, albeit a bit fidgety. Before heading inside, Bram looks over his shoulder at Kato.

"Will he be okay?"

Kato glares, but I nod. "Yes, I believe so."

Bram still seems a little skeptical, but ushers us inside and up the stairs to the room reserved for the prince, passing the other members of the Guard on the way. He knocks on the door. After a moment, Prince Ehren throws it open. He looks surprised to see us, but his expression quickly shifts from shock to a welcoming grin.

"You don't just throw the door open without asking who is on the other side," Bram admonishes, scowling.

Ehren rolls his eyes. "As if anyone could get past the guards and soldiers you've stationed every two feet."

I glance at Ehren. He's changed from his princely attire

into a basic pair of brown pants and a loose-fitting white shirt. No one would assume he's a prince. The look suits him. I switch my gaze to Bram and realize he, too, has changed into his more common clothes.

"They are not every two feet. You insisted on coming into town with six guards, including myself. Six. And while I do have villager soldiers posted, I don't trust them fully."

"Well, come in out of the hall and yell at me inside. No need to let the whole inn know what a fool you find me to be," Ehren says, throwing his hands in the air and stepping further into the room.

With a sigh Bram follows with me and Kato close behind. I shut the door and look around. The room of the inn is small and cozy. A bed is pushed along the far wall beneath a window, a small bedside table near the head of the bed with a washbowl and candle on top. The wall opposite the door has a dresser with a mirror. A wobbly table with two chairs sits in the center of the room and a worn easy chair sits in the corner opposite the bed. Candles and lanterns flicker around the room, making it very well lit despite the late hour. Ehren plops unceremoniously into the easy chair while Bram continues admonishing him.

"I know you don't care who you are, Ehren, but if you die on my watch, your father will have my head. And you know it."

"Fine, Bram. I'm sorry. I'll ask for five forms of identification next time anyone knocks on my door. Now, surely you didn't bring them"—he gestures to where Kato and I hover by the door—"up to my room so they can listen to you give me a rundown of security protocols."

"Right," Bram says, clearing his throat and turning to face us. "The accommodations are a bit sparse, but make yourselves comfortable and we will do our best to answer your questions."

I ease onto one of the wooden chairs, Kato choosing the

other. For a moment, Bram looks around the room and seems to realize that all the seats are taken.

"You can sit in my lap, Bram, if you need to," Ehren says, a smile dancing on his lips as he taps his thigh.

Bram closes his eyes and sighs, pressing his fingers to his temple. "I'm rather fine standing."

A smile twitches on my lips as Ehren shrugs. "Suit yourself."

"So, why are we here?" Kato asks coldly, and Bram's eyes snap open. "What do you want with us? You have one more chance to explain, and then we're leaving. Prince or no, I won't have you bothering me and my sister."

Bram studies Kato for a moment and then asks slowly, "What just happened at the bonfire—how long has that been an issue?"

"What?" Ehren says, leaping from the chair. "What happened at the bonfire?"

Bram makes a silencing motion toward Ehren, Kato ignoring him altogether.

"That was the first time."

"So it has never happened before that you are aware of?"

Kato shakes his head.

"What? What happened?" Ehren says, louder this time, enunciating every word.

"Has anything else ever happened? Something different but perhaps similar?"

"No, well, I—" Kato glances at me as he falls silent.

Bram's eyes shoot to me. "You, then? Have you ever had anything happen?"

I hesitate a moment before answering, "Not before today."

"But something happened today?" Bram presses. His eyes light up as the pieces click into place. "At dinner. Something happened at dinner. That is why you ran out so abruptly."

"For the love of all things holy, WHAT THE HELL HAPPENED?"

Bram sighs and turns to face Ehren. "While we were down by the bonfire, something upset Kato—"

"*You* upset me. It was you," Kato cuts in sharply.

"I upset Kato," Bram amends, "and he had flames in his eyes, and his hands were glowing like embers."

"Shit," Ehren breathes. He shifts his focus to me. "What happened to you at dinner? Why did you leave?"

"My hands were starting to glow with this weird silver light," I answer quietly.

Ehren lets out a long sigh and rakes his hands through his hair. "Shit. Shit. Shit," he mumbles, pacing the room. "She was bloody right." He pauses and looks up at Bram. "She'll never let us live this down."

"No, she will not," Bram replies with a sigh before turning his attention back to us. "Is there anything else besides what happened tonight? Anything at all, even something as simple as a bad feeling or something feeling off or unusual?"

I glance over at Kato. *I think we need to tell them.*

He shakes his head. *I don't know, Ash. I still don't trust them. We just met them.*

Come on, Kato. Something is happening with us, and I think they know what. I don't want those dreams to come true. Maybe they can help us stop it.

What if they make it worse?

I sigh. *Do we have a choice?*

Kato looks down for a moment and then back up at me. *I don't think we do, unfortunately.*

I look at Bram who is staring down at us, mouth open, his eyebrows knit in confusion. A quick glance at Ehren confirms he's just as baffled by our strange silence. I clear my throat.

"We'll tell you, but you have to swear to keep it secret."

"Were . . . were you two just having a conversation without speaking?" Ehren asks, his eyes darting wildly between us.

"What? Why would you think that?" I say, purposefully avoiding his eyes.

"You were!" Ehren says, his eyes going wide.

Bram ignores him. "We promise we will tell not a single soul unless you give us permission to do so. You have my word."

I nod and glance at Kato. He shrugs in resignation.

"Lately, for the past few months, we've had some . . . dreams. Nightmares, really." I pause and take a deep breath. "And in my dreams, there's a power inside me. It grows until I'm glowing with this odd, silver light. It consumes me, and I explode. Sometimes, I'm alone in a sort of empty village or void. Sometimes, I'm in a crowded place. Every dream is a little different, but every time it ends essentially the same."

I pause. Bram nods encouragingly and shifts his gaze to Kato. Kato inhales and then speaks softly.

"My dreams are similar. Only instead of light, it's fire. Fire shoots from my eyes and hands, destroying anyone and anything nearby. People scream out in agony but I can't stop it. My body heats, turning red and orange like a burning log, cracking under the pressure from the heat. And then I lose all control and fire bursts everywhere, like an explosion. And everything around me ceases to exist."

He lets out a long breath like he'd been holding it for his entire explanation. I reach across the table and grab his hand. He squeezes my hand in response. Bram studies us quietly, looking first at me and then at Kato. The silence in the room grows heavy. Finally, Ehren breaks it.

"It's just as bad as we thought. Maybe even worse."

"It would appear so," Bram says, stepping away and settling into the chair Ehren occupied earlier.

"What does it mean?" I ask weakly. "Do you know?"

"Yes and no," Bram replies.

"Well that was helpful," Kato mumbles. "So glad we shared our deepest secrets for that response."

"What is happening to you is unprecedented," Ehren adds. "If twins existed before in our realm, we know nothing of their existence. However, throughout time different Seers have prophesied your birth and your powers. Their accounts are few and far between and seem to contradict each other. Some claim you will destroy the world, whereas others swear you will save it. Your powers, and their source, vary from story to story as well. The only connecting factors are that twins will be born on the night when stars fall and that their powers would manifest after eighteen years."

Silence settles over the room once again. Ehren watches Kato and I like we could explode at any minute. Bram seems to be weighing his thoughts, deciding what, if anything, to add.

"Who was the 'she' you referred to?" Kato asks.

"My sister," Ehren says, clearing his throat. "What I told you at dinner was true. Winnie has been embedded among our palace scholars for years. Were she not a princess, she would likely be an official historian by now, despite being only sixteen years old. She stumbled upon some of the prophecies a couple years ago and has since devoted her time to researching and understanding your potential power."

"Did she give you any advice on how we could control it? Can we somehow stop our powers from overwhelming us?" I ask.

"There's no real indication that your dreams are premonitions," Bram replies matter-of-factly.

"But we clearly have powers of some sort. And if glowing hands and flames in eyes are only warning signs leading up to whatever we unleash tomorrow . . ." I trail off, shaking my head, not wanting to think about the possibilities.

"Your powers are manifesting. There is no denying that," Bram agrees. "But it appears you have some control over them. After all, your hands are no longer glowing and Kato's eyes have returned to normal."

"I would rather not take the chance if there's something we can do."

Bram nods and I turn to face Ehren. "Did your sister have any advice on how to control our powers?"

"Maybe."

"You're just full of positive information." Kato laughs bitterly.

"What I mean," Ehren clarifies, "is that she did find a few possible 'cures,' for lack of a better word, but with all the varied accounts it's nearly impossible to know which would be effective. One of the suggestions was to chop off your heads before you could manifest fully. I'm guessing you would prefer us to find an alternative method."

A smile plays at the corners of Ehren's lips, and, despite the seriousness of the situation, I fight back a smile of my own.

"Yes, I would prefer to keep my head," Kato grumbles, clearly less amused.

"There is a chance," Bram says, rising from his chair, "that certain magical artifacts could help to contain your power."

He nods to Ehren, who walks over to the dresser, opens a drawer, and begins rifling through the contents. After a moment, Ehren removes an ornate gold box from the drawer and carries it over to the table. He opens the lid to reveal two amulets lying on a green velvet lining. Both are on simple gold chains with a gem roughly half the size of my fist. One is a deep red, and the other a deep blue.

"These are the amulets of the sisters Laila and Adara. They were two of the most powerful sorceresses of their time. These amulets were said to help them contain and control their powers and kept their powers in check so they wouldn't be driven insane."

"And you think these will help contain our powers as well?" I ask, eyeing the amulets.

"My sister thinks it is a possibility, more so than the other options. Well, at least the options that leave you alive." Ehren flashes us a smile and winks. I can't help but roll my eyes, which only makes his smile grow.

"Will we have to wear these at all times?" Kato asks. "It won't exactly be easy to hide beneath my uniform."

"True. And no one would believe that someone of my status would own something this ornate."

"You, my dear, were seen publicly dining with the crown prince," Ehren says, grinning wickedly. "It would be bloody shameful if such a kind and benevolent prince didn't send you a lovely gift, especially once that magnanimous prince found out it was your birthday." This time Bram rolls his eyes. "And as far as you go, Kato, I can have you moved to my official detail. You can be by my side at all times. No one would even have the opportunity to question you if you're not mixed in with the other soldiers."

"It could work, I guess," I say slowly.

"I don't know that you have any other choice," Bram replies bluntly.

"Fine," Kato says, sitting up straighter in his chair. "Which one of these is mine?"

"Which one calls to you?" Ehren asks.

I lean forward and peer into the box, as does Kato. I study the jewels, watching how they catch the light from the nearby candles, twinkling like stars. And then I feel it. A slight, subtle pull from the blue gem. I cautiously reach and pull it gently from the box. It's surprisingly light. I slip the chain over my neck and let it fall into place. Something inside me hums. I look up from the amulet and find Kato studying me, his entire body tense, as if he's waiting for me to burst into silver light at any moment. When nothing happens, he reaches into the box and plucks up the red amulet, easing it on. I see his face relax into a slightly puzzled yet satisfied expression. I look over at Bram and Ehren to find them both watching us with eager anticipation.

"Do they appear to help in any way?" Bram asks, his eyes searching my face.

I nod. "I think so. But it's hard to tell. I feel more . . . I'm not sure how to describe it."

"At peace," Kato offers.

"Yes, at peace. Like something inside has stilled."

"Well, I'm putting that in the 'win' column," Ehren says, his grin returning.

"Let's just hope your sister interpreted those texts correctly."

"As much as I hate to admit it, my sister is seldom wrong," Ehren says with a hint of resignation.

"Let us hope that trend continues," Bram says.

"Now," Ehren says, clapping his hands together once, making us all start. "As I understand it, there is a festival down in the square with music and dancing and food galore. I say we drown our troubles with mead and fried foods and let ourselves forget all this for a few hours. What do you say?"

His enthusiasm is infectious and I throw back my head and laugh. "Why not?" I rise from my seat. "Mara's probably going mad looking for us anyway."

"I don't know, Ehren," Bram says, pushing up from the chair. "I'm not sure I can guarantee your safety in that crowd."

"Look at me!" Ehren cries, motioning dramatically at his clothes. "I look like your typical villager. Besides, by now most of them are deep in their cups and wouldn't recognize my father if he waltzed in with a full caravan, half a legion of soldiers, and his largest crown propped on his head."

I snicker and Bram shoots me a sharp look.

"He has a point," I say with a shrug. "I know many of the people down there and they won't notice or care. Not by this time in the festivities."

"See!" Ehren crows. "Astra agrees with me, and, if I may say so myself, she seems like a responsible individual. I do believe she and I are destined to be great friends."

Ehren meets my eyes, a genuine smile on his lips. I return his grin. I have a feeling, despite my initial reservations, he would make a very good friend.

"I can start being part of the prince's detail tonight," Kato offers, standing. "With you and I both on alert, I'm sure we can keep him safe."

Bram sighs. "You can say that because you've never seen him after several cups of mead, ale, and wine. But fine. Let's go celebrate."

Ehren lets out a rather un-princelike whoop and I laugh.

"I am regretting this already," Bram mumbles as he leads the way out the door.

We make our way down through the inn and back toward the bonfire. I'm not sure if it's the amulet pressing against my skin or the simple knowledge I've gained, but for the first time in a long time, I feel at ease. I just hope this feeling sticks around for a while.

CHAPTER SEVEN

We dance around the bonfire for hours. Bram sticks close to Ehren for the first hour or so until he finally concedes that not a single person in the crowd recognizes the prince for who he truly is. After all, Ehren's probably the least princely person in the crowd. He washes down every type of food he can with varieties of mead, wine, and ale, dancing with men and women alike, all while singing loudly off key. Bram constantly shakes his head, nursing his own tankards and doing his best to avoid dancing. Kato and I dance and laugh, forgetting our worries in good music and food, taking occasional turns dancing with Ehren.

Exhaustion from the day's events and the previous night's sleeplessness eventually catches up with us. The flickering flames of the bonfire are beginning to die, and dawn is only a couple hours away when we finally turn to leave. Bram ushers a staggering, drunk Ehren, who still sings loudly, back toward the inn while Kato and I make our way back home.

Neither of us speak. Whether it's from the exhaustion or simply from not knowing how to form the words to express how we feel, I don't know. When we reach our house it's dark and quiet, save for the snores of our father. I pause at the doorway and glance inside. I can just make out the sleeping form of Marco in the corner. My stomach drops. Kato walks through the door, but I hesitate.

Are you okay?

I'm fine. I just need a moment to myself. Go on. I'll be up in a minute.

Kato doesn't question me. He gives me a quick hug and crosses the room to head up to bed to get what little sleep he can before he needs to rise and be on duty. I lean against the coolness of the outside wall of my house and stare up at the night sky. It's another clear night. The silver stars glisten like diamonds scattered across a perfect sheet of deep blue silk. Something about the stillness and quiet of the night sky calms me, making me feel as if everything will be okay.

Today, I turn eighteen, and whatever has been building beneath my skin is about to be released. In my dreams, it's always night when I lose control. Something in me knows that whatever is about to happen will culminate within the next twenty-four hours, likely coordinating with the exact moment I was born. I reach up, my fingers tracing the amulet draped around my neck. Something about it helps to calm that swirling storm inside, giving me some measure of control, but it isn't enough to completely placate my fears. Whatever these powers are, they're strong. Strong enough that some of the few prophets who had foreseen my birth suggested killing me and my brother before the powers could manifest.

But worry will get me nowhere.

With a sigh, I push away from the wall and enter the house. I'm nearly at the base of the loft ladder when a rough hand grabs my arm. I gasp and try to jerk away but the hand pulls me back, tightening its grip as I crash into a hard body behind me.

A second hand reaches around me, pinning my arms to my sides.

"You can't avoid me forever, you little bitch," Marco slurs, his hot breath reeking of ale and mead.

"Let me go," I whisper hoarsely, struggling to get out of his grip.

He laughs. He spins me, pressing my body against the nearby wall, a hand on each arm, holding me firm so I can't move. His eyes rake my body hungrily and I shudder.

"Let. Me. Go," I say through gritted teeth. He only laughs. "I will scream."

His smile is cruel in the dim light. "Scream all you want. You're my wife and I'll do with you what I want."

"I'm not your wife yet," I spit. "And if I scream my brother—"

"Your brother will take time to get down that ladder. And your scream will wake your father who'll be on my side."

My mind races. I have no doubt that Kato could take on both Marco and my father if need be, but he's likely already asleep. And he needs his sleep. If I wake him, he'll be on guard the rest of the night, which isn't fair to him. I take a deep breath. While I may appear small and defenseless, the truth is that Kato taught me many ways to defend myself over the years. I hoped I'd never need to use any of those things, but, for the first time, his lessons might be useful. The first of his instructions that comes to my mind is, "Use your attacker's assumptions and prejudices against them. If they assume you're weak, let them think you're weak. When they've lowered their defenses, attack."

I let my muscles relax and drop my head in apparent resignation. Marco gives a pleased huff and loosens his grip slightly. I take the opportunity to give him a swift kick between his legs. He cries out, releasing me. Without hesitation, I dash past him to the ladder and climb as fast as I can with my shaking hands. Marco snarls and lunges after me, grabbing my ankle, trying to pull me off the ladder.

"Let go!" I hiss, tightening my grip on the ladder rung, kicking to pull my foot away.

"You little bitch," he growls. "If you think you can get away with that, you're very, very wrong." The hate in his voice sends chills across my body.

I kick again, managing to free my foot from his grip, but instead of climbing away, I kick down, hard and fast, into Marco's face. I hear a crack followed by a slew of swearing. I don't have to look to know my foot broke his nose. I race up the ladder, only glancing down once I'm safely at the top. Marco's hands cover his face, blood pouring out beneath them and soaking his beard.

"I'll kill you for this you bitch!" he roars as I disappear from the top of the ladder.

For a few minutes, I lay on my cot, heart pounding, half expecting him to climb into the loft and make good on his promise. But whether it was the threat of Kato, fast asleep a few cots away, or the simple fact that his drunken ass can't climb the ladder while battling blood pouring from his broken nose, he never appears. Finally, I drift off to sleep.

The next morning I wake with a start, the previous night's events flooding back into my mind. My breath catches, and I sit up. Light pours into the loft from the window revealing that all my siblings have already risen. I can hear the voices of my family in the house below but am unable to make out what anyone is saying. I rise from my bed and make my way to the washbowl in the corner. I splash some cool water on my face and debate whether or not it would be safe downstairs. Marco was pretty drunk when he assaulted me last night, but with a broken nose he's unlikely to forget what I did. It's a miracle my father hasn't already dragged me out of bed to face the consequences of my actions. He's likely too lazy to come up here. I decide it's best to avoid both Marco and my father as long as possible. Once I'm cleaned up and dressed, I crawl through the window and onto the roof.

Our house is, thankfully, not terribly high off the ground. As children, Kato and I escaped for nighttime adventures many times by climbing through the window and jumping off the roof. Jumping from the roof under the cover of darkness while the occupants of the house are sleeping has its advantages. The trick this morning is doing it without anybody inside the house seeing me.

I make my way to the corner edge of the roof farthest from the door and closest to town and peer down, taking a steadying breath. I say a quick prayer to the gods and leap. I land on the ground with a soft thud in a crouch. I hold my breath for a moment before slowly rising and glancing over my shoulder. With a sigh of relief, I see the curtains are down. Without another moment of hesitation, I hurry toward the town square before anyone can notice I'm missing. I reach out to Kato as I walk.

Are you with the prince?

I'm on duty at the inn. Ehren is still sleeping, the lucky bastard.

So, are you officially part of his guard detail? Or will that come later?

Bram talked to Commander Jetson first thing this morning and had me officially switched to the prince's Guard while he's in town. By the way, did you see Marco's face this morning? Apparently, he tripped and fell into a table last night and broke his nose. Dried blood and a crooked nose suit him.

That's not what really happened.

How could you possibly know that?

I know because . . . I'm the one that broke it.

What happened? He was asleep when we got home last night. His tone is cold.

I hesitate.

Astra? What the hell happened?

I promise I'll tell you everything in person. I'm heading into town right now.

Fine. I'll see you soon.

Most of the town stayed up late last night, drinking far too much, so, despite the late hour of the morning, not many people roam the streets. I'm surprised to see Mara is one of the few out and about. Guilt surges as I remember having abandoned her twice last night—once at dinner and then again at the bonfire. Her hurt expression when she notices me approaching tells me she remembers, too.

"Good morning, Mara," I say quietly.

"Good morning," she replies stiffly.

"Look, I'm sorry about leaving you last night. I really am. Things are insane right now." It's a pathetic excuse and we both know it.

"You know I'm always here for you. If you need to talk about your arranged marriage or complain about being a twin or whatever, you can always come to me. We've been friends for our entire lives. I may not understand why you felt the need to yell at the crown prince of Callenia and run from a dinner with him, but I am willing to listen to you and support you. You know that, right?"

I feel tears brimming in my eyes as I look at the hurt etched on my friend's face.

"I know, Mara. And I'm so sorry. I sincerely am." I pull her into a hug. "I promise I'll fill you in on every detail of my life."

When I draw away from the hug, Mara is smiling.

"What are your plans this morning? The library's closed for

the holiday, right? Perhaps we can have a cup of tea and just talk?" she asks.

"I'm actually going to meet Kato at the Briar Hog right now, but I can meet up with you later."

She forces a tight smile. "Well, do you mind if I walk with you?"

"Of course not!" I smile, looping my arm through hers. "I wouldn't expect anything else."

Her smile is genuine as we begin walking. After a couple moments she says quietly, "I saw you, you know."

I scowl in confusion. "Saw me when?"

"Last night at the bonfire. After you left with Kato and Bram. When you returned with the prince."

"Oh, I didn't see you," I mumble, my guilt resurfacing.

"I figured as much. I was getting ready to leave when the four of you arrived."

"You should've joined us."

"You looked happy and carefree. It's been a while since I've seen you that way, so I figured I'd let you be. Besides, by that time, I was tired."

"Well, if you see us together tonight, please, feel free to come over."

Mara nods and we walk quietly for another moment, letting awkwardness wash over us.

"Happy birthday, by the way," she says, elbowing me gently. I smile. Somehow, with everything else going on, I forgot today's my birthday. "How does it feel to be eighteen?"

I laugh. "The same as it felt to be seventeen." That isn't entirely true. "Though, I suppose I won't technically be eighteen until it's almost midnight."

Mara waves me off. "Oh, semantics. It's your birthday. You're eighteen. You know, most people don't actually know the exact second they were born like you and Kato do. Most people wake up the morning of their birthday and start announcing to the world they're another year older." I laugh again. "By the way, I received word from Madame Gosspick this morning that your dress is ready. I'll pick it up and you can come by my house before the festival tonight to get ready. Okay?"

"That sounds perfect, Mara," I reply, realizing we've arrived at the inn. I slip my arm from hers and wrap her in a quick hug. "I'll see you later. I promise."

She smiles and squeezes me tightly. "I'll hold you to that. Tell Kato happy birthday for me!"

I promise and she turns, walking back to her house as I enter the inn.

The inn is dusty and dark. Most of the windows are shuttered, so it isn't very well lit. Not that it needs to be. There isn't much to see. My brother and a few of the soldiers on duty are the only ones seated at the tables. Kato sits at the table closest to the stairs with two other soldiers, playing cards. I vaguely recognize the blond soldier to my brother's right but can't recall his name. The dark-skinned soldier on Kato's left, however, is almost as familiar to me as Mara.

"Is Kato taking all your money?" I tease and Pax looks up at me, grinning as I approach.

"Hell, no! I learned a long time ago to never bet against your brother. He never loses," Pax replies, drawing a card from the deck.

I laugh. Little does Pax know, when we were children, I would stand behind him and secretly tell Kato what cards Pax held in his hands. That was the reason he never lost then. But that cheating has turned into skill over the years, and I have no doubt Kato does win most hands.

"Mara says to wish you a happy birthday," I relay to Kato as he puts down a card and draws one from the deck.

He looks up, grinning. "I knew she would remember!"

"Of course she remembers. She's your sister's best friend. Forgetting your birthday would mean forgetting Astra's birthday and she's too good a friend to do that," Pax says, rolling his eyes before grinning up at me. "Happy birthday, by the way."

I give Pax a nod of thanks as Kato laughs, waving him off.

"Sure. Sure. That may be true, but she still didn't have to wish me a happy birthday. I'm telling you, she's most definitely falling in love with me." He splays his cards on the table. "Royal flush!"

The blond soldier grumbles and tosses his cards down. Pax smacks his onto the table, swearing. Kato just leans back in his chair, grinning.

"See? I told you! He never loses!" Pax laughs, motioning to my brother's cards.

For a moment I stand awkwardly, debating what I should do next. It's not like I can just waltz upstairs to Ehren's room. I've already wished Kato a happy birthday and, since he's technically on duty, pulling up a chair to watch their game probably isn't the best idea. I'm saved by Bram coming down the stairs. He pauses when he sees me, a smile spreading across his face.

"Astra! What a pleasant surprise!" he greets, walking over to the table. Pax and the other soldier sit a little straighter. "I was just about to head to the bakery and get a few things for Prince Ehren to eat for breakfast."

"Does Jaxon's porridge not seem appeasing to his royal highness?" I ask, eyes glinting.

"Unfortunately, it does not. While the prince is perfectly content with stew, he has never been a fan of porridge," he pauses briefly then asks, "I don't suppose you would like to accompany me?"

Out of the corner of my eye, I see Pax's eyebrows shoot up

in delighted surprise as he flashes my brother a mischievous, knowing grin. Kato kicks Pax under the table, and I bite back a laugh as Pax yelps.

"Of course! I would be more than happy to walk with you," I reply, pretending not to notice.

"Excellent!" Bram turns and addresses Kato. "This puts you on duty with His Majesty. Go upstairs and guard his door in my absence." It's almost startling to hear Bram's voice shift from the casual tone to which I've become accustomed to an authoritative voice of a commander.

Kato doesn't hesitate. He stands, giving Bram an affirmative nod. "Yes, Sir." Kato begins to walk toward the stairs, but pauses, looking back over his shoulder. "Would His Majesty like any coffee this morning? Jaxon has some prepared. It's quite strong."

"Yes, I think that may be exactly what he needs this morning."

Kato nods and makes his way to the kitchen.

Bram turns back to me, offering his arm. "Shall we?"

I accept with a smile. As we walk outside, Pax calls to one of the other soldiers lingering nearby to join their game in Kato's absence.

"How are you this morning?" Bram asks, his eyes searching my face as we walk.

"I'm good."

"Any bad dreams last night?"

I shake my head. "Actually, no. Last night was the first night in months I haven't had a nightmare."

Bram gives a satisfactory nod. "It seems the amulet is working."

He speaks quietly enough I know no one else could have heard him, but talking about it still makes me uncomfortable. He senses my unease.

"We can wait until we are in private, away from anyone else, before we discuss anything if you wish," he offers gently.

"That's not necessary. Not that I want to declare anything to the entire town. It's just, well, I've never really said anything to anyone before. It's odd to talk about it."

"You've never even talked with Kato about it? It seems as if you two share everything."

I can feel his eyes watching me as I stare straight ahead, avoiding his gaze. I whisper, barely audible, "We've never discussed it out loud."

Bram releases a slow breath. "Ah. I see. Ehren was correct last night, then, wasn't he? You and Kato, you can communicate without speaking. You can talk mind to mind." His voice is as quiet as mine.

I swallow and nod before stopping just outside the bakery door and look up directly into Bram's eyes. "No one knows. Not Mara. Not Pax. Not our parents. No one."

Bram smiles softly, holding my gaze. "I am excellent at keeping secrets."

We stand, not moving, holding our gaze for a moment before Bram breaks away, leading me inside the bakery.

The bakery is a little busier than it was yesterday, but we are still able to get a good selection of baked treats without waiting too long. As Esme fills a basket with our goods, her eyes constantly flit between me and Bram, trying to figure out exactly what relationship a lowly scholar could possibly have with the prince's Captain of the Guard, who is in full uniform today.

Once Bram pays, we make our way back to the inn, chatting casually about useless things such as the weather. When we enter the inn, a quick glance at the table shows that the simple card game now has five players. Coins sit in the middle of the table. With Kato gone they're willing to play for money.

Pax catches me watching and flashes a winning grin. His eyes dart to Bram next to me and he waggles his eyebrows. I fail at hiding my smile as I shake my head. Bram, thankfully, seems unaware as we go upstairs.

I expect to find my brother outside Ehren's room, diligently guarding the door, but instead, stationed outside the door are two of Ehren's personal Guard, decked in official royal uniforms. Kato, it turns out, is inside. Bram dismisses the Guards, ordering them to wait at the end of the hall, allowing no one to pass. Bram opens the door for me and I slide in. Kato sits at the table next to four mugs and a pot of coffee. Ehren lies on the made bed, fully dressed in another blue and gold tunic, with his arm slung over his eyes.

"Get up," Bram orders.

Ehren groans. "Did you get me food?" he asks, not bothering to move his arm and look for himself.

"Food and company," Bram replies, setting the basket of baked goods next to the coffee.

At that, Ehren drags his arm off his face, opening his eyes and turning his head just enough to see who Bram means by "company." When his eyes fall on me he grins, easing into a sitting position.

"Well, I must admit, seeing your face is more pleasant than having to see Bram's face. It's definitely better motivation to get out of bed."

Ehren staggers across the room and collapses in the chair next to Kato. He eyes the basket then switches his gaze to the coffee, pouring himself a cup. He takes a couple gulps of the hot brew before grabbing a poppy roll from the basket and taking a big bite.

"So, what is the plan for the day?" he asks, his mouth full.

Bram rolls his eyes. "Can you at least pretend to have some decorum?"

Ehren shakes his head. "Not until I've had at least two cups of coffee." He makes a mock "cheers" gesture with the coffee mug before washing down his roll with another gulp.

Bram sighs and I stifle a laugh. Kato hides his smile by taking a sip of his own coffee.

"It is decent coffee," Kato mumbles into his mug.

Bram just shakes his head in resignation, pouring a cup of coffee, which he offers to me. I take it and pluck a sweet bun from the basket before settling in the easy chair. Bram pours himself some coffee, grabbing a roll. He leans his back against the dresser, setting his mug down on top. Ehren pours himself a second full mug and gulps it down. When he's finished, he pushes his chair back and stands. He has a much more princely air now that coffee has pushed aside whatever effects linger from the previous night's events.

"Now then, I'm assuming that you two," he says, gesturing to me and Kato, "are doing fine so far this morning as the village exploded in neither flames nor light while we all slept. Is that correct?" We nod. "Any weird dreams or anything else?"

"None for me," I reply, shaking my head

"Same," Kato agrees. "I actually slept well for the first time in ages."

"Excellent. Excellent," Ehren says, clasping his hands behind his back, pacing the room like a general planning for a battle. "So, it seems that sweet Cadewynn—gods bless her—was correct in assuming the amulets would help control your powers, at least to some extent. The question remains as to whether or not it will be enough to contain whatever is threatening to burst out tonight."

"Is there anything more we can do?" I ask. "Now that we know the amulets work, is there anything similar we can use to help contain the power more?"

Ehren pauses his pacing and looks at me, his face grim.

"Cadewynn did provide a few spells that we can prepare that may help to absorb any power that you emit into the air."

Kato scowls. "What do you mean 'absorb power'?"

"Essentially," Ehren responds, resuming his pacing, "according to my sister, the mixtures, spells, potions—whatever you want to call them—will draw any magic or outburst of power to them instantly. It could help to reduce the damage when, hopefully if, one or both of you are unable to control your power, and you . . . Well, you know." Ehren makes an exploding motion with his hands.

I let out a slow breath. "Will the spells even work if we don't have magic yet? Don't you need magic to create spells?"

Bram answers me from where he still leans against the dresser, arms crossed. "Some spells, yes, require magic. But there are spells, such as these, that should be able to be wielded by anyone. At least, that is if the princess is correct. I have seldom known her to be wrong, though, so I have no reason to doubt that these spells will work exactly as she says."

I nod, weighing their words. "So is there anything else for us to do between now and tonight?"

Bram shakes his head as Ehren says, "Nothing but go about our normal days. I have official royal duties to attend to. Basic meetings with important people so I can pretend like I have reason to be here beyond why I am actually here. Bram and Kato will be accompanying me as part of my Guard. You're welcome to come along, but I'm sure you would be quite bored. I know, because I'm going to be bored."

"I guess I'll go see Mara," I murmur, mostly to myself.

"Mara? She's the lovely girl who came to dinner with you last night, correct?" Ehren asks.

I smile. "Yes. She'll be pleased to hear you called her 'lovely.'"

Ehren laughs. "She was lovely! And she was a very good

friend, defending you after you rushed off." My stomach turns with fresh guilt. "But, of course, we fully understand why you left as you did." He turns to Bram. "Well, shall we be off? The sooner we start, the sooner we will be done."

Bram nods, pushing off from the dresser as Kato and I rise from our chairs. As we walk toward the door, Kato stops abruptly, facing me.

"You never told me how you broke Marco's nose."

Bram and Ehren turn their attention to me. Bram's face is etched with concern and Ehren's in cautious delight.

"Who," Ehren asks, doing a horrible job of hiding his amusement, "is Marco, and why did you break his nose?"

"Marco," Kato answers for me, "is an associate of my father's who my father brought home to marry Astra, over my dead body."

I nod. "I've been avoiding him as much as possible but last night, after the festival, Kato went on to bed and I remained outside the house to collect my thoughts. When I went inside, I assumed Marco was sleeping but when I started to go to bed, he grabbed me from behind and pinned me to the wall."

All amusement vanishes from Ehren's face, replaced with cold displeasure. Bram sets his jaw and a deadly calm washes over him. Kato's eyes flash, and I know that if Kato had any control over his powers, Marco would be incinerated in a pillar of fire.

"What the hell, Astra? Why didn't you yell for me?" Kato asks, his voice controlled and even.

"I would have woken the whole house. You were tired and I figured you needed your sleep so—"

Kato cuts me off by slamming his fist into the closest wall. "Damn my sleep! You should have yelled for me!"

"And, what, had you and Marco engage in a full-out brawl and wake the whole damn village?" I snap. "I handled it!"

"By breaking his nose," Bram muses, his tone unreadable.

I nod, taking a breath. "Yes. First, I kicked him, um, between his legs"—Ehren lets out a low whistle—"and when I tried to climb up the ladder to bed, he grabbed my ankle and I kicked his face, breaking his nose."

"What if he had followed you up the ladder?" Kato demands, seething.

"Then you definitely would have woken up and beat his ass. But there was no way he could climb up the ladder as drunk as he was, let alone with blood pouring down his face."

"Remind me never to make you mad," Ehren mumbles, no hint of joking in his voice, rather a tone of awe. His voice becomes more cheerful again as he adds, "Do you want me to have him killed? I can have him killed. I'm a prince. I have power like that." He grins but we ignore him.

"How did you get out of the house this morning? It does not sound as if Marco is one who would have just let you go. Not after embarrassing him," Bram asks, his eyes locked hard on my face.

"I may have avoided facing him by climbing out the loft window and jumping off the roof . . ." I let my voice trail off, glancing away.

Ehren laughs. "I knew I liked you. I should marry you right here, right now. How do you feel about being a princess?"

I can't hide my blush. Kato shoots Ehren a mirthless look and Bram's lips tighten, clearly unamused.

"You should be able to feel safe in your own home," Bram says, his voice so quiet I barely hear him.

"I normally am," I insist, meeting his gaze. "But the last couple of days have been the exception. Thankfully, Kato trained me to protect myself."

Neither of us break our gaze until Kato speaks, his voice broken. "I never wanted you to have to use what I taught you,

Ash. And most of what you know is knives and weapons. With your size, I never expected you to fight hand to hand. I'm always supposed to be there."

I reach out and cup my hand against my brother's cheek, fighting back tears. He places his hand on top of mine, closing his eyes. Ehren shifts awkwardly, looking everywhere but at me and Kato. Bram just looks down, allowing us our moment. Kato takes a deep breath and I drop my hand.

"Well, everything worked out this time, but next time, Ash, next time, call for me. Even if you can handle it yourself."

I manage a weak smile and nod my agreement. Kato turns, opening the door, and we filter out into the hallway. Bram comes to an abrupt halt, glancing toward the room across from Ehren's.

"Wait one moment," he mutters, entering the room, which must be his.

He returns a moment later with a small silver dagger in his hand, the blade the length of my palm. The handle is simple save for a small diamond in the center, directly above the blade. In his other hand he holds a black sheath for the dagger. He slides the dagger inside and hands them to me.

"Take these. Then, the next time he lays his hands on you, you slit his throat."

I swallow and accept them, looking up into his eyes. "Thank you."

"The sheath clips inside a boot to help conceal the dagger and keep your hands free," he explains, his eyes dropping down to the worn black boots peeking out beneath my dress. He opens his mouth and I wonder if he's about to offer to help me secure it in my boot, but Kato offers first. I smile at my brother as he takes the dagger and kneels down to place it in my boot. Ehren turns away, shoving his hands in his pockets.

Bram locks his eyes with me once more and I feel heat

rising in my cheeks. When Kato stands, we resume our way down the stairs, the two Guards at the end of the hall joining us. I bid them farewell and rush off to Mara's house, my chest filling with a glow that has nothing to do with the power I have inside.

CHAPTER EIGHT

*M*ara hadn't been expecting me quite so early, but is thrilled nonetheless when I show up at her door. She's even more thrilled when I tell her that Prince Ehren called her "lovely." This, naturally, sends her gushing about how wonderful he is.

"Did you know," she asks, her face glowing, "that every year at Winter Solstice he goes down to give presents to all the children in the city outside the palace? Even the orphans!"

"I didn't know that," I confess, smiling.

"It's true! He told me last night at dinner that it's one of his favorite parts of the holiday." She continues rambling, relaying random facts she learned last night. I nod along. After a few minutes, my eyes begin to glaze over as I struggle to concentrate on her words. Mara declares we need tea and drags me into her garden for some "fresh air."

"So, what are your birthday plans?" she asks, taking a sip of her tea as we sit at a stone table outside.

"Nothing, really, beyond spending the day with you and the festival tonight."

"No plans with Bram?" she drawls, smiling mischievously around her teacup.

"No," I reply, a little too sharply. "He has a job, you know, guarding the prince."

"Mm hm. But surely he gets some breaks. I heard the two of you were at the bakery this morning."

"Heard from whom?"

"Esme. I went in to get a few things and she seemed very interested in what was going on between you and Bram. She says you two were together yesterday morning as well."

"We were not in there together yesterday," I huff, ignoring the fact my cheeks are turning red. "Esme is just a hopeless gossip. We just happened to be there at the same time."

"But he paid for your order and you left together." She sets her teacup down and stares at me with a knowing smile.

"I . . . yes . . . technically that is true. But it wasn't planned!"

"And this morning? Was that planned?"

"I didn't plan ahead of time to go to the bakery with him, no. However, when I went to see Kato this morning, Bram was there and he requested I go with him to pick out some breakfast pastries and whatnot. It would've been rude to turn him down."

"Very rude indeed, I'm sure," she teases.

"Mara!" I yell in frustration, nearly spilling my tea. Mara grins.

"I'm sorry, Astra! I know I shouldn't tease you. You seem genuinely happy with him. It's nice to see you happy."

I can't help but shake my head and smile. "Thank you, Mara. You're a good friend."

"Plus," she says, sipping her tea, "if you win the captain of Prince Ehren's Guard that puts you in an excellent position to help me win the prince."

It's my turn to laugh.

Something rushes over me, making the world tilt and spin. I

grab the table with both hands and squeeze my eyes shut in an attempt to steady myself.

"Astra, are you okay?" Mara asks, her voice thick with concern.

I don't respond at first. I wait a moment until the feeling fades, leaving behind a loud ringing in my ears. I slowly open my eyes to find Mara staring at me, her eyes wide with fear.

"You're so pale," she whispers. I can barely hear her above the ringing. "Are you okay?"

I attempt a smile I'm pretty sure looks more like a grimace. "Aren't I always pale?"

"I'm serious, Astra," she says, firmly. "Do you need to lie down?"

"Actually, that sounds good. I think the lack of sleep from the past couple of nights is catching up with me."

I rise slowly from the table, feeling slightly unsteady. Mara is next to me in an instant, offering me her arm for support.

"You can rest in my bed," she says in a motherly tone as she leads me back inside. "I have a few errands to run, including picking up your dress. When you're done resting, we can start to plan out the rest of your birthday and get ready for the feast tonight."

I nod my agreement but can't quite find the strength to speak. The ringing is making my head throb. Once we're in her room, she says something but I can't quite focus enough to process the words as I collapse onto her bed. As soon as she leaves, I let sleep consume me.

I STAND in a field with white wildflowers as far as the eye can see. A warm breeze winds around me, rustling the flowers and whipping my hair into my eyes. The sun is high in the sky above me, not a cloud to be seen. I turn, searching for someone. Kato, perhaps. I'm not really sure. Regardless, I'm alone. I spin and see that the field stretches in every direction with no end in sight. A crushing panic rises in my chest. Then, I hear that familiar voice. The one that always seems to haunt my dreams.

"Soon," it says. Just one word, spoken in a low purr, sending chills up my spine. "Soon."

The world around me fades in a flash of bright silver light. I open my eyes with a gasp to find Mara standing over me, her eyes filled with concern.

"Thank the gods!" she sighs, her voice shaky. "I've been trying to wake you for five minutes but you've been out cold!"

I push up onto my elbows. My mouth feels dry and my head pounds nearly as hard as my heart. "Sorry," I mumble, my voice hoarse. "I guess I just really needed the sleep."

"Apparently!" She narrows her eyes and asks, "Are you feeling okay? Do you need anything?"

"I'm a little thirsty," I reply weakly.

She reaches over to her bedside table and pours water from a floral painted pitcher into a cup and hands it to me. "Here. Drink as much as you need. We need to start getting ready if you're up to it."

The concern fades from her eyes, replaced with excitement.

I gulp down the contents of the cup before asking, "Already? How long did I sleep?"

"You've been out almost all day! It's nearly dusk!" she responds, walking over to her closet to shift through her dresses. "I thought about waking you for lunch but I figured you needed the sleep more than food. The feast starts in just over an hour." She pulls a sleek, dark blue gown from her closet and holds it up against her body. "How does this look? Do you think it would work for tonight?"

I nod. "You would look beautiful in that. You would look beautiful in anything."

"But is it worthy of a prince?" she prods, wiggling her eyebrows.

I chuckle, pouring myself another cup of water. "I hate to break it to you, but the rumor that the prince came to our village to find a commoner wife is completely untrue."

She sighs dramatically as I gulp down the water, my headache easing a bit. "I figured as much, but one can always hope." She turns and hangs the dress back in her closet and pulls out a bright red dress. "Why is he here? Did he really just want to meet you and Kato?"

I shrug. "I'm not entirely sure," I lie. "I think business just had him traveling nearby and the temptation to meet the infamous twins was too great to resist."

She nods, accepting my lie without question and trades the red dress out for the blue she held earlier. "I think I will wear this one. Your dress is over there," she says, pointing across her room to where my new dress is draped over a chair.

As I rise from the bed, I notice my strength has returned to normal. I dress quickly, taking care to hide my amulet from Mara's view as I slip into my dress. I study my reflection in Mara's full-length mirror. The dress seemed perfect before, but now it truly is. I still can't believe this dress belongs to me. Mara steps up behind me, grinning.

"You look amazing," she says. "Except for your hair. Let's fix that." She directs me to the chair. I obey her instructions and take a seat, sitting as tall as I can as she goes to work. I can't see what she is doing, but she brushes and tugs my hair for what seems like an eternity. Finally, she stops and crosses in front of me, studying my head through squinted eyes.

"What?" I ask, feeling self-conscious.

"It needs something," she says, drawing out the words. "I just don't know . . ."

She snaps her fingers, rushes over to her dresser, and digs through one of her many jewelry boxes. She returns with a hair pin that resembles a small tiara.

"I can't wear that," I insist, eyes wide.

"You can and you will," she says firmly, leaning forward and sliding it into my hair. "Consider it your birthday crown."

I smile at her and she motions for me to look in the mirror. I walk over and barely recognize the girl staring back. Mara has certainly worked magic. She goes to work on her own hair, chatting away about all the things she's planning to eat at the feast. I bob my head in agreement, adding in my own ideas as necessary.

Where are you?

Mara and I are still getting ready. We're almost done. We'll be there soon.

And you're okay?

Yes. I'm fine. No need to worry him. A little sleep never hurt anyone. *Why?*

I tried reaching you earlier, but you never responded. I was concerned.

Sorry. Mara let me sleep a bit this afternoon. All day really. I'm all rested now.

Good. I'll see you soon.

I focus back on Mara who is going on about spiced apples.

"And you know, you can't beat apples spiced with rum. It's one of the best parts of Kriloa."

"That and the honey mead," I amend, licking my lips.

"Yes. Honey mead is an excellent addition to anything!" She stands up, gesturing to her hair. "How does it look?"

"Worthy of a prince," I tease and she giggles.

"Well then," she says, looping her arm in mine. "Let's go find a prince, shall we?"

The last night of Kriloa is by far the busiest and most popular. Even people who haven't attended the previous nights' festivities will attend tonight. Long wooden tables are set up every few feet, each laden with every sort of food imaginable. Nearby, large hogs, chickens, sheep, and other delicious animals are turning on spits over fires. While some vendors will still have wares and food for sale, tonight most of the food is free. Every food merchant and family in town with resources to spare helps to provide the feast. It's a night of celebration, not one where money is to be made.

The crowd is thick, making it hard to navigate. It's almost impossible to locate anybody now that dark has almost completely fallen. After several fruitless minutes of trying to find Kato by standing on my tiptoes, I give up and reach out to him.

We're here. Where are you?

Right near the bonfire. There's a table reserved for the prince and his Guard.

Is there room for me at this table?

Of course. You and Mara have been marked as Prince Ehren's special guests.

Mara's going to love that.

I grab Mara's arm and guide her toward the bonfire. "I think I saw Kato this way," I explain as we push our way through the crowd.

It takes a little effort, but we manage to find the pocket in the crowd where Ehren sits, surrounded by seven of his Guard, all dressed in sharp uniforms. Three are positioned standing behind him, and four sit with him at the table, two on each side. One of the seated Guard is, naturally, Bram. The other, I realize with a start, is Kato. I wonder when he was issued an official Guard uniform. The uniform suits him well, though. I assume Mara's gasp and murmured "Is that Kato?" means she agrees.

Bram stands as we approach, his eyes frozen on me.

"Good evening ladies," he says, clearing his throat. "Please, join us."

We take our seats with a nod of thanks. Mara can't seem to take her eyes off Kato, and, judging by his smug expression, he notices.

"What do you think of your brother's new uniform?" Ehren asks, gesturing to Kato.

I force my expression into disinterest and shrug. "Eh. I've seen better."

Ehren and Bram laugh while Kato scowls, shaking his head, but even he's unable to hide his smile. I grin and give my brother a wink.

"I think he looks very handsome," Mara counters, her eyes shining. It's difficult to tell in the dim light, but I swear Kato blushes.

Before anyone else can weigh in, a loud bell rings over the noise of the crowd and people begin to fall silent. Mara's father stands on a small, raised platform not far away, everyone's gaze shifting to him. He beams at the crowd and his voice booms.

"Good evening, citizens of Timberborn!" Several voices call out from the crowd, returning the greeting. "Tonight we have a special guest who has agreed to start the feast tonight. It is my pleasure to introduce His Royal Highness Prince Ehren Andrewe Daniel Montavillier, Crown Prince of Callenia!"

The crowd erupts into applause and cheers as Ehren rises, waving at the crowd, and makes his way up onto the platform as Mara's father steps down.

"Greetings, people of Timberborn!" he calls out, his voice clear and resonating across the crowd. He is met with a host of cheers. He grins, his natural charisma shining. I can tell he's made for this.

"It has been my great honor to be a part of your annual celebration of Kriloa. I must say it has been one of the best Kriloa celebrations I have had the privilege of attending." This brings another round of cheers. After a moment of basking in the celebratory praise, Ehren holds up his hands, silencing the crowd. "You have been warm and welcoming to me, and I cannot show my appreciation enough. That said, let the feasting begin!"

A cheer roars through the crowd, so loud it makes the tables vibrate. As Ehren makes his way back to the table, grinning, people begin lining up near the small fires where the meat has been prepared so they can load their plates before heading back to their tables for the rest of the food. I rise to head over to a nearby fire where there is a large roasted pig, but Bram motions for me to sit. He and Kato disappear into the crowd, along with Ehren and a couple of the other Guards. Kato and Bram return shortly, each holding two plates. Kato places one of the plates in front of Mara with a sheepish grin and Bram hands his second plate to me. Ehren arrives with them and plops down in his seat.

"I hope you appreciate those plates, ladies," Ehren yells above the crowd, "because it meant I had to carry my own plate." He winks at us and I laugh.

"Somehow, I think you'll live," I tease. Ehren's eyes twinkle with surprised delight at my banter.

I pile my plate high with food until I can't see it. I dig in, listening to the easy conversation swelling around me from the crowd. I'm seated a little too far down to be able to follow whatever Ehren is saying (Mara, on the other hand, seems to be hanging on his every word), but I catch occasional clips of conversation. He seems to be regaling anyone within hearing distance with tales of his heroism, complete with dramatic hand gestures. Every so often Bram rolls his eyes.

Once we have all cleared our plates, trays of desserts start to make their rounds. I rise from my seat and wander through the crowd until I locate a table with a collection of cakes. I opt for a small rum cake topped with fresh berries and sugar. I add it to my plate and turn to find Bram directly behind me.

"Let me guess. You are incapable of making your own decisions and have come, once again, to see what I am getting so you can copy me."

He throws his head back and laughs. "As much as I hate to disagree, you would be incorrect." He reaches across me and selects a small chocolate cake covered in sugar. "I came for this."

I grin and we head back to the table together. This time, instead of sitting down near the prince, he takes a seat next to me. We sit so close our arms brush. I concentrate on eating my cake, trying to hide the blush rising in my cheeks.

"Are you having a good birthday?" he asks, his voice low and warm.

"I am, especially now that I have cake," I say, turning my face toward him. We're barely an inch apart. This close I notice he has little specks of gold mixed into the brown of his eyes. My heart skips a beat and rushes to catch up.

"Good. That's good."

I pull my gaze away, back to my nearly finished cake. "This cake is really good," I mumble, happy for the distraction.

"Yes," Bram agrees, shifting slightly. "Mine is quite delicious as well."

Somewhere nearby, lively music starts up, small pockets clearing throughout crowd for people to dance. Ehren claps his hands, rising from his seat.

"Music! Excellent!" he looks over to Mara who is poking at

a pudding. "Would you honor me with a dance?" he asks, extending his hand with a slight bow.

Mara's eyes light up as she leaps to her feet. "Of course!"

Ehren leads her to the nearest dance area. Bram leans in to me. "He'll get himself in trouble if I don't stick near. Would you care to dance?"

My stomach flips and I can't quite find the words so I just nod. Bram stands, offering me his hand. With a smile, I accept and am soon swept away in the music and gaiety of the moment. It doesn't take long before Kato and the other Guards join with partners of their own. Only one Guard, a handsome young man with dark skin, hangs back, content to watch, his eyes protectively following Ehren as he mingles with the crowd.

The bright and cheerful music swells around us. We dance and dance and dance, switching partners on occasion. I dance twice with Ehren, once with Kato, and once with one of Ehren's Guards with bright hazel eyes and roguish grin. Pax even makes an appearance, stealing a dance. The rest of my dances are reserved for Bram, who seems just as pleased as I do with the arrangement. After about our dozenth dance, Ehren declares it's time for a drink. We all heartily agree, except Mara who is busy dancing with one of the handsome Guards.

"I'll be right back," Bram whispers, leaning closer to me.

He leaves me near the edge of the bonfire feeling breathless and light. I'm so focused on watching him fade into the crowd, I don't notice Marco slink up beside me until he grabs my arm, his nails digging into my skin so hard he draws blood. I gasp in pain and spin to face him.

"You didn't think you could avoid me forever, you little bitch," he murmurs in my ear as I try to jerk away, my eyes frantically searching for Bram or Kato. "You're not getting away with what you did."

"I heard you fell into a table," I snap back with more vigor than I feel.

He tightens his grip and I inhale sharply. "You're going to pay for it. But not here." He jerks me away from the bonfire and into the crowd. I try to fight him off but there are too many people.

"Let me go!" I scream, but he only laughs.

I look around wildly, but no one around us seems to realize I'm being taken against my will. They're all too caught up in their own celebrations to pay any real attention.

Kato! I scream inside my head. *Kato!*

What's wrong? Where did you go?

Marco! He— I'm cut short as Marco thrusts me out of the crowd and into a dark, forgotten alleyway.

What! Marco is here? Where are you? Did he take you? Astra? His voice sounds as panicked as I feel.

I don't know where I am. It's too dark. I'm in an al—

Marco shoves me to the ground so hard I'm surprised nothing breaks. I remember the dagger in my boot and try to reach for it, but Marco kicks me in the stomach before my hand can even graze the hilt. I gasp, curling into a ball. Before I can recover, he kicks me again, this time on my back. Pain rattles through me, tears stinging my eyes.

ASTRA! WHERE ARE YOU?

An alley. Away from the crowd.

Marco smashes his foot down on my left hand with a crack. I can't contain my scream and Marco clearly derives pleasure from my pain.

Astra! Astra! We're coming!

Marco's boot connects with my face, the coppery tang of blood flooding my mouth. He kicks again and again, each time hitting a new spot. I curl up and try to protect myself as best I can as tears stream down my cheeks. I don't know how much more I can take. Finally, he pauses and I gasp for breath.

"You thought you were so wonderful and clever, sneaking away this morning without me noticing, didn't you? But you know what? You're not nearly as clever as you think." I move quietly and slowly, my hand sliding toward the dagger in my boot. "You know why? Because I found you. And now, not only do you have to pay for breaking my nose, you have to pay for sneaking away, too." My hand grasps the handle of the dagger. I steady my breathing as Marco leans down. "I will make you into a good, submissive wife if it's the last thing I do." He reaches out a rough finger and traces it down my cheek.

I strike using every ounce of strength I have left, stabbing the dagger into his neck. It's sloppy but effective. He stumbles back, choking on his own blood as it bubbles out of his mouth. I scramble to my feet and back down the alley, afraid to take my eyes off of Marco as his hands fumble to grab hold of the dagger.

"Astra," Kato's voice echoes down the alley. It takes me a second to realize he's physically there and not just in my head. I spin, wincing, and find him, Ehren and Bram materializing into the alley behind him. Kato rushes to me and I collapse into his arms, weeping and shaking.

"He found me. I couldn't get my dagger at first but . . ."

Kato cradles me close. "It's okay. I'm here. We're here."

Bram stalks past us, pulling his sword from its sheath with a hiss. He stops and stands above Marco, who looks up, terror evident on his face.

Bram speaks, his voice hard and quiet so I can barely hear his words to Marco. "You will never lay your hand on her or any woman ever again."

In one smooth motion, he plunges his sword into Marco's chest. Marco's eyes go wide before his body goes still. Bram removes the sword and wipes it clean on a patch of grass before leaning down and pulling the dagger from Marco's neck, cleaning it as well. Bram approaches me tentatively, his eyes searching me in concern. I pull away from Kato as much as I can, relying on him to keep me upright.

"Are you, did he . . ." Bram struggles to find the words. He starts to reach his hand to my split lip but draws back at the last moment.

"I think I'll be okay," I whisper. "He didn't break anything important. At least, I don't think so. A few fingers, maybe a rib or two. I can't really tell."

Bram nods and shifts his eyes to Kato. "Do you have a town healer?"

Kato nods. "We do, but I don't know where she is in this crowd tonight. I'll look for her, though."

I shake my head. "No, I'll be fine. Let's just get back to the festival. I'll just sit on the sidelines and watch."

Bram's brow furrows. "Are you sure that's the best idea?"

"Yes. It's my birthday. Our birthday." I smile up at Kato and he smiles back, but I can tell it's forced. "I want to celebrate."

The truth is I need a distraction. I want to forget.

"I will have Cal dispose of the body," Ehren says, his voice cold. "Makin can help him."

Bram nods.

"And I think you should definitely see a healer," Ehren adds. "I've seen too many seemingly simple injuries go unattended only for them to turn out ten times worse later because they weren't managed properly."

"I can find her but—" Kato breaks off and looks down at me.

"I will stay with Astra," Bram offers.

Kato hesitates but Ehren places his hand on Kato's shoulder. "Right now, Kato, I don't think there's anyone safer for her to be with."

Kato nods and releases his grip as Bram reaches for me. I take a step away from Kato and collapse against Bram, my legs giving out. Without hesitation Bram scoops me up, cradling me against his chest.

"I will wait here with her until you find the healer and make sure no one stumbles across the body before we take care of it. Go find the healer."

Kato gives me one last glance and then rushes off.

"I will go get Cal. And Makin. They should be back where we just were," Ehren says, turning to leave.

"You can't go back into that crowd without any protection," Bram argues.

"Bram," Ehren says firmly, authority ringing in his voice. "Stay here with Astra. That is a direct order." His voice softens sightly as he adds. "I'll be fine. It's almost as if I was trained by the best swordsmen in the kingdom."

Bram gives a small huff as Ehren winks, wandering off to find and retrieve the Guards he needs to get rid of Marco's body. Bram carries me over to the wall of whatever building we're near and sinks down, helping me sit up next to him. I lean against the building and gaze up at him.

"Thank you," my voice hoarse. "Thank you for the dagger. Without it, I don't know what might have happened." I glance away from the intensity of his gaze.

"I'm sorry you had to use it," he replies. "I'm glad you had it, though." He hesitates. "Do you want it back right now?"

"No, I . . ." I look back at him and then down at my hands in my lap. It's then that I notice the smears of dirt and blood now staining my perfect gift.

"My dress is ruined," I mutter, fighting back another rush of tears. I rub at a stain near my knee.

"It is a pity. You look beautiful in it."

I shift my eyes to his and he holds my gaze.

"Yesterday," he says, "I confirmed that Ehren's favorite color was blue and told you I would tell you mine at dinner. Since you left early, I never got to tell you. It used to be green, almost the exact shade of your dress, actually."

"Used to be?" I ask breathlessly. "What is it now?"

"Now," he says, his voice rough as he lifts a gentle finger to brush a loose strand of hair from my face, "it's the color of your eyes."

It feels like my heart is about to flutter out of my chest as he leans in. He's barely a breath away when the ground beneath us begins to tremble. He jerks back, glancing around in confusion as his hand flies instinctively to his sword. The rumbling grows and everything around us begins to shake. The crowd not far away begins to panic, cries of "Earthquake!" floating our way. The wall behind us lets out a loud CRACK as it starts to split. Bram jumps to his feet, pulling me up with him as debris crashes around us.

"We need to get away from the building!" he shouts. No sooner has he spoken than debris from the roof behind us plummets down, barely missing us. He tries to scoop me up again, but I shake my head.

"I can walk."

"Astra," he protests.

"I can walk. Just help me a little." He nods and helps me limp out of the alley toward the chaotic crowd.

Everywhere we look people are screaming and running, crashing into each other. If someone falls, they're trampled. Bram keeps us near the outskirts of the crowd but steers away from the buildings and falling debris the best he can.

Kato, where are you? We had to leave the alley. The building was collapsing. I look around in the ensuing chaos and try to figure out exactly where I am. *We're headed toward the houses. Good. I'll find you. Stay out of the crowd. I didn't find the healer, but I'm coming back to you anyway.*

"Kato is coming," I yell to Bram and he nods.

Bram's eyes furtively scan the crowd and I know he's searching for Ehren. If anything happens to the prince, Bram will never forgive himself. Thankfully, Ehren's face flashes in the crowd long enough for us to spot each other. Minutes later he's by our side. The world finally stops trembling. People stop running and screaming, but still seem eager to be anywhere else.

"Astra, your hands," Ehren murmurs in disbelief and I look down. My hands and arms have started to dimly glow.

"No, no, no," I cry, watching as the glow creeps up my arms. I can feel the cool light spreading all over. I hear a scream and I look up to see Kato rushing toward us, flames flickering in his eyes and his whole body glowing like an ember. He rushes to my side as the crowd clears around us, eyes locked on us in horror.

"It's happening!" he says, his voice shaking with terror.

I break my gaze away and look up at Bram who's watching us, fear and something else I can't quite describe in his eyes. "The spells," I force out. "Did you set up the spells?"

He nods, eyes wide, unable to find words. I swallow and pull away from him.

"You need to go. You need to get away," I insist, my voice trembling.

Bram reaches for me, but I shake my head and take another step back, grabbing Kato's hand. It burns, but I don't release it.

"Go!" I yell at Bram. My glow is brightening and more people are staring. "Go! Get out of here!"

Bram shakes his head firmly and takes a step toward me. "No. I am not leaving you."

"Don't be stupid!" I scream, stepping away, Kato going with me.

"The sky," Ehren chokes.

I shift my eyes to him and he's staring up. I follow his gaze, but it takes me a moment to see what grabbed his attention. Silver streaks shoot across the sky, one after another until the sky is nothing but falling stars.

That's when I burst into light.

I can see nothing around me save for blinding silver light. Someone—Bram, I think—yells my name, but I'm unable to respond. I can't speak. I can't move. I can't even feel. I am completely consumed. And then, just as quickly as it started, everything goes black.

Part Two:

Journey

CHAPTER NINE

I'm three, maybe four years old, sitting on the floor of my home, a fire roaring in the fireplace. Kato sits across from me, his face scrunched in concentration as he draws on the floor with the ashen tip of a half-burnt stick. After a few moments, he sits back, grinning.

"There," he says, pointing at the roughly drawn shape on the floor. "Guess what that is."

He crosses his arms across his chest and watches me as I turn my head and shift, trying to view his drawing from different angles. "Ummm, is it . . . a bear?" I twitch my eyebrows up in question.

"No!" he cries. "Come on! Look at it! It's so easy."

I furrow my brows and slide so I'm sitting next to him, looking at the sad shape from the same angle it was drawn. "Ummm . . ."

"Come on, Astra! You can figure it out."

"I don't know, Kato. It looks like a bear."

"It's not a bear."

"Are you sure? Because, look"—I point at the top of the

animal I can see as nothing more than a bear—"this is his back."
My fingers trace the outline down to four uneven lumps at the
bottom. "Those are his legs." I slide my fingers up to a circle at
one end. "His head, and there's his tail," I conclude, pointing at
the opposite end.

Kato cocks his head, scowling. "It's not a bear."

I throw my hands up in the air. "Then what is it? I give up."

"It's a rabbit."

"How is that a rabbit?" I giggle. "Rabbits have big ears.
Those are tiny."

"It's not funny!" Kato yells.

"Sorry," I say, but I can't stop giggling. "Maybe it's a rabbit
bear!"

Kato tries to hide his smile. "There's no such thing as a
rabbit bear!"

My giggles are almost uncontrollable and I'm not sure why.
"Maybe you just discovered the first one!"

"Astra, stop laughing!" Kato cries out, but even he's starting
to laugh. Within a few seconds we're both rolling on the floor
giggling.

The memory blurs and fades and everything starts to shift.
Suddenly, I'm not at home anymore but in front of the library.
I'm a little older than before. Kato stands beside me, holding my
hand. We're both staring up at the building like it could come
awake and consume us at any moment.

"I don't want to go to school," I whisper, not taking my eyes
off the library.

"You're going to be so good at school, though. I can feel it,"
Kato says, giving my hand an encouraging squeeze. "You'll
probably have a lot more fun in there, studying, than I'm going
to have training."

I look at Kato and scowl. "I doubt it. At least you'll be
outside. I'll be trapped in there for the rest of my life." My eyes

dart back to the building, as if looking away for too long will make it come to life.

"You don't know you'll be in there for the rest of your life. Lots of girls end up leaving and doing other things. Pax says his sister only had to go to school full-time for a couple years before they told her she could start training for another job. She helps her mother mend clothes now."

My eyes go wide and I look back at Kato in horror. "That's worse! I don't want to be a failure!"

Kato's eyes meet mine, his expression soft. "You're never going to be a failure, Ash. You're the strongest, smartest, most amazing person I know." I smile back at him before he adds, eyes twinkling, "Other than me, that is."

I gasp in feigned shock, letting go of his hand to punch him playfully on the arm.

He laughs. "See, you've got this!"

"Yeah, I guess," I concede. "I just . . . I'm going to miss you, Kato. We've never been separated before."

When I look into his eyes, I can see my own sadness and fears reflected there. He reaches out and grabs my hand again, giving it a firm squeeze.

You know you'll always have me. Just reach out anytime you need me.

I smile, fighting back tears. *I know. But what if I can't hear you when you're all the way on the training field and I'm locked inside the library?*

I don't think distance matters. Our bond is too strong.

He gives my hand another quick squeeze before he speaks out loud. "I need to go. I've heard the commander doesn't like it when boys are late, but I'll see you at dinner."

As I turn to say goodbye, a mist rises up around me. The world fades and turns to a gray smoke. I hear my name being called, echoing like it's far away. It's not Kato, but the voice is familiar. I can't quite place it, though. But as the sound of my name fades like the memory, I find myself outside, in the forest right by our village. Kato and I are seven years old. I'm glaring at him, arms crossed, while he tosses daggers at a target he's carved in a tree several yards away.

"I just don't think it's fair that you get to learn all about how to use weapons, and all I get to do is read about them."

"Honestly, I don't think it's fair you get to learn all about weapons and all I get to do is use them." He flicks his wrist and a dagger goes flying through the air, landing dead center in his target.

I throw my hands in the air in frustration. "What good is knowing all about weapons but not knowing a thing about how to use them! How is knowing that Thalri of Gizmeck was the first to use throwing daggers like these as a form of combat actually going to help me defend myself with them? Or how is knowing that silver from the mines of Heldonia is the best for creating weapons? Or the knowledge that the Veil Hags of Greyknoll were known for creating the most powerful magical weapons? How is any of that useful?" I say in one breath.

Kato listens intently as I speak, and then pauses, considering his answer, before he leans down and picks up another dagger. "Well," he says, weighing the dagger in his hand, "knowing those things lets you understand the weapons. Knowing their history makes them more powerful. It gives you an edge."

His hand flicks and the dagger goes flying, landing directly next to the one he threw before. He smiles in satisfaction.

"But how, Kato," I say, my voice almost a whine. "How can I have an edge if I'm never even allowed to touch a weapon? Knowledge can only take you so far. At some point you have to put that knowledge into action or it's worthless."

Kato turns to me, studying my face before he speaks,

choosing his words carefully, "Okay, fine. I guess you have a point. I'll make a deal with you. You teach me all the things you're learning at school—all the prophecies, all the histories, everything—and I'll teach you all the weapon skills I'm learning." My face lights up. "Deal?"

"Deal!" I lick my lips in eager anticipation. "What can I learn first?"

Kato laughs. "Well, if we must start this very second, why not start with throwing daggers since they're right here?"

I nod eagerly and he hands me a dagger. Then, just as he's beginning his instruction, smoke curls around me, pulling me away and into another memory. This time, I've jumped ahead two more years. I'm standing at the edge of the woods, grinning, holding a dead rabbit in front of me by its ears. Kato's weaving through the trees toward me, toting two rabbits of his own.

"Ha!" he crows once he's caught up to me. "I got *two* rabbits. You have to do my chores for a week!" He puffs his chest out in triumph.

"Wrong!" I declare, eyes sparkling. "*You* have to do *my* chores for a week!"

He shakes his head. "Nuh-uh. The bet was that whoever caught the most rabbits would have to do the other twin's chores for a week. I have *two* rabbits," he says, waving the rabbits in my face until I swat him away. "You only have *one* rabbit."

I laugh and skip over to a nearby tree, lifting two more dead rabbits. Kato's mouth drops open. "Hey! You cheated!"

"I did not cheat!" I argue, bringing the rabbits over and dumping all three in a pile at his feet. "I caught *three* rabbits. I just hid two of them for a big reveal."

"Yeah, but that one rabbit is small. Like really small. And that other one is just medium. My rabbits are both big."

"It doesn't matter," I say, shaking my head and placing my

hands on my hips. "The bet wasn't who could get the biggest rabbits or the most meat. The bet, dearest brother, was who could catch and kill the most rabbits."

He frowns, crossing his arms. "I still don't think it should count."

"No," I counter, "you just hate to lose. Now, come on. Let's get these rabbits back home. Maybe Mama will make us a meat pie for dinner!"

A mist rises up around me, blocking what happens next. I expect another image to appear, but I see nothing but curling wisps of silvery gray. I can hear voices mumbling somewhere nearby but can't make out what they're saying. I'm not able to recognize or place the voices. I try to concentrate but no matter how hard I try, I just can't make them come into focus. I hear a laugh behind me and turn. I'm in another memory now.

I'm twelve, maybe thirteen. It's winter and a light snow covers the ground. This time, Kato and I are joined by Pax and Mara. Pax and Kato are wearing their uniforms, having just come from training. Mara has on a long dress, the hem of which is already soaked. She grips a fur shawl around her shoulders as she watches Pax, Kato, and I in a full-blown snowball fight.

"Come on, guys," Mara whines, shivering. "It's really cold!"

I screech as a snowball thrown by Pax narrowly misses my head. I throw the snowball I have prepared in my hand at Pax, and he dodges it. As I reach down to scoop more snow, a snowball smashes against the back of my neck. I gasp and snap up, the snow dripping down my neck into my dress. Kato lets out a whoop from behind me. I spin to admonish him when another snowball smacks me directly between my shoulder blades.

"Hey! No double-teaming!" I laugh. "Come on, Mara! I need help! Otherwise the boys will win!"

Mara shakes her head. "Call me crazy but I don't enjoy having ice thrown at me."

"It's not ice! It's snow!" Pax laughs.

"There's not much difference," she replies stubbornly, scowling. "Snow is just what they call ice when they want you to like it."

"Come on, Mara, how often does it snow? Maybe once or twice a year? If we're lucky," Kato says.

"Lucky?" she huffs. "That's far too often if you ask me."

Kato shakes his head and turns his attention back to me a second too late. I'd taken advantage of him being distracted by Mara to build a large snowball, which splatters in his face.

"Oh!" Pax cheers from behind me as Kato just stands there, eyes closed, grinning. "And the winning blow for the evening comes from Astra!"

Kato laughs and shakes his head like a dog, snow flying everywhere. "I'll get you for that one!"

I squeal and take off running across the slippery snow, Kato not far behind.

The snow scene fades from view and is replaced by Kato and I wrapped in thin blankets, huddled in front of the fireplace. It's the next day. Our snow day had been fun, but our lack of proper layers resulted in us both getting sick.

"I think I'm dying," Kato grumbles.

"You're not dying." I sniffle.

"You're one of the smartest people I know, but you're wrong. I am definitely dying."

I roll my eyes. "If you're dying, I'm dying, too."

"Fine. I concede. We're both dying."

I just shake my head at him, too miserable to fight. Plus, it does feel a little like dying. I lay my head on his shoulder and he places his head on top of mine and we just stare into the fire. We're about to drift off to sleep when Mara's voice calls out.

"Hello?"

I pull away from Kato to lift my head and turn to see Mara

moving aside the cloth in the doorway to come inside. She's wearing her fur shawl again and carrying two small packages wrapped in brown paper and tied with twine. Her eyes find us by the fire and she exclaims, "Oh no! You two look terrible!"

"Thanks for the confidence boost, Mara," Kato groans, lying down on the floor and pulling his blanket over his head.

"Sorry! Sorry!" She makes her way toward us cautiously. "I just saw your mother in town with Beka and she told me you two were ill. I brought you an herbal tea mix that's supposed to work like magic." She holds up one of the packages in her hands.

I start to rise to take it from her, but she motions for me to sit back down. "No, no! You stay there. I can make you some tea." She turns and scans our sparse house. "Do you have any teacups or anything?"

I go into a fit of coughing, so I just motion to a shelf to her right bearing a small assortment of dishes, including mugs. Mara nods and grabs two mugs from the shelf. "And a tea kettle?"

"There's water in the kettle over the fire," I reply hoarsely.

Mara nods and brings the mugs and the packet over, giving Kato and I a wide berth. She unwraps the package and sprinkles a colorful mixture into each cup before carefully removing the kettle and pouring water into each mug. A sweet smell floats up with the steam.

"There now!" she says, sounding pleased. "Just let that steep for a few minutes and give it a try! It will have you feeling better soon!"

Kato shifts and peeks out from his blanket. "What's the other package?"

"Oh, this one is for Pax. Apparently, he's not feeling well, either. Maybe next time I tell you we should go inside out of the cold you three will listen to me."

Mara, Kato, and the fire fade as another memory blurs into focus. I'm walking out of the library, just weeks shy of turning sixteen. On my left is a tall young woman, a couple of years older than me with dark skin and hair. It's Kayla, my mentor for my first few years. To my right is a young, fidgeting girl with curly blond hair and brown eyes who has just been assigned to me as my first trainee.

I bid the girls goodbye and turn to head toward Mara's. Kato catches my eye instead. He's half-walking, half-running down the main road, caked in dirt and sweat. I start walking toward him and he rushes up to me.

"You will never guess what happened today during training!" he says, his whole face glowing.

I scan the amount of filth he's covered in and guess. "Were you all thrown in a mud pit and forced to fight to the death?" I notice a splash of red near his collar and narrow my eyes. "Is that blood?"

"Um, maybe?" he looks down, trying to see what I'm seeing. "If it is, it isn't mine."

"That's not exactly comforting."

"It doesn't matter," he says, shaking his head. He looks back at me, his expression pure and utter joy.

"Well, tell me, then!"

"Commander Jetson pulled me aside today and told me he wants me to do my testing! I'll get to be an official soldier! He even says I'll be put in charge of training some of the younger boys!"

"What?" I cry with happy disbelief. "But you're not even sixteen yet! You're not supposed to take your test until you turn eighteen!"

"I know! I know! But Commander Jetson says I show promise and he's making an exception for me to take the test in two weeks, once I'm officially sixteen!"

"Oh, Kato! That's amazing! If you weren't so gross and filthy right now, I would hug you!"

He ignores my words and throws his arms around me anyway, squeezing me tight. I squeal and try to wriggle from his grip, but he laughs. I laugh in response. When he releases me, I look down at the dirt and grime now smeared on my dress. But I can't be mad. Instead, I just laugh some more, shaking my head.

"Well, I suppose we both have reason to celebrate," I say, grinning. His eyes brighten when I add, "I've just been made a mentor!"

"Ash!" He pulls me into another hug. "That's amazing! It's what you've always wanted!"

I nod as he releases me. "I know! And this means that my dreams of becoming our village historian may come true!"

There's a flash of light and the scene is gone. It's night now. I'm seventeen, climbing out of the loft window and onto the roof. Kato sits in his usual spot at the edge, staring off at nothing. I sneak nimbly across the roof and sink down next to him.

"You know, when you're planning a great night escape you're supposed to take me with you," I say, bumping my arm against his.

He looks at me and smiles, but it doesn't go to his eyes. "I couldn't sleep."

"Nightmare?" I ask, tentatively. I've just started having my own nightmares. It's why I'm awake.

He nods. "Yeah. Nightmare. It woke me up and I couldn't get back to sleep."

I rest my head against him and just sit, staring over the quiet, sleeping village. When he speaks again, it's mind to mind.

Do you ever think about what it means that we're twins?

What do you mean?

I mean, we're literally the only twins ever born in our king-dom. Not just in our village. Not just in our lifetime. You and I, Astra, are the only twins to ever exist.

Twins might exist in other places.

But they don't exist here. What does that mean for us?

It means you and I are one of a kind. It means we are the luckiest people in the kingdom because we have each other and we always will. And if anything gets thrown at us, we will be okay because we won't have to go through it alone.

He grabs my hand.

You're right. As always you're right.

Of course I'm right.

I give him a teasing smile, but he avoids my gaze, looking down at our linked hands. I study his face in the moonlight for a moment.

You think something is coming, don't you?

He nods. *I do.*

And then, the world fades to nothing.

CHAPTER TEN

I'm trying to decide if I'm dead. If I am dead, I shouldn't be able to feel, not like I can feel right now, at least. My eyes are still closed—at least, I'm pretty sure they're closed—but I'm aware of every inch of my body. My skin feels alive, overly sensitive to everything, feeling every sensation at once. My mouth is dry, a metallic tang on my tongue. My throat aches. I want to scream, but I can't find my voice. It feels trapped deep within me, somewhere, hiding. I long to open my eyes, but it's taking incredible effort, as if the muscles have forgotten what they're supposed to do.

When I finally manage to crack them open, the light is too bright. I snap them shut. I lie there for a moment, listening, searching for any familiar sounds or a familiar voice to give any indication of where I am. I need to know what's happening. I can make out someone humming and the general clattering of things being moved around, but it's not enough to give me answers. I struggle to remember what happened, but my memories blur together. I can see flashes of faces, hear snippets of conversations, but they swirl together, indistinguishable from one another.

I lie there, motionless, for I don't know how long. Maybe I am dead. Maybe I'm just in a dreamless sleep. All I know is that I can't lie here forever not knowing anything. I force my eyes open again and refuse to let myself close them. The bright light assaults them but, after a moment, starts to slowly dim as a blurry face comes into focus. An older woman with a lined face and kind blue eyes peers down at me. Her gray and white hair is pulled into a frazzled bun with almost as many hairs flying about as are contained. She gives me a wide smile. I attempt to ask her who she is, where I am, what happened, but when I open my mouth all I can manage is a weak wheeze.

"Here, my dear," she says, handing me a clay cup. "Drink some water."

I try to lift my hand to take the cup, but I am unable. The woman smiles and raises the cup to my dry, cracked lips, tipping it back for me. I gulp the water, the cold liquid burning my throat.

"There, there. Take your time. I have plenty more." Once the cup is empty, she pulls it back and sets it on a table next to my head.

"Who . . . ?" I croak, barely audible.

"My name is Healer Heora. I'm sure you have many other questions. I promise you, they will all be answered in time. However, for now you need your rest. Your body has been through quite the ordeal and needs more time to heal."

She reaches to the bedside table and picks up another cup and tips it to my lips. This time, instead of water, a thick, bitter liquid fills my mouth, making me gag.

"I apologize. The tonic is not the best tasting, I fear, but it does the trick." She smiles gently, her eyes crinkling.

The effects of the tonic are almost instantaneous, tugging

on my consciousness, drawing me back toward the bliss of sleep. I force myself to focus, to fight and manage to get out one more word.

"Kato?"

"Your twin is fine. He is resting as well." Her eyes shift and she gives a slight nod to my left.

I use every ounce of power I have to turn my head enough to find my brother. He's lying on a small bed a couple of yards away, a white blanket pulled up to his shoulders. His black hair looks like spilled ink against the white pillow. His eyes are closed, but his chest rises and falls smoothly. I long to reach out to him, but the tonic is fighting to pull me under.

"He is doing well. He has already woken and taken his tonic and, like you, will be better soon. Likely even sooner than you as he had fewer physical injuries. Now, my child, rest. Heal."

I close my eyes and fall into a dreamless sleep.

When I wake later, it still takes effort to force my eyes open, but it isn't quite as difficult as it was previously. This time a young girl with long dark hair stares at me. Her eyes open wide and she scampers out of the room like a frightened mouse.

My skin still feels overly sensitive and raw. My body is heavy as if someone had filled it with stones, but I rally my strength and manage to push myself up onto my elbows. I glance over to where Kato had been before and see he's still there, but this time, he's sleeping peacefully, curled on his side with his body turned toward me. I realize with a start that I have no idea what time of day or night it is. I'm not even sure *what* day it is or how much time passed while I slept.

I try to think back to the last thing I remember doing, and the memories tumble into my head in flashes: the bonfire, Marco, glowing hands, flames flickering in Kato's eyes, the silver light, Bram, Ehren. I'm still sorting through the memories when Healer Heora shuffles into the room, the girl cowering behind her.

"Now, now," she clucks. "Lie back and rest. You've got a good bit of healing left to do, though I will admit it's good to see you've regained a bit more of your strength."

She pours water from the silver pitcher on the bedside table into a cup and hands it to me as I settle back against my pillows. My hand is heavy, but I manage to lift it and take the water, gulping it down. I wipe away some dribbling water with my other hand as Healer Heora takes the cup back. She hands it to the girl and whispers something to her before she scuttles away again.

"You'll have to forgive my granddaughter. Her mother thinks she has the gumption to be a healer one day and insists I let her shadow me. I'm not entirely sure she has the proper manner for it, but only time will tell."

"How long have I been here?" I manage, my voice so raw I barely recognize it as my own.

"Here? Let's see, you've been here a little over two weeks now. Sixteen days to be precise."

I nod. Or, at least, I think I do. "So, it's been two weeks?"

"Oh, you've been out longer than that, I'm afraid, but not by much. Your journey here was three or four days and before that you were with another healer." I open my mouth to ask for more details but she shakes her head. "No more questions. You need rest and someone who was there, not someone like me who only has incomplete, secondhand information."

She makes her way across the room to a table in the corner and begins mixing ingredients.

"Bram?" I ask weakly.

"Heavens, child! Don't say that name! I barely got that young man out of here! His duties called him away temporarily, he and the prince both, but I sent word that you've woken so

I'm sure we will see him again soon." She gives a low chuckle and turns and walks toward me, holding out a cup with red liquid inside.

I take the cup and down it. It's the same sticky, bitter tonic from before. I grimace. Somehow, I think it tastes worse. The healer gives me a sympathetic smile.

"Your brother was asking after you. He was very pleased you were starting to wake. He required slightly less healing than you but still needs his rest."

With that, she leaves the room and lets me drift off to sleep.

The next couple of days I drift in and out of sleep, each time managing to stay awake a little longer, my healing progressing nicely. Healer Heora begins bringing me warm broth in addition to water and gradually reduces the amount of tonic I have to force down. Each time she assures me that Kato is doing well, we just keep waking at different times. When I awaken on the third day, I glance over to find Kato's bed empty. I sit up and, for the first time since falling ill, I reach out.

Kato?

Astra! Are you awake? I can feel his excitement as if it were my own.

Yes, where are you?

I'll be there in a minute. Don't get up.

I hear a door open and close in a nearby room, accompanied by heavy, hurried footsteps. When Kato's face appears in the doorway, healthy and vibrant, I break down in tears.

"Hey, now! None of that!" he says, rushing to my side.

He sits on the edge of my bed and I throw my arms around him, sobbing into his shirt. In response, he returns the hug and holds me until I calm down. I draw back and wipe at my tears with the back of my hand. When I look up at him I see tears on his cheeks.

"No, now, we can't both fall apart."

He gives a short laugh. "Sorry, I guess I'm a sympathetic crier."

I laugh and he says, "Gods, I missed that laugh." His eyes grow dark and serious. "I was beginning to wonder if you would be okay. Healer Heora kept telling me you were fine, but you always looked so pale and, I don't know, like you were going to sleep forever. I told her to wake me up whenever you woke, but she refused."

"Well," I say, looking him over. "It seems she knows what she's doing since we're both alive."

"I suppose so."

For a moment we sit and stare at each other. Finally I ask, "Has she told you anything about what happened?"

He shakes his head. "All I know for sure is that Ehren and Bram brought us here because she's supposed to be one of the best healers in the kingdom. I know something happened that requires their attention, so that's why they're not here. They're out there, somewhere, dealing with whatever it is."

"What about—"

"All right. Enough chit chat," Healer Heora interrupts, entering the room with a smile. "Time to see if you can get around a bit. I've prepared you a bath and when you're done, you can eat. Come, come!"

Kato stands and offers me his hand. With his help, I ease from the bed. My legs are shaky and unsteady, but, with a little help from Kato, I make it into the main room and then the small washroom without incident. Kato leaves and Healer Heora helps me undress and get into the small washtub. The water is warm and feels soothing against my skin. She leaves me be for a while to soak and clean myself. When I'm done, I feel exhausted but refreshed.

Healer Heora allows me a bit of fruit and tea before leading me outside to a little herb and flower garden where Kato sits at a stone table with his own half-finished plate of food and tea. He rises and helps me to the spare seat. For a while, we say nothing. We're happy to simply be awake and together. The healer's granddaughter, who Kato informs me is named Hanna and is ten years old, joins us. It's evident by the way she starts chattering on and on about the various plants and flowers growing around us that her shy streak is over. We smile and engage her until her grandmother comes and shoos her back inside. She then forces me back inside as well and helps me to my bed.

"You're doing much better," she says as I accept a small cup of the tonic. There's barely more than a sip. "A couple more doses and my work will be done."

I smile and lay back on the pillow. It doesn't take long before sleep claims me. I'm woken a few hours later by the smell of rabbit stew. I'm alone in the room, but I can hear Kato's voice drifting from the main room of the healer's house. I ease from the bed and make my way across the room, feeling a little stiff but fine overall. When I pull back the curtain separating the room from the rest of the house, I find Kato, Hanna, and Healer Heora seated around the table. Healer Heora meets my gaze with a welcoming smile.

"There's stew in that. Help yourself and join us," she says, motioning to the fireplace where a black iron pot sits next to a couple of wooden bowls and spoons. I quickly ladle stew into a bowl, grab a spoon, and join them. Kato breaks me off a chunk of bread from the loaf in the center of the table.

As we eat, Healer Heora tells us stories from her childhood. She casually chats about her older brother, who defended our borders against Paravalian invasions before losing his arm and retiring in honor, and her older sister, a stunning beauty who was married to a lesser court noble, and even her youngest sister who was a respected scholar in their village. She has the natural cadence of a storyteller and holds our attention long after our dinner is finished. She only stops sharing stories when someone knocks on the door. Hanna rises from her seat and answers. My heart stops when Bram strides in. His eyes scan the room, looking for Healer Heora. When he finds her, he opens his mouth to speak but no words come out as his eyes slide from her to me.

"Good evening, Captain," Healer Heora greets him. She turns and adds to Hanna, "Why don't you get our guest a bowl of stew? Then you and I will go check our herbs in the garden and give these three a few minutes to catch up."

Hanna obeys and Healer Heora pushes up from the table and shuffles toward the door. Bram never takes his eyes off my face, barely blinking, as if I'll disappear if he looks away. He sinks down at the table across from me and doesn't even glance at Hanna when she places a bowl of stew in front of him before heading outside.

"You're okay," Bram finally chokes out, his voice unsteady and quiet.

I reach my hands across the table and place them on top of his. "I am, and I think that may be partially due to you."

He glances down at our hands and gently folds his fingers into mine.

"I'm alive, too," Kato says, clearing his throat. Bram jumps and jerks his hands back. "You know, just in case anyone cares."

Bram sheepishly slides his gaze to Kato. "I am sincerely happy about your recovery as well."

"So, what exactly happened? Healer Heora won't tell us anything," I ask.

Bram clears his throat and digs into his stew. "What do you remember?"

"I remember everything up until I burst into flames," Kato answers. "After that, not much."

"Same for me. I remember the stars falling and my body glowing but then it's just black."

Bram pauses, enjoying a few more bites of stew before answering, as if he's deciding what information to share first. "Well, for one, this time the stars really did fall from the sky. They weren't just silver streaks in the heavens. There are reports from all over the kingdom of the stars crashing to earth. Two of them fell within a couple miles of Timberborn."

I gasp. "Was anyone hurt?"

Bram nods, tearing some bread. "Yes. Most of the injuries were mostly superficial, though, and no one from Timberborn was killed by the stars, although there were a few deaths as a result of the earthquake. Both Mara and Pax, as well as your family, are okay aside from your basic cuts and bruises," he says, reading the question on our faces. We breathe a quick sigh of relief.

"What about outside of Timberborn?" Kato asks hesitantly. "What damage was there?"

"We are still collecting information from around the kingdom about other areas and how they were affected. From what we have gathered, at least a dozen stars fell, most outside of cities and villages, keeping injuries and deaths at a minimum. It seems that the heaviest starfall was in the south of the kingdom, closest to Timberborn with the north affected the least."

"Did we—did we hurt anyone with our magic?" I ask, terrified of the answer.

Bram shakes his head. "I think the amulets did their job of containing your powers. We were unable to go near you for a few minutes while you glowed and burned, but everything was otherwise okay." He looks down at his bowl, going silent. When he looks back up emotion is written all over his face as his eyes meet mine. "After you stopped glowing, you just collapsed. Both of you did. We thought you were dead."

He stops, his voice wavering.

"But we weren't. We were okay," I whisper, reaching out and placing my hand over his. His eyes drop to our hands and he intertwines his fingers with mine.

"You were alive but not really okay. You were so cold I couldn't even touch your skin," he shifts his gaze to Kato. "And your skin was hotter than fire." He looks back at me. "You were barely breathing. We were afraid that you were dying slowly. Pax found us and helped us locate blankets to wrap you in so we could touch you and get you to a healer. Your village healer was dealing with a lot of injuries, but she did what she could, which honestly wasn't much. She kept checking on you all through the night and through the next day but wasn't able to figure out anything. She was able to help some of your injuries from . . . earlier but had no idea what to do with magical injuries. She recommended we come here, to Healer Heora. She claimed Healer Heora came from a long line of healers and might have knowledge about injuries caused by magic. As soon we were able to procure a wagon, we traveled here, and Healer Heora began her work.

"I stayed for a few days, but Ehren had to go back to Embervein. Our trip to your village, as you've probably guessed, wasn't exactly sanctioned, and he needed to go home and smooth things over with his father. It was only when he got back to the capital that he realized how far-reaching the damage was. He sent orders for me to find out what I could. That is when I left, but I made sure to keep communication with Healer Heora open so I could monitor your healing while performing my duties for Ehren."

"So, all this time we've been recovering, you've been traveling Callenia, looking for falling stars?" I ask, trying to process the influx of information.

Bram nods, but I can tell there is something he isn't saying.

"What is it, Bram?" I press.

"I haven't just been studying the damage from the stars. When your power awoke, something else happened."

"What?" Kato asks uneasily.

Bram looks from me to Kato and then settles his gaze back on me. He exhales and says slowly, "Magic is awake again."

CHAPTER ELEVEN

*K*ato and I gape at Bram, barely blinking, for several minutes as we process everything he's told us.

Finally, Kato finds his voice. "What do you mean magic is awake? I thought magic faded out and disappeared centuries ago."

"That's what everyone thought," Bram replies. "But, apparently, it wasn't really gone. It has just been lying dormant. And now, it is awake."

"But awake how?" Kato presses.

"Well, there have been literal bursts of magic reported all throughout the kingdom. Families with ties back to magic wielders are showing an aptitude for magic that hasn't appeared in generations, many of them performing uncontrollable magic without meaning to. Parts of the land that were once known for being imbued with magic seem to be magical once again. There have been reports of Seers having visions and Healers able to heal without the use of herbs and medicines. We have yet to confirm their accuracy. There are also rumors claiming some of the magical species, long believed to have been extinct, are starting to emerge, but, once again, those may just be stories from wishful thinkers."

"What happened to us, what we did, is that what brought magic back? Did we do this?" I ask.

Bram shrugs and gives a slight shake of his head. "We aren't sure. We do know that there were surges of magic all around the kingdom that correspond with your . . . event. Whether you actually caused magic to awaken with your powers or whether magic awakening is what caused your powers to manifest in the first place, we aren't really sure."

Kato swears, leaning back in his chair. I swallow and shake my head in disbelief.

"For now," Bram continues with a sigh, "all we can do is continue to investigate all the claims of magic from around the kingdom and use that information to figure out our next steps."

"So, that's what you've been doing? Traveling from place to place, from town to town to see which claims are true and what are just rumors?" I ask.

Bram nods. "Essentially. We are also trying to contain the rumors. If our neighboring kingdoms were to realize magic has returned, well, we have no idea how they might react. Ascaria has always been very anti-magic, and, if the history books and scrolls are to be believed, they are known for mass slaughters of magical people and creatures. In recent generations, we have managed to build a fragile peace with them. We have little to no doubt that peace will be out of the question if they discover we have magic. We will be lucky if they don't immediately attack in an attempt to wipe magic out again before anyone can wield it against them."

"So," Kato says evenly, "Callenia is the only kingdom with magic? It didn't awaken everywhere?"

"Honestly, we aren't sure. King Betron has chosen to deny

magic has returned. He refuses to address the issue and has threatened death upon anyone who speaks openly about it or suggests it may be more than rumors. Ehren has reached out to his personal spy network, spread throughout many kingdoms, but if he has received anything definitive it has not reached me."

"Wait," Kato says, scowling. "How can the king deny magic? From what you've said, it's fairly undeniable at this point."

Bram shakes his head with a sigh. "He is a powerful, mighty king, and a good leader, but he does not like things he cannot control. Magic is one of those things. For him, denial seems an easier solution than facing down a problem he is not prepared to deal with. But his denial could be deadly for everyone, especially if magic reaches beyond our borders."

"The Dragkonians," I breathe, color draining from my face.

Bram nods grimly.

"What are the Dragkonians?" Kato asks, looking from me to Bram.

Bram motions for me to answer.

"The Dragkonians were a brutal race of creatures, bred through dark magic. Dark sorcerers combined their own souls with those of dragons to create one of the most vicious species or races ever known. To be killed outright by them was considered a mercy. They preferred to play with those they captured, torturing them in unimaginable ways, driving many of their captives insane. They did it all without fear of consequence, for no one was able to stand against them. A single Dragkonian could take out an entire army. It took several strong sorcerers and sorceresses banding together to trap the Dragkonians on the Isle of Atroxmorte. Unable to procreate without humans, they eventually died off."

Kato pales. "And you think they could come back?"

"We don't know," Bram whispers. "Everything is still new, constantly changing. We have no idea what things or creatures magic may have brought back or even what new things may have been created. The Isle of Atroxmorte has been abandoned and considered uninhabitable for centuries. Its location was chosen because it was far from any kingdoms. Even once we have a grip on the magic within our own kingdom and an indication of whether magic has indeed returned other places, we will probably still have no idea what that isle holds since we have no eyes on it. And if they have returned, we have no guarantee that the magical wards that once made it a prison are still holding."

Kato swears again and Bram nods his agreement, his mouth a tight line.

"So, what can be done? What is being done? With the king in denial, what are you doing with the information you're gathering?" I ask.

"Right now, I am reporting all my findings and suspicions back to Ehren. He is doing his best to assemble all available information and provide solutions without his father knowing, but he is only the heir to the crown, not the crown itself. His resources, while vast, are limited. Without the king's approval, we won't be able to act on our findings without facing consequences from the king."

I swear under my breath.

"And, even as the king's son and heir to the throne, Ehren is at risk. If his father were to even suspect what Ehren is doing, that he is involved . . ." Bram releases a long sigh.

"Surely King Betron wouldn't hurt his own son?" I gasp.

I can see the worry in Bram's eyes as he looks at me.

"I honestly don't know. I would hope not. I would hope

that, at the worst, he would only disown Ehren, but his denial runs so deep . . ." He looks away, shaking his head. "I hope to the gods that he sees sense soon, for the sake of the kingdom."

The door opens and we all jump. Bram's head spins to look at the door, his hand going to the sword strapped at his side, but it's only Healer Heora and Hanna coming back inside with a basket of freshly gathered herbs. She smiles at us and Bram relaxes.

"I'm sorry to interrupt your discussion," she says, her voice gentle, "but I'm afraid my patients still need their rest. You are welcome to stay the night, Captain."

Bram gives her a grateful nod. "When will Astra and Kato be able to travel?"

"Kato would be fine to leave at any time. Astra will be at least another day, as her body requires more time to heal." Bram nods as Healer Heora continues, "And even after they leave my care, there are still some medicines and tonics they may need. I will prepare some for you to take with you when you go."

Kato and I stand and begin to head to the little room that has become our own while Healer Heora and Hanna busy themselves sorting and putting up the herbs they've just gathered. I'm about to slip behind the curtain to my room when Bram calls my name. I pause, turning to him. Without another moment of hesitation he strides across the room and gathers me in his arms. His lips crash against mine, warm and inviting. When he pulls away, I stare breathlessly up into his gold-speckled brown eyes.

"I never thought I would be able to do that," he says, his voice rough.

I respond by lightly touching my lips to his again before whispering, "I'm glad you had the chance."

Healer Heora coughs pointedly from her corner of the room and Bram releases me, red rising in his cheeks. "Sleep well, Astra."

When I finally pull back the curtain and enter the room, I feel like I'm glowing. Kato is watching me, a smile dancing on his lips.

"How long do you think I have to wait for my glad-you're-still-alive kiss?" Kato teases. "Do you think Bram will give me mine in the morning?"

I scowl at him, but there's no real ire in it. He chuckles, eyes shining. I'm about to retort, but I stop as a thought strikes me. I stare at Kato, puzzled.

"How did you know he kissed me? The curtain was closed."

Kato's face grows serious, but his eyes still twinkle. "I can feel you now, in some ways, through the bond if I focus."

I furrow my brows. "What do you mean?"

"I'm not sure how to describe it, exactly, but I can sense you now in a way I couldn't before. And when you have a strong emotion, like you just did when Bram kissed you, I can feel it. I could almost see it through your eyes but not quite. Like I was watching you through a dense fog."

"You could feel it? Like Bram was kissing you?" I ask, horrified, my face growing warm.

Kato throws back his head and laughs. "Gods, no! It's not that strong. I couldn't feel it in the same way you could. It wasn't like it was physically happening to me." His eyes sparkle as he softly adds, "I could feel how happy it made you."

I smile. "It did make me happy." I pause, thinking. "I wonder why I can't feel you."

Kato shrugs. "Maybe you can. You just haven't had a need to, yet. I first discovered I could feel you when you were still sleeping. I tried to reach out and speak to you, but I couldn't quite get through. But that's when I realized that I was linked to you now in a different way. I thought, at first, that this new bond had replaced the old bond, changed it so we could no longer speak mind to mind. I was incredibly relieved when you reached out to me."

"So, you think if I try to reach out and connect with you through the bond, without speaking, that I might be able to sense you as well?"

He shrugs. "It might be worth a try. Go ahead. Try."

Kato eases down onto the edge of his bed, hands by his side with his palms pressed against the mattress and locks eyes with me. I take a deep breath and reach out with my mind like I would when I want to talk but keep the words to myself. At first, there's nothing. I'm about to shake my head when suddenly, I feel something. It's like seeing a dim light at the far end of a dark hall. I follow the trail and the feeling grows. All at once I feel a warm rush of emotions. I inhale sharply. It's almost overpowering. I feel . . . love. Not the kind of love I might feel for Bram or any kind of romantic love. This is a love I recognize better than any other kind. It's the love I have always felt for Kato, that strong, overwhelming, unchangeable love that I could only ever feel for him, for my twin, the other half of my soul. Though, this love isn't my love for him. It's his love for me. Tears well in my eyes.

Kato . . .

He smiles, tears in his own eyes.

I love you, Ash.

I love you too, Kato.

You're never allowed to almost die again, do you understand? And if it so happens that something ever injures both of us at the same time, and we almost die again together, you are most definitely not *allowed to take longer to recover. Understand?*

I laugh softly. *Understood.*

"You two are supposed to be in bed," Healer Heora chides as she slides into the room, balancing a tray with two cups in her right hand.

"Sorry," I apologize, crawling into my bed while Kato swings his legs up, lying back on his own.

"I've prepared you each a tonic," she says, handing me one of the cups and turning to hand the other to Kato.

Kato groans while I down mine. "I thought I had healed enough not to take that horrible tonic anymore."

"Your tonic," she explains, "is more of a sleeping tonic than a healing tonic. With all the news you two received this evening, sleep may be more difficult. That tonic will help to ease your worries."

"So, you know what's happening?" I ask as she takes back my cup and I settle into bed.

"I have heard the occasional twitterings and bits of gossip, and even warnings about things that are taking place across the kingdom from other patients who have come to me the past few weeks. And I have felt age-old, long forgotten magic inside me that I thought was only a rumor passed down by wishful thinkers in my family. I know things are brewing and that your trials have only begun, but I am not privy to exactly what those trials may be."

"You have magic?" I ask, and she nods.

"Yes. I wasn't able to heal you through tonics alone, child," she says softly.

She holds out one of her hands and closes her eyes. I wonder what she's doing until her hand starts to glow. The glow is different from mine and Kato's. Healer Heora's glow is a soft, warm light, a healing light. She opens her eyes and the glowing fades, a weary smile on her lips.

"Now," she says, straightening and taking Kato's cup. "It is time for sleep."

Neither of us argue.

CHAPTER TWELVE

*T*he next morning, I wake before Kato. Hanna and Healer Heora are busy grinding herbs and mixing various medicines.

"Your handsome young captain is in the garden," Healer Heora offers without looking up from her work.

I thank her and make my way outside. The day is beautifully warm. I easily find Bram, strolling casually through the garden, his back toward me. Quietly, I advance toward him. He turns to face me moments before I reach him, surprise flashing on his face.

"I didn't hear you," he says, schooling his features. "You must have incredible stealth to have been able to sneak up on me." His mouth twitches into a teasing smile and I laugh.

"Or you just have a lot weighing your mind," I counter with a smile.

He nods. "There is no denying that." He glances behind me toward the house. "No Kato this morning?"

I shake my head. "He's still sleeping."

"Well, I am not complaining. That means I can get a

couple minutes alone with you," he grins, reaching his arms around me and pulling me close. I tilt my face up toward his and he leans downs and brushes his lips across mine. He begins to pull back but I press my lips more firmly against his, hungry for more. He responds in kind, his hands pressing against my back and drawing me tight against his body. What started as a simple kiss quickly becomes more, a welcome heat rising in my chest.

"It's a good thing I haven't eaten breakfast," Kato's voice drawls from behind me, "or it would probably be coming up right now."

Bram jolts back, releasing me. My body feels cold from the absence of his so close to mine. I slowly turn to face Kato, my cheeks pink, grinning.

"Good morning, Kato!" I say, my voice overly cheerful and still a bit breathless. "I, uh, didn't realize you were awake already."

"That much is obvious," he mumbles, his eyes shifting to Bram standing awkwardly behind me.

Bram glances away, avoiding Kato's glare.

"Well," Kato says slowly after a minute, his eyes back on me, "Healer Heora says there's not much here in terms of breakfast but she's given me some coins to go into the village if you'd like to come with me. Unless, of course, you and Bram have other, more important things you need to be doing."

His eyes sparkle with mischief.

"I think we are done for now," I say with a grin, glancing over my shoulder at Bram who nods, "so, I can go with you."

"Would you mind if I accompany you?" Bram asks, addressing Kato. "I would like to see what rumors have surfaced in this area and assess any new information."

"That's fine, but no more kissing my sister," Kato says with a wink.

"You have my word as a Guard that I will not kiss your sister . . . while you are looking."

Kato laughs and Bram grins.

"All right. I find your terms acceptable. Now, let's get going. I'm about to starve to death."

The village, which Bram informs me is named Honeyhallow, is smaller and more intimate than Timberborn. While Timberborn had one main road that ran through the town with most of the shops and businesses on one end and homes at the other, Honeyhallow is set up more like a target, with a cluster of businesses in the center and homes spread around them. Healer Heora's house, it turns out, is situated close to the center of the village, so it doesn't take us long to reach the shops.

While Kato and I buy bread, fruit, cheese, and a few other things on a list provided by Healer Heora, Bram wanders around, chatting idly with the villagers. He fits in so well and I recall how I had no idea who he really was the first time we met. Once Kato and I have everything we need, we sit on a bench in the center of town, munching on sweet rolls while Bram wraps up his current conversation.

"So, Bram seems to make you happy," Kato says, tossing a bit of bread up in the air and catching it in his mouth.

I look over to where Bram leans casually against a building, chatting easily with a man and his wife. I can't help but smile.

"Yes, he does," I say, my voice quiet.

"That's good, Ash. I just hope that it works out."

I look at Kato and raise an eyebrow. "Why wouldn't it?"

Kato gives a noncommittal shrug before tossing another piece of bread in the air and catching it.

"No, what do you mean?" I press.

Kato sighs. "It's just . . . everything is changing. The world we live in today is not the world from a few weeks ago. Even things that seem the same may be entirely different. You and I literally exploded not that long ago. There's no way that power is just gone. It didn't just disappear."

"You don't know that for sure. Maybe it did," I whisper.

Kato looks at me, his face serious. "You know that's not true. You feel different. I know you do because I do. The power has shifted somehow. It's still in us. It just isn't as volatile anymore. We need to figure out where it went and how to access it."

I swallow and look away to avoid his penetrating gaze. I know what he means, what he's saying. Ever since I woke up, I've felt different. My vision is sharper. Food doesn't have the same taste it did before. I'm more sensitive to sounds and smells. Somehow, I feel everything more intensely and in a different way, like I'm viewing life from a different angle. But I've been refusing to acknowledge it. I keep telling myself it was an effect of the tonics and the healing process or that I'm simply imagining it. I know I can't pretend anymore.

"You know what I'm talking about, don't you?" His voice sounds sad, resigned.

I nod.

"We should find someone who can explain this to us and help us draw on our power so we can control it," Kato whispers.

I shake my head. "I don't know about that, Kato. I doubt there's even anyone who understands our magic. After all, magic has been gone for so long. There are no Masters anymore."

"Come on, Astra. We need to know how to control our power. And even if we can't find someone who grew up with magic and has mastered it, there has to be someone who knows something, even if it's just in theory. If we refuse to learn, refuse to master the power, who knows what might happen. If it goes uncontrolled for too long, we might explode again."

I take a deep breath. "You're right. I don't want to admit it, but you're right."

Kato gives me a playful shove with his shoulder. "It's tough being the twin that's wrong, isn't it?"

I laugh. "Don't get used to it," I say, shoving him back.

I look over to Bram and see him walking our way.

"Find anything interesting?" Kato says by way of greeting.

Bram shrugs. "Not much new information, but I was able to confirm a few things."

Kato nods, grabbing the basket full of supplies and food as he stands. Bram helps me up, intertwining his fingers with mine as we head back to Healer Heora's house. Kato shoots him the occasional dirty look, but Bram pretends not to notice. When we get back to the house, Healer Heora greets us with a smile.

"Did the market have everything?" she asks, peering into the basket as Kato sets it on the table.

"Everything on your list," Kato says, handing her a scrap of paper.

"Excellent. Excellent." She glances from the basket to me. "You should probably rest a bit my dear. I can provide a tonic for you, if you wish."

I shake my head. "I admit I am a bit tired but I don't know that I want to sleep."

Healer Heora surveys me for a minute and then concedes. "Fine. But I insist you at least relax some. Perhaps retire to your bed and read for a bit. If sleep calls to you on its own, so be it."

"That sounds good," I reply. "I will never say 'no' to the offer of a book."

Healer Heora nods and leads me to my bed. A few minutes later she returns with a small book bound in brown leather.

"I'm afraid it may not be the most entertaining read, but

you will likely find it informative," she says, handing me the book.

I take it from her eagerly. "What is it?"

"A book containing lists of plants and their medical functions."

I flip open to the first pages and find scrawling writing with sketches and diagrams of various plants.

"Hopefully, you won't find it too dull."

"On the contrary. I think this looks fascinating."

Healer Heora smiles. "Well, I'll leave you to your resting and reading. Let me know if you need anything. I'm teaching Hanna how to mix salves today so I'll be right out there."

I nod and dive into the book. Judging by the various handwritings, it appears the book had at least three, maybe four, main contributors. I hang on every word, drinking in and memorizing as much as I can. I have a little trouble making out some of the words smashed against diagrams or scrawled as afterthoughts in the margins, but overall I have little difficulty. At some point, Hanna brings me a small plate of cheese, bread, and fruit for lunch, but otherwise time passes silently without my notice. As I read, my body rests but my brain grows stronger. Reading is familiar and comfortable. By the time I finish the book, it's early afternoon. I go to give it back to Healer Heora and find her and Hanna putting their newly made salves in jars.

"Thank you," I say, handing the book to Healer Heora. She wipes her hands on her apron before taking it from me.

"You finished it?" she asks, sounding surprised and impressed.

"Yes, ma'am. I enjoyed it very much. Thank you for sharing it with me."

"What was your favorite plant?" Hanna pipes up.

"Oh, I don't know. There were so many interesting ones. I

really enjoyed learning about the White Eiyles. It has so many uses."

Hanna's eyes light up. "I love that one, too!"

I smile and glance over at Healer Heora who beams with pride.

"I think you definitely have a budding healer on your hands," I say with a wink toward Hanna.

Healer Heora gives an affirmative nod. "I think you may be right." Hanna looks up at her grandmother, her face glowing. "The young men are out back, if you want to see what they're up to. They wouldn't stop hovering, so I sent them outside hours ago. You may want to take them a bit of water. It's a warm day."

I nod and thank her, grabbing a couple cups of water before heading outside. Bram and Kato are on the side of the house opposite the garden in the area stretching between Healer Heora's house and her neighbor's, sword fighting. They're both so focused they don't notice me approaching. I stay silent and watch. I've observed Kato training many times with the other village soldiers. His skill is always evident, his form seemingly flawless. He's never failed to impress and I've never known him to lose a single fight. I have long suspected that when he skirmishes he holds back some of his skill, but now, watching him go against Bram, a trained soldier for the royal army, he isn't holding back in the slightest. And neither is Bram. They both move so quickly I can't quite track all their movements. Watching them is like watching a well-rehearsed dance.

After several minutes, they're both still going strong. With a smirk, I decide to help give Bram the upper hand.

Oh, Kato, if only Mara could see you now.

Kato misses a step and Bram knocks the sword from his hand. Kato throws his hands up and swivels to find me.

"That's cheating," Kato says, breathless, pointing at me.

I grin. He rolls his eyes and scoops up his sword while Bram saunters over. His face is red and his clothes are soaked in sweat. I hold out one of the cups of water.

"I thought you might like this."

"Thank you," he says, accepting the cup and gulping the water down.

"Is that other cup for me?" Kato asks, ambling over.

"Of course!" I say, handing him his cup.

"Good," he says. "Because it's clear you're playing favorites. Cheater."

He winks at me as he gulps down his water, and I roll my eyes in response.

"Did you two have fun?"

"Your brother is by far one of the best swordsmen I have ever met," Bram answers but Kato waves him off.

"I wasn't that impressive. I still don't think I've recovered completely, so I wasn't really performing at my peak. Bram's just being generous."

"If that was you at less than perfect, remind me never to make you mad when you're at the top of your game."

"Is he really that good?"

"He is extraordinarily skilled. I wish the soldiers in my command had even half his skill with a blade. There would never be a battle lost," Bram says sincerely. "One day, maybe once things have settled, I would love for him to join the Prince's Royal Guard."

"Doesn't Ehren get a say in that?" Kato asks, arching an eyebrow.

"Technically, Ehren can choose to dismiss or add anyone to his Guard as he wills, but he pretty much leaves it up to me to make the decisions. And all it would take to get Ehren to sign on is for him to watch you practice or fight for about two minutes."

Kato shrugs. "If you want, I suppose I can join. It would be an honor. Right now, I think I'm going to go inside and see if Healer Heora will allow me to use her washroom to clean up a bit."

"That actually doesn't sound like a bad idea," Bram agrees. "I think I'll go check on Solomon, and I may do the same."

Kato nods and heads inside.

"Who's Solomon?" I ask.

"Solomon is my horse," Bram answers with a smile.

"That dapple gray I saw you ride into town with Ehren?"

"That's Solomon! We've had many adventures together."

I glance around. Healer Heora doesn't have a barn of any kind, or any other place to keep a horse.

"Where is he?"

"A nice family a couple houses over had a spare place for a horse," he answers gesturing down the road. "I am paying them to board him. They are doing an excellent job caring for him, but I don't want him to feel like I have forgotten him."

"You're a good man, Bram," I say softly and he smiles. He glances around before he leans down, brushing his lips against mine.

"I promised I wouldn't kiss you with your brother watching, but he's not here now," Bram grins and I laugh.

"Well, on that note, I'll let you go. If you'll give me your cup, I'll take it back inside."

He laughs and hands me his cup. As he starts to walk away I yell, "Tell Solomon hello for me."

He glances at me over his shoulder, grinning. "I will."

I stand and watch him walk away for a minute before I go inside.

CHAPTER THIRTEEN

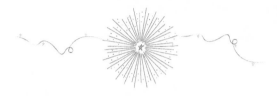

*A*ccording to Healer Heora, Kato is in the washroom. She and Hanna have moved aside all their herbs and salves and have started preparing dinner. Healer Heora invites me to join them, and I accept.

"I suppose you probably used to help your mother prepare meals at home," Healer Heora says as she crushes spices and I chop vegetables.

I nod. "Most of what we made was fairly simple, but my mother taught me all the basics. I have a younger sister, Beka, about your age, Hanna, and she would help." I stop chopping and stare off for a moment. "I wonder how they are now."

"The captain seemed to indicate your family was fine when you left your village," Healer Heora says gently. "I am sure they are equally fine still."

I offer her a grateful smile and go back to chopping. "My Mama has always been a strong woman. I'm sure she's surviving and doing fine, as are my sisters and my little brother. I've just never been away from home for this long. I've never actually been away from home at all." I fight back tears as an ache fills my chest.

"I understand. I remember when I left my family for the first time. I had just begun my work as a healer and had been accepted as an apprentice a town over. I was thirteen. I missed my family every day."

I look over at her. "How did you do it? Be away from home, from family?"

"I got through it day by day and each day it got easier. I have no doubt that one day it will be the same for you, especially since you have a piece of home with you through Kato."

"I didn't even realize until just now how much I missed home."

"I have some spare parchment and ink if you would like to write a letter when we're done prepping dinner. This soup has to simmer for a bit so there will be plenty of time. We can send it tomorrow."

I nod. "Thank you."

Kato comes out of the washroom and side-eyes me.

"Uh, oh. Are you sure you want Astra helping with food? She's not the best cook," Kato teases and I stick my tongue out at him.

"I'm just chopping vegetables. They're taking care of the actual cooking."

"Well, I guess that's okay then. Just don't get creative," he says with a wink. "Is there anything I can do to help?"

Healer Heora shakes her head. "Thanks to your sister's assistance we're almost done here." She pauses to think. "But if you wouldn't mind bringing in a bit more wood to add to the fire, I would appreciate it."

Kato nods. "Of course!"

As Kato goes out the door, Bram comes in. He gives me a nod before heading into the washroom. I add my chopped vegetables to the pot and take a seat at the table to write my letter while Healer Heora and Hanna put the finishing touches on the soup. Kato stacks firewood next to the fireplace, adding a couple small logs to the fire, before joining me at the table.

"What are you writing?" Kato asks, peering at my letter.

"I thought I might write a letter to Mama, let her know we're alive and everything."

"Oh. All right."

I nod, concentrating on writing. A thought strikes me and I pause, looking up at Kato.

"What exactly is the plan? Where are we going after we leave here? Are we going to Embervein or traveling around with Bram collecting information? Or are we going back home?"

Kato clears his throat. "Bram and I actually discussed that earlier while you were resting and we were going to run the plan by you after dinner. He thinks we should head to Embervein and I agree. They have a lot of resources there. We could have the entire royal library at our disposal. It's possible we would be able to learn about our power from ancient texts that can't be found in other libraries. Bram also says we might be able to locate someone who knows enough about magic to be able to guide us, so we can control our powers."

"Is that the safest option? With King Betron so against magic, I mean."

"There's no doubt it's risky, but unless we find some other leads between now and then, I don't see what choice we have. Even if we don't find exactly what we're looking for, we might at least find a place to start. Besides, from what Bram has said, I think Ehren could use our support."

I nod. "All right. I want to help Ehren. If it hadn't been for him giving us those amulets . . . I don't even want to know what would have happened. We owe him. But you have to swear that we'll leave if it gets too dangerous." I pause. "What happened to those amulets, anyway?"

"I have them," Bram says, coming up behind me. I turn and look at him. He's wearing a clean, loose white shirt and brown pants. His wet hair sticks up in several directions. It's the most casual I've seen him, and it makes my heart flip.

"You do?"

"Yes, I kept them with me." He nods to a brown bag in the corner. "You are more than welcome to have them back, especially if you think they will help."

"I don't know if they'll help anymore. My power—it's changed. Right now I feel like I have control over it, but I don't really understand it."

Bram nods. "Well, if you want yours, just let me know."

"Though," I add as an afterthought, "if I'm going to be in Embervein near King Betron it may be a good idea to have something like the amulet nearby, just to make sure my powers don't overwhelm me again. If that's even how the amulet works."

"So, you and Kato discussed our plans?" Bram asks, taking a seat next to me at the table.

"He gave me a quick rundown but not a lot of details."

"I would have given you more details if there were details to give."

"What sort of details do you want? Perhaps, now that the three of us have a moment together, we can solidify a few things. Create a backup plan if necessary," Bram offers.

"Well, for one, how safe would we really be so close to the king?"

"Honestly, it is not my first choice to take you to Embervein, but I am not sure where else you could find the answers both you and Kato need. Ehren and I will both be there, though, to make sure that you are both kept safe, along with other people I know we can trust," Bram says, his eyes dark and serious. He takes my hands in his. "I swear on my life, if I think there is even the slightest chance you or your brother would come to any harm I will get you out immediately."

The look in Bram's eyes is something undefinable. It's a mix of concern, determination and . . . something else. For a moment I lose myself in Bram's eyes, my heart threatening to flutter out of my chest.

Kato coughs. "No kissing, remember?"

I break the gaze and pull my hands back. "Well, that answers that question, I guess. What about supplies and clothes and things?"

"Well, while you were with the healer in your village, I had Mara and Pax gather a few things for you both, in case you were unable to return home," Bram answers. "Healer Heora has them here for you."

"That I do," Healer Heora confirms as she walks near us to put her soup over the fire.

"And any other supplies we need I can grab in town after dinner or first thing in the morning. That is, as long as Healer Heora still gives you the okay to leave," Bram says, glancing to Healer Heora for confirmation.

Healer Heora stands back from the fireplace, brushing her hands on her apron. "I suppose it would be fine. I would like for Astra to stay another day or two, just to err on the side of caution, but I can understand your desire to move on given your circumstances. I must recommend caution, though. Astra, and even Kato to an extent, is still healing. I have very little experience with magical injuries, so I can't be sure what effects the magic may have had on their bodies. Be alert. Be aware."

"I will," I agree, afraid she might change her mind.

"Good, then. I will prepare some medicines for you to take

on your journey." She gives us a soft smile, heading to her medicine corner.

"Well, I guess now that I know what we're doing, I can finish writing my mother," I say, looking down at my half-finished letter. I lift my pen to write, but pause. "Bram, you said Mara and Pax provided our things. Did my family come by at all?"

Bram shifts uncomfortably and glances toward Kato who avoids his gaze and mine. My heart sinks.

"What happened?"

"Well, everything was complete chaos immediately following your powers manifesting. We reached out to Mara and Pax because Ehren and I knew them. Initially, Mara went to your family to let them know you had been injured."

"Did she tell them about Marco?" I ask weakly.

Bram shakes his head. "No, she didn't know anything about him. Cal and Makin were able to dispose of Marco's body before anyone could find out what happened to him." I nod and he continues. "She informed them of your injuries and let them know you were in the care of the healer. She didn't tell them any details because she didn't have to. Almost everybody who was at the bonfire saw what happened to you two, and the rumors had already reached them."

"And no one had bothered to look for us? Find out more?" I can feel the tears welling up but I fight them back.

"Not that I know of. I will admit that my attention and focus were on you and it was a chaotic time, so it is possible someone was looking for you, but I just wasn't aware."

"What about after Mara went to the house? What then?"

Bram looks down at his hands in his lap. "When Mara returned with your things, your sister, Beka, I think she said her name was, came with her. She said your father was furious."

He looks back up at me, his eyes dark.

"What?" I ask. When he doesn't answer I look over at Kato. "What isn't he saying?"

"He's disowned us, Ash," Kato says, bitterness thick in his voice. "He didn't want to have anything to do with us or our powers or anything. He forbade anyone to visit us."

A tear slides down my cheek. "And you were going to just let me write a letter home to Mama like everything is just fine?" I spit at Kato.

"I didn't want to hurt you, Ash," Kato says, his voice softening, the edge gone.

I shake my head, wiping away my tears. I grab the letter I had been writing and wad up the paper, throwing it into the fire. I feel more tears threatening to spill, so I storm outside before I break down completely in front of Bram. I hesitate right outside the door for a moment before walking into the garden. After a moment of attempting to stifle my swirling emotions, I give in to them, crumpling to the ground as my tears tumble out.

After a few minutes, I'm aware I'm no longer alone but I don't get up or acknowledge who it is. Kato kneels beside me and draws me into his arms. I lift my head and look up into his eyes, which are also heavy with tears. For a moment we say nothing. We just sit there in the garden, suffering together, staring at the sky which has started to turn various shades of pink and orange with the setting sun. When Kato finally does speak, his voice is weak and broken.

"We'll get through this like we've gotten through everything else in our lives—together. The world can turn their backs on us, but we can always move forward as long as we have each other. We don't need anyone else."

"I know. Deep inside I know. We may not *need* anyone else, but I *want* other people, Kato. I don't want it to have to be us against the world."

"I don't want it that way, either, if we can avoid it. But know that I am always on your side. I will always be here. I will never abandon you, Ash." He hugs me tighter, adding with a hint of forced humor, "You're not going to be able to get rid of me, you know, no matter how many times you explode."

I manage a small laugh. "I guess that means you're stuck with me, too. I love you, Kato."

"I love you, too, Ash. Now, what do you say we go back inside? I need someone new to play cards with me, and Bram seems like a good option. I could use some money."

I look up at the twinkle in his eyes and give him a genuine laugh. He stands, helping me up. As we walk back toward the house, I freeze, my eyes widening in horror.

"I can't go back in there looking like this!" I cry, gesturing at my face, which I know is red and puffy from crying.

Kato turns around, assessing me. "Well, the good news is that if seeing you like that doesn't make Bram run then I think you're set for life."

I smack his chest with the back of my hand and he laughs. "Honestly," he amends, "you don't look too bad." I raise my eyebrow. "Well, you've looked worse."

"You're not helping, Kato!"

"Look, you can either hide out here for gods know how long, or we can just go back inside. Your choice."

I take a deep breath and close my eyes to think. I try to imagine exactly how bad I probably look and what I would want to look like for Bram. My head begins to ache thinking about it.

"Astra," Kato breathes, his voice filled with awe. "You're glowing."

My eyes snap open and I look down. My whole body glows with a silver light. But this light is different from what I felt before. It feels controlled and safe. It doesn't feel threatening—

it feels familiar, like I've always known and understood it. It feels cool and calm. I turn my hands over, just looking at the gentle glow. I focus on drawing it in, and it slowly fades. I look up at Kato who is gaping at me in disbelief.

"You . . . you can't even tell you were crying," he chokes out.

"What?"

"Whatever you just did, you look normal. Better than normal."

I reach my hand up and touch my cheek. It's not even damp from my tears.

"How?" Kato breathes, his eyes still wide.

"I . . . I don't know," I confess, baffled. "I simply wished, wanted to change, and it just happened."

Kato takes a step toward me. "That's incredible. Maybe these powers are going to be a good thing. Maybe all of this trouble will be worth it. If you ever figure out how you did that, you have to share. It's not fair if you're the only all-powerful twin."

I laugh. "Maybe. But no promises. Now, how about we go inside and play some cards?"

Kato smiles. "That sounds like an excellent idea."

He offers me his arm and I take it. Together, we head back inside, ready to embrace our new lives.

CHAPTER FOURTEEN

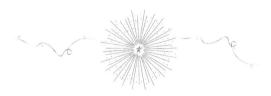

$\mathcal{I}$ stand in a small green clearing, wearing a long iridescent dress, my feet bare. I step to the edge of a pool of liquid silver, surrounded by butterflies that seem to have wings made of soft light. I squat down next to the pool and cup my hands, scooping some of the light. I lift it to my lips and take a sip. It slides down my throat, filling me with joy, happiness. I laugh, so carefree, as if all my burdens have been lifted. I'm about to lean down and drink some more when I hear my name. The voice echoes around the clearing. I search for the speaker, but I'm still alone, save for the butterflies.

"Astra!" the voice calls.

"Kato!" I laugh, recognition dawning. "Where are you?"

"Astra!" his voice echoes again.

I twirl, searching for him. I realize he's not here with me, but calling from someplace I can't see. His voice starts to draw me away. The clearing fades and gives way to darkness. I feel hands shaking me. I open my eyes to find Kato standing over me, gently shaking me by my shoulders. I blink and sit up.

"You were sleeping really soundly. You had me a little

worried," Kato confesses, crossing his arms, eyebrows knit in concern. "Are you okay?"

I nod, rubbing the sleep from my eyes and fighting a yawn. "I actually feel great. That's the first non-tonic induced sleep I've had in weeks."

Kato eyes me skeptically. "Because if you're not feeling up to traveling, we can wait another day. I'm sure Bram won't mind."

I shake my head. "I'm fine. I promise." I hop off the bed and spin. "See, I'm standing on my own and everything."

"All right, then," Kato concedes. "Your bag is at the end of your bed. Get dressed and make sure you have everything you need. Bram's in town right now gathering last-minute supplies. If you're sure you're good to go, we'll head out when he gets back."

I nod and he leaves to let me get ready. I open my bag and sort through the things Mara packed for me. The top dress, a heathered gray, is the only familiar dress of the three. The other two, one light blue and one light pink, aren't ones I remember owning. I think I vaguely remember seeing them among Mara's many dresses. I lift the pink dress, holding it up to my body. If it was one of Mara's, she had it hemmed and brought in to fit my smaller frame. With a grateful smile, I pack the dress back into the bag and look for something else that may be better for a day of traveling. I find a couple pairs of leather leggings paired with dresses open in the front to make riding easier. I change into one of the riding dresses and make sure everything else is securely packed.

I reorganize my tousled hair into a long braid and slip on my boots. Once I'm ready, I grab my bag and head out into the main room of the house. Healer Heora is in her usual corner, organizing many bottles of cures.

"Mrs. Malone from down the way traded me several eggs

for a salve. I prepared them for breakfast and made the boys leave you some," she says, gesturing to a plate of scrambled eggs sitting on the table.

I thank her and take my seat. The eggs are a little cold but still delicious. I'm shoveling them in my mouth when Healer Heora approaches me, several things in her hands. I swallow my current mouthful of eggs and look up at her. She sets a small corked vial on the table in front of me.

"Your body went through a lot with all the magical changes and it's still adapting. If you start to feel weak or weary, or if the same happens to Kato, a few drops of this should help." I nod and she places a second vial next to the first. "This is a special concoction meant to help restore magic if you've drained yourself."

I scowl. "What do you mean?"

She clears her throat. "From what I've read in journals kept by my healing ancestors who lived when magic was still alive, magic wielders can drain their energy. How much magic you can perform and how quickly your energy will drain varies from person to person, but everyone has their limits. This oil"—she taps the top of the vial—"is a way to help restore your energy a little faster and, in the event that you've overexerted yourself, it may save your life."

"Thank you."

She nods and sets a small leather pouch on the table. "I've also prepared a few other medicines for you to take with you. Mostly healing salves for cuts and bruises, some pain medicines, and other basic things you may need on your journey."

"Are they magical?" I ask, trying to peek in the pouch as she opens it and places the other two vials inside.

"Mostly, no. While I may have some healing magic now, magic is still too foreign for me to feel comfortable using it to make many medicines. Magic, while powerful with many great uses, can be dangerous if not wielded properly. It takes training and practice." Her eyes meet mine and I can feel the weight of her words.

"That said," she says, looking back down at the bag, tying it shut with a leather string, "some of these do have magical properties to them. Magic is the only way to heal magic, so, in some cases, it is unavoidable."

I nod, thanking her again. She gives me a soft smile and returns to her corner, gathering ingredients to make a new mixture for her shelf. I finish up the last of my eggs and wash my plate. I grab my bag and find Kato outside teaching Hanna a few sword tricks. Both use sticks in place of actual weapons. I smile and lean against the house, watching as Kato instructs.

"It's all about the footwork," Kato says, demonstrating the proper stance. "If you can stay quick on your feet, it doesn't matter if the other person is more skilled with their sword. Sometimes it's about dodging rather than striking."

Hanna nods and mimics Kato. "Like this?"

Kato smiles. "Pretty close! A little practice and I have a feeling you'll be undefeatable," Kato says with a wink.

A snort from behind makes us turn and I see Bram walking toward us with three horses. The one at the front is his own dapple gray. He also has a black horse with a white line on its nose and white around two of its hooves, as well as a white horse with a gray mane and tail. All three are saddled. He pauses a few yards away and leans against his horse. I walk over to him, smiling.

"This must be Solomon," I say, reaching up to rub Solomon's nose.

Bram grins. "It is. And I think he likes you. He has always had excellent taste." He pats Solomon's neck.

"I suppose the other two are for us?" Kato asks, looking past Bram to the spare horses.

"They are," Bram nods. "Are you familiar with horses? Have you ridden before?"

He looks from Kato to me. I shake my head but Kato nods.

"I've ridden many times. It was part of my training as a soldier," Kato says, walking up to the black horse, assessing him.

"Not really," I admit with a shrug. "I mean, I know the basics enough to be comfortable riding, but I haven't ridden more than once or twice. There wasn't much need for it in our village."

"Well, I can help you as needed," Bram offers, "but I have a feeling you will do fine. The hard part will be the aftereffects of riding."

"What do you mean?"

Kato laughs. "He means you'll be sore as hell by the end of the day."

I look at Bram and he gives a half shrug. "It is not pleasant but you will adapt. If you need to take breaks, let me know."

I nod and approach the white horse, giving her a pat. She responds with a soft snort and inclines her head toward me.

"Hey, girl," I whisper. "You don't mind if I ride you, do you?"

She gives another snort, nodding her head as she paws the ground with her hoof.

"I think she is on board," Bram laughs.

I grin. "What's her name?"

"Her name"—Bram points to white one I've chosen—"is Luna and that one"—he indicates the black horse—"is Twilight."

"Luna," I muse, rubbing her mane and looking into her clear blue eyes. "It fits her."

"Twilight suits him as well," Kato agrees, patting his horse.

"All right, now that we are all acquainted, let's load up and be on our way. If we leave now, we should be able to reach Meadowridge by nightfall."

Kato and I nod, grabbing our bags. Bram helps me secure mine to my horse, but Kato attaches his without any help. Once the horses are ready, we go back inside to say goodbye to Healer Heora and Hanna.

"I admit, I'll miss you. It's been nice to have people around," Healer Heora says, wrapping me in an affectionate hug.

"Thank you so much for healing us and helping us," I say.

When she pulls back, she gives a nod to Kato and Bram. "May you have safe travels."

"Thank you, Healer Heora," Bram says, bowing his head.

Kato pauses in the doorway and looks back toward Healer Heora and Hanna. "Now, Hanna, you practice that footwork. I expect you to be a worthy opponent next time we meet."

He gives her a wink and she giggles, promising to practice.

The first part of our journey passes without event. Although the sun is already high in the sky, it doesn't begin to get hot for several hours. My discomfort riding a horse, however, hits much sooner. I begin shifting atop Luna, attempting to be as stealthy as possible, but it doesn't take long for Bram to notice.

"If we need to take a break, just let me know," he offers, riding beside me.

"No, I'm fine. Well, not fine but I can manage. I don't want to slow our journey," I insist. "Besides, if I get off, I may not be able to convince myself to get back on."

Bram smiles. "Don't worry. You will adjust after a day or two. Until then we will just take it little by little." He squints up at the sky. "It looks like we are actually making good time. We can take a short break in an hour or two, eat a bit of lunch, and let the horses rest."

"Thank you."

"No kissing!" Kato calls from where he rides in front of us, his back to us.

"We're not kissing!" I yell back. "We're riding horses for gods' sake!"

Kato looks back over his shoulder, a mischievous grin on his face. "Oh, it's possible to kiss on horseback."

"Who have you been kissing on horseback?" I ask, arching an eyebrow.

Kato turns back around. "I don't kiss and tell."

I shake my head and laugh.

Bram grins and whispers, "He is right. It is possible. I will have to show you sometime."

He winks and I blush.

"I heard that!" Kato yells and we both laugh.

We ride along for the next hour, mostly quiet. I enjoy watching the changing scenery. It's so different from Timberborn, where we had mostly forests. Here, the land is spread out. We see the occasional farm or house from the road but mostly it's just stretches of green fields sprinkled with wildflowers.

When we finally stop, I'm more than ready. Bram helps me off my horse and we settle on the ground. Kato pulls out some crackers and dried meat from his pack and we share a skein of water. The break from riding is far too short. The next thing I know, Bram's helping me back onto my horse. As I swing my leg over the saddle, I wince. I briefly wonder if Healer Heora included any sort of healing salve that might help. Though, with the discomfort I'm feeling, it would likely have to be one of her magical mixes.

"So, Bram, we don't really know that much about you. Where did you grow up?" Kato asks.

"I grew up in the small farming village of Hounddale. In many ways, it is a lot like yours, just closer to the capital," Bram replies. "My father was a farmer, so we lived more on the outskirts but went into town on a regular basis, especially once we started our training and school. My older brothers only trained for a couple years each before they returned home to help my father on the farm, but I was determined to succeed. My father actually tried to keep me from training after only a year, but my commander convinced my father to let me stay. He insisted I had incredible potential. My father agreed to let me continue training, but I could tell he wasn't entirely happy. I knew he wanted me home. Even at that young age, I knew that being a soldier was my calling. Sword fighting, defense, crossbow, it was all like breathing to me. I lived for it."

"How did you become captain of Ehren's Guard?" I ask.

Bram grins, his eyes shining.

"Well, when I was thirteen, one of the captains for the royal army came to Hounddale looking for soldiers. They didn't recruit from our village often since we were mostly farmers, so I figured it was my only chance. Even though I was much younger than they were looking for, I applied. The captain laughed in my face and told me to go home, but when I insisted, he agreed to let me try out. In order to be considered, candidates had to go up against three highly trained soldiers. I beat the first two but failed against the third. The captain was so impressed he promised me he would return in a year. He left me with a few pointers, and I practiced as much as possible every single day until he returned. He kept true to his word, and I passed his tests with flying colors. I beat the first two in under two minutes and the third in under five.

"Ehren was in training at the time as part of his duties. Since we were nearly the same age and skill, we were often paired up. At first, he didn't care for me." Bram gives a little chuckle. "He was mad that I was more skilled than him and, I admit, I did like to taunt him. Ehren didn't care for most of the nobles' sons, and our mutual hate of them eventually drove us to be friends. Good friends. When I turned sixteen Ehren had me moved to his guard detail. I highly suspect he only did it so he could use the excuse that he had a guard with him after he would convince me to help him sneak off for a mischievous adventure. About three years later, when Ehren turned eighteen, he was permitted to have his own Guard. He made me the captain, and I've held the position ever since. Almost three years now."

"So," Kato muses. "While you're willingly sharing details about your life, what is your surname?"

I perk up, realizing with a rush of embarrassment I never thought to ask. Bram laughs.

"Actually," he chuckles. "It is Bram. Or, at least, that is part of my surname. My full name is Alexander James Bramfield."

"So your first name is Alexander?" I ask, shocked.

"Yes. It is." He looks over at me and smiles, his eyes sparkling.

"Why did you shorten it to Bram?"

"Well, I didn't. When I was training at the castle, Ehren started calling me Bram to annoy me and, over time, it stuck," he answers with a shrug.

"So do you hate the name Bram?" Kato asks.

"No, not anymore. It did annoy me at first, but it grew on me. Now, if you called me Alexander or Alex, like my mother, I would barely recognize it as my name."

"Interesting," Kato says, drawing out the word. "Any more secrets you want to divulge?"

Bram laughs. "I pretty much summed up my whole life story for you."

Kato side-eyes him. "So, that's a no, then?"

"Yes," Bram chuckles. "That would be a no." He glances between me and Kato. "Any secrets you want to share? I mean,

I already know your last name is Downs, you have both excelled at your various studies, and that you are the only twins in the entire kingdom, but that doesn't really tell me about who you really are."

I shrug. "I don't know what there is to tell. We had a pretty basic, unexciting life."

Bram smiles. "Well, what was it like growing up as a twin? That is something no one else can claim."

I glance at Kato and he gives a half-shrug. *Why not? Let's bore him to death with our life story.*

I hide my smile and share some of the fun memories Kato and I have from growing up as twins. Kato joins in and we go back and forth, often remembering particular details slightly differently, like which one of us was the first to hide a snake in the other's bed. Occasionally, Bram cuts in with his own personal stories about him and his siblings. Talking helps the time pass, and, before I know it, we can make out the outline of Meadowridge in the distance.

CHAPTER FIFTEEN

he sight of Meadowridge makes me realize how tired and sore I am. By the time we make it into the village, night has started to fall, but it doesn't seem to have affected any of the town businesses. Where Healer Heora's village had been different in that it was smaller and more spread out, Meadowridge is a busier, more cramped version of my hometown. The buildings are practically stacked on top of each other. The main road is cluttered with merchants selling their wares from booths with crowds of people swarming the streets.

After several long minutes navigating the crowd, we find a stable to keep our horses. A man with a large belly and dark, greasy hair leans against a wall underneath a sign that reads "Horse Boarding," nursing some sort of drink. Bram hops off Solomon and greets the man, who eyes Bram with distrust.

"It's a marke-and-a-half per horse to leave 'em the night and three markes if they need food and water," he grunts.

"That is fine," Bram says, pulling out a coin pouch. "I will throw in an extra half-marke per horse if you will brush them."

The man nods and Bram hands him the coins. The man counts the coins then calls out, "Boy!"

A young boy around eight or nine years comes running out. His clothes are worn and he's covered in dirt. He brushes his long, dark hair out of his eyes as he says, "Yessir?"

"We've got us some horses to care for, boy," the man says gruffly, motioning to us as Kato gets off his horse and Bram helps me off mine. I practically fall into his arms.

"Yessir," the boy says, eyeing us and easing in our direction.

I help Kato remove our bags while Bram squats down so he's at eye level with the boy. He holds up a quarter-marke coin. "Here, take this and if you take good care of these horses, I will give you another in the morning."

The boy's eyes light up and he takes the coin. He turns it over in his hands, his eyes wide. He looks back up at Bram, nodding emphatically. "Yessir! I'll take real good care of yer horse!"

Bram stands and gives the boy a nod. "Good." Bram looks over to the man. "Could you possibly direct us to the closest inn?"

The man gestures vaguely to our right. "Right down that way. The Drunken Goat," he grumbles.

Bram nods his thanks.

The boy and the man lead the horses into the stable as we head down the crowded street. Walking is now as uncomfortable as riding, so I'm extremely relieved when we come to a stone building with a wooden sign reading "The Drunken Goat: Inn and Tavern." Bram opens the door and we're met with a roar of noise and the strong stench of unwashed bodies, ale, and piss.

People are packed close together, but we manage to weave our way through the crowd to a small table crammed in the corner. I slide in, pressed up against the wall, with Bram right next to me and Kato across from me, our knees touching beneath the table, our bags crammed beneath our feet.

"Let's get something to eat," Bram yells, leaning in so we can hear him over the noise. "And then we can ask about a room."

Kato and I nod in agreement.

Despite the density of the crowd, it doesn't take long for a barmaid, her ample bosom practically spilling out of her dress, to notice us. She pushes between patrons, weaving her way to our table, a wooden tray loaded with empty mugs propped on her hip.

"Afternoon, gentlemen and lady," she says, nodding to us each in turn. "What can I do ya fer this evenin'?"

"We have been traveling all day and are starving," Bram answers, twisting in his chair to face her. "Perhaps you could bring us some food along with some mead?"

"I can do that fer sure! We have some delicious meat pies, if you'd be interested. They're individual per person and ready to eat."

Bram nods. "Sounds excellent. One for each of us, if you please."

"Alrighty. I'll have those up a minute." She gives Bram a wink and saunters off into the crowd.

While we wait, I watch the crowd around us, marveling at how different this town is from Timberborn. I hear music coming from somewhere and realize there's a minstrel playing a lute in the corner opposite us. A group of men at a nearby table start roaring with laughter and I jump, accidentally elbowing Bram. Kato laughs but Bram gives me a reassuring smile.

"Sorry," I mumble.

"Don't worry. You'll adjust soon," Bram murmurs to me, but I can barely hear him over all the noise.

This is a lot different from Timberborn, isn't it? Kato says in my head.

No joke. It's so loud I can barely hear myself think.

I'm sure once we've eaten something we can find somewhere quieter.

I hope so. This place is giving me a headache.

The barmaid pops up at the edge of our table again, her tray holding three small meat pies and three full mugs of mead. She places one of each in front of us.

"Anything else I can get for ya?" she asks, resting the tray at her side.

"Actually," Bram replies, "we were wondering if you had any rooms available for the night? Two rooms would be preferred."

"We should. I'll go check fer ya and I'll be right back."

She disappears into the crowd and we dig into our pies. They aren't the best I've ever had, but they aren't bad. Honestly, at this point I'm so hungry I don't really care. The mead is stronger than any I've had before, but I like it. We're nearly done eating when the barmaid returns.

"I have some good news and bad news for ya. Bad news is that we only have one room available, but the good news is that it has more than one bed. Will that suit ya?"

"I suppose that will have to do," Bram answers with a smile.

He and the barmaid negotiate a price for the meal and the room. She disappears, returning a couple minutes later with a key and refills of mead. By the time I finish the second mug of mead, I'm ready for bed. We manage to navigate our way through the swelling crowd, which somehow grew while we were eating. We make our way up a winding and very creaky staircase to a narrow hall.

"Let's see," Bram says, reading the number on the key. "Room 17."

We make our way down the hall, scanning doors for our number and discover our room at the very end. Bram unlocks the door and we step inside. The room is tiny and bare, with no windows, an oil lamp on the wall just inside the door lighting the room. Two thin beds rest along one wall only separated by a bedside table with a second small lantern on top. Directly across from the beds a dirty mirror hangs above a small wooden table bearing an empty washbowl and pitcher.

"Well, it's nice and cozy, I guess," I mumble as Bram closes and locks the door.

"It will do," Bram replies, surveying the room.

"You and Astra can take the beds tonight. I'm more than fine on the floor," Kato offers, sitting down on the edge of the nearest bed to remove his boots.

Bram shakes his head. "That's not necessary. I've spent plenty of time sleeping on floors."

"No debate. I'm taking the floor," Kato insists, kicking his boots off. "You had to sleep on the floor last night, and I've been sleeping in a bed for weeks."

"Very well," Bram concedes.

Bram glances around the room, his eyes settling on the empty wash bowl.

"I'll go fill this so we can at least clean up a little," he says, snatching it up and disappearing out the door.

Once Bram is gone, I collapse on one of the beds.

"You okay, there, Ash?" Kato teases, a smile playing on his lips.

"Yes," I say, sitting up. "But who knew riding a horse all day could be so exhausting!"

I remember the pouch Healer Heora gave me and pull it out of my bag, dumping the contents on the bed.

"What's all this?" Kato asks, coming over to my bed and sitting next to me. He picks up one of the bottles. "'Crushed

Bentlon Leaves: Use Sparingly for Pain - take small amount by mouth.'"

"They're medicines from Healer Heora," I reply, turning over bottles. I pick one up and squint at the label, trying to make it out in the dim light. "I'm hoping she might have something in here to help with soreness from riding all day."

Kato nods. "It was nice of her to send these." He pauses, watching me squint at another label before lighting the little lantern on the bedside table.

"There, that might help," he says as the lantern flame flickers, casting more light on the pile of medicines.

"Yes, it does. Thank you."

He picks up another vial and reads it to himself while I scan labels on my own. After a few moments of checking labels he holds up a jar. "I think this one might do the trick!" He tosses it to me and I read the label.

Healing Salve: Use for general muscle soreness or general aches and pains - apply generously to sore area.

"Yes, I think this may work." I open the jar and a sweet, minty aroma wafts up.

"Smells good at least," Kato says with a shrug. He stands up. "Well, I'll just step over here and stare at the door to give you some privacy."

I thank him and quickly apply the salve, rubbing it just about every place that aches, including my arms. I feel almost immediate relief. I suspect there really must be magic involved for it to work that quickly. When I'm done Kato turns around, eyeing the jar sheepishly.

"I don't suppose there's enough left in that jar for me, is there?" he asks.

I laugh. "Yes, there's plenty left."

I toss him the jar and focus on putting the medicines back in the pouch while he applies the salve. After a minute I hear Kato release a sigh of relief before he tosses the jar back on my bed. I add it to the pouch and turn around.

"That woman truly is magical," he sighs.

I laugh but agree as I tug off my boots, stretching my legs out and wiggling my toes.

"I don't know how people travel like this all the time. Sleeping in random beds, fighting crowds of people just to eat dinner, aching everywhere . . ."

"Well, I would guess people who travel a lot get used to it," Kato says with a shrug.

"Still, it must be exhausting." I collapse onto the bed. I figure there's no use in changing out of my clothes into anything else, not that I'm sure I even have any sleeping clothes packed. I can hear the rumble of the people in the pub below and wonder if I'll be able to sleep at all.

There's a knock on the door. Kato answers it, hand on the hilt of his sword. He relaxes when he discovers it's Bram returning with the water.

"Sorry, that took longer than anticipated," Bram apologizes, setting the water on the table. "I overheard a few men talking about magic nearby, and I listened in for a bit. I think it might be worth checking out if you two don't mind."

"It wouldn't bother me," Kato says. "Will it make our journey much longer?"

"Not really. I was originally planning on taking the northwest road up toward Embervein. The villages and cities that way are closer together, meaning we wouldn't have to camp out. Veering east to this town takes us on a road less traveled by merchants and we will have to make camp a couple nights. The village I want to visit is a two-days' ride from here." Bram shifts his eyes to me. "Would you mind if we had to spend nights camping?"

I shake my head. "No, that would be fine. I have a bedroll packed, and it's not like my cot at home was the epitome of comfort. You have a job to do, so please, don't let us get in the way of that."

"What she said," Kato says, pointing at me.

"Very well. Tomorrow we will head toward Wickbriar. The earlier we leave the better, so we should probably get some sleep."

I nod and settle beneath the covers on my bed. Kato extinguishes the lantern near the door, the small lantern between the beds casting flickering shadows on the wall. As Kato pulls out his bedroll and makes himself comfortable on the floor, Bram sits on the bed next to mine and removes his boots. I turn and face the wall, wanting to give some semblance of privacy as he makes himself comfortable in his bed. After a minute, he puts out the light and the room goes dark. Despite the raucous rumbles from the pub below and the awareness that Bram is sleeping barely an arm's reach away, I fall asleep rather quickly.

CHAPTER SIXTEEN

I'm in the glade clearing again, only this time I'm sitting on a small ledge overlooking the pool of light, dipping my bare feet into the cool liquid. I lift my foot and watch the liquid light drip down, making circles in the pool beneath. I tap my toes, creating more ripples across the smooth surface. Little glowing fish rise up from the depths of the pool and nibble my toes. I giggle, leaning over to examine them. That's when I notice my reflection. It's me but not me at the same time. The me in the reflection looks older, wiser. I wear a crown on my head with confidence. I can almost feel the power she emits.

"Hello," I say to myself, tilting my head.

"Hello," she echoes. Reflection me smiles, but there's no real joy in it. It's the kind of smile you would expect a cat to give a cornered mouse. "Don't we look beautiful."

I nod. "I suppose." I tilt my head the other way, as if she's a puzzle I need to solve. "Do I become you?"

"You can," she purrs. "If you want to be me, it's easy enough."

"What do I need to do?"

"It's easy. Just give in to your power."

As she speaks, ripples wrinkle her reflection as her voice echoes around me. The whole glade fades away to darkness.

When I open my eyes, it takes a moment to remember where I am. I'm lying on my side, facing a wall, a low glow casting shadows from behind me. I slowly roll over and see that Kato is seated on the other bed, leaning against the wall, his head tilted back, eyes closed. Bram is nowhere to be seen.

"Where's Bram?" I ask, sitting up.

"Really?" Kato replies without opening his eyes. "No, 'Good morning, beloved twin. How did you sleep'?"

I laugh and toss my pillow at him. He opens his eyes and turns his head toward me. "And now you're attacking me. I guess it's true what they say."

"And what's that?" I ask, crossing my arms and arching an eyebrow.

"That the road can really change a person."

I roll my eyes and Kato grins. He sits up straighter and adds, "Bram went downstairs to see if he could wrangle up any breakfast."

"Thank you. Was it really so hard to give me a straight answer?"

"Not easier but definitely more fun." His grin is contagious.

I decide to take the moments semi-alone to get up and check my appearance in the mirror. Despite having slept in my clothes I don't look as much like a wrinkled mess as I expected. I'm reworking my hair into a decent braid when Bram knocks on the door. Kato gets up to answer, but pauses with his hand on the door handle and glances over his shoulder at me and whispers, "You done primping? Can I let breakfast in?"

I glare at him in response and he grins, opening the door.

Bram strides into the room holding a tray bearing three bowls of a lumpy gray substance and three crusty rolls.

"All they had to offer was this porridge and some bread. They offered mead but I thought it might be a little early to imbibe." His eyes drift past Kato to where I stand. "Good morning, Astra. Did you sleep well?"

I nod as Kato shuts the door. Bram sets the tray on the table.

"Why does nobody care about how well *I* slept last night?"

Bram's lips quirk into a smile. "How did you sleep last night, Kato?"

"Why, I slept like a baby, Bram. Thank you for asking," Kato says with a slight bow.

I shake my head at him and grab one of the bowls, eyeing it with distaste.

"Looking at this I'm wondering if maybe the best option would have been washing it down with mead," I mutter.

Kato lifts his own bowl to eye level. "I think I have to agree." He dips his finger in and scoops some into his mouth. He makes a slight face and then gives a half-shrug. "It's not that bad."

I grab one of the rolls and use it to scoop some of the porridge. The porridge is mostly flavorless with a thick, lumpy texture that wants to stick in my throat as I swallow, and the roll is hard, almost impossible to chew. It's not great but I've definitely had worse in my life.

"I know it's probably not your ideal breakfast," Bram says, sitting on the edge of my bed as he eats his porridge. "But it will help keep you full while we travel."

We suffer through our breakfast, the last few bites a little difficult to get down, but we all manage. A few minutes later we're back downstairs in the tavern, our bags slung over our shoulders. The tavern is empty save for a man with a bushy gray and black beard behind the bar and a couple drunks snoring loudly in the corner. Bram thanks the man for our "pleasant stay," and he grunts in response.

The outside air is welcome after a night in the stuffy inn. I take a deep breath and sigh, looking up at the sky. It's earlier than I thought, barely dawn, the sky still painted with pastel pinks. The town merchants are starting to filter into the streets to set up their booths, but they don't seem to have the energy they showed when we rode in last night. The streets are much less crowded, so it doesn't take us long to reach the stable. The stout man is nowhere to be seen, but the young boy greets us with a smile.

"Morning, sir! I'll go get yer horse!" He disappears into the stable and returns, bringing the horses out one by one. "I took real good care of yer horses! I brushed 'em real good and made sure they got lots of good food!"

Bram gives Solomon's neck a pat. "I must say, they do look well cared for." He reaches into his coin pouch and the boy licks his lips in anticipation. Bram pulls out two quarter-markes and hands them to the boy.

"Thank ya, sir!" the boy says, his eyes bright.

"Spend them well," Bram says, winking. The boy bounds off down the street toward the merchants, presumably to spend them well as soon as possible.

"That was nice of you," I whisper to Bram.

He shrugs. "The boy did a good job."

We take a few minutes to attach our bags and then we're on our way. Even though it's early, it's already starting to get warm, bordering on hot, which does not bode well for a day of travel. After a couple hours, sweat is starting to bead on my forehead. Bram has refilled our skeins of water, and I'm tempted to gulp mine down, but I know I'll regret drinking it all too soon. At least today, riding seems to be much more comfortable. I'm not sure if my body is adapting or if Healer Heora's salve is still working its magic.

It's nearing noon when the road splits into two. Bram pulls Solomon to a stop.

"Are you sure you don't mind heading east?" Bram asks.

"We're fine with it. I promise," I insist.

"Trust me, we'd tell you if we minded," Kato adds.

"Okay, then. Onward we go!" Bram says as he urges Solomon toward the road on the right.

After a minute, Kato asks, "What magical things are actually happening in this town, if you don't mind sharing?"

"Well, there are actually a couple of things going on, which is why I felt it warranted attention. For one, there have been reports of magic wielders in the town. One of the town healers seems to have actual healing power now, and there also appears to be a Seer who is offering fortunes with incredible accuracy. Of course, those careers have often been known to claim magical heritage so they can charge more, which may be the case here. If they were the only rumors coming out of Wickbriar, I would probably just take note and check it out later but..." He glances away, trailing off.

"What else is there?" I ask nervously. "Anything dangerous?"

"Not exactly. It seems that some magical animals have been spotted," Bram says.

"Magical animals?" I ask, my interest piqued. "What kinds?"

"The details on that are a bit fuzzy. Chatter from drunk tavern patrons doesn't always yield a lot of details, and what details there are vary from person to person. But there are enough reports and sightings that it's worth checking out. We have yet to confirm that any of the magical species have returned, so being able to see it firsthand will be important for our records." He pauses and gives a slight shrug. "Of course, discovering they are only rumors could be helpful, too, I suppose."

I nod. In my studies I learned a little about the now-extinct species of magical creatures. Some were kin to humans like the Fae, Dwarves, Elves, and Nymphs. Others were animals, mostly magical variations of commonly found creatures, or unique species like Dragons, Unicorns, and Firebirds. And then, of course, there were those that fell somewhere in between the two categories—like Mermaids, Centaurs, and the Dragkonians that shared animal characteristics with human-like intelligence.

Some were little more than myths and legends, evidence and records scarce, and many scholars debated over whether they actually existed. Others were well documented. Regardless, any of these species and races depended on magic from the land in order to survive, so once magic disappeared, they did, too.

I muse to myself as we ride along what exactly the return of these species means. Were they created by this new surge of magic? Or had they simply gone away to a place we didn't know of where magic existed this whole time? My thoughts keep me so occupied I'm surprised when we stop to take a break.

The sun is now high in the sky, and my neck is soaked in sweat. Lunch consists of more dried meat and some fruit, but it's so hot I barely have an appetite. Judging by how little Kato and Bram eat, they feel much the same, so we're soon back on the road.

The day drags on and on. Within a couple hours after our break, I'm miserable at best. My discomfort riding a horse has returned in full force, and the sun is unbearably hot. By the time the sun finally decides to start sinking into the horizon, I'm eager to be off my horse.

Once night has fully settled, we stop to make camp. I practically fall off my horse I'm so relieved. Bram makes a small fire, insisting that while the day may have been hot, the cold will more than likely find us tonight. Kato goes through our bags and prepares a small dinner spread of cheese, fruit, bread, and more dried meat. I settle on the ground next to Kato and lean tiredly against him.

"You going to live, Astra?" he asks, looking down at me.

I just grumble, making Kato laugh.

"I admit"—Bram takes a bite of an apple—"that today was quite warm weather-wise, but we did make good time. If I am correct in my estimate, we should be to Wickbriar by early afternoon tomorrow, assuming we keep up this pace." He looks at me and offers me a half-smile. "I'm sorry it was a difficult day for you."

I reach out lazily for some cheese. "I'll adjust, I'm sure. I'm just not used to all this traveling. I do like the change of scenery, though."

"That is one nice thing about traveling—being able to see what all is out there." Bram pauses. "You know, when I was growing up in Hounddale, I was eager to leave and see as much of Callenia as I could."

"I know what you mean," Kato agrees. "I loved Timberborn but I always knew I wanted more. I never expected I would get the opportunity, though."

I sit up and look at Kato. "That's the second time you've said something like that. Have you always wanted to leave Timberborn?"

Kato shrugs, avoiding eye contact by fiddling with a piece of bread. "It's not like I felt trapped or anything, just like I was meant for more than being a village soldier. Like there was something out there calling to me." He finally looks into my eyes. "Didn't you ever feel that way? Reading all those histories and everything? Didn't it make you want to see the world?"

I shrug my shoulders. "Yes and no. Reading about other places could sometimes make me want to see them firsthand, but I thought I would always live in Timberborn and had made my peace with it. Reading was how I escaped our simple lives, and I think I convinced myself that was enough for me." I pause then add, "I did feel a certain restlessness, but I always assumed it was the power inside me."

"Maybe it was the power," Bram offers. "For both of you."

"What do you mean?" Kato asks.

"Well, maybe your fate was decided long before you were born, and that power was tied into your fate. Maybe your fate all along was to leave Timberborn, and the power inside of you was pushing you to fulfill whatever your destinies may be."

We take a few moments to mull over his words.

"Maybe," I finally concede. "And maybe whatever we find out in Embervein can help answer that question."

A few minutes later the food is packed up and our bedrolls are out. I collapse on mine and, once again, it doesn't take sleep long to claim me. I'm awoken a few hours later by a sudden chill. I open my eyes and sit up, glancing over at Kato and Bram, but they're both still asleep. I start to lay back down when I hear a sound behind me. I twist around and see a cloaked figure standing behind me. I open my mouth to call out, but the figure lifts her head and I see her face. It's me. Or at least the "me" from the reflection in my previous dream.

"Who are you?" I breathe.

My other self's mouth twitches up into a wry smile. "I should think the answer to that is obvious."

I shake my head, rubbing my eyes. "I'm dreaming," I mutter to myself. "I'm just dreaming."

"Yes and no," my other self says. "You're not exactly dreaming, but neither are you fully awake. You're in the realm of your subconscious, the in-between, if you will."

"Why are you here? And how am I talking to myself?"

"Well, while I may appear to be you, I am really just a manifestation of your power."

"My power?"

"Yes. The power inside you is powerful and ancient, as is the power inside your brother. Long ago, Fate set into motion the course you are now on."

"So, Bram was right," I muse to myself. "It is Fate."

Other me nods. "Indeed. And in order to fulfill your destiny, you must embrace and wield your power."

"How? I don't even know how to access my power."

"Soon, you will find someone to guide you. When you find this person, cling to them. Trust them."

I scowl. "How will I recognize them?"

The other me smiles brightly, her eyes meeting mine. "Your soul will know without a doubt. Trust it. Trust him."

I open my mouth to ask another question, but she disappears without another word. I startle awake and find myself lying on my bedroll. I blink and sit up, looking around. Kato and Bram are exactly how there were in my dream, but no one else is in sight. I lay back down, but sleep is restless the rest of the night.

CHAPTER SEVENTEEN

*a*s soon as light begins to appear in the sky, I give up on any more sleep and rise. I pack up my bedroll and strap it on Luna. I'm poking the embers of last night's fire with a stick and eating an apple when Bram wakes. He sits up, stretching, glancing my way.

"Had trouble sleeping?" he inquires.

I shrug. "A little." I debate telling him about my dream but decide against it. I don't need him to question my sanity. "I slept okay at first but couldn't go back to sleep once I woke up."

Kato groans from his spot on the ground. "Is it morning already?" He rises, rolling his neck. "I guess the sooner we get going the sooner we get to Wickbriar."

As he starts packing up his bedroll I reach out to him.

Kato, have you been having any more dreams?

He pauses and I can see him weighing his words. *Not nightmares.*

But your power, have you been dreaming about it?

Have you?

You're not answering my question.

Honestly, I don't remember. Ever since I spent two weeks sleeping I'm not sure I dream anymore. If I do, I forget as soon as I wake.

He studies my face. *Are you having nightmares again?*

I shake my head. *No nightmares.*

I don't want to tell him about my dream last night, but I'm not sure why. I know my brother well enough to recognize when he's keeping secrets, and I know he's holding something back. But he doesn't press me, so I offer him the same respect. I suppose we're allowed a few secrets, even as close as we are.

By the time sunrise officially comes, we're on the road. It's cooler today, thanks to cloud cover, but by the way Bram keeps glancing at the sky, I'm not sure the clouds are a good thing. A couple hours into our journey, the skies begin to darken and thunder rumbles around us. The rain starts as little more than an annoying drizzle and slowly escalates until we're in a downpour.

Being soaking wet adds a whole new level of discomfort to the journey. We all agree there's no point in stopping, so we power on. We don't even bother stopping for lunch. Occasionally, the rain lets up for a few minutes at a time but most of the day, we ride in rain. Finally, the rain stops, but the clouds remain, keeping the sun from drying us off quickly.

Early afternoon, we start seeing houses closer together as we ride into Wickbriar. This village reminds me a lot of Timberborn as we ride into the main square. A few residents are milling about, conducting business.

"I'll see if I can find someone to direct us to the nearest inn and stable," Kato says, hopping off his horse.

He saunters over to a very pretty girl with waist length brown hair. Judging by the way she's flitting her eyelashes at Kato he's definitely getting more than directions to the nearest inn.

"I take it Kato never has problems with the ladies," Bram chuckles, watching their interaction.

I grin. "He's never engaged in any sort of serious relationship that I know of, but he's never had problems charming girls."

Kato waves at the girl and makes his way back to us, grinning. "Jaima Beth says that if we continue heading down the main road we'll see the inn in a few minutes with a stable for the horses connected."

"If it's not that far, I think I'd rather walk," I say, sliding off Luna.

Bram nods, dismounting Solomon. The three of us walk side by side down the road until we find the stable. It's nice and cozy. A young man in his thirties greets us.

"Afternoon! I suppose you're looking for a place for your horses to rest a bit?"

Bram nods. "Indeed. We'll need them here at least one night."

"Are you staying at the Crooked Rooster?" the man asks.

"We plan to, as long as they have room available," Bram answers with a nod.

"Well, anyone who stays at the Rooster can leave their horse for free as long as needed, no charge for boarding. Food is one marke per horse."

Bram pays the man three markes and we leave our horses in the stable where they start munching on grass, and we head next door to the Crooked Rooster. We open the door and find the tavern area about a third full. A middle-aged man with a brown beard and a gray cap greets us from behind the bar.

"Evening! Looks like you got caught in that rainstorm we had roll through here earlier."

"We most certainly did. I don't suppose you have any

rooms available where we could clean up and change into dry clothes?" Bram replies.

"I have several rooms available. How many do ya need?"

"Three," Kato answers, then lowers his voice to add, "A little privacy might be nice for once."

I can't help but agree. We receive our keys and head upstairs to our rooms. Kato and I have rooms next to each other, and Bram is directly across the hall from me. I go inside and am tempted to collapse on the bed, but my desire to get out of my wet clothes and eat win out.

A few minutes later I emerge from my room wearing a blue dress, my hair wound into a bun at the nape of my neck. I head downstairs and find Kato and Bram seated at one of the tables with three mugs. I join them, taking a seat next to Bram. He gives me a warm smile.

"We went ahead and ordered you some cider," Bram says, pushing one of the mugs toward me. "The food should be here in a moment."

"Thank you." I smile, wrapping my hands around the mug.

The man with the beard approaches our table with three steaming bowls of soup and a loaf of seeded bread. He sets them on the table. "Let me know if you need anything else!"

I take a spoonful of my soup. It's delicious, which is a very welcome change from the last inn. It's some sort of meat broth with hearty vegetables and seasonings. The bread is equally amazing.

"So what's the plan?" Kato asks, dipping some bread in his soup.

"Well, as it's already early evening, I doubt there's much we can find out, but I say we mingle with anyone on the streets, gather some basic information, and follow up on anything tomorrow," Bram replies.

We agree it's the best plan and finish up our food. We're

happy to discover there are a decent amount of people on the streets this time of day. We start making our way around the town square casually chatting with people. Bram warns us to keep our questions non-specific so people don't get suspicious or guarded. Kato takes it upon himself to chat with as many of the young women as possible. I'd never noticed how much of a flirt my brother was before and can't resist rolling my eyes. Bram and I stick together for a while, but eventually split up to cover more ground before it gets too dark and everyone retreats indoors. I'm distracted watching Bram when someone bumps into me.

"Sorry, love," a voice says.

I spin around and come face-to-face with a handsome young man near my age with messy, bright red hair hanging just past his chin. His shockingly bright emerald green eyes shine with mischief. He flashes me a wide grin.

"Then again, perhaps I'm not too terribly sorry if it means I get to meet you." He has an accent with a pleasant lilt that enchants me for a moment.

"You seem a bit familiar. Do we know one another?" I ask, narrowing my eyes at him as I try to place his face.

"'Tis more than likely, love. I've been all over. But I hardly ever stay in a town for more than a day or two. I've got a travelin' spirit buried deep in my bones."

"Wait," I say, a memory clicking into place. "You're a performer, aren't you?"

"Aye, that I am." He eyes me, a touch of his previous frivolity replaced by wariness.

"You were at the Kriloa festival in Timberborn a month or so ago, weren't you? You did magic tricks."

He suddenly seems a bit uneasy and guarded. "Aye. What of it?"

"I just . . . you were very talented."

He grins, flashing his white teeth as he relaxes. "Well, thank you, love. I work very hard at my trade."

"But your magic," I press, "it seemed like more than tricks."

The man shifts his gaze over my shoulder, his face falling. "Now, there you're wrong, love. No real magic."

I glance behind me to see what changed the man's cheerful expression to one of cautious restraint. Bram is walking toward me, his face in a determined scowl. I turn back to my conversation.

"Please, if you know anything about real magic, I have questions."

He shakes his head, taking a step back, looking almost afraid. "No can do. Trust me, I would more than love to help a lady like you, love, but I'm afraid I rather prefer my head on my neck."

I knit my eyebrows in confusion. "What do you mean?"

"What are you doing here, Alak?" Bram demands from behind me.

"Evenin', Captain," the man, Alak, replies, his voice cool. "Your prince seems to have given you a longer leash to sniff out magic users, is that it? Gonna drag us back as prizes, are ya? Or are you going to slit my throat right here in the very public town square?"

Alak's eyes flit downward and I realize Bram has drawn his sword.

"My business is none of yours, Alak," Bram replies in a voice colder than any I've heard before. "But I have absolutely no interest in dragging you anywhere, except perhaps a shallow grave. You should thank the gods we are in the middle of a crowd, or you would be dead already." He turns to me and adds, "We should head in."

I scowl in confusion, turning back toward Alak. "Please, if you really can use magic . . ."

Alak laughs bitterly. "Love, you're one of the prettiest sights these eyes have seen, but I'd have to be crazy to admit or even hint at magic in front of the prince's very own Captain of the Guard."

"We aren't out for blood. I swear. Why would we be?"

"For one, the captain is always out for blood when it comes to me, love." Bram mumbles agreement under his breath as Alak continues, "For another, from what I hear, the king is less than happy that folks are saying magic has returned and he is more than happy to silence those rumors in any way possible. I can only assume the prince and his lackeys"—his eyes slide to Bram—"are on the same side as our king."

"What if I can promise you that no harm will come to you?"

Alak laughs again, shaking his head. Bram gently grabs my elbow. "Come on, Astra, you won't get any information from him. Nothing worthwhile anyway."

I sigh and start to turn away, thinking that Bram must be correct. Alak suddenly goes still and his eyebrows shoot up, his eyes locking on me. "Astra? Your name is Astra?"

I scowl and turn back to him. "Yes. Why?"

"And that other lad, the tall one with the dark hair stealing all the ladies' attention, who is he?" He nods toward Kato.

"It is none of your concern," Bram snaps, his voice hard.

"He's your brother, isn't he? Your twin?" Alak's eyes search my face. I could deny it, but I can tell he already sees the answer in my expression, so I nod.

Next to me Bram raises his sword and points it directly at Alak. A few nervous villagers glance our way, but Bram doesn't back down. "Go away, Alak. We don't have time for your games. I *will* run you through. Just give me an excuse."

"Lower your sword," I hiss. "Or none of these people will talk to us."

With a grunt, Bram complies, sheathing his sword. Alak looks from me to Bram. Bram's jaw is set and his eyes are filled with something akin to hate. Alak crooks his finger for me to come a little closer. I start to take a step forward, but Bram's hand is on my arm again, his grip tense. I give Bram a puzzled look but step forward anyway, jerking my arm from his grasp. Alak shoots Bram a victorious look over my shoulder and leans in to whisper in my ear.

"If you really want to know about magic, love, I can help you, just not near the good captain. Meet me tonight at midnight just outside town at the edge of the forest. I'll tell you what you need to know. But you gotta come alone. No captain. No brother. Understand?"

I nod and pull away.

Alak turns and waves over his shoulder. "See ya later, love."

After he's gone I turn to face Bram, whose expression is still cold. "What was all that about? Why were you acting so defensive?"

"Whatever he told you, Astra, you can't trust him." Bram's face is all seriousness.

"Why not? How do you know him?"

Bram just shakes his head and looks away. "It's getting dark. We should head back to the inn. Get some rest and start again tomorrow." Bram strides away, leaving me little choice but to follow.

Once we get back to the inn, we convene in Bram's room for a few minutes, compiling the information we gathered. There have been several reported sightings of magical creatures in the forest. Most of the villagers also firmly believe that a teen girl by the name of Sara is a Seer and that the town healer is showing clear signs of magical abilities. We agree that we will start with finding the Seer and Healer first thing in the morning and then make a trip into the forest. Kato and I stand to leave when Kato pauses, turning to me.

"Who was that you and Bram were talking to? He looked familiar."

"He's a charlatan street urchin," Bram snaps while I say, "He was the magician we watched at Kriloa by the bonfire."

Kato, realizing he's stepped into something, puts his hands up in surrender. "Forget I asked."

"He might have real magic, Kato," I say quietly, avoiding Bram's eyes,

"What? Really?" Kato looks from me to Bram. "Then why aren't we talking to him?"

"Because he's not trustworthy. Anything that comes out of his mouth is more than likely a manipulation or trick," Bram answers. "I should go out right now and rid the world of him, to be honest, but he's likely already scampered away to some new hole."

I dodge Bram's eyes, knowing for a fact that Alak is still in town and will be waiting for me outside the village in just a few hours.

"Sooooo, it sounds like you have some sort of history?" Kato drawls.

"Yes," Bram says, his voice clipped. "A history I would rather forget for now."

"But if he does have magic, if he can help . . . ," I start, knowing I will feel less guilty about my rendezvous if I can get Bram on board even a little.

"No," Bram snaps.

I go silent and look down. Kato scowls. Bram sighs and runs his hand through his hair.

"I'm sorry," he says quietly, looking at me, his eyes heavy and sad. "I know Alak. He cannot be trusted, Astra. He's nothing more than trouble. You cannot believe a word he says.

He works his own agenda and doesn't care about the consequences. Doesn't care how many people he hurts."

Genuine pain shines in Bram's eyes. I feel guilty for drawing out the conversation with Alak and agreeing to meet him, though it doesn't change my mind. I know Alak is the person my dream me mentioned, and I'm not about to let whatever feud exists between Bram and Alak get in the way. I step toward Bram, taking his hands in mine. I look up into his eyes.

"I trust you Bram. I really do. I'm sorry."

He leans down and lightly brushes his lips on mine. Kato coughs behind me but doesn't say anything. After Bram pulls back he whispers, "Have a good night."

Kato and I walk into the hall and head to our separate rooms. I remove my boots and collapse on the bed, ready for a night of good sleep. My body is exhausted but my mind is wide awake. I know Bram and I trust Bram, but there's something about Alak. I feel like he's really telling the truth. I trust him, with all my soul.

CHAPTER EIGHTEEN

I'm not sure exactly when I fall asleep, but one minute I'm snuggled in bed and the next I'm staring at the dream version of myself standing in the corner of my room.

"Why are you in bed?" she demands.

"Because I've had a long day and I'm tired."

"You need to go."

"Is it time already?" I pause, adding. "Bram says—"

"Bram doesn't know everything, especially when it comes to this and other magical matters. You need to go."

I hesitate and open my mouth to argue but she cuts me off.

"Go. Now!"

I wake with a start to an empty room. I sit up in bed and debate with myself for a moment before I surrender and put on my boots. I go to leave the room but freeze with my hand on the doorknob. I cross over to my bag and dig until I find the dagger buried in the bottom. Disjointed images of the dagger stabbing into Marco's neck flash through my mind, and I close my eyes tight, willing them away. I inhale slowly to clear my head.

"You won't need to use it," I mutter to myself. "It's just a precaution. You know you can trust Alak."

After a few more deep breaths, I slip the sheathed dagger into my boot and head out to meet a stranger in the woods.

A few patrons linger in the pub below, but I manage to sneak through without anyone noticing me. Even though I'm mostly unfamiliar with this town, it's laid out enough like Timberborn that it doesn't take long for me to find my way to the edge. Roughly half a mile separates the town and the nearby forest. I take a deep breath and start across the field, my heart hammering in my chest.

As I near the tree line, I debate turning around since I don't see anyone, but a figure appears at the edge of the trees, little more than a dark silhouette against the night. I don't even know if it's Alak. It could be someone very dangerous. I pause and the figure steps forward. I can just make out his features in the silver moonlight. I breathe a sigh of relief when I realize it's Alak. Which, I realize, shouldn't really comfort me since I have no idea who this man really is, and what little I do know came as a warning from someone I trust.

"Hello, love," he says as I approach. "I was beginning to wonder if you were going to make our lovely little rendezvous."

"Sorry," I apologize, stopping a couple feet away. "I drifted off. It's been a long day."

"I can imagine so, especially if you had to ride in the rain." He pulls an apple from his pocket and takes a bite. "Don't mind me. I always like a little midnight snack."

"Whatever suits your fancy, but I came out here to find out what you know about magic, against the advice of someone I trust very much, I might add. So, can you help me or not?"

Alak swallows and runs his tongue across his teeth. "I figured the good captain would warn you away. Good to see you have your own mind and will. I like a willful lass." He winks at me and I swallow nervously. "I do appreciate you coming alone. Helps build trust. Though, I suspect the real reason you're alone is because you didn't bother to tell anyone you were coming, am I right?"

Even in the dim light from the moon I can see the mischievous twinkle in his eyes.

"You are correct. Which means they could discover I'm missing at any point, and it won't be good. So, can you help me or not? I've seen your tricks. They were more than just sleight of hand. You had real magic a month ago, didn't you?" I say with more bravado than I actually feel.

He pauses, all mischief gone, and takes a thoughtful bite of his apple before he slowly replies, "Aye, love. I had real magic then and I have it still, though it's a fair bit stronger now."

I breathe a sigh of relief. My mission tonight may be worth the risk after all. "How did you access it before magic was awakened? How do you control it? Can you help me control my power?" My questions spill out uncontrolled. He laughs and holds up his hands.

"Slow down, love! I can only answer one question at a time!" he chuckles. "To start with, I come from two long lines of powerful magic. One on my mother's side and one on my father's. It's made me more . . . receptive to magic, I imagine. I haven't always been able to wield it, and my magic tricks were indeed sleight of hand and illusion for many years. It's only been more recent that I've been able to do any real magic. It started small. Little bits here and there. That night in Timberborn was the strongest I had felt. That is, until magic broke free from wherever it's been all these years.

"As to how I knew what to do with magic, it's in my blood. When I was a wee boy, my mother used to tell me tales about magic. All the stories that had been passed down through the generations, including how to access and use magic. My mother passed on when I was but ten years of age, but her stories stuck. She always put a great importance on our history. She was proud of it. My father was a bastard, but when he would get drunk, he would ramble sometimes about his family's history. Only time that man was useful. He died shortly after my mum."

"It must have been hard to lose both parents so young," I whisper.

"Well," he says, munching his apple, "it certainly wasn't ideal, I'll give you that. Losing my father wasn't bad but my mother was another story. Made me who I am, though, and I don't regret that." He clears his throat. "Anyhow, to answer your other question, I might be able to help you. What can you do with your magic?"

"I don't really know. It's all so new and powerful. I've only accessed it once, well, twice if you count when . . ." I let my voice trail off. "You know who I am, don't you? You recognized my name. That's why you offered to help me."

"You got me," he says. "I've heard many rumors about you and your brother. Both before and after—shall we just call it the incident? I'll admit, I'm curious. What exactly does your magic do, and how are the two of you linked to everything that has been happening?"

"I really have no idea. I know of no magical heritage. I only know that Kato and I were born with this power inside and it all came to the surface the moment we turned eighteen. I can feel it inside me now but have no idea how to draw it out. I've read stories of magic wielders that went insane from not using their magic, and I'm terrified that the same might happen to us if we can't figure out how to use it," I confess, my voice trembling. Alak notes my distress with guarded concern.

"All right, love, give me your hand," Alak says, tossing the last bit of his apple to the side and reaching out both his hands toward me.

I tentatively raise my hand, but pause, pulling away.

"I'm not gonna hurt you, love," he says, his voice low and soft. My eyes meet his, a gentle sincerity reflecting back. "Trust me, love."

My heart beats wildly as I take a deep breath and offer him my hand. He cups my hand in his and closes his eyes. His hands are warm and rough, but gentle. I'm about to ask what he's doing when I feel it. My magic is awake and swirling inside, responding to his touch. My hand starts to glow. Alak gasps, dropping my hand and jerking away. He looks up at me, eyes wide as my hand stops glowing and the magic quiets.

"Are you okay? Did I hurt you?" I ask, taking a step toward him.

He shakes his head. "No. No. I'm fine." He rakes his hand through his hair. "It's just . . . you're very powerful. I knew you had a fair amount of power. I could sense the moment you and your brother rode into town. But your power is kind of hidden behind a shield. It's masked."

"Is that bad?" I ask weakly. "Does it make me bad?"

"No," he says firmly, almost defensively. "No, love, it most certainly does not make you bad. Magic is neither good nor evil. It's merely a tool. A weapon, perhaps, like a sword. A sword on its own is not evil, but it can be wielded for evil, for selfish purposes. But it can also be used to help those who need defending. Magic is the same way. Magic as powerful as yours is no exception. It's not inherently good or bad. You can choose what you want to do with it. You seem like a good person, so I can only assume your magic will be likewise."

I nod. "So can you help me control and use it? What you did just now, how did you do that?"

"Well, like I told you, I come from two lines of magic. One, on my mother's side, is natural magic. People, like you, who were born with magic. My father's line were Syphons."

"Syphons?"

"Aye, Syphons." When he sees that I have no idea what that means, he continues. "Syphons aren't born with their own magic. They depend on the magic of the earth, magical creatures, magical relics, and other magic wielders. They can draw out the magic of someone or something and then wield it themselves. That's what I just did to you."

I clasp the hand he had held against my chest. "You stole my magic?"

"Borrowed," he says, defensively. "I borrowed a slight bit of your power. Believe you me, I have no desire to try to drain you. With your immense well of power, I would likely die before I could kill or harm you."

"Can Syphons do that? Kill someone by draining their power?" I ask, horrified.

"Aye, but I would never do that, love. I swear it. Most Syphons never would."

I jump at movement out of the corner of my eye. I swear I saw something near Alak's discarded apple but at second glance, there's nothing there. I chalk it up to nerves and exhaustion and turn my focus back to Alak.

"So, can your Syphon powers help me learn to release my magic?"

"Not really sure. I can definitely draw your magic, which might help you learn about it or at least find where it lies within you. And I can teach you what few things I know about magic. And my Syphon powers also allow me to sense magic more acutely than most, which is how I was able to sense you and your brother so keenly, so I could possibly help you find a better, more reliable teacher. But I need something in return."

I sigh. I should have expected this. "What would you require?"

"Take me with you on the road."

His response surprises me, given Bram's reaction earlier. For a moment I think he's joking, but his eyes are earnest.

"With the king bearing down on magic, I've sold everything I own, save for one horse," he explains. "I know my money won't last much longer, so staying here and paying for every night and every meal isn't a permanent solution as long as I can't perform my tricks. I'd rather not resort to who I used to be before I had my performances. There's also safety in numbers."

I frown. "I don't know what Bram will say about that."

Alak grins. "Seems like he cares a good bit about you, love, and might just do whatever he needs to do to make you happy. I'm sure if you ask, he will comply."

I go to answer him, but out of the corner of my eye I see Alak's apple move. I freeze, gasping as a creature suddenly appears, batting and nibbling at the apple. It's about a foot long with shimmering white and silver fur, a slightly bushy tail and ears easily twice the size of its head.

Alak follows my gaze and grins, his eyes bright. The little creature looks up at us with wide, glowing blue eyes and gives a little bark. His whole body shimmers and he disappears, reappearing perched on Alak's shoulder. I give a little shriek which makes Alak laugh.

"What is that?" I ask, eyeing the little creature, who's leaning forward, his little black nose sniffing wildly.

"Felixe is a Fae Fox," Alak says cheerfully, reaching up to scratch the little fox between his massive ears. The Fae Fox makes a little sound somewhere between a squeak and a purr.

"He's magical?" I ask as the fox disappears from Alak's right shoulder and reappears on his left.

"Obviously." Alak chuckles, his eyes sparkling with amusement. "Fae Foxes were one of the most common familiars when magic was alive. They're very loyal companions," he says, stroking the fox who, in turn, licks Alak's cheek.

"Can I pet him?" I ask.

"Course, love! If he'll let you."

I reach out. The fox leans forward, wiggling his little black nose as he sniffs my hand. I start to move my hand to pat his head but jerk my hand back when he gives a squeaky bark. I try again, slower. This time he lets me stroke his fur. He's so soft. He leans into my touch and makes a purring sound. He disappears and he's on my shoulders, rubbing his soft furry face against mine. I jump slightly, but it doesn't seem to bother him.

"It seems he likes you, love," Alak grins. "Felixe has good taste. After all, he did choose me. Didn't you, boy?" Alak reaches out and scratches Felixe's chin and the fox jumps fluidly onto Alak's arm and scampers back up to his shoulder.

"He chose you?"

"Aye. It's how familiars work—they choose their magic wielder, not the other way around."

"Where did you find him? Or where did he find you?"

"He found me my first week at this village." Alak pauses, his face thoughtful. "Finding you a familiar may help with your magic. Familiars are known for being able to channel their master's magic and sooth outbursts. This forest is filled with magical creatures."

"And you can find those creatures?" I ask, brightening.

"I can sense them. But like I said, they would need to choose you. But with as much power as you have, I'm sure you could draw one to you easily enough. And I can help you, if you make the deal."

I let loose a breath. "Okay, fine. You help me and my brother learn about our magic and how to control it, and I'll make sure you come with us. I'll find a way to convince Bram.

If you agree to help us find magic wielders and magical creatures along the way, you may be able to prove useful enough even Bram will be on board."

Alak's smile fades into a concerned frown. "Why exactly are you searching for magic? I'm assuming that since you're overloaded with magic yourself you're not in cahoots with the king."

I shake my head. "No. Prince Ehren is on the side of magic and is working under his father's nose to help magic grow stronger, undetected. Bram is trying to find magic before the king's soldiers so we can protect it."

Alak considers my offer. Felixe disappears off his shoulder and reappears by the apple, which he lays next to and begins to gnaw on.

"Fine," Alak says at length. "I'll help you with your mission if you help protect me from the king and help me get to Embervein safely." I nod and he reaches out his hand. "Shake on it?"

I grab his and give it a firm shake. My magic sings at his touch, but if Alak notices, he gives no indication. He makes a clicking sound with his tongue. Felixe's ears perk up and he appears on Alak's shoulders before slowly fading away.

"Well, now that's settled, I suggest we both get a good night's sleep. Shall we head back to town together, or do you not trust me?" He grins wickedly.

"I'll trust you until you give me a reason not to."

He shrugs, his eyes shining. "That's fair."

We walk side by side until we reach the edge of town. He's staying in a different inn further down the road, so he turns to part ways.

"Alak, what happened between you and Bram, anyway?" I call after him. "Why does he hate you so much?"

Alak's expression goes dark. "That, love, is a story for

another day. And it's not my story to tell. Suffice it to say I do have many regrets in life. What happened between the good captain and I is one of the deepest of them. It wasn't entirely my fault, what happened, but he blames me all the same, with reasonable enough cause." He dips his head. "Goodnight, love. I'll see you in the morning." And with that Alak fades into the night.

I make my way back to the inn, exhaustion growing with every step. The pub is mostly deserted as I slink up the stairs. I'm almost to my room when a figure appears out of the shadows.

"Kato!" I cry quietly, my hand flying to my racing heart. "You scared me to death!"

"Where were you?" he asks, his voice firm and arms crossed across his chest.

"I . . . How did you even know I was missing?"

"I couldn't sleep and was looking out my window when I saw you returning." The accusatory tone is sharp. "You went out and met that guy that Bram was warning us about, didn't you."

"Yes, but, Kato, he can help us," I insist.

"Bram said he's trouble."

"He might be. In fact, I am positive he is, but he's also able to help us. He understands real magic. I trust him."

"You trust him? You trust this stranger over Bram, who's risked his life for you?"

Kato's words sting but I nod.

"I do trust him." I look at Kato steadily. "Do you trust me?"

"Of course I do, Ash," Kato says, his voice sounding hurt.

He drops his arms by his sides, and I reach out and grab his hands.

"Then trust me. I really think Alak can help us. I *know* he can. I don't like hurting Bram this way but . . . I don't know. I just feel really strongly about this."

Kato sighs and draws me into a hug. "Okay, fine. But if this guy hurts you, I'm going to kill him myself. Got that?"

I laugh softly. "Deal." I pull away. "Now, I'm going to bed."

Kato wishes me goodnight and disappears into his own room. I head into my room and fall asleep the second my head hits the pillow. I don't wake, not even in my dreams.

CHAPTER NINETEEN

I'm awakened the next morning by pounding on my door. I roll out of bed, squinting and rubbing my eyes in an attempt to adjust to the bright morning light streaming through my window so I don't kill myself stumbling across the room to open the door.

"Astra!" Bram yells through the door, his voice tinged with anger.

I freeze halfway across the room.

Bram pounds again. "Astra! Open this door!"

Grimacing, I crack open the door, peeking out into the hall. Bram stands there red-faced, jaw set, eyes flashing.

"May I come in?" he asks, his voice hard.

I nod, unable to find words. He storms past me into my room. I shut the door and slowly turn around.

"Kato told you," I whisper, avoiding his gaze.

Bram nods, crossing his arms. "What were you thinking, Astra? I warned you not to trust him!"

"I know, Bram, and I'm sorry!" I say, lifting my eyes to his.

"I really, truly am! But Alak has magic and he knows how to use it. I need someone like him to help me. So does Kato."

"That's why I am taking you to Embervein. Once we arrive, we can find someone to guide you and Kato. Someone with credentials. Not some . . . common criminal!" Bram spits, waving his hand in frustration.

"I know. Maybe when we get to Embervein we can find someone else, someone better, but people have been known to go insane from not using their powers. I don't want that to be me or Kato. The sooner we can get a grip on our magic, the better."

Bram sighs, his body relaxing as his hands fall to his sides, but hurt still shines in his eyes as he asks, "Don't you trust me?"

I take a step toward Bram. "Of course I do," I say, tears welling in my eyes. "I trust you with my life."

Bram steps toward me and places his hands on my shoulders. He looks into my eyes. I'm not the only one fighting back tears.

"Then trust me, Astra. Alak is bad news. He cannot be trusted. You have no idea what he is capable of."

My chin trembles and my tears threaten to spill. "I do trust you, and I trust that you have a very good reason to dislike Alak. But I need you to trust me, too. Can you trust me?"

He opens his mouth but closes it without speaking. He takes a deep breath and nods.

"I do trust you, Astra. I do."

"Then trust me. Trust me, Bram. I don't know what bad blood there is between you and Alak. All I know is that for the first time I feel like I may have found a way to control and understand my power. I don't know how to explain it, but Alak is the key. Please, Bram. Please, understand," I plead.

He leans his forehead against mine for a moment.

"Fine," he breathes. He pulls back a couple inches and

looks down at me. "I do not like him near you and I will never be entirely at ease with him around. I never want you alone with him again, understand? I won't let Alak be the reason I lose someone else I love."

Questions flood my mind, but I push them aside, nodding. "That's fine. I can do that."

Bram sighs. "Good. We will stay long enough for Alak to teach you what you need before we continue to Embervein." I cringe and his eyebrows shoot up. "What aren't you saying?"

"I promised Alak he could travel with us to Embervein," I mumble, my voice barely audible.

Bram releases me and jerks away, yelling, "What?" He stares at me in disbelief, the anger flickering in his eyes again. He turns away from me, running his hand across his face in frustration.

"Why the hell would you do that?"

"It was the deal we made," I say weakly. "He'll teach me how to control and access my powers if we help him get to Embervein."

Bram spins back to me. "I don't like this. I don't like this at all. How could you make that deal, knowing I didn't trust him?"

I've never seen Bram this angry, this hurt. But I know what the me in my dreams told me. I know Alak is the person who's supposed to help me with my magic. But I can't explain that to Bram without sounding insane.

"I just know this is what I have to do. I know it's not a great reason but it's the truth. Can you accept that?" I take a step toward him. "Please?"

I feel a tear slide down my cheek. Bram pauses and then strides toward me, wrapping his arms around me. He holds me tightly. I lean into his embrace.

"I don't like it, Astra," he says into my hair. "But if it's what you need, then so be it." He leans back and looks down at me.

"Next time you make a deal with a devil, take me with you. Okay?"

I nod, giving Bram a small smile. He smiles back and leans in, kissing me. The kiss is eager and hungry. I respond in like as Bram pulls me closer, tighter against him. Heat courses through my body and I crave more. I flick my tongue across his lips, and he responds with a sharp gasp. He pulls back slightly, looking down at me with an indescribable intensity in his eyes. He places his hands on either side of my face, caressing my cheeks with his thumbs. Our breathing is heavy.

"Astra, I—"

"Everyone alive in there?" Kato yells through the door as he knocks lightly.

Bram quickly releases me and steps back, blinking like he's waking from a dream.

"Guys?" Kato says, knocking. "Don't make me break this door down."

I shake my head and laugh. Bram clears his throat and calls out, "We're alive."

My hand absentmindedly reaches up and touches where Bram's lips were moments before. Bram sees the motion and smiles shyly.

"Well, do I get to come in?" Kato calls.

You have the worst timing.

Oh, am I interrupting something?

Kato's feigned innocence makes me laugh. I walk over to the door and open it. Kato grins, his eyes darting from my face to Bram's.

"What are we doing in here? Unsupervised, with no chaperones . . . ," Kato drawls, staggering into the room. He plops down on my bed. "Well?"

I roll my eyes, but Bram's face is turning redder by the second.

"Well, whatever was happening is over now. Give me a few minutes to freshen up and I'll meet you two downstairs."

Bram nods. "Fine."

Bram walks to the still open door as Kato sighs dramatically, bouncing up off the bed.

"Okay. Whatever. Keep your secrets," Kato says with a wink at me. "See you downstairs."

Kato bounds out the door, shutting it behind him, shooting me one last grin before it closes all the way. I take a few minutes to straighten my rumpled dress and fix my hair. I decide to just braid part of it back out of my face, leaving the rest down. Once I'm satisfied with my appearance, I head downstairs. Bram and Kato stand by the door.

"We thought we might see what breakfast we can find around town and do a little more investigating," Bram says as I approach them.

"That sounds good. I'm more than happy to avoid more porridge."

The clouds from yesterday are gone, replaced by a beautiful blue sky. Several people are out and about, and we make pleasant conversation with a few people as we head toward a small bakery.

"Well, well. Look who we have here," a familiar voice pipes up from the corner of the bakery as we step inside.

I look over and find Alak sitting at one of three tables, leaning back in his chair, his feet propped up on another chair, ankles crossed. He has a half-eaten sticky bun in his hand. Bram's hand immediately goes to the sword hanging loosely at his side but he doesn't draw it. Alak's eyebrows twitch up in amusement.

"And here I thought we were all friends," Alak says in a tone of feigned hurt. "Or," he says, his amusement growing as he looks from me to Bram, "maybe you don't know yet, Captain?"

"I know," Bram growls. "I am not happy about it."

"Well, can you kill each other later?" Kato says, pushing past Bram to the bakery counter where a young woman is watching us, wide-eyed. "I'd like to eat breakfast before we draw swords, if that's okay with you."

Alak grins and takes a bite of his sticky bun. Bram lets out a huff and turns his back to Alak, sliding his hand around my waist, pulling me almost possessively to the counter. We make a selection of treats, Kato choosing three different kinds.

"Maybe we should eat outside," Bram suggests, glancing pointedly at Alak.

"That's fine!" Alak says, hopping up as he pops the last couple bites of his sticky bun in his mouth. "I like outside, too."

Bram grits his teeth and strides outside, doing his best to ignore Alak. Kato follows, focusing on shoving a sweet roll in his mouth. I shrug apologetically to Alak, following them outside, Alak not far behind.

"So, team, where are you starting today? What's on the agenda?" Alak asks with a clap of his hands.

Bram ignores him and turns to me. "Let's go sit over there," he says gesturing to a tall tree in the center of the town.

I nod and the three of us go over and take a seat in the shade of the tree. Bram and I sit with our backs against the trunk of the tree and Kato sits cross-legged facing us. Alak trails behind and stands over us, arms crossed.

"You can't ignore me all day," Alak says, lips pursed.

"I'm sorry. Is not ignoring you part of the deal that was struck for me last night without my knowledge?" Bram asks harshly and I wince. Alak, however, doesn't seem put off in the slightest.

"Naw, mate. Not part of the deal. Just trying to live up to my part of the bargain by using my talents to aid your cause."

"What talents?" Kato asks, his mouth so full of food I can barely understand him.

"Didn't Astra tell you that in exchange for letting me travel with you and helping me out, I will help you two learn how to access and control your magic while aiding you, Captain, with your mission to find all the magic out there before the king?" His eyes dart from face to face. "Well?"

Bram clears his throat. "And how exactly can you help me find said magic?"

Alak's eyebrow arches as he glances at me. "You didn't cover much, did you?"

"There wasn't much time," I mumble.

"Well, then," Alak says, grinning. "I guess I'll explain. I have Syphon blood, which allows me to sense magic in people, creatures, objects, places, and anywhere else it might be. I can also tell the extent of the magic."

That gets Kato's attention. "You can tell how magical someone is? Like how powerful they are?"

"Yes."

Kato perks up, sitting very straight, his eyes bright. "Can you tell how powerful I am?"

Alak surveys Kato and nods. "I could, if I touched you. But if you're as powerful as your sister, which I very much suspect would be the case, I would rather not."

"You touched her?" Bram growls.

"He touched my hand, for gods' sake. And I offered it to him willingly. Will you relax?" I mutter. Bram lets out a long breath.

"The point is," Alak says, "that I can help. Just tell me where you want to start."

Bram considers Alak for a moment and finally concedes.

"Fine. What do you know about a Healer or Seer in this village?"

"Both gone or in hiding."

"Why?" I ask, surprised.

"Because," Alak replies, dropping down to join us on the ground. "Some of the king's men started sniffing about, asking about magic and the like, and anyone with real magic decided it would be best to disappear or hide."

Bram leans back against the tree. "We're too late, then."

"Now, there is a young girl, daughter of the blacksmith, that has some magic. I don't know who knows about her yet, but I can sense it," Alak adds.

I look down to tear off a bite of a sweet bun and I feel Bram jump beside me. Kato swears as Bram demands, "What is that thing and where did it come from?"

I look up and see that Felixe has appeared on Alak's shoulders, his little nose sniffing the air frantically. Alak grins.

"This 'thing' is a Fae Fox," Alak replies proudly. "And his name is Felixe."

Felixe sees me and disappears from Alak's shoulder, appearing in my lap. I scratch the top of his head. "Hey there, Felixe," I say softly and he gives a happy yip.

Felixe turns to Bram and starts sniffing. Bram extends a tentative hand toward him. Felixe flattens his ears and body and lets out a growl.

Alak laughs. "I don't think he likes you, mate!"

Bram pulls his hand back, scowling. "Are there more of these creatures?"

"Oh, there are plenty of magical creatures in the woods. Enough that you may even find one that likes you." Alak grins and Bram tenses. "So, do you want to start in the woods or with the blacksmith's daughter?"

"Since we're in town, let's go ahead and find the blacksmith," Bram says standing and offering me a hand up. Felixe disappears from my lap as I stand.

"Excellent choice," Alak agrees, standing up. Kato rises as well.

"I'm assuming you can lead the way?" Bram asks, everything about him tense and stiff.

"I would love to, mate!" Alak says, bounding down the road.

We have no choice but to follow. Alak weaves his way through the town, obviously knowing the route. The blacksmith's shop is hot, the air filled with black smoke. Alak walks up to a middle-aged man with a thick black beard wearing a stained apron.

"Morning, Anton! How are you this morning?" Alak calls out and the man smiles.

"Not bad. Not bad. How are you?"

Alak flashes a smile. "I must say, I'm having an unusually excellent morning so far."

Bram shifts uneasily beside me. His movement draws the man's attention. Alak notices and waves us off. "These are just my friends. They'd like to meet Eissa."

The man shakes his head firmly and turns his back. "No. I'm sorry, but no."

"We want to help your daughter," Bram says, taking a step forward.

The man spins around, shaking his head.

"No. Leave my Eissa alone. It was nothing. Just imagination."

"Please," I say softly. "We only want to help."

The man looks at me, a little of his panic fading. He's still uneasy and unsure, though. I take a step forward, slowly, like I'm approaching a wild animal.

"Does your Eissa have magic?" I ask and the man blanches,

shaking his head. "Because I have magic, too."

The man studies my face. "Show me."

I take a deep breath and turn, looking at Alak. I've never purposefully drawn my magic before. Somehow, I know Alak can tell.

"Take a deep breath and focus," Alak instructs, stepping toward me and placing his hand on my shoulder. "You can do it."

I feel a spark of magic ignite at his touch, and I think it has less to do with his Syphon powers and more to do with the fact my magic recognizes his. I turn back to the blacksmith and close my eyes.

"Just focus and envision what you want to happen." Alak's voice is steady and comforting in my ear.

I do what he says. I focus. I breathe. I imagine my hands glowing. I take another deep breath. I feel the power beginning to stir. I reach for it, pull. I hear a gasp and open my eyes. My hands are glowing with a faint silver light. The blacksmith's eyes are wide. I smile and drop my focus, the light fading with it. Alak smiles at me. I ignore Bram's obvious discomfort.

"Very well. You may meet my daughter. But not now. There are too many curious eyes. Tonight. Come to my house for dinner. You can meet her then. In private. Our house is the fourth one off the main road."

"Thank you, Anton," Alak says while I nod my gratitude. Anton gives us a nod as he turns back to his work.

"Now, if you don't mind, I have a lot to do."

We thank him for his time and walk away. He busies himself immediately. Once we're safely away from him, Kato turns to me, his eyes shining.

"You did it. You used your magic," he says, excitedly.

I grin. "I did. Well, kind of. I made my hand glow. I'm not

really sure that counts since I didn't actually do anything with the magic."

"It's more than I've ever done," Kato points out, a touch of bitterness in his voice.

"Your magic should work the same," Alak offers. "You just need to focus."

"But not here," Bram snaps. He turns, looking me in the eye. "That was reckless. You don't know who could have seen you."

"I know, but it worked, didn't it?" I say, excitement winning out over guilt.

"Magic isn't something you should have to hide," Alak says sharply.

Bram glares at him. "Maybe not, but you saw how hesitant that man was to tell us about his daughter. You know about the others going into hiding. There's a reason for that. I'm just suggesting some caution. Astra could have lost control."

"You're suggesting I don't know what I'm doing. If she had put us at risk I could have absorbed some of her power. And she has to learn sometime," Alak snaps. "You can't keep her hidden away forever."

"Sometime does not have to mean 'right this minute in the middle of town square,'" Bram snaps back. "And I am not hiding her away. I am protecting her from people like you who will inevitably hurt her."

"Stop!" I command and they both look at me. "Not here, for gods' sake."

My eyes dart nervously around but it doesn't seem anyone has noticed. Bram straightens and Alak sneers.

"Well, I don't care when or where, but I definitely want to see what I can do with my magic," Kato says with a shrug.

"Maybe we can practice in the forest," I offer. "No one should be around."

I glance at Bram and he nods, relaxing a bit. "That's not a bad idea."

"Excellent! Well, since we don't have any plans until dinner, I suggest we make a day of it. The inn where I'm staying makes excellent sandwiches with bits of meat. I say we get some of those, a bottle or two of mead, and some other food, whatever fits your fancy, and we have lunch taken care of. We can spend all day in the forest, exploring, practicing, whatever. What do you say?" Alak grins.

"Sounds good to me!" Kato says, matching Alak's grin.

Bram grunts his agreement. He needs a break from Alak, or he's going to lose it again.

"Why don't we split up?" I suggest. "Alak, you get sandwiches and mead. Kato can go back to the bakery and get us some breads and cakes while Bram and I get some fruits, vegetables, cheeses, or whatever else. Does that work?"

"Works for me, love!" Alak says with a wink.

Kato shrugs. "Sure."

"Great. We can meet at the tree where we ate this morning when we're ready." They all nod and we split up, Alak blowing me a kiss as he walks off just to make Bram's eyes flash.

Once we're on our own, Bram slides his hand into mine.

"I am sorry," he says, his voice low. "I loathe Alak, and as much as I realize you may have a need for him, I cannot change how I feel toward him."

"Why, Bram?" I inquire gently. "What did he do?"

He shakes his head. "It is a long story." He smiles at me sadly. "Maybe I will tell you one day, but today let us focus on the task at hand."

He stops, pulling me against his chest and kissing me. When he pulls back his eyes are shining, and I'm suddenly breathless.

"I care for you deeply, Astra. It may seem ridiculous, seeing as how we haven't really known each other all that long, but it is true all the same." My heart flips.

"I care deeply for you, too, Bram." I stand on my tiptoes and give him a quick kiss.

He smiles down at me. "I have seen what Alak can do to people. I don't trust him. I am afraid he will end up hurting you."

I tilt my head. "I understand that, Bram, but you have to trust me. I promise I will be careful, but you have to let me make my own decisions. I think I proved well enough with Marco that I can defend myself. Not that I want to," I add quickly when his eyes darken, "but I can."

"You have the dagger?" he whispers.

I nod and glance down briefly at my boot. "I do."

He nods, satisfied. "Hopefully, you won't have to use it again, but never go anywhere without it. Especially around Alak."

I agree, and he kisses me lightly again before we start walking, hand in hand, to gather our share of the supplies.

CHAPTER TWENTY

*I*t's mid-morning by the time we gather under the tree with our supplies. Alak leads the way into the woods, whistling the entire time. Once we're out of town, Felixe appears and bounces along with us, occasionally disappearing and reappearing further in front of us, chasing butterflies and other insects.

The forest itself is alive with magic, calling to me the moment I step beneath the canopy of trees. Magic pulses through the air, making my own magic feel alive and vibrant. The further we go into the forest, the stronger the magic grows. I can't hide my smile.

Can you feel it? Kato asks, looking around in wonder.

I nod, my grin growing. *I can.*

I reach out my hand, touching the magic in the air around me. My skin tingles, absorbing or responding to the magic in some way I can't quite describe. Bram looks from me to Kato curiously before glancing over at Alak, who watches us with a cocky grin, Felixe perched on his shoulder.

"What is it?" Bram asks.

"Magic," I breathe. "There's magic everywhere."

A screech echoes above us, drawing our attention to a bird with shimmering blue feathers flying above us, a trail of gold streaking behind him. He lands on a tree branch high above and looks down at us, giving another screech.

"What is that?" Bram whispers, eyes wide.

I shrug, eyes bright. "I'm not sure, but I'm positive it's magical."

"It's an Indigo Lovelin Bird," Alak replies. "They're known for being a good omen."

"Oh! I remember reading about them. Aren't their feathers supposed to be lucky?"

"Indeed," Alak replies, arching an eyebrow. "I'm impressed. You know your magical creatures."

"I know some of them from reading and studying, but I'm sure what little I know doesn't even begin to touch the surface of what's out there. Timberborn's library was limited."

"Astra's brain can store knowledge better than anyone I've ever met," Kato adds. "If she's read about any of the animals we'll see, she'll remember them."

I smile and look at Alak. "How do you know so much about magical creatures?"

"What, a handsome fellow like me isn't supposed to know about such things, eh?" I shake my head, smiling. He grins. "I think it's part of my magic. For some of these creatures I can sense what they are, like they want me to know and are reaching out to me. Others I know about from stories and lore. Thanks to my mum, I've always had an interest in my magical heritage."

Bram scoffs and I scowl at him. Before I can ask why he's being so rude, Felixe starts yipping excitedly. He disappears from Alak's shoulders and reappears in the brush a couple yards away, still yipping. Felixe spins in a circle and magically jumps from the brush to Alak's shoulder to mine and back to the brush.

"I think he wants us to follow him," I giggle.

"Well, what are we waiting for?" Kato asks, grinning and bounding off after Felixe with the rest of us not far behind.

Felixe races through the forest, jumping back to us anytime he gets too far ahead. We follow without question. Felixe halts, his nose in the air, sniffing frantically. He looks back to where we've frozen a few feet away, and I swear he smiles. He gives a quiet yip and slinks to a slight ledge, peering down. We creep forward and follow Felixe's gaze down into a small clearing. I gasp in delight. Down below is a whole skulk of Fae Foxes. Several kits tumble together, yipping, playing, and nipping at each other's tails and ears. A couple more are off to the side trying to catch butterflies. Nearby are a few adult Fae Foxes, watching over the kits. One is licking the long ears of one of her kits.

For several minutes, we squat at the edge of the clearing watching the kits play. They pop in and out of sight and reappear in random places, often looking around as if they're baffled by their new location. Then they just shake their heads and go right back to playing.

Eventually the wind shifts and one of the adult Fae Foxes catches our scent. Her eyes flash to where we're hiding. She lowers her whole body to the ground, flattening her ears as she growls. The kits all perk up and stop their play. The other adults appear next to her, and, one by one, the kits pop behind them. After a moment of making it clear that they're not to be messed with, they bound away, disappearing into the forest.

"That was amazing," I whisper, standing straight.

Alak grins as Felixe appears on his shoulder. "Fae Foxes are wonderful creatures."

Felixe yips his agreement.

We make our way down to where the skulk of foxes were moments before and follow their path out of the clearing. Just on the other side of the trees we find another clearing, pulsing with magic. I instantly know that we've reached the heart of the forest.

This clearing is slightly larger than the last one, with a large pond in the center and plenty of sunlight shining down. Several brightly colored plants are scattered everywhere, most gleaming with magic. Everything looks vaguely familiar and, with a start, I realize this is the glade from my dreams. I walk over to the pool and peer down and am slightly disappointed to see it's only water and not light.

"What the hell are you doing?" Bram asks from behind me.

"What do you think, mate?" Alak's voice replies. "I'm goin' for a swim."

I turn and see Alak pulling his shirt over his head. His bare chest, bearing several white scars that stand out against his tanned skin, isn't exactly what you would call toned, but he's made of lean muscle that's all soft edges. Alak catches me looking and grins.

"Like what ya see, love?" he asks. Heat rises in my cheeks as I pull my gaze away. "It's all right. I know I'm lovely to look at," he adds with a wink.

Bram glares at him, but I shrug. "Eh. I've seen better."

Alak bursts out laughing at my feigned nonchalance as he kicks off his boots. "That's the spirit, love!"

He starts to take off his pants, but Bram puts a stop to that rather quickly. "Alak, I know you are not seriously debating taking off another article of clothing with a lady present," he mutters.

Alak rolls his eyes. "Fine. Wouldn't want to make anyone feel inadequate."

I blush at his words, but Bram only glowers. Alak walks to

the edge of the water, wading in until the water is nearly up to his shoulders.

"How is it?" Kato asks, eagerly.

"It's rather nice," Alak calls back. "A wee bit on the chilly side but nice."

Kato grins, pulling off his shirt. "Excellent."

He pulls off his boots and strides to the pool, plunging right in. He walks out to Alak and motions for us to join him. Bram comes and stands next to me, his eyes on the pool of water.

"Care for a swim?" he asks.

I grin and face Bram. "Really? You're going to swim?"

He laughs, his eyes sparkling as they meet mine. "Sure. Why not?"

He slowly, somewhat nervously, pulls off his own shirt in one smooth motion. Alak may not be toned, but Bram fits the definition flawlessly. His chest is lined with taut muscles fitting a captain of the prince's Guard. I'm left literally breathless. Bram smiles softly under my gaze.

"No kissing!" Kato yells from the water.

"I second that!" Alak cheers with a wicked grin. "No kissing, unless, of course, you have kisses to share with everyone."

"That is *not* what I said," Kato counters, laughing as he splashes Alak.

"Aye, I know, mate," Alak says. "I was merely amending the terms."

I look away and laugh. As Bram leans down to take off his boots, I nervously lift my dress over my head. I'm wearing a simple chemise underneath but I feel nearly naked. I lay my dress across some nearby rocks and sit down to take off my boots. Bram offers me his hand and I take it, my heart pounding. When we wade into the water, I gasp, shocked by the ice-cold water.

"It's nice, isn't it?" Alak asks, grinning.

"It's freezing!" I shiver.

"But a good freezing! It makes you feel alive!" Alak throws his arms wide and does a backward dive, splashing us all.

I shriek, laughing. When he pops back up I splash water in his face and he grins. Even Bram seems to relax after a few minutes in the water. Since I don't know how to swim, I stay in the shallow water, observing the plants, fish, and other wildlife. I spot a couple types of fish I'm certain are magical, as well as a shiny, metallic beetle I'm almost positive can be used in healing potions, a glowing salamander whose skin secretes some sort of magical oil, a butterfly with glowing wings, and dozens of other plants and fauna. I'm examining an underwater plant growing in the shallows with shiny green leaves lined with silver veins when Alak swims up to me.

"Do you know what that is?" I shake my head and he plucks one of the leaves and holds it out to me. "Eat it."

I raise my eyebrows. "Eat it? You want me to just eat a random plant?"

"Yes," he replies, grinning. "Don't you trust me?"

I cautiously take the leaf from his hand, holding it between two fingers. I slowly start moving it toward my mouth, watching Alak's face. I pop the leaf in my mouth and chew it, making a face. It's extremely bitter. I'm about to spit it out when a strange feeling washes over me. Alak takes my hand and pulls me deeper into the water.

"Duck under," he instructs quietly. "You can breathe under the water."

Without hesitation, I immerse my head in the water. Sure enough, when I go to take a breath, I can breathe. I laugh and little bubbles float up. A couple curious fish swim up to me and float directly in front of my face. I take a couple more breaths, enjoying the underwater world. When I feel the effects of the leaf fading, I pop back up above the surface, eyes shining.

"That was amazing!"

Alak grins. "I thought you might like that."

"What did you do?" Kato inquires eagerly, wading over to us.

I pluck a leaf and hand it to him. "If you eat this you can breathe underwater."

His eyes go wide as he grabs the leaf from me and pops it in his mouth. "This is disgusting," he gags. He forces it down and then dives under the water. When he resurfaces a minute later his face is glowing. "Magic is amazing."

Bram swims over to us. "Will it work for me?"

Alak cocks his head. "Are you about to trust me now, mate?"

Bram glares.

"Aye, it should work for you," Alak says with a laugh. "That's the wonder of magical plants. No matter who you are, you can benefit from them, even if you don't possess a lick of magic."

I hand Bram a leaf and he holds his hesitantly in his hand before placing it on his tongue. He chews it for a moment and then swallows. He ducks under the water. I chew a leaf and go under with him. The water is perfectly clear, and, for a couple minutes, we grin at each other under the water, eyes dancing. We all spend the next half hour mostly underwater, marveling at the wonderful new world teeming with life. I'm following a turtle when the ground drops off underneath my feet. I'm sinking. I look up and see the sunlit surface getting farther and farther. I feel a surge of panic as I realize I only have one, maybe two, breaths left.

Kato! I'm falling! I lost my footing and I'm sinking!

Where are you?

I take a breath and know it's my last. I turn and see Kato diving under the water, but he's at the other edge of the pool.

Bram is even further. I start struggling in the water, trying to pull myself up when an arm loops around my waist, hoisting me up. When my head breaks the surface of the water, I gasp. Alak's arm stays around me until I'm firmly seated on land. I collapse, shaking. Bram and Kato are by my side seconds later, Alak shifting to the side so they can reach me.

"Are you okay?" Bram asks, dropping next to me.

I nod. "Yes, I'm fine. I'm okay."

He wraps his arms around me and holds me close. "I should have known better than to trust you," he growls at Alak.

"No, Bram," I argue, pulling back slightly. "It was my fault entirely. I wasn't watching where I was stepping. Alak saved me."

Alak offers Bram a weak smile.

"Thank you," Bram says with a stiff nod.

"All in a day's work," Alak says with a shrug. "Now, who's up for a bite of lunch? Swimming and rescuing drowning damsels have worked up my appetite."

Bram and Kato put their shirts back on, but Alak seems perfectly content to remain shirtless. I also leave my dress off, hoping the patches of sunlight will dry me off enough that I won't soak my dress when I put it back on. We spread our lunch out on the ground and sit in a circle around it. Once we're sufficiently stuffed, Alak stands, brushing crumbs off his hands.

"All right, now if I remember correctly this trip to the woods was to serve two purposes. One, we were looking for magical critters and whatnot. I think we've pretty well fulfilled that purpose. The second was to help you two wield your magic. So, what do you say? Want to give it a try?"

Kato and I nod eagerly and stand, facing Alak. Bram leans against a tree, watching carefully.

"All right," Alak begins. "I want you both to keep in mind

that I am still relatively new to this magic thing as well. I can only teach you what I know, what I understand. The basics should be the same for your magic as mine, but I cannot make any promises since your magic is different and much stronger. Got it?"

We nod and he continues. "Okay. First you need to find the source of magic inside you. Once you know where it dwells, you can reach for it. This forest is filled with enough magic that it should make the task that much easier. Magic calls to magic, so follow the trail."

Kato and I close our eyes. I block out the sounds of the forest and focus on my breathing as I search for my magic. I find a hint of it, a thread, and I follow it. I feel my magic surfacing little by little. I gasp when I tap into my magic, my eyes flying open. A moment later, Kato does the same.

"You found it?" Alak asks, inclining his head and we nod. "Okay, now slowly, very slowly draw it out. Focus. You don't want it to overwhelm you. Control it."

My hands begin to glow silver and Kato's red.

Alak lets out a long breath, eyeing our hands nervously.

"Now most magic is rooted in a particular skill or focus. Many people believe it's linked to the elements—water, earth, wind, fire, and spirit. Others believe that some magic comes directly from the gods. Knowing what kind of magic you have helps you know how to manipulate it. Focus, find that element or skill, and bring it out. Envision what you want to do and make it happen."

Next to me, Kato knits his eyebrows, concentrating as a small flame flickers to life in his hands. His eyebrows shoot up and he looks at me, grinning. "I did it!"

"Now, control it," Alak says through his teeth. "You don't want fire to get out of hand in a forest." He glances to me. "Now, you try."

I take a deep breath and pull on my power. I hold out my hand, palm up. I imagine taking my light and forming it into a ball. A small orb of silver light forms, hovering above my palm.

Alak smiles. "Good. Now, let's see what you can do with that magic, but be careful not to use too much too quickly. How long your magic lasts and how quickly it drains you is tied to how well versed you are with the type of magic you're performing and how much physical energy you have. The better you get to know your magic, the longer you can go without draining yourself."

Kato makes his flame grow a little and tosses it from hand to hand, manipulating the shape to make various animals. I raise my orb of light higher into the air until it's floating several feet above us, making it grow until it's roughly the size of my head. I hear Kato swear from beside me. I take my eyes off my orb to find he's set a nearby bush on fire. Instinctively, I reach out with my magic, dousing the flames with liquid silver light.

"Perhaps we should call it a day," Bram suggests, eyeing the smoking remnants of the bush. "We need to head back into town soon anyway. Hopefully finish drying off."

A thought pops into my mind, and I focus my magic again. A cool wind rushes around me, whipping my hair into my face. When the wind ceases, I'm completely dry. I grin. Kato closes his eyes and does the same, only he's surrounded by a warm wind. Alak grins, snapping his fingers, and his clothes go from damp to dry. I smile at Bram and reach out with my magic, my cool wind drying him.

"Thanks," he says, looking down at his dry clothes.

I slip back into my dress and Alak sighs. "Well, I do prefer as few clothes as possible but if everyone else is dressed, I suppose I should be as well." He winks at me as he grabs his shirt and puts it on.

We take a few minutes to pack up the remains of lunch

before weaving back through the forest. We soon realize that we were a lot deeper than we thought. It takes us nearly an hour to find our way out. As we cross the field between the trees and the town, we decide to meet back up at our inn in a couple hours to go to the blacksmith's house together. Alak gives us a wave as he disappears, heading toward his inn.

When we get upstairs, Kato declares he's going to take a nap, and I can't help but think how wonderful that sounds. As soon as my door closes behind me, I lie down and fall into a dreamless sleep.

CHAPTER TWENTY-ONE

I wake up after a couple hours, feeling refreshed. I'm more aware of my magic now. I can feel it coursing through me, purring beneath my skin, begging me to use it. I take a deep breath and hold out my hand, calling forth the orb of light I created in the forest. This time it takes less thought and effort. I smile, concentrating on the light as I slowly manipulate it into the shape of a butterfly. The silver butterfly flutters off my palm and soars above my head. I blink and make multiple butterflies in multiple sizes. Soon I've filled the entire room with them. They look so happy and free. I wish for a moment that I could fly with them. Suddenly, the ceiling looks closer. I glance down and see that I'm hovering a couple inches above the ground, a silver cloud beneath my feet, lifting me in the air with gentle grace. I give a little gasp and I falter, sinking slightly.

"Focus," I mutter to myself. I regain my balance and lift a little higher. Pure happiness bubbles inside me, and I can't help but laugh. I slowly lower myself back to the ground, allowing the butterflies to fade away. For a moment, I just stand there, smiling. I owe a lot to Alak for all he's taught me in such a short time. I can't wait to see what more he can teach me.

Alak. I feel a swarm of guilt. Bram did loosen up a bit while we were swimming, but I know he still isn't happy with the arrangement I made behind his back. It's this guilt that guides me across the hall to knock on Bram's door. At first he doesn't respond. I'm about to turn and go back to my room when I hear footsteps inside. The door cracks open and Bram peers out.

"Astra?"

He opens the door a bit wider. His shirt is half untucked, and his hair is tousled.

"I'm sorry. Were you sleeping?" I ask, slightly embarrassed.

"I was earlier, but I have actually been awake for a few minutes." He clears his throat. "Come in."

He opens the door the rest of the way and gestures me inside. His room is roughly the same size as mine with the same table, chairs, mirror, bed, and bedside table. Bram shuts the door while I stand awkwardly in the middle of the room. Bram studies me for a moment.

"Is everything okay?"

I nod, offering him a smile. "I'm fine. I just wanted to apologize again for this whole situation with Alak."

Bram's lips form a tight smile. "I admit I was less than happy this morning, but after I saw him help you and Kato in the woods, I can't deny that he might actually be useful. Not to mention that he does have a skillset that can help lead us to magic before the king." He reaches up and smooths down his hair absentmindedly. "Though it may be a challenge for me to remain civil to him at times."

"And that is more than understandable," I offer, taking a step toward him.

"Thank you for understanding," he replies, stepping toward me.

He reaches out to me, and I place my hand in his. He pulls me close and leans down, kissing me. I return the kiss eagerly. The kisses can't come fast enough. It's almost as if time around us has frozen. We're the only two who exist, the only two who matter. My hand grips the edge of his untucked shirt. He pauses, pulling back slightly, his breath rough and heavy.

After a moment's thought, he pulls his shirt off in one smooth motion. I reach out and run my hand across his muscled chest. I look up into his eyes and he smiles at me. I tilt my face up toward him and his lips crash against mine. He lifts me up and stumbles toward the bed. He lays me down on the bed and settles next to me. My heart races. We lie face to face. I trail my finger across his chest, a soft moan escaping his lips. I swallow hard. My lips graze his and we're at it again. Hungry, eager kisses. His hands slowly begin to explore my body, sending chills of pleasure coursing through me. I want more. I need more. But something in me is terrified. Something in me makes me pull back. Bram brushes hair out of my face.

"Are you okay?" Bram asks gently, his voice rough.

I nod. "I just need a moment."

"Take as many moments as you need," he replies, his smile gentle.

I snuggle into his chest and lie there, enjoying his warmth and listening to his heartbeat, which races as quickly as mine. He doesn't protest. He just holds me tight, tracing his fingers up and down my back. I'm not sure how long we lie there without speaking, but I would be happy like this forever. We're interrupted by a knock on the door.

"Bram, you in there?" Kato's voice asks through the door.

Bram jolts to his feet while I swear under my breath. Bram turns and looks at me, his eyebrow quirking up.

"I don't believe I've heard you curse before," he muses with a grin.

I grin mischievously. "Sometimes the occasion calls for it."

He tries to hide his amused smile, but it shines in his eyes anyway. He leans down and scoops up his shirt from the floor, slipping it over his head. Kato knocks again.

"Bram?"

"Maybe if we don't answer he'll go away," I whisper.

"Tempting," Bram replies, his lips twisting into a smile.

I think he might actually let Kato just walk away, but he strides to the door. I sit up, my hands flying to straighten my hair.

Bram opens the door barely a crack. "Yes?"

"Hey, I thought it was probably about time to meet up with Alak and head to the blacksmith's."

"Yes, you are more than likely correct. Give me just a moment. I will meet you downstairs. "

"Okay, I'll grab Astr—" Kato starts, turning away from the door.

"No! Wait!" Bram pauses awkwardly. "I will get her. I need to . . . discuss something with her first."

"You do, do you?" Kato asks, his voice thick with suspicion.

"Yes. I promise we won't be long."

I can't see Kato's face, but I can imagine the incredulous look he's giving Bram right now. Bram closes the door, leaning against it as he releases a long breath I suspect he was holding the entire time.

"That was uncomfortably close."

Astra, dear sister, are you what Bram is hiding in his room?

I'm sure I don't know what you mean.

So, if I knock on your door right now, you'll answer it,

No, but only because I don't want to see your face right now.

Right.

Okay, fine. Yes, I'm in Bram's room but nothing happened. I swear.

So you weren't kissing?

Okay, kissing happened.

And everyone was fully clothed?

I don't reply.

Astra, was everyone clothed? His words are clipped.

I was fully clothed the entire time.

And Bram?

He may have lost his shirt. But that's it.

'Lost his shirt . . .'

Yes. Are you mad? Please don't kill him.

I can feel a laugh through the bond. *I won't kill him. Just hurry up.*

I look up at Bram who is studying me.

"He knows." Bram says it as a statement, not a question.

I nod. "He sure does."

Bram curses and I grin. "He promised not to kill you."

Bram shakes his head, running his hand through his hair. I stand and lightly kiss his lips.

"Well, kissing you is worth the risk." He kisses me again, pulling away reluctantly. "We should probably get going."

He takes my hand and leads me downstairs. Kato is leaning against the doorway to the street, arms crossed. He pushes off from the wall as we approach.

"So," he drawls, "how was your afternoon?"

"Better than yours," I say haughtily as I parade past him and out the door, pulling Bram along with me.

Kato's eyes narrow slightly at Bram, who gives Kato an apologetic shrug as we slide past, but he doesn't say anything else. Outside we find Alak walking our way, Felixe perched on his shoulder. We meet him halfway and Felixe pops over to my shoulder.

"Hey, Felixe!" I say, scratching Felixe's chin. He yips happily in response and pops back over to Alak.

"You better not steal my fox," Alak says, pointing his finger at me.

"I can't help it if he likes me better," I grin.

Alak grins, eyes glinting. "Definitely cannot blame the fella for that."

"Shall we get to this dinner?" Bram cuts in sharply, glaring at Alak.

We nod and begin our journey to find the blacksmith's house. It doesn't take us long. His house looks a lot like where I used to live—open door and windows with a large piece of cloth serving as a door. The curtain is pulled back, however, and we can see into the house. A middle-aged woman with long dark hair notices our approach and greets us with a tight smile.

"Hello! Please, come in! Anton told me to expect you. My name is Marta. Make yourselves comfortable!"

She busies herself in the kitchen area but gestures to the open area of the house where four children play. The children eye us warily. The oldest is a girl probably ten years old, holding the youngest, a toddler around two years old, in her lap. A boy around five and a girl around eight sit nearby playing a game of checkers.

"Do you mind if I watch you play?" Bram asks, sitting down near the game. The boy shakes his head but doesn't speak, his big brown eyes fixed on Bram's face in wary suspicion. "Thank you. I can always use some tips on this game. Cards I can play, but checkers I lose every time."

I walk over to Marta and offer to help her with the final meal preparations, but she waves me off. "No, no. You're guests in my house. It's not often we get guests. Please, have a seat! It's my pleasure to have you here."

She offers me a sincere enough smile that I decide not to push her. I walk over and sit down next to Bram. He smiles at me and reaches his arm behind me. I rest my head on his shoulder and watch the game. After a few minutes, Anton enters the house, covered in soot. His wife greets him with a kiss before he comes over to us, wringing his hat in his hands.

"Hello," he says, inclining his head slightly. "If you'll just give me a moment to wash up."

"Of course, mate!" Alak replies. "Take your time!"

Anton offers Alak a weak smile and disappears into the only side room. His wife begins bringing food to the table. The children jump up and help her. Bram and I rise from our spot on the floor. I feel even more out of place in the busy shuffle. I can tell Kato feels the same, sensing his growing unease through our bond.

"Please, have a seat," Marta says, motioning to the table. "My husband will be out shortly."

We take our places around the small table. The children load their plates and take them to eat on the floor in front of the fire. We fill our plates at the hostess's request, and Anton joins us a moment later. Marta has prepared us a roast of some sort with vegetables, spiced fruit, and rolls. We eat in mostly awkward silence. The only one of us that appears to have any sort of skill at conversation is Alak, who seems perfectly at ease.

"This fruit is absolutely delicious! Did you grow it yourself?" Alak asks, stuffing his mouth.

Marta shakes her head. "No, we're very lucky to have the Braylin Woods nearby. It provides us with many delicious fruits and vegetables."

Alak asks more questions, complimenting every portion of the meal, and Marta always responds, her smile growing. When the meal finally ends, Marta and the older children go about cleaning up the meal. I once again offer to help but am denied. Once everything is cleared, Anton stands.

"Lita," he says, addressing the oldest girl as he pulls a coin purse from his pocket. "Why don't you take Gillian and Codi

into town and get some sweet cakes. Bring one back for Eissa."
The oldest girl, Lita, takes the coin purse from her father with a
wary nod. She motions for the younger two and they follow her
out, the youngest clutching her hand. Once they're gone, Marta
closes all the windows and pulls the cloth across the doorway.

"Eissa," Anton says gently, motioning to the little girl that
remains. She slowly walks toward her father, her big brown
eyes watching us. Anton places his hands on Eissa's shoulders.
"This is my daughter, Eissa."

"Hello, Eissa. It's very nice to meet you," I say, kneeling
down to be eye level with her. I can feel the concerned gaze of
her mother watching me from across the room. "Can I show
you something?" Eissa nods her head.

I hold out my hand, folded into a fist, my fingers facing up,
and concentrate. I take a deep breath, finding and molding my
magic. I slowly unfold my fingers, revealing a silver light
butterfly on my open palm. The girl's mouth gapes in delight
as her eyes go wide, sparkling. The butterfly stretches its
wings before fluttering into the air. Eissa's eyes follow its path
as it floats around the room. She reaches her hand toward it,
and I allow the butterfly to land in her own outstretched
palm.

She giggles. "It's like a real butterfly, only it's cold!"

The butterfly flies back to my own palm. I close my hand
and the butterfly disappears. I look up at Eissa.

"Can you do something like that?"

Eissa looks at each of her parents before slowly nodding. "I
can't make a butterfly, but I can do something kind of like that."

"Can you show me?"

The delight that shone in Eissa's eyes moments before is
slowly being replaced by fear. Her eyes dart from her father's
face to the strange men standing behind me.

"No need to fear us, love," Alak says comfortingly. I can't

see what he does but judging by the flash of delight crossing Eissa's face, Alak performed some sort of magic.

"I have magic, too," Kato says. Out of the corner of my eye I see him call forth a small flame and mold it into a little cat that sits safely in his palm licking its paw. When Kato makes the kitten disappear in a flash of smoke, Eissa looks expectantly at Bram. Bram kneels down next to me.

"I don't have magic like they do," he explains, his voice smooth and comforting. "I am here as a protector of magic. This sword," he says, placing his hand on the hilt of the sword strapped to his side, "serves Prince Ehren, who wants nothing more than to protect magic for the good of the kingdom."

Eissa takes a deep breath and nods. "Okay," she whispers. "I'll show you."

She holds out her hand. There's a flash of color and a flower unfolds in her hand. First, it's just a couple of leaves but then a purple bud appears, slowly blooming, the petals stretching and twirling until a complete flower sits in her palm. She looks up at us, eyes bright.

"That is truly beautiful magic," Bram says softly.

"That's not all I can do!" Eissa says eagerly, all traces of her former fear and hesitation gone.

"Really? What else can you do, love?" Alak asks, kneeling on my other side.

She looks excitedly at each of us. "If I touch the ground and think real hard, I can make plants grow. Make them grow a lot faster than they're supposed to. And I can make them grow without seeds."

"Well, that is quite handy!" Bram declares. "I think I need to talk to your parents now, okay?" Eissa nods as we stand.

"Why don't you see if you can catch up with your brothers and sister, eh?" Anton says, offering Eissa a small smile. She nods and skips off.

"Is she in danger from the king?" her mother asks quietly once Eissa is gone, wringing her hands.

Bram nods. "I won't lie to you. It is possible." Anton swears and Marta's hand flies to her mouth, tears welling in her eyes.

"What do we need to do?" Anton asks, his voice firm.

"For now, keep her powers as quiet as possible. Allow her to use them, but only sparingly when you are sure you are alone," Bram instructs in the voice of a commander.

"Is that wise, allowing her to use her powers?" Anton asks, scowling.

"If she doesn't use her powers, if she tries to keep them inside, her power could become out of control," I answer. "Allowing her to use it sparingly will actually help her stay hidden."

Bram nods. "What Astra says is true. We are traveling back to Embervein to help the prince. If you need anything, please, reach out to me. I am Captain Bramfield, Captain of Prince Ehren's Guard. Any messages sent to me will remain confidential. The prince and I, along with the help of others who support magic, will do our best to protect you."

Marta nods, a tear sliding down her cheek.

"Thank you," Anton says, gripping Bram's shoulder in appreciation.

Bram gives him an assertive nod. "Now, if you don't mind, we must be on our way. We need to leave first thing in the morning to get back to Embervein as soon as possible."

Anton and Marta thank us again as we duck out of the house and begin our trek back to our inns.

"So, where do you want me to meet you in the morning, assuming our deal is still on?" Alak asks, eyeing Bram as we pause outside his inn.

Bram avoids eye contact with Alak but responds. "Dawn at the stables next to our inn." He raises his eyes to look at Alak, adding, "If you aren't there, ready to go, we will leave without you."

"Message received, Captain," Alak says with a fake salute.

Bram turns away shaking his head as Alak disappears inside his inn. As we continue walking toward our own inn, Kato turns to Bram.

"What is the plan?" Kato asks. "Are we heading directly to Embervein? Or are there more stops along the way?"

"Well," Bram replies, "I would like to get to Embervein as soon as possible. Especially since it seems the king's denial of magic is causing fear and putting magic users at risk. If I recall correctly, there is one village, Hollowcreek, between us and the most direct road to Embervein. It's roughly a day-and-a-half to a two-day ride to Hollowcreek and another day or two from there to Embervein."

"If we ride directly through Hollowcreek without stopping, can we reach Embervein in three days?" I ask.

Bram considers my words for a moment before answering. "It is possible. If the weather is good and the terrain smooth. We would need to cut down on breaks and keep our nights short, but we could potentially make it to Embervein in three days."

"Good. Can we try that? The sooner we get to Embervein, the better."

Bram nods. "I agree." He glances over at Kato. "What do you think?"

Kato shrugs. "It sounds good to me. I've learned to listen to Astra. She's seldom wrong."

I shoot Kato a grateful smile.

"All right. Then we leave tomorrow at dawn and make our way to Embervein as quickly as possible," Bram concludes.

When we get to our inn, Bram walks me to my door. Kato narrows his eyes at Bram but disappears into his own room without a word. Once we're alone, Bram presses his lips to mine. I'm no sooner leaning in to the warmth of his lips before he pulls back, his eyes bright.

"Good night, Astra," he whispers, his voice warm.

I'm tempted to kiss him again, to ask him to come into my room with me and continue what we started earlier, but he turns away and strides across the hall to his room. He turns and gives me one last look, making my stomach flip, before he disappears into his room. I open my door and fall on my bed, heart full and head filled with wonderful thoughts.

CHAPTER TWENTY-TWO

*D*awn comes entirely too early. I manage to wake up in time, but it takes effort to pull myself from my bed. I dress quickly in another riding outfit and braid my hair. Knowing we'll be riding all day, I preemptively apply some of the magical salve to make the journey easier to bear. I still feel half asleep, however, when I arrive downstairs. Bram is nowhere to be seen, but Kato stands nearby, leaning against one of the tables while sipping from a mug.

"Mead this early in the day?" I tease, hiding a yawn.

"Nope. Coffee." Kato reaches behind him and pulls another steaming mug from the table, handing it to me.

"Thank the gods," I mumble, taking a sip of the hot, bitter liquid.

"I figure if we're going to be riding all day we need all the energy we can get," Kato says, taking a long sip. "Bram's getting the horses ready as we speak."

I just nod and gulp my coffee. Once we're done, we head outside to find Bram standing with all three horses. I walk over to Luna and begin attaching my bag.

"Good morning, girl," I whisper to Luna, rubbing her neck. "Are you ready to stretch your legs?" She snorts and gives a short whinny.

As we mount our horses a voice calls out, "Don't you be leaving without me, now. I'm here at dawn, bags packed and ready to go, as promised."

I look down the road and see Alak riding toward us atop a speckled brown mare with a white and brown spotted mane. Felixe is curled up, seemingly asleep, in front of Alak on the horse's back. Alak pulls up next to me. Bram looks disappointed Alak made it in time.

"Morning, Captain, Kato," Alak greets, giving each a nod in their turn. He looks at me and grins. "Morning to you, too, love."

"Good morning," I reply, returning his smile.

"Well, now that formalities are out of the way, shall we go?" Bram says, already agitated.

It's going to be a long journey.

As we ride, we briefly fill Alak in on the plan. He doesn't seem all too thrilled about riding practically nonstop for three days, but since he doesn't have much choice, he agrees. Bram takes the lead. Kato takes the rear, leaving Alak and I in the middle. Kato insists that having them on the ends is the best defense against any attacks should they come. Apparently, the road we're traveling is known for bandits. Bram glances over his shoulder at me and Alak so often I'm sure his neck will be sore by the time the day is over.

"Oi, mate!" Alak eventually calls out to Bram. "Keep your eyes on the road in front of you!"

Bram glares in response.

"Don't worry," Kato calls from behind us. "If he looks at Astra wrong, I'll set him on fire."

Alak scowls and shakes his head.

"You better not," I call back to him. "You'd hurt his horse."

Kato laughs. "I'll find a way to spare his horse."

"Be careful of Felixe, too," I add, shooting Alak a grin.

"Naturally!" Kato laughs

"Great to know my horse and fox are more well-loved than I am," Alak mumbles with a grin. "But if they help spare my life, so be it."

"What's her name?" I ask, nodding to the horse.

"Fawn," Alak replies with a gentle smile. "I've had her since I was a boy. When I got her she was but a foal and the spittin' image of a young fawn. I used to tease her that she was a fawn rather than a horse and the name stuck."

"It does fit her very well," I reply.

"Aye, it does," Alak agrees, giving her a loving pat.

"You said you had to sell another horse. Did you have that one as long?"

Alak shakes his head. "No. I had only had Peanut for a little over a year. I got him around the same time I got my cart and tent you saw me with in Timberborn. That cart was too big for just Fawn to pull." Alak pauses, thinking for a moment. "It wasn't easy to part with him, though. He was a good horse. But without a cart to pull, I didn't have need for him anymore and without my trade I didn't have the money to care for him."

"At least you have Fawn."

He offers me a sad smile. "Aye, at least I have Fawn."

We ride along in silence for a while before Alak starts singing. At first, he's singing under his breath to himself, but once he realizes his singing is annoying Bram, he starts belting out his songs. Judging by the way Bram grips the reins so tightly his knuckles are white, it's taking every ounce of his self-control not to openly react to Alak. When Kato joins in on one of Alak's off-key melodies, he jerks his head around, eyes flashing.

"Really, Kato?" Bram snaps.

Kato shrugs and continues singing. Bram looses a long breath.

"You okay?" I ask gently, riding up next to him.

"I'm fine," he replies, forcing a smile. I arch my eyebrow and he laughs. "I will live. I am used to my men singing when we travel. Singing is actually a good way to pass the time and works as a good distraction. I just wish that, perhaps, it was a little more on-key and not quite as loud."

I laugh. "I can't disagree with you there." I pause, then ask, "What was it like traveling as part of the Guard? Did you travel a lot?"

"At first we didn't travel much. When I was officially part of the army, but not yet part of the Guard, I traveled as one of the men, among the soldiers. It was very different from the Guard."

"How?"

"Well, for one, the Guard is a smaller, more intimate group. We know each other better. Once I was made Captain, I went from being a common soldier or guardsman to being a leader. I won't lie, it was a bit of an adjustment. Especially considering some of the men I was put in charge of were older with more years of experience."

"But surely Ehren chose you for your talent, and no one could deny that."

Bram inclines his head slightly, "Yes, Ehren had seen my talent firsthand and knew I could do the job justice, but not everyone under my command wanted to believe that was the only reason. When I was first appointed, many outside the Guard wanted to believe it was favoritism from Ehren since our friendship was clear and well known. Most within the Guard knew me well enough to know that rumor wasn't entirely true, but a few men were disgruntled."

"What did you do?"

Bram can't hide the grin. "Ehren set up a challenge. He declared that any man that could best me in the sword ring could have my position."

"I take it no one was able to beat you." I grin.

Bram gives a soft chuckle. "No one lasted more than a minute. After that, no one, within the Guard or out of it, doubted me or Ehren again."

As we ride, Bram shares a few more stories about his life in the Guard, while Alak and Kato bellow behind us. The farmland around us shifts into more and more trees, helping to offer a little shade from the climbing sun. We're making good time when an arrow shoots in front of us, narrowly missing Bram. He snaps to attention, his hand flying to his sword.

"We're under attack!" Bram yells, unsheathing his sword as more arrows shoot from the surrounding trees. "Get behind me," he orders, his voice full of authority.

I fall back next to Alak, who's wide-eyed and silent. Felixe is also on full alert, his ears perking up as his nose sniffs the air. Another arrow whistles by and Felixe disappears. I glance over to Kato who also has his sword drawn, his eyes searching the trees. I hear Alak loose a long breath as he closes his eyes.

"Where did they go?" a deep voice calls from the forest as another voice cries, "They disappeared!"

Bram's eyebrows knit in confusion. Kato glances over at Bram. Both are still tense. I look over at Alak who grins and winks at me. I open my mouth to speak, but he slides a finger up to his lips silencing me. It takes Bram and Kato only a second longer to figure out that Alak is using his magic to hide us.

A few figures appear at the edge of the forest on either side of us.

"Where did they go?" a thin man mere inches from Kato asks. "They were here a second ago."

Kato moves his horse as quietly as possible so he's right up against Alak and Bram does the same, easing toward me. A few more men appear from the forest. There are a dozen in total. I hold my breath, afraid to make any sound. Down the road in the direction we came from, a small flame suddenly bursts to life in the center of the road. Several of the men swear.

"Devils!" one of the men yells and several more make religious signs, looking to the heavens.

The flame rises into a tower before taking the form of a dragon. The men scramble into the trees, some even dropping their weapons. Once we're sure the men are gone, we start to edge down the road on our way. Bram once again takes the lead with Kato at the rear. Felixe reappears on Alak's shoulders, pressing up against Alak's face. After several long minutes I finally speak.

"Making us disappear, how did you do that?" I ask Alak quietly.

Alak looks at me, his eyes shining. "My particular magic tends to lean toward illusions." He holds out his hand and makes a coin appear. He flips the coin into the air and it disappears.

"So that's how you were able to do all those magic tricks at the festival," I muse.

"Indeed. I was already a master of perceived illusion, but my actual magical gift made it all the better. And more profitable until the king stifled that." He reaches up and strokes Felixe, who seems to relax a bit. "I think that may be part of the reason Felixe and I get along so well. We're both masters of illusion."

"How many different kinds of magic are there?"

Alak shrugs. "I'm not sure. The old magic was rooted largely in the elements, but over time magic evolved and took on a life of its own, combining elements and growing. Your magic is old and powerful and somehow a beast of its own. My magic has been passed down through the generations. Legend claims that illusion magic was a gift from the god Dolus. Not that I'm limited to only illusions, mind you, but they are what I'm best at. Just like your magic is tied to light and Kato's to fire, but with practice you can both expand your power to do many things."

I nod. "That makes sense."

"How do I move past just fire and on to other things?" Kato calls out, riding up on the other side of Alak.

"Practice, plain and simple," Alak replies with a shrug. "Start with what you know. Master your skill and practice and, like with anything else in life, your skill will increase."

Kato looks a little disappointed, but nods, falling behind us again. We ride mostly in silence the rest of the day. Even though there are no more signs of bandits in the woods, we're all still a little on edge from their attack. Like planned, we don't even break for lunch. We nibble on whatever food we can easily reach from our packs as we ride. Alak constantly complains because Felixe keeps snatching his lunch and disappearing. We're still in a heavily wooded area as night starts to fall. We ride until it's fully dark and are simply too exhausted to continue. We dismount and make camp.

"We should take shifts watching guard in case there are any more unwelcome guests," Kato suggests. Bram readily agrees.

"I'll take first watch," I offer, munching on some cheese.

Bram opens his mouth to argue. "I'll take watch with her," Kato offers before Bram can object. "And then you and Alak can take a shift."

Bram doesn't seem entirely pleased with the prospect, but he gives a reluctant nod. "Fine."

"It'll be a great chance for us to catch up," Alak offers with a wry grin.

Bram grits his teeth and bites back his response. After we've all had a bit to eat, Bram and Alak lie down on their bedrolls and drift off to sleep while Kato and I take watch. Save for the sounds of forest life around us, it's quiet. There's not much to do. For a while, Kato and I take turns drawing in the dirt with a stick, having the other person guess our drawing, but even that gets old. After a couple hours Kato suggests I go ahead and rest, and I comply, too tired to argue. I pull out my bedroll and fall fast asleep.

I'm awoken the next morning by someone gently shaking my shoulder. I open my eyes to find Bram looking down at me. I sit up and stretch. The first hints of morning light are just starting to appear in the sky.

"I know it's early, but the sooner we can get on the road the better."

"That's fine. Give me a minute to wake up, and I'll be ready to go," I say, attempting to hide a yawn.

"Breakfast?" Kato asks, tossing me an apple. I catch it and take a bite. Felixe appears in my lap and blinks up at me.

"Are you hungry, little guy?" I ask him with a laugh, and he responds with a sharp yip, eyeing my apple. I bite off a chunk and hand it to him. He grabs it in his muzzle and gnaws on it, making cute little grunting sounds.

Once Felixe and I have finished our breakfast, I help load my pack and we're on the road. I expect Felixe to jump back over to Alak, but today he seems content to remain on my shoulder. His presence is somehow comforting. Alak keeps eyeing me warily with a slight scowl until, after a couple hours of traveling, Felixe finally decides to pop back onto his shoulder.

"Oh, you think I want you back, you little traitor," Alak grumbles, smiling as he gives Felixe a little scratch. Felixe nips his fingers playfully.

"I don't think he likes being called a traitor," I laugh.

After a few hours of travel, we reach Hollowcreek. It's not an especially busy town so there's not much of a crowd to navigate. Alak gazes longingly toward the tavern we pass but, as agreed, we make no stops. After we cross through the town, we eat lunch while riding. Thankfully, we come in contact with no more bandits, and the day passes quickly, the landscape turning back into rolling fields of farmland.

When we finally stop to make camp, night has already fallen. We camp on the side of the road at the edge of a cornfield. Bram and Kato both agree that taking shifts again would be our best option, even though we are less likely to be attacked in a cornfield than the forest. Bram seems less than happy with having been paired up with Alak the night before and suggests he and I take first watch.

"Why?" Kato challenges. "So you two can kiss all night?"

"Kato!" I cry, my cheeks reddening slightly.

"Oh, you know it's true," he says, waving me off.

"I'd actually prefer to take first watch, myself," Alak says. "I don't much like getting up so early. I'd rather be up for a few more hours and then sleep until time to leave."

"Are you sure?" Bram presses, scowling.

"I'm positive," Alak insists.

"So, Alak and Astra take first shift and you and I take second?" Kato confirms with Bram.

Bram lets out a long sigh. "I suppose. Though one of the trained soldiers should be on each shift."

"We have magic, mate," Alak replies, waving him off. "We'll be fine."

Bram reluctantly agrees. Once we've all had a little to eat, Bram and Kato get out their bedrolls.

"If you so much as touch her, I will kill you in the morning," Bram growls to Alak before he lies down.

Alak gives Bram two thumbs up, grinning in a way that I'm sure doesn't comfort Bram in the slightest. It takes a while for Bram to finally fall asleep, but eventually he surrenders, leaving Alak and I essentially alone.

"At least your captain doesn't snore. That's one point in his favor," Alak mutters.

"Bram is a good man. He just doesn't like you."

"Yeah, I got that."

"And you still won't tell me why?"

Alak shakes his head. "I told you, it's not my story to tell."

"Fine."

We fall silent for a few minutes before Alak offers, "Why don't we practice magic?"

"Right here?"

Alak shrugs. "Sure. Why not? We've got a few hours to kill and if we keep just sitting here doing nothing, I'm going to fall asleep. And if I fall asleep and something happens your captain will never forgive me. I'm actually surprised he hasn't found a reason to kill me yet. So, what do you say? Magic?"

"All right. Fine." I turn to face Alak. We sit cross-legged, knee to knee. "What do you suggest?"

His eyes glint mischievously. "Let's play a game. I'll perform a bit of magic and you copy it."

I nod. "Okay. I can try that."

Alak presses his palms together in front of his face in a prayer-like motion, his eyes closed. He opens his eyes and slowly opens his hands, cupping them, revealing an apple. I take a deep breath and hold out my hands. I concentrate and an apple made of light appears in my cupped hands.

"Okay, good," Alak says, "but now try to make it look like a real apple."

I close my eyes and concentrate. When I open them, a realistic apple sits in my hands. Alak grins.

"Excellent."

We repeat the process again and again, each time the magic getting slightly more complex. The hours pass quickly, and, before I know it, it's time to trade shifts. I'm about to wake Bram when Alak places his hand on my arm.

"Thank you for bringing me along. You've given me a purpose and I really appreciate it."

I offer him a tired smile. "You've really helped me a lot with my magic in just a short amount of time. We owe you."

Alak meets my eyes, hesitating. I can tell he wants to say something, but it takes him a few moments before he voices it.

"We will most likely reach Embervein tomorrow," he says, choosing his words carefully, "and it's possible you won't need me anymore. I know the good captain would prefer you to find another teacher. One he trusts. I have a feeling the prince won't be all too happy to see me, so we'll likely part ways."

"You've pissed off Bram *and* Ehren?"

Alak grimaces. "Unfortunately, yes. I wish I could change my past, but I can't."

"If you were given the choice, would you want to stay with us, continue helping me and Kato, or go your own way?"

Alak chews his lip in thought for a moment. "Honestly," he says slowly. "I would rather stay with you."

I look in his eyes and I can see the earnestness there. "Then I will convince Bram and Ehren to let you stay."

"Really?" he asks, surprised. "Just like that?"

I nod. "I have no idea what you did to make them hate you, but I trust you."

His expression softens. "Thank you, love. You have no idea what this means to me."

"I'm really just doing it so your fox will stick around," I say, motioning to where Felixe lies a few feet away, curled up sleeping.

Alak throws his head back and laughs. "All right, love. Whatever you need to tell yourself."

I smile as we wake up Bram and Kato. Before I turn over on my bedroll to go to sleep I take one last glance at Alak. He's watching me. He gives me a wink and turns to face the other way. I smile and close my eyes.

The next morning I wake up all on my own. Bram and Kato are packing the horses and Alak is still sleeping, Felixe curled up against his side.

"Good morning," Bram greets me.

I walk over to him and he gives me a quick kiss on my lips.

"No kissing," Kato teases. "Why is that so hard?"

I stick my tongue out at Kato and Bram kisses me again, his lips lingering a little longer this time. It makes me hungry for more, but Bram pulls away.

"We should wake Alak and be on our way," I mutter.

Bram scowls. "Or we could see how far down the road we can get before he misses us."

"Bram . . . ," I scold.

He throws his hands up in mock surrender. "Fine. I'll wake him."

I reach out and grab Bram's arm. "No, let me. I want to try something."

I close my eyes, focusing my magic. A ball of water forms above Alak. I let it drop, drenching him. He snaps awake, sputtering.

"What the hell?" he yells.

I burst out laughing, and he spins to face me, eyes flashing.

"That was you? I expect this behavior from him," he says, motioning toward Bram, "but I expect more from you."

"Sorry," I giggle. "I thought you'd be impressed I woke you with magic."

"Impressed, sure. Pleased, not so much," he laughs. He

stands up and snaps his fingers, his clothes magically drying. "Lucky for you I have a bit of my own magic."

"And, as happy as we all are about that, we need to get on the road," Bram says.

Alak rolls his eyes and packs up his gear and we're on our way. The sun rises exceptionally hot and we're all sweating by mid-morning. I use my magic to create a cooling wind, but even it doesn't have lasting affects against the sun.

"Maybe you should try dousing us all in water," Alak mutters under his breath.

"Don't tempt me," I mutter back.

It's at that point Alak decides to start singing his traveling ballads again, and Bram snaps at him to shut up. Felixe barks defensively at Bram.

"How much longer do we have?" Kato asks, shifting atop his horse.

Bram glances around, assessing our position. "A few more hours. We should be able to reach Embervein by nightfall."

Nerves rise, my stomach turning. I've known all along we were traveling to Embervein, but now that we're so close, I'm worried. Being so close to the king is terrifying. Kato must be able to sense my nerves down our bond.

We'll be okay, Ash.

How do you know?

Because we'll be together. And we'll have Bram and Ehren and whoever else they have gathered.

And Alak. We have Alak as well.

I suppose.

You don't trust him, either?

I trust him but not as much as I trust Bram and Ehren. I know they'll stick by our sides and work with us. I have a feeling Alak will run as soon as he feels threatened.

I don't think he'd do that.

Are you sure?

I'm not sure at all, but I don't want to admit that to Kato. I want to trust Alak, despite the fact I know very little about him. Still, I know that despite any reservations, I *do* trust Alak without question.

He didn't run in the woods when the bandits attacked. He could have just used his magic to hide himself, but he hid us all.

I suppose that's something. But my point stands. We have allies and we will be safe in Embervein. If we even get the slightest hint we aren't safe there, we'll leave. Got it?

Got it.

Our bond falls silent. Alak is still singing, Bram's expression murderous. I edge up next to Bram, and he smiles at me.

"Are you ready to see Embervein?"

"I suppose."

"It really is a wonderful city. I can't wait to show it to you." He senses my unease and adds, "Don't worry, I will keep you safe."

I offer him a weak smile. "I trust you." I pause. "Will we be staying in the palace?"

"Ideally. My room is in the castle near Ehren's. Most of the guest rooms are at the opposite end of the castle, but I am sure we'll be able to get you and Kato rooms near mine."

"What about Alak?"

"The stables always have space." Bram glances at me side-eyed, and I give him a stern look. "Fine. I can't make any promises, but it is possible we can find him a room near you and Kato. Though Ehren won't be happy about it."

I fight the urge to ask again what Alak did. Bram glances over at me and smiles sadly.

"I promise, I will tell you why, one day. It is just very difficult to talk about." I accept his answer with a nod.

We fall silent and ride side by side. Having him close is

comforting and helps soothe my rising nerves. After a couple hours, we're able to make out Embervein in the distance. My stomach flips. Alak must be feeling similar nerves because he falls silent. Felixe goes jittery, switching from Alak's shoulder to the horse and back, even occasionally appearing on my shoulder.

When we reach the main village outside the castle walls, Bram starts smiling, happy to be home. His ease helps. At the gate outside the castle all it takes is a wave from Bram, and the guards, who clearly recognize him, let us through.

"No going back now," Alak mumbles as we pass through the gate.

Bram leads us to the stables and dismounts. Solomon gives a happy huff, recognizing his home. A young boy of about twelve with a head of shaggy blond hair rushes up to Bram.

"Hello, Captain!" the boy greets Bram, grinning.

"Hello, Peter," Bram responds with a smile.

"Did you have safe travels, Sir?"

Bram gives the boy a nod. "Indeed we did. These are my friends and they will need to keep their horses here while they visit Prince Ehren at the castle," Bram adds, motioning to us. I dismount and Kato and Alak follow suit.

"Yessir," the stable boy replies. "I will take good care of them while they're here. What are the horses' names, if you please?"

"This is Luna," I say, stepping forward and handing Peter her reigns.

"And this is Twilight," Kato says, doing the same.

Peter turns expectantly to Alak who hesitates.

"It's all right, Sir. I promise I'll take good care of her."

Alak swallows and nods. "All right, then. This is Fawn." Alak relinquishes the reins, watching Peter with wary eyes.

"Give them all a good rub down and a good meal. They've

been traveling hard for the past three days," Bram instructs, and Peter nods. "You can send our bags inside."

Bram leads us out of the stable and toward the palace. I stop at the base of the castle steps and stare up at it. It towers above me. I suddenly find it hard to breathe. Bram slides his hand into mine, intertwining our fingers.

"I'll be right here beside you," he promises, giving my hand a little squeeze. "Are you ready?"

I swallow and nod as he leads me up the stairs. A few people acknowledge and greet Bram as we walk. Kato is a step behind us, Alak slinking along not far behind. We come around a corner into a wide long hallway and I see a familiar face. In the middle of the hallway stands Ehren. He's dressed in a blue silk tunic with a circlet crown on his head and a sword strapped to his side. He's talking to one of his Guard who looks past Ehren as we approach. Ehren turns to see what drew the Guard's attention, and a tired, relieved smile spreads across his face when he sees us. He dismisses his Guard and rushes down the hallway to us.

"Thank the gods you're back!" Ehren says, gripping Bram's shoulders in greeting.

"It's good to be home," Bram smiles.

Ehren's eyes slide down to my hand in Bram's and gives me a sly smile. "Well, it seems you've not only recovered but grown rather close to Bram, eh?"

I smile. "It's good to see you, too, Ehren."

His eyes go over my shoulder to Kato. "We should send that Healer a gift basket!"

All humor vanishes from Ehren's face and anger flashes in his eyes. His hand draws his sword in one smooth move.

"What are you doing in my palace?" he spits, pointing the sword at Alak who throws his hands up defensively and ducks behind Kato.

"Ehren," I shout. "Please, he's here as my guest."

Ehren's eyes flash again, and he glances at me, loathing for Alak etched in his features. "Do you have any idea what he did?"

I shake my head. "No, no one will tell me."

Ehren shifts his gaze to Bram. "You knowingly have allowed this?"

Bram glances at me and then nods. "We have a good reason." His eyes glance around at the few people around us who have all stopped to watch. "Reasons best not discussed here. Is there a place we can go to discuss developments?"

Ehren sheaths his sword. "Fine. I will let you live for now," he addresses Alak, "but one wrong move and you're dead."

I can tell by his tone Ehren isn't exaggerating in the slightest.

Gods, I hope I never fall on Ehren's bad side, Kato says in my head.

Same here.

"Trust me," Bram says. "I have promised him the same."

Ehren relaxes slightly and glances back to me. "I suppose you want a room near Bram?" I blush and Ehren takes that as answer enough. He motions to a servant farther down the hall who rushes to him immediately. "Please, prepare rooms for these three immediately as close to mine and Captain Bramfield's as possible." The servant nods and shuffles off. "Let's give them a moment to prepare your rooms. In the meantime, let's adjourn to mine and go over all the developments."

We agree and follow Ehren as he winds through the palace. With each step I take, I can't help but feel I'm taking one step closer to my destiny.

Part Three:

Embervein

CHAPTER TWENTY-THREE

*P*rince Ehren's private quarters are so massive you
could easily fit three of my house inside. Chairs,
couches, and tables fill the main room. Books are scattered
across every surface and stacked on the floor in random piles. In
the center of the room is a long table covered with books and
papers. Ehren leans his back against this table, his jaw clenched
as he eyes Alak with evident distaste.

"Okay, explain to me why that traitor is with you," he
demands, crossing his arms. "I'm assuming if you've allowed
him to live this long he must be important."

"He has magic," Bram states simply.

"All the more reason to kill him," Ehren says, and Alak's
eyes go wide.

"I thought you were supposed to be in favor of magic," Alak
protests weakly.

Ehren's eyes narrow. "I'm in favor of magic when it's not in
possession of someone like you. You cause enough trouble
without it. I don't even want to imagine the devastation you can
wreak with magic at your disposal."

"He's helping me and Kato learn to control our magic," I interject, stepping forward. "He's already helped us a lot."

Ehren looks at Bram. "Is that true?"

Bram tenses. "Anything Astra says you can believe."

Ehren lets out a long breath. "Okay. Fine."

Felixe decides now is a good time to appear on Alak's shoulder and Ehren jumps, swearing loudly. Even Bram can't hide his amused smile.

"What is that thing?" Ehren asks, pointing at Felixe.

"Come on, Ehren," Bram grins. "Don't tell me you don't recognize your standard Fae Fox?"

"A what now?"

"Felixe is a Fae Fox," Alak replies in a hoarse whisper. "He's my familiar."

Ehren's eyes go wide, mouth gaping open. He looks at Bram, his eyes bright. "So magical creatures are returning? You've confirmed it?"

Bram nods. "We have been able to confirm a good bit."

"Tell me everything," Ehren demands, and so we do.

Bram fills Ehren in first, relaying his findings and discoveries regarding the various locations where the stars fell. Ehren marks them on a map and cross checks it against information he's received from other sources. Kato and I share our experience with Healer Heora, Bram adding additional details. Ehren scribbles furiously in a black leather journal. Every so often he stops whoever is speaking and asks for clarification, but he mostly lets us talk while he makes notes and nods along. When we reach the part involving Alak, Ehren glares at him, but his eyes go wide when he hears all that happened in the magical woods. When we finally get him all caught up, Ehren collapses in a nearby chair, flinging his crown carelessly on a couch.

"Well, it seems the world really is returning to how it was, magic-wise," he mumbles.

"Has your father come any closer to accepting it?" Bram asks.

Ehren lets out a huff. "Far from it. The more proof he's presented with the more he denies it. He's starting to send out soldiers to 'take care' of any rumors and has threatened to imprison or behead anyone claiming to be able to do magic."

All the blood drains from my face, and Bram wraps his arm around my waist. Ehren notices and jumps to his feet.

"Don't worry. I'll make sure my father doesn't suspect you —any of you—while you're here. Despite his actions, there are many people within these walls that believe in and support magic. We're gathering as much information as we can."

Ehren walks over to the table and sorts through scrolls until he finds what he's looking for.

"I've marked as many confirmed cases of magic as I can," he says, spreading out a map of Callenia, several locations marked with red ink. "I've sent out trusted soldiers to some of these areas to help protect people and cut off my father's soldiers. Unfortunately, there's no way to protect them all. I have reports from people who didn't have powers two days ago and suddenly woke up with power this morning. It's exhausting trying to stay one step ahead."

As he speaks, I can see the pure fatigue on his features.

"What can we do to help?" I ask, taking a step toward Ehren.

He thinks a moment. "Well, you could actually help my sister, if you're willing. She's buried deep in books about magical lore and histories, trying to decipher what was real and what was legend. She's attempting to predict what might happen next, or, at the very least, trace magical family trees down to people alive today who may possess magic."

My eyes light up. "I would love to help your sister."

"I figured you might," Ehren grins. "There's not much we

can do about the magic that's already here, and I can't go up against my father directly. Not yet, anyway. What we can do is stay one step ahead using knowledge my father is choosing to willfully ignore. Knowledge can be a great and powerful weapon when wielded well."

Ehren turns his attention to Kato. "Would you be willing to serve on my Guard? The more people I have close to me that I trust, the better."

Kato nods. "Bram and I have been discussing that as a possibility."

"Good. Good." Ehren looks at Alak, his expression darkening. "You just stay out of trouble."

Alak nods meekly, but I cut in with, "Alak has Syphon blood."

Ehren scowls. "What does that mean?"

"It means he can sense magic more keenly than most. He can actively seek it out and confirm whether someone or something is magical."

"It is true, unfortunately," Bram confirms. "I have seen it firsthand."

"I'm more than willing to serve in any way that I can," Alak says with a slight bow.

"Fine. I'll take that under consideration. For the time being, however, you keep to yourself. Understood?"

"Yes, Your Majesty."

I open my mouth to ask another question, but it turns into a yawn. Ehren laughs.

"I suppose you're all eager for a good night's sleep."

Ehren strides to the wall and pulls a tasseled rope. A moment later there's a knock at the door and a servant enters.

"Are the rooms for my guests ready?" Ehren asks in a very princely tone.

"Yes, Your Majesty," the servant says with a low bow.

"Very good. Please escort them to their rooms."

We bid Ehren goodbye and follow the servant down the hall. Bram goes with us, even though his room is only one down from Ehren's. The servant leads us to a suite of rooms. Our suite has a large sitting area, with plenty of seating options, as well as a table, bookshelves, and a balcony overlooking a garden. Off the main room are three bedrooms, each with their separate washrooms inside.

"This is incredible," Kato mumbles, looking around. The servant leaves, shutting the door behind him.

"Being a friend of the prince has its perks," Bram says with a smile. He glances over at Alak. "Just remember this room can easily be revoked in exchange for a dungeon cell."

"Trust me, mate, I'm not going to cause any trouble," Alak mumbles, walking toward one of the bedrooms.

"Well, I bid you all good night," Bram says with a nod, giving me a quick kiss before he leaves.

We each choose our rooms. Mine contains a large four-poster bed with curtains, a settee, a dresser with a mirror, bedside tables, and a small writing desk. I even have my own personal balcony. My washroom is nearly the same size as my room. I'm tempted to ring for a full bath but opt to just wash my face using the bowl provided on one of the bedside tables. I undress and slip into a simple nightshirt. I'm ready to crawl into bed when there's a tentative knock on my door.

"Who is it?"

"It's me, Alak," Alak's voice whispers, followed by a gleeful yip. "And Felixe."

I look around the room and see a red silk robe hanging next to the bed. I slip it on and crack open the door. Alak stands just outside, Felixe perched on his shoulder.

"What do you need?" I ask.

"May I come in?"

"Why?"

"I just . . . I just want to talk to you for a moment."

I hesitate, but the look on Alak's face convinces me to open the door wider. Alak strolls in, looking around my room. I glance out into the sitting room, half-expecting to see Kato, but it's empty.

"Well, what is it?" I ask, turning to Alak.

"I just wanted to thank you for standing up for me with the prince. You didn't have to, but you did, and I appreciate it." My irritation fades away at the earnestness in his voice.

"Oh, well, you're welcome. You've helped me a lot. I'm happy to return the favor."

He gives me a nod. "Okay, well then, that's what I came to say, so . . ." He trails off and walks to the door.

"Wait," I stop him. He turns, his eyebrow arched in curiosity. "I know you don't feel it's your place to tell me what happened between you and Bram and Ehren, but is their anger justified?"

Alak takes a deep breath and releases it slowly. "I'm inclined to say yes."

"If or when I find out, will it change my opinion of you?"

Alak's shoulders sag. Given his normal confident swagger, it's off-putting. He turns away from me and walks toward the balcony.

"I can't really say, love," he mumbles quietly, his back still to me. "But it is entirely likely." He turns to face me, something akin to agony written on his face. "Do you remember me telling you that I was orphaned at the age of ten?" I nod and he continues. "I had to do a lot to survive and it made me . . . not the best person. Every move I made in life was entirely self-serving. I never thought about or prepared for the future, at least not more than one day at a time. I was foolish and foolhardy. I made a lot of mistakes, and one of the biggest mistakes I've ever made affected Bram and Ehren. And not in a good way. There isn't a day I don't regret it, and I have few regrets.

"I wish I could say that when I knew Bram and Ehren I was a different person, but I can't. Not really. I'm still that same person at the core. I'm still self-serving. The choices and circumstances of my youth have molded me into the man I am now, but what happened that day made me want to change. In the years since then, I've made an effort to better myself. I'd like to think I've succeeded. But I can't erase my past."

He pauses and meets my eyes. "I sincerely hope that you can hold on to the version of me you've gotten to know, but if you can't, if my past erases everything good about me, then I'll understand. If I can't forgive myself for what I've done, I can't expect other people to forgive me, either."

I'm at a loss for words. I just stand there, looking at him, at the pain in his eyes, unable to say or do anything to comfort him.

"Anyhow," he says, forcing a smile that doesn't reach his eyes. "I'll leave you with my thanks and that cryptic explanation and allow us both to get some sleep."

Felixe gives an agreeing yip and disappears from Alak's shoulder, popping onto the foot of my bed. Alak scowls at his familiar.

"This isn't our room, Felixe. Come on," Alak calls, clicking his tongue.

Felixe cocks his head and yips before turning in a circle a half dozen times, curling into a ball as he closes his eyes. Alak puts his hands on his hips, narrowing his eyes at Felixe.

"Felixe! Not our room."

Felixe opens one big, blue eye and peers briefly at Alak before closing it and snuggling into a tighter ball. Alak looks at me, and I bite my lip, trying to hold in my laugh. Alak gives an exasperated sigh but can't hide his own smile.

"You're a little traitor, you are," he says, wagging a finger at Felixe, who ignores him entirely.

"I'm sure he'll pop back over to you after a few minutes," I offer, my eyes glistening with glee.

Alak throws his hands up in surrender. "Fine!" He laughs and then sobers slightly. "I guess I'll see you both in the morning."

He saunters out the door and I close it behind him. I stroll over to my bed, giving Felixe a scratch between his ears. He makes a contented purring sound.

"You're a good judge of character, I think," I mutter to the little fox. "If Alak wasn't worth the time, you wouldn't trust him."

Felixe opens his eyes, lifting his head slightly to look up at me with these big blue eyes. He gives a soft yip. I smile.

"That's what I thought."

I hang up my robe and slide beneath the covers. The bed is cozy and comfortable. It doesn't take long for me to fall fast asleep.

CHAPTER TWENTY-FOUR

*T*he next morning, a rustling noise wakes me. I slowly open my eyes, taking a minute to remember where I am. When I realize I'm not alone in my room, I bolt upright. At the foot of my bed stands a maid about my age with dark hair and eyes.

"Sorry if I woke you, miss," she says with a pleasant smile. "I was just bringing in some dresses for you and wanted to see if you needed help with anything." She gestures to the wardrobe, which is open, bearing several colorful dresses.

"Oh, um, no that's fine. Thank you," I mutter, rubbing sleep from my eyes.

"My name is Kara, miss, and I'll be here for anything you need. Perhaps I may draw you a bath?"

I glance toward the washroom. "Yes, actually, a bath would be wonderful."

She nods and scurries off to the washroom. A few seconds later I hear running water. I slide out of bed, stretching, and make my way to the washroom which is already filling with steam.

"We have water pumps that bring the heated water directly into the room," Kara offers, reading my somewhat puzzled expression.

Kara busies herself preparing my bath, adding various oils and placing soaps on a small table next to a large, ivory tub. I stand awkwardly by the door watching. Once the tub is sufficiently filled, Kara turns off the water and faces me.

"Do you need any assistance?"

I shake my head. "No, but thank you."

She gives a short nod. "I will allow you your privacy then. Your breakfast is on a tray in the sitting room, along with a fresh pot of tea. If you need help dressing or finding your way, please don't hesitate to ring."

I give her a grateful smile. She leaves with a small bow, closing the washroom door behind her. I undress and sink into the welcoming warm water. For several minutes, I lie there, enjoying the first truly relaxing moments I've had in weeks. The smells of the oils wrap around me. Eventually, I reach for the soap and go about washing my body and hair. When I'm done, I'm appalled at how filthy the water is. I quickly pull the plug at the bottom of the tub, hoping that draining the water quickly enough will prevent a dirt ring on the otherwise flawless white surface. I decide to dry off using my magic, glancing around tentatively, although I'm quite positive I'm alone. I call forth my magic, much in the same way I did when I dried myself off after swimming in the glade. I wrap the towel around my body, slipping back into my bedroom.

I throw open the wardrobe doors, gaping at all the beautiful dresses. I select a red one as well as some undergarments. I dress quickly. I discover a little pair of red silk shoes that match the dress and slip them on, finding them amazingly comfortable. I debate calling Kara back to help me do something with my hair but decide to braid part of it, pulling the hair out of my eyes and face, and leave it down in the back. I look at myself in the mirror and am startled at my reflection. Somehow, this look suits me. With a smile, I open my bedroom door and stroll into the sitting room.

The room is filled with glowing mid-morning light, making it warm and welcoming. I feel a warm breeze and look over to the main balcony. The doors are open and the curtains are billowing in the breeze.

"Morning, love," Alak's voice calls, startling me.

My eyes dart to a sofa directly in front of the balcony where Alak lounges, wearing nothing but a casual pair of white linen pants.

"Really? You couldn't be bothered to put a shirt on?" I sigh.

Alak shrugs. "Why should I? I have no plans to leave this room."

I roll my eyes and walk over to the table in the center of the room, which contains a steaming pot of tea and a tray piled high with breakfast pastries.

"You're really going to stay in here all day?" I ask as I pour a cup of tea and select what looks to be a strawberry pastry.

"That's the plan. I have direct orders from his princeliness to stay out of the way, if you recall."

I take a bite of the pastry and find it absolutely heavenly. "Why don't you come with me when I go to visit the library and meet Princess Cadewynn?" I offer.

Alak sits up, slinging his arm over the back of the sofa as he twists to face me. "I feel rather confident that the prince would prefer me to stay as far away from his sister as possible."

"That may be true, but it's likely we can use your help. There are probably hundreds of texts to sift through, and who knows what all we'll be looking for. Another set of eyes would be handy, and you may even be able to find magical texts detailing your Syphon abilities or illusion magic."

Alak lets out a long sigh. "All right. Fine," he says dramatically, bouncing up off the couch and walking toward his bedroom door. "But if the prince finds out and has me beheaded, it's on you."

"Deal," I laugh.

Alak disappears into his room, and I devour my danish, washing it down with tea. I'm debating stuffing my face with a second pastry when Alak strolls back into the room. He's replaced his white linen pants with a sleek pair of black leather pants and a gray shirt. He's pulled his red hair back and tied it off.

"Are you ready to go now, or do you need to eat a few dozen more danish?" he grins.

"I'm fine," I say, standing.

We're halfway to the door when Alak casually asks, "Do you even know how to get to the library or are we going to wander around aimlessly until we find it?"

"I was thinking perhaps the latter . . . ," I confess. "I guess I could ring for my maid."

Alak shakes his head. "I think we'll be able to find it. If we struggle, we can ask someone on the way."

He throws the door open and strides into the hallway.

"You just want an excuse to roam around the castle," I say, following him.

He grins at me. "Would you believe me if I told you I actually know how to get to the library?"

"What? How?" I ask, not bothering to hide my surprise.

"I've been here before, love," he answers with a wink.

The castle is full of long winding hallways and corridors, but Alak does seem to know how to navigate them. He leads me down a long flight of staircases to the lowest level of the castle and down another long corridor. I'm starting to wonder if he really has any idea where to go when he halts in front of a massive pair of carved oak doors, announcing that we've arrived. I stare up at the doors, my stomach in knots.

Alak leans down, whispering in my ear. "Are we going in or was this our end goal?"

I scowl at him and pull away, pushing one of the doors open. What I see inside steals my breath. I'm in a massive room that stretches at least three floors with bookshelves stretching from the floor to the domed ceiling above. In the center of the room is a winding golden staircase leading to additional levels. Neatly arranged library stacks take up most of the room with a few tables stretching down the aisles they create. I'm staring up at the stories and stories of books when a sharp voice draws my attention.

"May I assist you in some way?"

I startle and turn to see a thin woman in a floor length brown dress approaching me. Her dark gray hair is pulled into a tight bun, and she's peering at us through a pair of spectacles.

"Oh, yes. My name is Astra Downs and I . . ."

Her eyes light up with recognition. "Ah, yes. His Majesty Prince Ehren mentioned you would likely be coming by today to meet Princess Cadewynn." Her eyes narrow as she notices Alak hovering behind me. "I did not realize, however, that you would be accompanied by anyone else."

I glance at Alak apologetically and then look back at the librarian.

"Is it okay if he comes with me? He has a great interest in histories," I lie, Alak giving an emphatic nod.

The librarian stares Alak down for at least a full minute before she finally concedes.

"So be it." She turns on her heel and begins walking away. "Follow me."

She walks much quicker than I expect as we weave in and

out of stacks of books and tables. She leads us off the main room to a hall of alcoves. She stops outside one and motions us inside. Seated just inside the alcove at a table loaded with scrolls and tomes is a girl a couple years younger than me. She's leaning over a large book, golden curls tumbling forward.

"Your Majesty," the librarian says, clearing her throat. When the girl doesn't look up, she adds, "You have visitors."

The girl's head jerks up and she stares at me with wide blue eyes. Her face lights up as she bounds from her chair, rushing over to me. Once she's in front of me, I can easily understand how my maid was able to find me a large collection of dresses with such short notice. The princess is almost the exact same size and height as I am.

"You must be Astra!" she gushes.

I nod and the librarian, sensing we are in good hands, begins weaving her way back to whatever she was doing before we interrupted.

"You must be Princess Cadewynn," I say weakly.

She smiles. "Oh, please call me Winnie. All my friends do, and I do so hope you and I are to be friends!" Her eyes fall on Alak standing awkwardly at the alcove door and she scowls. "Who is that? Is he with you? I wasn't expecting anyone else."

Alak takes a step forward, offering the princess his most charming smile. "No one ever seems to be expecting me, love. My name is Alak."

"He is with me, if that's all right," I add.

Princess Cadewynn nods. "Oh, yes! I seldom get visitors here in the library, so the more the merrier! What would you like to look at first? Or perhaps I should just give you a tour of the library, so you can know the layout?" She speaks so quickly it's almost hard for my brain to follow.

"Uh, a tour would be nice," I say at length.

She grins and gives a little clap. "All right, follow me!" She floats by, gesturing for us to follow.

"These are the alcoves meant for studying whatever you need in peace," she says gesturing down the corridor where her own alcove is located. "You're welcome to share mine or use your own."

I nod and follow her further into the maze of the library. She takes us room by room. There are separate rooms for census records and tax records and criminal records. One room just records every birth and death. There's a massive genealogy room filled with books of family trees and a room full of general histories. She even leads us to a room that includes records from every town in Callenia. I stare around the room wide-eyed.

"So these are all the records for every village for every day?"

She shakes her head. "Not exactly. Each town historian sends us the highlights for each year. They mostly confirm death and birth details, but there are occasional entries that elaborate on specific events worth noting. Like, your birth, for instance. There's a whole entry detailing when you and your brother were born." She pauses, tilting her head in thought. "And, I suppose with everything that's happened in past months there will likely be some specific entries this year confirming those details."

She leads us into another room rivaling the size of the main room, only this room is filled with ancient looking scrolls and tomes.

"These," she says, her voice trembling with excitement and her eyes glowing, "are where we keep our magical records." She gestures around the room. "You'll find specific magical genealogies and entire books of prophecies, magical histories, descriptions of magic, and basically anything else you could ever want to know about magic."

I slowly walk to the center of the room, gazing around in awe.

"It's amazing, is it not?"

"It truly is," I breathe.

"So, let's say someone knew he was from two lines of magic, would it be possible for him to find his family tree in this room, so he could learn about his ancestors?" Alak asks casually, his eyes scanning the books nearest him.

Princess Cadewynn nods. "Yes, as long as he knew his family names back to the time of magic. These genealogy records stopped being kept once magic faded away but if you—or he—needed to trace back from his parents, you could start in the regular genealogy room and work back to this point."

Alak offers her a grateful smile. "Thank you."

Princess Cadewynn leads us back to the main room.

"This room is mostly reading for entertainment purposes and holds the books and scrolls my father and other palace guests seek out the most. Most of the fictional accounts actually hold some truths and are always worth looking into. But I'm sure you know that." I nod and the princess grins. "And that's the library. Shall we go back to my alcove? I can show you what I was looking at."

I nod and follow her. Alak veers off into the genealogy room, but I continue back to the alcove with Cadewynn.

"These are most of the scrolls and the books that contain information about you and your brother," Cadewynn explains, resuming her previous seat at the table.

My eyes go wide as I sit across the table from her, picking up the nearest paper, scanning to find where I'm mentioned. It doesn't take me long.

On the final eve of celebration, two babes shall be born of one womb. And with them, a great power shall awaken that shall shake the core of the earth. And the power that shall manifest when the babes come of age will awaken beasts of darkness and power long forgot, and havoc and devastation shall spread across the land, until nothing good remains.

I lay the paper down and stare at it. "Well, that's unpleasant."

Cadewynn sighs. "I know. But they're not all bad." She shuffles through a pile near her and finally holds a page out to me. "Read this one."

And the twins, born on one night of one mother, shall be blessed by the gods and shall bring about an era of peace and prosperity of a magnitude never known before.

"Okay, well that makes us sound a little better," I mutter, handing the paper back.

Cadewynn nods. "It's very confusing. I'm hoping that maybe you might be able to shed some light once you've read more."

"Well, I'm more than happy to try."

I dig in and start sifting through the texts. For every one I read like the first, claiming we are destruction and death, there's another text countering it, calling us saviors and praising us for the good we will do. After a couple hours of sorting and shifting, Cadewynn insists it's time for lunch.

"Madame Linwood doesn't allow us to eat in the library, of course, but we can have a lovely lunch in one of the gardens, if you like," she suggests shyly.

I agree and she rings for a servant. Once the servant has disappeared to fulfill her request, Cadewynn turns to me.

"Shall we check on your friend and see how he fares? We can invite him to join us."

I nod and we navigate our way to where Alak sits, buried beneath genealogy books.

"You know, you can take these books back to an alcove to study," Cadewynn offers. "You might be more comfortable."

"I might do that in a bit. I'm still sorting and looking for exactly what it is that I need, but once I've narrowed it down, I'll make myself more at home," Alak replies with a smile.

"And you're welcome to leave the books in the alcove so you don't have to search for them. Just let Madame Linwood know, and she'll let them be." Alak gives her another grateful nod. "Anyway, we were about to eat some lunch in the garden and wondered if you would want to join us."

"Thank you for the offer," Alak replies, "but I'm good for now. Some of us actually did eat a dozen pastries for breakfast." As he says the last bit, his eyes slide to me and he grins.

"Very well. If you change your mind, please feel free to join us."

Cadewynn leads me out of the library toward what feels like the opposite end of the castle. The walk proves to be worth it when we enter a beautiful garden. Just inside the garden is a round table, decked out with a small feast. We take a seat and I fill my plate. There are several chilled meats to choose from along with bread, an assortment of cheeses, and several different fruits and vegetables. I'm about halfway through my plate when Cadewynn's eyes light up.

"Ehren! Join us!" she calls, and I turn to see a grinning Ehren striding toward us. He's accompanied by two sharply dressed members of his Guard, who I recognize immediately as Bram and Kato.

"Don't mind if we do," Ehren says, taking a seat beside his sister.

Bram grins at me as he slides between me and Ehren. Cadewynn eyes Kato with interest as he takes a seat between her and me. Ehren seems to notice as well.

"Winnie, this is Kato Downs, the newest member of my Guard and Astra's brother," Ehren says, gesturing to Kato.

Cadewynn's eyes go wide with delight.

"You're the other twin," she whispers almost reverently.

Kato grins. "That I am."

"I cannot believe how lucky I am to meet you! I mean, you have no idea how much I've longed to meet you! I've read so much about you, and I read a lot. I never imagined that I'd be able to do or see half the things I read about, so you can imagine how big an honor—"

"Winnie, breathe," Ehren laughs.

Cadewynn's cheeks grow pink as she looks down. "I'm sorry." She looks back up at Kato. "I tend to get overly excited."

Kato's grin spreads. "There's nothing wrong with that." He reaches across the table, filling a plate with food. "Believe it or not, Astra can get rather excited about similar things. I've gotten used to hearing her gush on and on."

I shrug when Cadewynn shifts her gaze to me. "It's true."

"I knew you two would get along well." Ehren grins.

"It is rather nice to have a like mind in the library. It makes it much less lonely to have Astra there. It's even nice to have that other young man in the library, even if he's off on his own," Cadewynn says innocently, buttering a roll.

Ehren's eyes flash, though his voice remains steady. "Alak is in the library?"

I nod and stare him down. "Yes, I thought it would be better to put him to use in the library than to leave him shirtless and sulking in the room all day."

"Shirtless?" Bram sputters beside me, choking on his lunch.

"Yes," then I add, "but, for the record, he fully dressed before we came down."

Ehren still doesn't look entirely pleased, so I quickly change the subject. "So, Kato is part of your official Guard now?"

"He is," Ehren affirms. "He swore his oath this morning."

"What did the other Guard members think?"

Bram grins. "A few seemed a bit disgruntled, but once your brother showed his skill, there were none left questioning his position."

I knocked them on their asses. Kato says in my head and I stifle my laugh.

Bram grabs my hand under the table. I lean ever so slightly toward him in response.

"So," Bram says quietly, "are you finding interesting things in the library?"

I look up at him and nod. "A lot of confusing, conflicting things, but I've only just begun."

Ehren suddenly goes stiff, his gaze just past my shoulder. I turn with Bram and see two soldiers, dressed in uniforms similar to Bram and Kato's but black instead of maroon.

The king's Guard. Kato answers my unasked question.

I suck in my breath and my heart beats faster. Bram shifts noticeably closer to me, wrapping his arm around my waist.

"Good afternoon Your Majesties," one of the men says with a sneer.

"Good afternoon, Hamlin," Ehren replies curtly. "And you too, Pelion."

The Guard, Hamlin, looks toward Cadewynn. "It's quite pleasant and unusual to see you out of your library, Princess. Though, should you be out and about without any guards?"

"I wasn't aware I would need any guards in my own palace garden, especially since I am currently accompanied by my brother and two of his personal Guard," Princess Cadewynn replies, sitting straighter. "There was no danger to me before you entered the garden. Are you suggesting that you now pose some sort of threat? For your presence is the only thing that has changed."

Both men look taken back by her sharp words. Hamlin holds up his hands defensively and bows his head. "I meant no offense, Your Majesty."

Cadewynn glances away with disinterest, and the Guard's eyes fall on me, shifting to Kato. Kato tenses.

"You have a new Guard and a lovely new guest. How . . . interesting," Hamlin muses to Ehren.

"Yes, both are guests here at the palace at my request," Ehren replies stiffly.

"And one of your guests is already a Guard?" Hamlin's eyebrow arches.

"Yes," Bram growls from beside me. "And if you ever have a chance to see his skill, you will understand why. Perhaps a demonstration is in order?"

"Please, not during my lunch," Cadewynn says, sounding bored.

Hamlin sneers. "Very well. I wouldn't want to disturb your lunch." He inclines his head to me. "I look forward to meeting you both again later."

Once they're gone, Bram relaxes slightly. Ehren, however, is still scowling.

"They'll cause nothing but trouble. I can guarantee by end of day, my father will know you are here."

"Is that bad?" I ask, nerves swelling.

Bram's thumb strokes my hand. "Don't worry. We will take care of it."

Ehren nods. "Yes, in fact, we should probably get on that now."

He stands, Bram and Kato following suit.

"Stay in the library," Ehren instructs. "And, as much as I hate to suggest it, keep Alak close."

Bram leans in and brushes his lips quickly against mine. "Don't worry. I promised I would keep you safe and I meant it."

Ehren leads Bram and Kato out of the garden, leaving Cadewynn and I alone.

"Should I be worried?" I ask her quietly.

"Not yet," she replies, then her eyes begin to glisten. "Though, if you've already won the heart of Bram, I say you have nothing to worry about."

I blush and look down at my plate. Cadewynn giggles. "It's nothing to be ashamed of. He's very handsome and one of the best men I know."

We sit in silence for a few minutes, but when we realize neither of us have much of an appetite left, we decide to head back to the library. We find Alak still buried in genealogies. I quickly fill him in on our interaction with the king's men.

"If his princeliness and his dear captain think I should stay with you, far be it from me to argue," Alak says, gathering up his books.

The three of us settle down in the alcove, buried in our texts. I start shifting through the prophecies that Cadewynn has been studying, believing that they're most closely linked to current events and the near future. My hope is that I can perhaps figure out how my own magic works as part of a larger picture. The prophecies, however, are all over the place and nearly impossible to decipher. It doesn't take long for my head to start aching.

"I'm going to go take this book back and grab another one," Alak says, breaking the silence. He stands and stretches, cracking his knuckles before grabbing a large book and leaving the alcove.

I lay down the text I was reading and am reaching for another when I hear Alak yell. I jump up and run out of the alcove with Cadewynn on my heels. Once in the corridor, I freeze, coming face to face with at least a dozen of the king's Guard.

CHAPTER TWENTY-FIVE

$\mathcal{T}$he throne room is grandiose to say the least. The floors are blood red marble with onyx columns shooting to a domed ceiling that depicts a previous king victorious on a bloody battlefield. King Betron sits on a colossal golden throne, staring down at us in cruel amusement. He has brown hair and a thick beard, his blue eyes cold and calculating. Next to him sits an elegant woman with blond hair and green eyes, who looks at us like she couldn't possibly imagine anything less interesting.

The soldiers who dragged Alak and I from the library still surround us, their presence a threatening shadow. Cadewynn is being detained outside the throne room by the king's Guard. My heart pounds so hard I wonder if the men closest to me can hear it. Beside me, Alak stands stiffly, but I can sense power rippling from him, like he's collecting it to full strength should we need to escape. I am reaching down inside my own well of power when bootsteps echo behind me. I don't dare turn away from the king to see who's approaching.

"Here's the other one, Your Majesty," the familiar voice of Hamlin sneers, shoving Kato to my other side.

If I thought I could feel power coming from Alak, it's nothing to what I sense from Kato. He's a coiled snake ready to strike.

"Father!" Ehren's voice thunders across the throne room, ringing with power. "What exactly are you doing?"

The king smiles mirthlessly. "Last time I checked, I was king, and I did not need to explain myself to my son."

"Last time I checked, my friends weren't dragged needlessly before you without cause," Ehren spits.

"Watch your tone, boy." The king's mouth tightens into a thin line of displeasure.

"Pardon me, Father, but I must inquire as to why exactly you feel the need to drag three of my guests here without ceremony."

Ehren's voice is controlled venom. Anyone less than a king would be shrinking away from Ehren, but his father merely looks amused.

"I just wanted to meet our guests. After all, it is rare that strangers to our court are made guardsmen overnight. Would you care to explain?" King Betron asks with a wry smile. "At the very least, introduce me to these guests, who are apparently important enough to have been housed in one of our top suites."

Bram materializes next to me, pressing between me and Alak.

"Astra is my betrothed, if it pleases you, Your Majesty," Bram states, bowing his head to the king and grabbing my hand.

My heart leaps into my throat, and I do my best to school my features to hide my shock. I swallow and force a smile as the king's eyes slide to my face.

"Indeed," King Betron drawls, sounding less than convinced.

"Yes, Your Majesty. And her brother, Kato, is by far one of the best soldiers I have ever encountered. It only seemed natural to find him a place at the palace so his sister would not be without family." Bram squeezes my hand reassuringly. "If you would like to see proof of his skill, I am sure he would be more than willing to go up against any of your own Guard."

"That I may have to see at some point." The king's eyes focus on Alak. "And who is the redhead? Another brother?"

"Our cousin," I blurt out, my voice holding more authority than I feel. The king's cold eyes lock on my face and it takes all my power not to show fear. Instead, I take a half step forward. "He is like a brother to me, Your Majesty." How my voice is steady I have no idea, but I continue. "We have no other family, and with him being so dear to our hearts, we simply could not leave him behind."

The king weighs my words. His mouth curves into a smile once more as he peers down at us, like a cat who's cornered its prey.

"And when is this wedding?" he asks Bram.

"We have no official date set"—the king's eyes flash a temporary victory and Bram, sensing a trap, amends—"but we were thinking mid-summer, should it please you."

The king settles back against his throne, casting his gaze back to Alak, "You, cousin, you approve of this union?"

"Yes, Your Majesty. We would be fools to oppose it."

Alak's voice sounds stilted and odd. I barely recognize it. It takes me a moment to realize he's masking his accent.

"And you, brother, you approve as well? Or is your guardship buying your support?" King Betron demands, looking back to Kato.

Kato takes a step forward, looking the king directly in the

eye. "We could not imagine a better match. The guardship was offered after the fact. As Captain Bramfield said, I would be more than happy to prove my skill."

I can feel the edge in Kato's voice more than I can hear it. Through our bond I sense a surge of hate for the king.

"That won't be necessary," the king concedes with a wave of his hand. "Well, my son, now that I have met your guests and new guardsman, I feel a bit more at ease with strangers in my home. Congratulations on your betrothal, Captain. You may all go."

The king dismisses us with a flippant wave of his hand, whatever game he was playing on pause for now. Bram slides his hand around my waist and leads me from the throne room, Kato and Alak on our heels. As we pass by Hamlin he shoots me a bitter, disappointed look. Cadewynn rushes to us as soon as we exit, eyeing the king's men escorting us with distaste.

"They wouldn't let me in but I heard everything. Congratulations on your engagement announcement," she says brightly. "I do love weddings!"

I offer her a weak smile. Ehren storms next to his sister's side, glaring at the king's soldiers until they move further down the corridor.

"Shall I take them back to the library?" Cadewynn asks Ehren quietly.

Ehren shakes his head, still eyeing the guards disappearing around a corner. "No," he looks from me to Kato to Alak. "Your suite might be the safest for now."

"Me as well?" Kato asks stiffly.

"Yes," Ehren replies firmly. "If for no other reason than to keep an eye on your sister." He takes a breath and drags a hand down his face. "I'll be returning to my room for the rest of the evening, anyway." He turns to Cadewynn and adds gently, "You can return to your library."

She smiles gratefully. "I think I will. It's frightening outside the library walls."

Ehren gives a slight laugh. "That it is, dearest Winnie. That it is."

She offers us all one last smile before floating away to the library. Bram doesn't remove his arm from around me all the way to our suite, and I'm happy he doesn't. After the experience with the king, his touch is comforting. I expect Ehren and Bram to leave us at our door, but both follow us inside. Once the door shuts, Ehren collapses in the nearest chair.

"Shit. Shit. Shit."

"I know," Bram agrees.

"What?" I ask, confused, eyes darting from Bram to Ehren.

Ehren looks up at me. "This means my father suspects something is going on. Worse, he suspects you. He never would have made such a production otherwise. He wants me to know he's watching. This is not good at all." He shifts his gaze to Bram and a grin spreads across his face. "Good thing you're good at thinking on your feet. Congratulations on your impending marriage."

Bram takes a deep breath and turns to face me. "About that, I couldn't think . . . I knew the king would likely accept that. You don't have to . . . What I mean is . . ."

"Captain Bramfield, are you rescinding your promise of marriage?" I inquire, arching an eyebrow and placing a hand on my hip.

"I . . . no." Bram's cheeks turn red as his eyes brighten. "Are you saying that you would be willing to marry me?"

My stomach flips. I laugh. "Yes. I would love nothing more."

I catch a hint of tears in Bram's eyes as a grin spreads across his face. He pulls me close and presses his lips firmly to mine. I throw my arms around his neck and weave my fingers into his hair.

"I'll allow it, seeing as how you two just got engaged and all," Kato's voice cuts through, "but I was pretty sure we had a 'no kissing in front of Kato' rule."

Bram pulls back and I drop my arms, my hand sliding into his.

"Forgive me," Bram says with a mock bow toward Kato.

Kato grins. "Congratulations, Ash."

"I'm happy for both of you, but we have a serious matter on our hands," Alak interrupts, scowling.

"I really hate to agree with the rabble, but he's right," Ehren sighs. "We need to be on both the offensive and defensive now. We've been making things up as we go, but now we need a plan. And about five backup plans to go with it." He leans his head back against the chair and closes his eyes, pinching the bridge of his nose.

"What do you need from me?" I ask.

Ehren opens his eyes and stares at the ceiling a moment before shifting his eyes to me. "Just continue helping Cadewynn. She's been looking into prophecies trying to figure out where most magical occurrences are likely to be. She's also been trying to sift through all the magical genealogies in the hopes we can find those with magic in their blood before my father. It's a lot and she can use all the help she can get."

"I can help with that, too," Alak offers meekly.

"Fine," Ehren says with a reluctant nod. "I don't particularly like the idea of you near my sister, but we need all hands on deck." His eyes narrow. "But you so much as touch my sister or talk to her in the wrong way or anything remotely close to what you did to Isabella, and I don't care who's 'cousin' you're pretending to be, I will drive a sword through your heart myself and no hole will be a safe place to hide this time."

Alak blanches. "Isabella was—"

"Don't you dare say her name," Bram yells, jerking away from me and lunging toward Alak, who scrambles away, throwing up a magical shield between him and Bram.

"I'm sorry. I'm sorry," Alak sputters.

I sweep across the room to Bram's side and slide my hand back into his. "Come," I insist gently, pulling him toward my room.

We go inside, shutting the door behind us. Bram sits down on the edge of my bed, shaking his head.

"I am sorry," he mutters, looking away from me. "I shouldn't have lost my temper like that."

"I think it's time you tell me why you hate Alak. Now," I say firmly, crossing my arms.

Bram looks up at me, his expression broken, tears in his eyes. He swallows and nods.

"Isabella was my sister. When I left to be a soldier, she was sad to see me go, but she supported me. After a year of being apart, she found she wanted to visit me and see Embervein, so she took a job and saved every marke she could. It took her almost a year, but she did it. She was just shy of fifteen at the time.

"She loved being in Embervein. She was really meant for this life. Ehren and I were just building our friendship and Isabella helped smooth over our differences. It helped that she was beautiful, and I'm pretty sure Ehren fell in love with her the moment he saw her. Her plan was to visit for a couple weeks before returning home, but neither Ehren nor I would allow her to travel alone. Ehren helped find her a place at the palace, working in the library and studying with Cadewynn. They became as close as sisters, despite Isabella being nearly five years older.

"A few months later, Alak came to town."

With this Bram's voice shifts from an affectionate tone to one of loathing. He stands and walks to my balcony, hands clasped behind his back. "He enjoyed conning the sons of nobles, so Ehren and I found him amusing. We trusted him and considered him a friend. He was an artful flirt, so it didn't take long for Isabella to fall for him. He stole her heart with his cunning words, enticing smile, and that stupid accent. Somehow, Alak conveyed to her that he intended to marry her one day when she was old enough. So she . . . she gave him everything." Bram's face goes stern as he struggles to continue.

"You mean, she—"

Bram cuts me off with a sharp nod. "Yes. And then he went around bragging about his conquest and dragging her name through mud to anyone who would listen. He destroyed her reputation and wanted nothing else to do with her. Her disgrace and heartbreak were little more than a joke to him. And, come to find out, it was all for a bet he had made with a nobleman's son.

"When Isabella found out, she—" His voice breaks as he sinks back onto the edge of my bed, his head in his hands. When he looks back up at me, there are tears on his cheeks. "We found her the next morning lying in her bed on blood-soaked sheets, wrists slit."

I gasp, my hand flying to my mouth. "Gods, no."

Bram nods and takes a deep, shuddering breath. "When that bastard found out, he ran. I know the decision was Isabella's, and I can't imagine that Alak had any idea she would do something so drastic, but I can't help but blame him for her death."

I sink down on the bed next to Bram and wrap my arm around him. He holds me and I kiss him. These kisses are different. There's a longing, a need to be comforted. They slowly grow more and more intense. Bram lifts me up and lays me down on my bed. My breath is unsteady as he lies next to me, kissing me hungrily. His fingers fumble to undo the buttons on his Guard uniform and he tosses the jacket aside. I slide my hands under his shirt and trace my hands over his muscled chest. He groans and shifts on top of me. I pull his shirt all the way off and flick my tongue across his lips. Suddenly, he jerks away, sitting up, his breath ragged. I kneel behind him and wrap my arms around him.

"What's wrong?" I whisper, kissing his neck.

"I love you, Astra."

My heart flips.

"I love you, too, Bram."

He shifts to face me. "I want you," he says and a heat rushes through my body. He kisses me and that heat increases. He pulls back again. "I want you, but not now. Not here. Not like this."

I look at him, disappointment and confusion on my face.

"Please, understand. I want to be able to love you fiercely and wildly, but I can't do that here. Not with your brother in the other room. Not out of a sense of needing comfort. I want to fully devote every thought and emotion to you, to pleasuring you."

I smile and nod. "I will hold you to that."

He laughs. "I expect you to."

He rises from the bed and walks over to the balcony, looking outside. "Embervein makes a beautiful home. I can't wait to share it with you."

He turns back to me, grabbing his shirt from where it landed at the foot of the bed and slips it back on before fetching his jacket and buttoning it. He stands straight and tall, looking as regal as ever. I walk over to him, and he cups my face in his hands, kissing me tenderly.

"I could stay here and kiss you all day, Astra, but now I

need to go. I need a plan in place to make sure you're safe." He kisses me again and I nod.

When we walk back into the sitting room everyone tries to act like they had no idea what was going on in my room. Alak is lounging on the sofa in front of the balcony again and he sinks further down as Bram walks out. My hand absentmindedly straightens my hair and dress while Ehren waggles his eyebrows at me. I roll my eyes and he laughs.

Are we going to talk about what just happened?

No.

So . . . maybe later?

No, Kato.

We don't keep secrets.

There's nothing to tell.

Right . . .

Fine. Later.

Ehren pops up from his chair. "Well, Kato and I have discussed a few things. I'll let him catch you up if you're done with Bram," he says with an over-exaggerated wink.

"Nothing happened," Bram says slowly and firmly.

Ehren puts his hands up in surrender. "I just figure you were in there for a little longer than necessary . . ."

"Nothing happened." This time Bram's voice is frighteningly cold.

"Message received," Ehren mumbles. "Let's go reconvene in my room and see what good we can do with all the information we've gathered. Hopefully, we're still one step ahead of my father."

Ehren gives me a parting nod as he and Bram leave. I turn to Kato.

"What did you and Ehren decide?"

"He's going to have members of his personal Guard stationed near you as often as possible. Guards of his and

Bram's choosing that he knows and trusts to protect you and magic, allowing you to use it freely in their presence but adding an extra layer of protection from the king and his men," Kato explains.

"Will you be one of them?"

Kato shakes his head. "No, I volunteered but Ehren thinks having me constantly by his side will prove his faith in me. He's also going to work out a safe house for us to flee to should the need arise."

"You should learn wisping," Alak offers, rising from the couch.

He studies my face and something he sees must tell him what I know. His face falls. His lips part as he locks his eyes with mine.

Kato doesn't seem to notice and cuts in with, "What's wisping?"

Alak shakes his head, forcing himself to focus. "It's what Felixe does."

As if summoned, the Fae Fox appears on Alak's shoulder. Alak gives his head an affectionate scratch.

"You mean, appearing and disappearing at random?" I ask.

"Essentially. Wisping is immediately transporting yourself from one location to another through magic. If you can master the skill, you can wisp away at any moment, and it could mean life over death. Enough practice and, with your amount of magic, you can even transport others with you."

Kato nods. "Can you do it?"

"I've only tried short distances, but yes," Alak replies. He disappears and reappears on the balcony. He walks back inside. "With your power, you could probably travel miles, possibly even countries. Of course, it helps to be able to picture exactly where you're going to land. Otherwise, there can be all sorts of issues and complications."

"But we can do that? Just travel like that?" Kato says, snapping his fingers. His eyes flash with something that looks a lot like hunger.

"Yes, with practice, focus, and concentration. It might be tricky to practice with the king watching you, but we can start small in this room and go from there," Alak offers. "Being able to leave the palace grounds without detection through wisping to practice magic would definitely be a plus."

"Good. What else can we do with our power besides run?" Kato demands.

"You mean offensive magic? Attack magic?" Alak asks hesitantly.

"Yes," Kato says at the same time I ask, "Is attack magic necessary?"

"One thing I learned training as a soldier," Kato says, addressing me, "was not just to defend or to hide but to go on the offensive. If the king comes after us directly, we would be fools not to use every weapon in our arsenal which, for us, includes magic."

"But the king is already wary of magic. Using it against him could only make it worse," I argue.

"Perhaps. But he wouldn't be able to pretend it didn't exist anymore," Kato replies a bit too casually.

There's a knock on the door and I move to answer it, but Kato stops me.

"Who is it?" Kato calls out.

"Winnie."

I grin and rush to the door, throwing it open. Cadewynn stands in the hall, her arms loaded with books, papers, and scrolls. Behind her is a servant laden down with even more.

"I figured if you couldn't return to the library today, I might bring some of it to you," she says cheerily as she marches into

the room, depositing her load on the table. The servant stacks
his on the table as well and leaves with a bow.

I walk over and begin shifting through the papers. "Thank
you! This is very helpful! I should be back in the library with
you tomorrow."

"Oh, good! It was nice to have a friend." Her eyes glance
over to Alak. "Well, two friends." Alak smiles weakly but keeps
an obvious distance. "I brought the books you were looking at as
well as a couple others I thought you might find useful."

"Thank you. I appreciate it," Alak says, leaning away, his
eyes darting to me.

The princess suddenly notices Felixe perched on Alak's
shoulders. Her eyes go wide. "Is that a Fae Fox?"

Alak nods, but makes no move closer to her. She seems to
notice his darker demeanor and doesn't push the issue.

"Well," Cadewynn says, backing toward the door. "I'll
leave you be. I'm sure you'll want to look at those in depth.
Perhaps bring your Fae Fox with you tomorrow, just don't let
Madame Linwood see him. She won't care for animals in her
library. I'll see you in the morning."

"Goodbye, Princess Cadewynn," I say as she opens the
door.

"Please, do call me Winnie," she says, smiling as she closes
the door.

Kato glances at the table. "Well, that looks a bit boring. I'll
leave you to it. I'm going to go in my room and see what magic I
can conjure. Let me know if you need me."

"Try not to set your room on fire, please," I call after him as
he strolls across the room, shooting me a rude gesture over his
shoulder.

Alak approaches me tentatively, reaching for one of the
genealogy books as he takes a seat. Felixe darts down his arm
and begins sniffing the parchment.

"Did he, did Bram—" Alak begins, deliberately avoiding eye contact.

"Yes," I cut him off sharply.

He lets out a shaky breath. I look up at him. His expression is broken, tears welling in his eyes as he meets my eyes. For a moment I hold his gaze.

"Astra, please," he begs, his voice trembling. "I had no idea she would do that. Even then, as horrible as I was, I would have never let things get so out of hand. If I could go back and change everything, I would."

"So it's true? You seduced Bram's sister for a bet?" I ask, my voice quiet but sharp.

Alak flinches. "It's not that simple. There are details that Bram and Ehren don't know—details I've never told a living soul. I truly cared for Isabella. I did. She was my first love. Things just . . . got out of hand. Everything went wrong so quickly, and I didn't handle things well at all. In the end, it's my fault. I did everything wrong and I take the blame."

"And then you ran instead of facing the consequences?"

"Yes. I was terrified of Bram and Ehren. They would have killed me without a thought. Honestly, they had every right to do so. I told you my self-preservation was strong." He pauses, gaining control of his voice, but a tear slides down his cheek. He doesn't even bother wiping it away. "I've often wished they killed me that day, because the guilt I've lived with every day since has been a fate worse than death."

"How can I trust you?" I ask, my voice barely audible.

He swallows and holds out his arms, wrists facing up. At first, I don't see anything and then, there's a shimmer across his skin. He has scars, once deep slashes, on his wrists. I gasp, meeting his eyes.

"Some fool saved my life." He laughs bitterly, pulling his hands back.

"How do I know those are real and not the illusion?" I whisper, and immediately regret my words as hurt flashes across his face.

Alak closes his eyes, opening them slowly. "I wanted to die. I deserved to die. But when I didn't die, the scars were just a physical reminder of what I did to Isabella. So I hid them. Before my magic returned, I used to wrap my wrists with leather bands. But now," he turns his wrists up again and the scars shimmer away.

"I need you to believe I am sorry and that I regret everything that happened. I need you to believe that I would never do it again, to you or Princess Cadewynn or anyone else." His voice is shaking and his eyes pleading. "Please, Astra."

"Why does it matter what I think?" I say at length.

"Because it does. Because, for whatever reason, you trust me. You're the first person to ever trust me so wholeheartedly and without any real reason or proof that I should be trusted. Because you've defended me. Because you make me believe that I can be the better person I've been trying to become all these years. Because . . . I can't take disappointing you and losing you. Your friendship means everything to me."

His eyes search my face desperately. I place a hand over where his lays clenched on the table. I feel him relax as I meet his eyes with a steady gaze.

"I believe you," I whisper. "Gods help me, but I believe you."

"Thank you," he says weakly. "You have no idea . . . thank you."

"Now, let's sort through this and see what we can find out before it's too late," I say, pulling my hand back to gesture at the piles of texts on the table.

CHAPTER TWENTY-SIX

*W*e spend the next half hour sorting through the piles of materials. We divide everything according to category, so we can shift through the information more efficiently. The genealogies go at one end, with histories in the middle, and prophecies at the other end. Everything is nearly sorted when I pick up a parchment and scowl in confusion. At first glance it looks like an older dialect of Callenian, but the more I look at it, the more confused I become.

"What's that?" Alak asks, nodding at the paper in my hands.

"I have no idea what language or dialect this is written in. I don't recognize it at all," I reply.

Alak walks around the table and peers over my shoulder.

"That's Yallik," he says, the word rolling off his tongue.

"What?"

"Yallik. It's the dialect commonly spoken in the Athiedor region."

"But the Athiedor region is part of Callenia. Why would their dialect be so different?"

"Athiedor may be part of Callenia now, but for generations it was its own country. There was even a period of time when it was part of Paravalia. Many people in Athiedor still feel they should be their own country, which has kept Yallik and other parts of their culture strong," Alak explains with a wave of his hand.

"How do you know so much about Athiedor?"

Amusement flickers across his face. "Are you serious?"

Suddenly, it clicks. "Your accent. You're from the Athiedor region."

He chuckles. "Aye, love. I am. Or at least my mother was, though I spent a good many years there myself when I was growing up."

I hand him the page. "So you can read this?"

He takes the page and scans it a moment before replying. "Aye, I can. It's a slightly different dialect than I'm accustomed to, but I can read it."

Alak takes a seat and leans over the parchment, studying it for several minutes, a scowl growing deeper and deeper on his face. I stand behind him and look over his shoulder.

"Hovering isn't going to speed this along, love," Alak mutters.

"Sorry," I apologize, but I don't move. "I'm just trying to figure out what's making you scowl so much."

"This date," Alak replies, tapping numbers at the top right corner of the page. "It doesn't make sense."

"Why not?" I ask, leaning over to look at it more closely. "I may not be able to read Yallik, but that looks like a pretty standard date."

"That's not the odd part. This entire page is an account involving magic, but, by that date, magic was supposed to be gone, faded away entirely."

"Are you certain?" I ask breathlessly.

"Fairly certain. There was apparently some sort of sparring that took place between two feuding families, and then there was a Healer involved." As he speaks, he runs his finger along portions of the text. "The sparring was essentially a magical duel, and when it speaks of healing, it sounds like actual magical healing."

I collapse into the chair next to Alak. "So magic didn't disappear entirely. It still existed in Athiedor. At least part of it," I mutter in disbelief.

Alak's eyes scan the bottom of the page and his eyes go wide. "I don't think it was just Athiedor. Listen to this, 'And such things are common enough here, as they are on the Isle of Naskein and in the Hundan Valley.'"

I shake my head, bewildered. "So all this time there have been pockets of magic?"

Alak nods, leaning back in his chair. "It would appear so."

"You said you spent some years growing up in Athiedor. Do you recall any magic?"

Alak shakes his head. "No, but I was relatively young." He pauses and then continues. "I told you my father was a real bastard. When he married my mother, they lived in Northern Callenia. After I was born, my father sank more into drinking than ever before, and when I was somewhere between a year and two years old, my mother fled with me back to her family. We lived in Athiedor with my mother's family until my father found us and dragged us back when I was around nine."

"And you haven't been back to Athiedor since then?" I ask.

He opens his mouth and then closes it, looking down. "Once. For a few months. After the . . . incident. I fled Embervein with the intent of finding my family and essentially hiding out with them. But my guilt got the better of me and I ended up wandering around Athiedor for a few months until I felt it might be . . . safe to return."

"And you didn't notice any magic?" I press.

"I—" he looks up at me, realization dawning on his face. "When I was wandering around Athiedor, that's when I started performing."

"Your magic tricks? You started that in Athiedor?" I ask, excitement edging my voice. "Maybe you tapped into your real magic and didn't even realize it. That would also explain why you were able to start using magic before it awoke everywhere else."

"I think you may be right. This means that there could be skilled Masters of magic out there. We just need to find them!" Alak's voice sounds equally excited.

"Do you have any contact with your family in Athiedor?"

Alak shakes his head. "No, but I know the village where my mother took me, and I remember my aunt's name. Hopefully she's still there. I can try to reach out to her."

I nod enthusiastically. Before we can discuss any further plans, Kato strolls into the room. He glances at the table of neatly organized material.

"Well, it seems you've been productive."

"Actually, we think we may have discovered that magic didn't disappear entirely. There are possibly pockets of magic that never faded and within them those that truly understand magic," I relay, my eyes shining.

Kato's eyes go wide. "That's excellent news! Do you know the exact locations?"

I shake my head. "Not yet, but Alak is going to contact his family to see if they know anything."

Kato rubs his hands together eagerly. "Good. I can't wait to access the full extent of my powers and see what exactly I can do."

Alak stands and walks to Kato. "In the meantime, we can

work on honing your skill. A lot of magic is just practicing. Do you want to try wisping?"

Kato nods, and I stand and join him. "I definitely wouldn't mind learning that myself."

"Okay," Alak begins. "Let's start small. Pick a spot within just a few feet and concentrate on moving to that spot. Focus all your energy and magic. Envision yourself moving and don't fight against your magic. Let it guide you as much as you guide it."

I pick my spot and close my eyes. I pull at my magic and do exactly what Alak says, but when I open my eyes I haven't moved. Neither has Kato. We try again and again for the next hour, but the most we accomplish is exhausting and frustrating ourselves. Eventually, Kato just bursts into a controlled pillar of frustrated flame before extinguishing and collapsing into an easy chair.

"Why is this so difficult?" he complains.

"Don't worry. You'll get it. It's all about doing it once. Then, once you've figured out that first time, it will come easier the next time and so on and so forth until it's little more than a reflex," Alak says.

There's a knock at the door and Kato sits tall, tensing.

"It's just me, with some food," Bram's voice calls through the door.

"Thank the gods," Kato mumbles, leaping up to answer the door. A second before he reaches the door, Alak wisps directly in front of Kato, opening the door himself, his eyes twinkling.

"You think you're so damn clever, don't you," Kato growls at Alak.

"I only think the truth, mate." Alak grins.

Bram strides past both of them bearing a tray of food. Behind him follow a couple servants with more trays and a pitcher of mead. Bram pauses, looking down at the table that's mostly covered in books and papers.

"Sorry," I wince. "Give me a minute."

"I'll have Ehren arrange for another table to be brought in," Bram says, his eyes glittering with amusement as I hurriedly gather the books and papers, moving them to a couple of the easy chairs at the other side of the room

"That would be helpful," I concede as Alak and Kato help me clear.

As more of the table resurfaces, Bram and the servants start laying out the food. Once all the trays have been deposited, the servants leave with a bow.

"I hope you enjoy dinner. It was all prepared especially for you by the kitchen staff. One of the perks of living in the castle," Bram says with a wink

Kato and Alak don't hesitate, quickly filling plates with roast goose, steamed vegetables, spiced fruits, and breads. I walk over to Bram and greet him with a kiss.

"Are you going to be joining us?"

"I can, if you don't mind the company," Bram replies with a smile.

"Do our opinions count?" Kato asks, his mouth full. "Because if you're going to keep kissing, then I'd rather you not. It's ruining my appetite." He winks at me and I roll my eyes.

Bram laughs. "I promise. No more kissing during dinner."

He takes a seat at the table and I take the seat beside him. The food is delicious, by far some of the best I've ever had. I devour my first plate and am considering a second when Kato, who has fully committed to second servings of everything, speaks up.

"So, were you and Ehren able to create a workable plan?"

"We have the makings of one. We received word not long ago from some credible sources that confirm our theory that magic has returned everywhere, not just in Callenia. We are hoping to find allies both outside and within our kingdom. Now, we just need to make contacts," Bram replies.

"Alak and I may be able to help with that," I interject and Bram raises his eyebrows. "Cadewynn brought us some research and among it was a page written in Yallik that Alak was able to translate. It's a record of magic that took place barely fifty years ago in the region of Athiedor. It also alludes to magic in Naskein and the Hundan Valley.

"Really? That's information we didn't have before. It also gives us a good place to start. Athiedor is part of Callenia, so that would be the easiest place to start," Bram muses.

"Already on that, mate," Alak says with a grin, which instantly fades with a sharp look from Bram.

"Alak has family in Athiedor," I explain.

"Very well," Bram concedes. "Naskein is technically part of Portia but governs itself as part of a religious order that revolves around magic. I can imagine they would be willing allies. I am surprised we did not think of contacting them before now. The Hundan Valley might be trickier."

"The Hundan Valley is in Gleador, isn't it?" I ask. "I thought they were allies."

"They are allies as far as trade and general peace go, but they aren't fans of us crossing into their territory and vice versa. Their border is under constant observation. The king most likely has sources and spies in Gleador, but Ehren doesn't have access to them. It could take some time to build those relations, time I fear we don't have."

"Well, let's start with what we have and go from there," I suggest with a shrug.

Bram stares off, lost in thought. I grab his hand.

"Would you like to go out on the balcony?" I ask softly and he nods.

The evening air is warm and welcoming. This is the first time I've actually gone out onto the balcony and the view is extraordinary. I walk to the edge and peer at a stretch of garden below, complete with a trickling fountain in the center.

"Not a bad view," Bram says, walking up beside me.

I turn and look up at him and he smiles down at me. I reach up and touch his check. "What's wrong?"

He gives a short laugh. "Where do you want me to start?"

He sighs and turns away, looking down into the garden, his hands gripping the balustrade.

"I'm hesitant to trust Alak with the negotiations with Athiedor," he confesses. He glances at me. "Are you sure he even translated the Yallik correctly?"

"I understand why you don't trust Alak, and I cannot blame you, but I trust him," I say quietly.

Bram's expression is heavy. "Even now that you know his past?"

I hesitate. I can see the raw emotion Bram is attempting to hide. I know Alak hurt him in a way that is irreparable, but I can also see a side of Alak that Bram refuses to acknowledge, a kinder side that's been broken and molded by his past.

"Yes," I answer at length, choosing my words carefully, "because our past does not define us. Rather, it is our choices that we make to better ourselves despite our past and the mistakes we've made. I truly believe that Alak regrets what he did and everything he has done since that day has been to atone for the better."

Bram reaches out and takes my hands in his, looking deeply into my eyes. "I trust you and if you trust him, that's enough for me." I arch an eyebrow and he chuckles. "Okay, admittedly it may take a little more for me to fully trust him, but I promise to try. For you."

I look up at him, and he kisses me again. I can taste his longing. He pulls back with a sigh and presses his forehead to mine.

"I don't want to leave you," he whispers, wrapping his arms around me.

I lean into his embrace and rest my head against his chest. "Then don't."

He holds me closer, and I can hear his heart racing. We stand there for a moment before he pulls back with a sigh. "I really should get back to Ehren. We have a lot of things to figure out. I need to let him know what you and Alak discovered."

"Fine," I reply, giving him a quick kiss. "But promise me we'll spend some time together soon."

"I promise," he says with a smile.

He takes my hand as we go back inside. Alak is nowhere to be seen. Kato leans back in his chair, his hand resting on his stomach.

"Did you get enough to eat?" I tease as Bram and I approach.

Kato pats his stomach. "I don't think I've ever been so full in my life."

"Glad to see you enjoyed dinner," Bram says with a smile. "If you're done I can send up some servants to clear everything."

"That would be good, thank you," Kato groans.

I walk Bram to the door, stealing one last kiss before he leaves. I turn back to Kato, who's closed his eyes.

"Is Alak in his room?"

Kato nods without opening his eyes. "I believe so."

I stroll over to Alak's door and knock. After a moment he answers, a curious expression on his face. "Yes?"

"Is Felixe in there? I was looking for him." Alak arches an eyebrow and I laugh. "Can I come in?"

Alak opens the door all the way and steps back, gesturing with his hand for me to enter. I step inside and he hesitantly closes the door while I glance around his room. It's essentially the same as mine only lacking a balcony. He doesn't even have a window, so his room is lit by lanterns alone.

"So, what can I do for you, love?" he asks, shoving his hands in his pockets.

"Why are you hiding out in your room?" I ask point-blank.

Alak looks down and shrugs. "There wasn't much need for me out there anymore. I've been composing letters to send to Athiedor." He nods to a desk in the corner of his room.

"The lighting is better in the main room," I point out, but he just shrugs again, still avoiding my eyes.

"You don't have to avoid Bram," I say quietly.

Alak gives a bitter laugh. "I beg to differ. I'm not sure my magic is faster than his sword, and I really don't want to test that out."

"We're on the same side, and Bram realizes that. We don't know how many allies we have so we need to make peace with the ones already available."

Alak finally meets my gaze and offers a weak smile. "Well, I guess a tentative peace until he finds people he can trust is better than nothing at all."

"Well, I just wanted to let you know," I mumble. "I'm going to go sort through some more texts before bed and maybe practice some magic if you want to join me after you're done with your letters."

"Thanks, I might do that."

I turn to leave, but pause and turn to Alak. I concentrate my magic and form a silver orb of light about a foot in diameter between my hands. I lift the ball in the air and float it over Alak's desk.

"It will be easier for you to write with better lighting."

Alak locks eyes with me, his expression laced with more emotions than I can sort.

"I don't deserve your friendship, love," he says quietly, "but I'm more grateful for it every second."

"Fate plays interesting games, doesn't she," I say with a wink.

Alak smiles a true, genuine smile that lights up his eyes. I hold his gaze, lost in his emerald eyes. After a moment, I blink and turn, leaving Alak to write his letters, feeling a sort of pleasant satisfaction and warmth.

CHAPTER TWENTY-SEVEN

I wake when the sun is but a whisper of light on the horizon. I'm tempted to roll over and catch another hour of sleep, but my mind is already wide awake. Somewhat reluctantly, I get out of bed and throw open my wardrobe. As I spend a few minutes sifting through the dresses, I can't help but think about how much Mara would love them. Guilt washes over me when I realize I haven't written her at all. I know if she were in my shoes, I would have gotten at least a dozen letters from her. I choose a simple pale green dress before sitting down at my desk to write Mara a letter.

I start writing, all the details spilling out. I'm hesitant to put down specifics about magic in case my letter is intercepted, but I speak as candidly as I can while giving Mara as much information as possible. I fill her in on my engagement to Bram, Kato's promotion to Ehren's Guard, and even a little about Alak. By the time I'm done, I've filled almost three full pages. With a smile of satisfaction, I dig through the desk looking for a seal of some sort, but I can't find one. I suspect that I could easily ring for Kara or another servant to assist me, but I decide to check with Alak first on the off chance he procured what I need when he wrote his letters last night.

The sitting room is dark and empty as I stroll through to Alak's door. I knock softly. There's no response. Assuming he's sleeping, I turn away, deciding I'll just sort through some more texts until he wakes up. I've only taken a few steps when his door creaks open behind me.

"Astra?" Alak's groggy voice calls out.

I turn around. Alak leans against his doorpost, wearing nothing but his linen pants, his hair sticking up everywhere. I'm not sure if it's a trick of the morning light, but Alak's scars look slightly more pronounced than usual. I wonder if he's been using his illusion magic to dim these scars as well.

"Sorry if I woke you. I was just wondering if you had a seal or anything to send a letter," I say, meeting his eyes.

"Are you sure you didn't just want to see me fresh out of bed, love?" Alak grins. "Because you don't have to make an excuse for that. You're welcome in my room any time, day or night."

I roll my eyes, ignoring the way my heart picks up a little speed at his words. "Do you have the supplies or not?"

"I do," he says, beckoning me into his room.

Inside his room, I find Felixe snuggled down in the blankets on Alak's unmade bed. He raises his head and greets me with a little yip before curling back up and closing his eyes. I sit down on the bed next to him, scratching him between his ears as Alak closes the door.

"Sorry if I woke you up, too," I whisper.

"You really do just keep me around for Felixe, don't you?" Alak accuses, crossing his arms.

I grin up at him. "You figured it out."

He shakes his head at me in mock disappointment. "I guess it's a good thing he's my familiar, or you'd probably just kick me out and keep him. But as it is, if you want Felixe, you have to keep me around, too."

"Pity," I tease, rising from the bed and making my way over to the desk. The letter materials are on top. I scoop them up and seal my letter. Once I'm done, I turn to Alak.

"Thank you. I'll let you get back to sleep."

"Naw, you're good. Once I'm awake, I'm up for the day. No fighting it. How about we ring for some breakfast? Then we can finish looking over those texts out there and take them back to the library," Alak suggests.

"All right. That sounds good. I'm almost done reading all the prophecies involving me and Kato, and I'm ready to move on to something less depressing."

"They can't be all bad."

"You would think," I mutter. "But even the ones that praise us and talk about how we're going to be the salvation of a nation just pile unwanted expectations on me."

Alak offers me a weak smile. "You are extraordinarily powerful. It may seem like a demand you can't fulfill, but you do have the power to do it."

I sigh. "It's just that Fate has already decided my destiny, and the more I read about it, the more I feel I have no choice. I can either save the world or destroy it."

"See, love, that's the thing about Fate. She doesn't really get to decide every little thing. You still get to make your own choices. It's your choices that decide the path that Fate takes, not Fate that forces you to take your path," Alak says, waving his hand.

"I don't think that's how it works. Otherwise, what would be the purpose of all those prophecies?"

"Those prophecies are just possibilities. Maybe that's why they're all so different. You haven't chosen your path yet, so your future isn't set. The decisions *you* make mold your future, not some random words written by strangers hundreds of years ago," Alak argues.

"Those words aren't just written by strangers. They're written by Seers, people who actually had visions of what is going to happen—people who have spoken with the gods. And while some of these things haven't happened yet, some obviously have. Like me being born a twin with this power. I had no choice in that."

"Okay, sure," Alak concedes with a shrug. "Maybe you had no choice in being born, but other people made choices up to that point. Your parents made a choice to get together and have a child. Yes, perhaps Fate intervened and made sure that it was you and Kato that were born as twins, and maybe it was Fate that gave you your power, but that does not mean Fate gets to decide every move you make for the rest of your life. Just because she set you on a road doesn't mean you have to travel down it. If you don't want to be the savior of the world, then, by all means, change your name, your appearance, everything about yourself, and go live on your own where no one will ever find you. You want to overthrow the world? Do that. But whatever you do, do it because it's what you want to do, because it's what you feel is right, not because some bloody prophecy decided it for you."

Alak speaks with such earnestness, I stop and truly consider his words. His eyes lock with mine, and I can feel his fervor.

"Let me give you an example," he says. "Let's say you stumble across a prophecy that says you're meant to be with an extraordinarily handsome red-head from the Athiedor region. That you're meant to marry him and combine your power." He waggles his eyebrows and I roll my eyes, fighting a smile. "Would you just throw in the towel and break off your engagement with Bram? Just because a prophecy says it was supposed to be?" I remain silent, weighing his words. "Likewise, if another prophecy says your marriage to Bram would surely bring about destruction, would you call it off for no other reason?"

I shake my head. "I guess I see your point. But I still think some of those prophecies hold water. There's just too many to ignore them all."

Alak nods. "I suppose. But don't let them weigh you down, love. Just because they may be right in some aspects doesn't mean you have to base a single decision on any of them."

I release a long breath and smile. "Thanks, Alak. Believe it or not that actually helps a bit."

Alak gives me a smug smile. "Anytime you need some words of wisdom, you just come to me, love."

I laugh. Alak opens his bedroom door and saunters out into the sitting room with me a couple steps behind. The room is filled with a beautiful golden light from the rising sun. While I was in Alak's room, some servants came, leaving behind a tray of breakfast pastries and a steaming pot of tea on the small table Ehren sent up last night after dinner. Kato stands next to the tray, dressed sharply in his Guard uniform. As Alak and I approach the table, Kato's eyes narrow at Alak and his jaw locks.

"No, mate! It wasn't like that!" Alak says quickly, holding his hands up in a defensive position.

I'm confused for a moment before I realize what it must look like. After all, it's barely dawn and I'm coming out of Alak's room. It would probably look better if Alak had bothered to put on a shirt.

"I needed supplies for my letter," I say, holding up my sealed letter and offering Kato a weak smile.

"You needed letter supplies before dawn from Alak?" Kato asks sternly, arching an eyebrow.

"Yes. I woke up this morning and couldn't get back to sleep, so I wrote a letter to Mara. I didn't have everything I needed, but I figured Alak probably did since he was writing letters last night," I explain in one breath. "Come on, Kato. What else would I be doing in there? It's Alak."

Alak narrows his eyes at me. "I feel like I should be offended by that."

"Fine," Kato concedes, but shifts his gaze to Alak. "You could at least put on a shirt."

"I could, mate," Alak says, strolling up to the plate of pastries and plucking up a sweet bun covered in sugar. "But if I did, I wouldn't be me."

Kato sighs, shaking his head. "You two stick together today. I'm off to train with the Guard and whatever else Bram and Ehren need me to do. As agreed on yesterday, other members of Ehren's Guard will be with you throughout the day. Don't go anywhere without them." Kato looks at me firmly with his last statement. "If you need me, just contact me."

"I will," I promise.

"I mean it, Ash. I'll stop whatever I'm doing and be there in seconds."

"Kato, when have I ever needed you and not reached out?" I demand, crossing my arms.

Kato arches an eyebrow as he answers, "Yesterday, when the king's Guard dragged you into the throne room comes to mind."

I grimace. "I wasn't in danger. Not really. Had you not been dragged in moments after me, I would have reached out to let you know."

"It only would have taken moments for the king to have had your head," Kato says fiercely.

"And how would it have looked if my brother suddenly knows about me being brought before the king, despite being in a completely different part of the castle? You don't think the king would have found that the least bit suspicious? Oh, and by the way, I don't recall you reaching out to me when you were dragged before the king. The bond works both ways, brother."

Guilt flashes across Kato's face. "Fine. You're right. I promise to keep you updated as well."

I glance over at Alak, who has been standing there, stuffing his face while watching in amusement as Kato and I go back and forth.

"Don't let me get between you two," Alak says, eyes sparkling as he reaches for another pastry. "I haven't been this entertained in weeks."

Kato just shakes his head. "I'm done with my lecture. I'll see you both later."

"Wait," I call out as he turns to leave. "Can you take and post my letter as well as Alak's? The sooner we get them out, the better."

"Fine. Give them here," Kato replies, holding out his hand. I place my letter to Mara in his palm while Alak fetches his letters. Once he has the letters, Kato gives a parting nod to Alak before leaving.

Once we're alone, Alak eyes me expectantly.

"What?" I demand, examining the pastries and selecting a cinnamon bun covered in icing.

"I'm just waiting to see if you'll explain that whole conversation, or if I have to ask," Alak says. When I don't answer and instead take a bite of my cinnamon roll, he throws up his hands. "Fine. I'll ask. How is it that you could have told Kato you were being taken and vice versa?"

By the way his eyes are glittering, I suspect he already knows the answer. "Why does it matter?"

"Why does it matter?" he laughs. "It matters because if you two can do what I suspect, it's a very rare talent."

"And what is it you think we can do?" I ask, purposefully avoiding his eyes as I pour a cup of tea.

"You can communicate without speaking and across distances, can't you?"

I take a deep breath, releasing it slowly. "Yes. We can."

Alak pumps his fist in the air, grinning victoriously. "I knew it! How long have you been able to do it? Just since magic returned or before?"

"Since always," I admit.

I've surprised Alak with this bit of information, and I find some small satisfaction in that. I take a sip of my tea, but it's too hot, making me jerk back.

"You know, you can use your magic to fix that," Alak comments, nodding to the cup. "Controlling temperatures is an excellent way to release your magic in a non-obvious way and keep it from building up. Just barely tap into your magic and control it."

I look down at the cup of steaming tea and focus for a second before taking another tentative sip. It's the perfect temperature. I smile.

"See, not all magic has to be big." Alak smiles, pouring his own cup and changing the temperature to his tea as well. "That's a good cuppa." He looks up at me. "Does your captain know?"

"That the tea is good? Most likely."

Alak rolls his eyes. "No, that you can talk to Kato mind to mind." I nod. "Well, that explains why he and the prince would be willing to let you out of their sight. If either of you are in trouble, it only takes a second for you to communicate. In the meantime, it makes you look more relaxed in front of the king, like you really have no reason to be worried."

I shrug. "I suppose. Though we still can't go anywhere without guards, apparently."

Alak waves his hand. "Eh, what's a guard or two?"

"I suppose they'll be along soon. You should probably go get dressed."

"You finding me hard to resist?" Alak teases with a roguish grin.

"Hardly. We'll just need to leave shortly after they arrive, and I think that Ehren will happily kill you for parading around in front of his sister without a shirt on. Kato was close enough to killing you this morning."

"Indeed. I suppose you have a point," Alak concedes, rising. "I'll go make myself presentable."

After he disappears into his room, I enjoy a berry tart while I finish my cup of tea. I'm sorting the papers when there's a sharp knock on my door. My heart quickens as I cross the room and crack the door open just enough to peer out into the hall to see two of Ehren's Guard. I open the door a bit wider. I vaguely recognize them as the guards that were stationed outside Ehren's door in Timberborn. One has dark brown skin and eyes, with hair that's so short his head is nearly shaved completely. The other has naturally tanned skin with short, curly blond hair and bright hazel eyes.

"Good morning, Ma'am," the latter says, grinning. "My name is Makin Pareli and this is Callon Browen. Captain Bramfield assigned us to you and your friend for the foreseeable future."

I hide a smile. "Yes, he said he might do that. Please, come in," I say, motioning them inside.

"I could have introduced myself," the other mutters as they slide past me into the room. "I'm more than capable."

"Then do it next time," Makin replies.

"Would you prefer I call you by first or last names?"

"Whichever suits you," Callon says quickly, then adds, "but I'd be perfectly happy if you're content to call me Cal."

"And you can call me Makin, ma'am," Makin says with a nod.

"Well, please call me Astra. I don't think anyone has ever called me ma'am in my life, and I find that I don't really care for it," I say, wrinkling my nose in feigned disgust. Both men grin.

"We can do that," Makin grins.

"Alak should be out in a moment. We have plans to visit Princess Cadewynn in the library once he's ready. While we wait, please help yourself to any of these pastries. I think the kitchen must think we're feeding an army in this room each day."

"We're fine. Thank you," Cal says, bowing his head.

"Speak for yourself," Makin grumbles. "I'll never turn down food."

I hide my smile and return to sorting papers while Makin grabs some pastries. After eyeing him for a moment, Cal hesitantly joins him.

"I take too long to get dressed and you've gone and found two men to replace me," Alak bemoans, marching back into the room.

"I can't help that you're easily replaced."

"Oh! That cuts deep, love," he replies, dramatically throwing his hand over his heart.

"Meet Cal and Makin," I say, gesturing to each in turn. "They're our new escorts."

Alak surveys the guards and they size him up in turn. I can't help but roll my eyes.

"Alak, can you please help gather the materials we no longer need?"

"Aye," he says, breaking eye contact with our guards. "I suppose we can take a good bit of this back."

We spend a few minutes sorting through everything. In the end, we're taking back nearly a third of the materials.

"Are you sure you want to take back all these prophecies?" Alak asks as we gather the items in our arms. "Maybe there's something you missed that might help."

"No," I reply, meeting his eyes and smiling. "No point in studying things that will only drive me mad. Besides, someone convinced me to ignore what Fate thinks and just make my own decisions."

His lips part and his eyes shine. "Brilliant person that was."

"Eh," I reply with a shrug. "He has his moments." Alak grins.

We make our way through the castle under the guidance of Cal and Makin. When we enter the library, Madam Linwood eyes the books in our arms.

"I suppose you need those returned to their shelves?" she asks, staring us down through her spectacles.

"If you don't mind," I reply, inclining my head.

She huffs. "It is my job, you know. Just set them there." She makes a sharp motion to the desk behind her. She looks at the guards accompanying us today and her eyes narrow. "I expect everyone to be quiet and respect the library."

Cal and Makin nod quickly. She gives a little sniff and mutters something under her breath about her library becoming a party zone. Cal and Makin exchange curious looks as I lead the way back to the alcove where I found Princess Cadewynn yesterday. When we walk in, her head bobs up from her book.

"Oh! I'm so glad you came back today! I was a little concerned that you wouldn't be able to after what my father did yesterday." Her eyes slide to the guards behind us. "Ah. I see my brother is adding his protection." She offers Cal and Makin a smile.

"Yes, he thought it might be best," I reply with a nod.

"They helped us carry back some of the things you brought us last night. We left them with Madame Linwood."

Cadewynn's eyes brighten. "Did you find anything useful?" Her eyes flit from me to Alak.

"Interesting how that bit of Yallik made it into your selections." Alak grins.

"Were you able to translate it?" she asks eagerly. When Alak nods she claps her hands. "I knew you would be able to! Was it what I thought? I don't know much of the language myself, but I was almost sure it mentioned magic."

"Do you have more? If you do, I would be more than happy to translate," Alak offers.

Cadewynn grins in a way that makes me think Alak may regret making that offer.

"There are a lot of records and such from that region. Not everything would be important, but there are some other entries that may be helpful. I can show them to you."

Cadewynn leads Alak to an area with scrolls and papers from Athiedor, Cal going with them. I go to gather multiple genealogies to locate magical families, Makin tagging along. When I return to the alcove, Alak and Cadewynn have already returned. Cal leans against the alcove entryway.

"It will be far too crowded with you in here," Cadewynn addresses Cal and Makin. "Feel free to sit in the hall and play cards if you wish."

Makin grins. "Well, if you insist."

Cal rolls his eyes but follows Makin out into the hall, pulling a deck of cards from his coat pocket. Once the room is less crowded, we dive in. Cadewynn and I scour record after record of family trees, comparing more modern trees to those of magical families from the same towns. We decide to focus on those nearest Embervein in the hopes that we can find allies and magic users sooner rather than later. Alak bends over stacks of papers and works tirelessly. After a few hours, Cadewynn and I have scribbled a few names down on paper, and Alak has found a couple brief mentions of magic, albeit nothing terribly specific. We decide to take a short lunch break in the garden again, and this time Alak joins us.

CHAPTER TWENTY-EIGHT

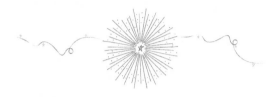

*T*he servants lay out another great spread for lunch, which thrills Makin. I half expect Bram and Ehren to show up again, but they don't. Neither, thankfully, do any of the king's Guard. Lunch is over far too quickly, and we're back in the library. Cal and Makin seem bored, and I can't help but pity them.

"I'm sorry you're stuck guarding us all day. It can't be any fun," I apologize as Makin follows me to return some books and grab new ones.

"I've been through worse," Makin replies with a smile.

"Still, I know it's dreadfully boring."

"You're not that much less interesting than following Ehren around all day," Makin offers. "And you're infinitely better to look at."

I laugh and Makin grins. He insists on carrying the books back for me. When we renter the alcove Alak swears.

"What is it?" I ask, rushing to his side to see what he's found.

Alak throws his hands up. "Nothing! Again! It's just pages

and pages of nothing." He props his head up on his hand, his face in his palm. He drags his hand down his face with a growl and looks up at me. "Sorry. I just . . . I've got a bit of a headache. I'm not used to being this inactive."

Cadewynn smiles at him sympathetically. "Sitting in a library definitely isn't for everyone. Perhaps there's another task with which I could help you?"

Alak considers her question, but I'm the one who answers. "Do you know of a place within the castle where we can practice our magic away from the prying eyes of your father?"

"Yes, I do!" Cadewynn says, glowing.

Alak instantly perks up. "Where?"

"Beneath the library, actually."

"There aren't any books or anything stored down there? Because magic can be unpredictable at times," Alak clarifies.

Cadewynn shakes her head. "It's mostly a large empty room. I have no idea what it was used for. To be honest, I haven't been down there much. It's very dark and dreary."

"Can you show us?" I ask, exchanging an eager look with Alak.

"Of course!" Cadewynn hops up from her seat. "Follow me!"

Cadewynn winds through the library, leading us to a back corner room filled with journals and records. She goes to the far right wall that holds two candelabras. She turns the left one a quarter turn to the left and the one on the right a quarter turn to the right. A portion of the wall shifts out. She places her fingers on the edge and gives it a yank, revealing a dark passageway. She turns to us, grinning.

"Holy shite," Alak mutters peering down the dark winding stairs just inside the door.

I glance around and make sure no one's watching before I

summon a small orb of light in my hand. Cadewynn gasps, her eyes going wide with surprise and delight.

"Shall we?" I grin, taking a step into the stairwell.

The others follow. Cal enters the stairwell last, pulling the door mostly closed behind him, leaving it open a crack so we won't be trapped. The stairs wind down a story or two before finally coming to an end in a wide, open room. I push my orb into the center and make it grow until the silver light illuminates the entire area. The room is made of simple stone walls with a stone ceiling held up by stone columns. Off the main room are a couple small alcoves that a quick inspection proves are just as empty as the room.

"Well," Cadewynn asks, her voice echoing, "will it do?"

Alak grins and strikes a stance, rolling his neck. He reaches out his hands and stretches his fingers. Sparks shoot from his fingertips, small at first, but they grow as he tosses them in the air like fireworks. Cadewynn gasps and claps her hands. Cal takes several steps back, and Makin swears under his breath. Alak looks at me and our eyes meet. I can feel a surge of magic within me. I walk over and join him, lifting my palms, silver butterflies rising and filling the room. Cadewynn stares around in wide-eyed wonder.

Alak looks at me, his eyes wild with magic. "Try wisping," he encourages. "There's plenty of room."

Nodding, I focus on a spot across the room and take a deep breath. Alak wisps across the room. I can feel his magic, but when I try to follow, I can't. After several attempts, I hear Cadewynn gasp.

"You flickered," Alak explains when I shoot Cadewynn a puzzled look.

"I flickered?"

"Aye. You faded in and out for a second. I thought you had it."

I smile and am about to try again when a slightly panicked voice rings through my head.

Astra, where are you?

I'm in a room beneath the library. Is everything okay?

Yes. Bram, Ehren, and I came to check on you but couldn't find you. Where is this room?

It's hidden. There's a passage with a secret door in one of the record rooms. Where are you?

Near the alcoves.

Find the alcove where we were studying. There are books and papers spread all over. I'll send someone up to guide you down here.

All right. See you soon.

I turn to Cal and Makin. "Would either of you be able to navigate through the library back to where we were and show my brother how to get down here?"

The two guards exchange a quick look.

"I could try," Cal offers with a shrug. "Though I'm not that familiar with the library's layout."

"I can go with him," Cadewynn pipes up.

"Are you sure?" I ask and Cadewynn nods.

"We'll be right back."

Cadewynn and Cal disappear up the stairs, and I go back to my attempts at wisping.

"Focus," Alak says. "You can do this. You're so close. I can literally feel your magic trying. Don't try to force your magic. Let it lead you."

I close my eyes and focus. I gather my magic and envision the movement. Dizziness and nausea overwhelm me. I hear Makin swear and suddenly I'm off balance, falling, stumbling. I hiss as my ankle twists underneath me, and I fall hard against someone's arms. I open my eyes to see Alak's face inches from mine, his eyes glowing.

"You did it," he whispers.

I look around and realize I wisped all the way across the room, losing my balance somewhere along the way. When I started to fall, Alak caught me. Grinning, I pull away from Alak, but a sharp pain shoots through my ankle. I lean on Alak for support to keep from tumbling to the ground. He loops his arm around my waist to steady me.

"You okay, love?" he asks with genuine concern.

"Yeah, I just—"

"What are you doing?" Bram's voice cuts across the room and Alak's attention jerks away from me, his grip tightening slightly as Bram strides into the room followed closely by Kato.

"I wisped across the room but lost my balance. Alak caught me," I say, eyes twinkling.

"You wisped?" Kato asks eagerly.

I nod with a proud grin. "But I twisted my ankle a bit, I think."

Bram reaches toward me, and Alak practically throws me into his arms, backing away quickly.

"What are you doing down here?" Ehren asks from where he stands at the bottom of the stairs. He looks around, eyes tracing the edges of the room. "And where the hell are we?"

"We thought it would be a good place to practice magic inside the castle without the king knowing," I reply.

Ehren nods, stepping further into the room, still looking around.

"It's not a bad plan. I don't think my father knows about this place. And even if he did, I doubt he would suspect we know about it." His eyes settle on me and he adds, "Just be wary."

"I don't like that there appears to be only one way in or out," Bram mumbles, his eyes scanning for another exit.

"Technically," Alak cuts in, holding up his finger, "if they can both learn to wisp, we can leave at will. In fact, we can even come down here without opening the door above, leaving no indication we're down here."

"Well, I know my goal now," Kato says, licking his lips and rubbing his palms together. "How did you do it?"

"I followed Alak's advice and let the magic do the work. I stopped trying to force it, and it just worked," I reply with a small shrug.

"Okay. Okay. I can do that," Kato mumbles. He closes his eyes for several moments, and opens them again, swearing when he discovers he hasn't moved.

"Let your magic guide you," Alak says. "Just ask it to do what you want and let it work."

Alak demonstrates, popping up next to Kato, then back to the other end of the room. "Follow my magic. Can you sense it?"

Kato scowls. "I think so."

He tries again. I see him flicker slightly a couple times before he finally disappears and reappears next to Alak. He stumbles slightly but catches himself. He spins and finds me, grinning wildly.

"Did you see that?" he cries. "I did it!"

I return his grin. "Now we just need to hone our skill."

"That's all wonderful, but it might be best we not stay down here much longer," Bram suggests. "If anyone were to look for any of us, it could make things difficult. We wouldn't want them to start searching and find this area."

"True," Ehren says with a nod. "We were just coming to see if you had found anything."

"We've found a couple family lines in nearby villages that go back to magical roots," Cadewynn answers. "The list is up in the alcove."

"We probably should go back up," I add. I glance over at

Kato and Alak. "We can come back down here later, after dinner perhaps."

"Fine," Kato says, but I can tell he's disappointed.

"Can you get up the stairs with your ankle?" Bram asks gently and I nod.

"It's just a little sore. If you help me, I should be fine."

Bram looks over at Alak. "I don't suppose you have any healing magic?"

Alak shakes his head. "Negative, mate. Wish I did."

"I'll be fine," I insist. "I'll just rest for a bit and it will heal itself. Besides, I still have the ointments and salves from Healer Heora up in my room. I'm sure there's something in there that will prove useful."

I call my orb of light, shrinking it to a manageable size to light our way up the stairs. Despite my reassurances that I can make it on my own, it's actually more difficult than I anticipated. The narrow stairwell makes it hard for Bram to support me, and I end up mostly hopping up the stairs. We spill into the small room, relieved to find it undiscovered. Cadewynn leads everyone back to the alcove and fetches the list of names we compiled.

"I'm sure we'll be able to find more, but it's a tedious process," Cadewynn says as Ehren studies the names.

"Well, this gives us a good starting point. Most of these people we can reach in less than a day's travel. At least two of these families are listed as being here in Embervein," Ehren muses, handing the list to Bram. "We should be able to check with the Embervein families this evening and set out in the morning for some of the others, don't you think?"

Bram glances toward me, and I can tell he doesn't want to leave me. Ehren catches the look as well.

"Of course, anyone is welcome to join us, but the smaller the party the faster we can travel," Ehren adds.

"I'll be more than fine here," I interject. "I'll just stay out of the way." Bram glances quickly at Alak, and I shake my head. "I thought we covered that."

"Sorry," Bram mumbles. "Old habits die hard."

Ehren exchanges curious looks with Cal and Makin, but none of them dare to say anything.

"Winnie," Ehren says, addressing his sister, "I almost forgot. We actually had another reason we were seeking you out. Father has requested our presence tonight at a formal dinner."

"Oh, gods," Cadewynn sighs. "Let me guess, several nobles' sons will be in attendance? All of them single and more than happy to wed a princess?"

"It's more than likely."

Cadewynn tilts her head back and looks up at the ceiling. "Some days I truly hate being a princess."

Ehren attempts to hide a smile. "Try being a crown prince, set to inherit the throne."

Cadewynn shoots him a look of disbelief. "Right. When you tire of all the most beautiful girls in the kingdom throwing themselves at you everywhere you go, let me know."

"Not all of them are beautiful," Ehren replies, faking a grimace and shiver.

Cadewynn throws a small book at Ehren and he dodges, laughing. Makin also chuckles and Cal rolls his eyes.

"You're a pig!" Cadewynn laughs.

Ehren's expression sobers. "But you know, eventually, Father will more than likely force me to take a bride of his choosing whenever he finds a situation that suits his needs. Even if I decide a bride isn't what I want."

Ehren glances briefly toward his Guards as Cadewynn nods sympathetically and whispers, "I know."

I shift and accidentally put pressure on my hurt ankle. I hiss and jerk my foot back up. Bram scowls.

"We need to get you up to your room so you can rest your foot," Bram insists and my ankle hurts too much to argue.

"Fine, but can you help me take some of these things up to my room to study further?" I request.

"Of course," Bram answers. A quick nod to Cal and Makin has them stepping forward to grab whatever I require. I direct them to the materials I need, and even Kato steps in to help. Alak gathers his own papers. After a few minutes, we have everything collected. I try to limp away on my own, but after several sharp pangs, I finally surrender to allowing Bram to carry me the rest of the way.

"Just set me on that couch," I say when we enter our room. "The one by the balcony."

"Are you sure you wouldn't rather your bed?" Bram asks.

"No, I'm not an invalid. I just have a sore ankle. I'll be fine on the couch. It will be easier to study out here. I just need the pouch of ointments from my bag," I insist and Bram complies, helping me get situated on the couch.

"I'll get the medicines," Kato offers, ducking into my room.

Bram kneels on the floor next to me. "I'll have to accompany Ehren to his dinner tonight, but I will come by after if that is acceptable."

"That sounds more than acceptable," I smile.

Kato returns with the pouch. I dig through and find a small jar of salve marked for sprains and quickly apply it. Relief is almost instant.

"It feels better already," I assure Bram, making him relax.

He leans forward and kisses me gently, brushing hair from my face. "Rest. I will see you later."

He stands and looks over to where Cal and Makin stand by

the table. "You two, stay here and stand guard outside the door."

"Oh, please don't make them stand outside. They can stay in the room," I protest.

Bram glances at me. "Are you sure?"

"If you'd rather me stay in the room alone with Alak . . ."

Bram's eyes flash and I duck my head to hide my smile.

"Excellent point." He turns back to Cal and Makin. "You are not to leave this room until one of us returns."

Cal and Makin exchange a quick look but agree.

"We really should get going if we're going to find these families before we have to be back for my father's dinner," Ehren says, waving the paper.

Bram nods. "Indeed. We will see you all later."

A few moments later, Bram, Kato, and Ehren are gone. Cal and Makin settle in a pair of chairs and start up a game of cards while Alak pours over the things he brought, cursing under his breath at regular intervals. The extensive family trees are far too large for me to read while lounging on the couch, so I opt to read through scrolls of magical instruction. Most are simple records of magic performed and the effects of the magic, but occasionally I stumble across step-by-step instructions on harnessing and using magic.

"Why would you use twenty words when five would do?" Alak yells in frustration, throwing a scroll. I glance over at him, eyebrows raised. He looses a breath. "Sorry."

"Sounds like you need a break," I reply.

"I just don't understand why these record keepers feel the need to blather on for pages and pages about trivial things," Alak growls, gesturing in frustration. "And with all that blathering they *still* manage to withhold just enough information, so I can't even pinpoint the specific villages they're talking about."

"So you've found more information about magical regions?" I perk up.

"Aye, I have. There are several references to sister cities, which, given the context, I assume refer to other magical cities," Alak says, shifting through pages of records as he speaks. "So far I haven't been able to find any names or specific locations." He tosses a paper back onto the table and leans back in his chair.

"Why don't you come over here and look at these records for a bit? I think you'll find them more useful."

I start to shift into more of a sitting position, but Alak motions me to stop. "You're fine."

He sits on the floor in front of me and leans his back against the center of the couch. I hand him one of the pages I've already read.

"This is much more pleasant," he muses after a moment. "Thank you, love."

We sit for several more minutes, studying the magical texts, before there's a knock on the door.

"Dinner!" a voice calls and Makin bounds across the room, throwing the door open.

A servant with a large tray bearing four large, steaming meat pies and a loaf of bread strides into the room. A second servant follows behind with a pitcher of mead.

"Is there anything else you need?" the first servant asks, placing his tray on the spare table.

"I think that should be all," I reply. They bow and leave.

Alak rises from his seat on the floor and offers me his hand. I take it and rise slowly, testing my ankle before I put my full weight on it. It's still sore and sensitive, but no longer sends shooting pain up my leg.

"Are you good?" Alak asks, releasing my hand.

I nod and walk to the table with only a slight limp. Cal offers me a meat pie, and I accept with a smile.

"Do you always get to eat food this good?" I ask.

"More or less," Makin replies. "It's an advantage of being one of Prince Ehren's Guard. On typical banquet nights, when we all gather in the great hall for dinner, we get to be seated at one of the better tables."

"And even when we aren't eating with everyone, we still get plenty of good food, even when we're on the road," Cal adds. "Ehren has always been kind and generous."

"It's good to know that Ehren treats you well. How did you become members of his Guard? Have you always been soldiers for Embervein?" I ask, taking a large bite of my pie.

"I have," Cal answers. "I was born in the city and worked my way up through the soldiers. I know both the prince and captain well, having been near their age. When Ehren formed his Guard and made Bram captain, I was asked to become part of his original Guard. I accepted without hesitation."

"Are you from Embervein as well?" I ask Makin. He shakes his head.

"Nope. I'm from a small village to the northeast, about a two-day ride. When I heard the prince was forming a Guard, I saved everything I had to come and volunteer my services." Makin grins. "Of course, it wasn't easy. I had to prove myself just to make it into the basic rank of soldiers, and then I had to complete the testing to even be considered for the Guard. Once I did, I had to verify my loyalty to Prince Ehren and show I could get along with the rest of the Guard. I was fortunate enough to finally be accepted." He glances over at Cal and grins. "Thankfully, I made a friend who helped pave the way." Cal looks down, a slight hint of red tinging the tips of his ears. "I'm one of the few of the Guard that was neither born in Embervein nor trained side by side with the captain and prince." Makin pauses and looks at me evenly. "Much like your brother."

I feel a wave of guilt. "I suppose having some random soldier from a small, no-name village sweep in and be handed a Guard position was unwelcome."

Makin avoids my gaze while Cal looks at me directly, carefully weighing his next words. "It was . . . unusual and unexpected. There's no doubt about that. But your brother's skill is unmatched. The only man I've ever seen with his level of skill is Bram, and, even then, I suspect your brother could overtake him if he ever felt the need. That level of skill is rare, and Ehren would have been a fool not to want him by his side."

"But, like you said, it's not just skill, is it? It's loyalty," I add.

"Loyalty goes more than one way," Makin counters. "We were in Timberborn. We witnessed what happened firsthand. The prince and our captain are as loyal to you as you and your brother are to them. Those types of life and death situations breed loyalty quickly."

"It is an honor to serve with your brother," Cal adds. "It is also an honor to know you as well, and we will happily serve you as both a friend of the prince and future bride of the captain." He tips his goblet of mead toward me in a toast, Makin doing the same.

I offer them a small smile. "Thank you. I appreciate that. I really do."

CHAPTER TWENTY-NINE

I'm fast asleep in my bed when I'm woken by a gentle kiss on my cheek. I sit up quickly and almost smash my head against Bram. He laughs as I smile.

"You're back," I whisper.

He leans in and kisses my lips.

"Yes, I'm back. I'm sorry it took so long," Bram says, sitting down on the edge of my bed. "I probably should have waited until morning to come see you, but I couldn't wait. It's been a long three days."

"I'm glad you woke me. I've missed you so much." I lean forward and kiss him again. "Tell me how your trip went. Unless, of course, you're wanting to get to sleep. I'm sure you're exhausted from your travels."

"I am quite exhausted, but I'm not ready to leave you quite yet," Bram confesses.

"Well, then, come here and lie down next to me," I say, patting the empty space of bed to my right. Bram raises his eyebrows and glances hesitantly to the bed. I'm afraid he's going to turn me down, but he eases onto my bed, sighing as he leans back on the spare pillows. I snuggle down next to him, resting my head on his chest, and he wraps his arm around me, pulling me closer.

"So," I murmur, "tell me all about your trip."

"It went well. Of the three names you and Cadewynn found for us, we were able to locate two," Bram says, stroking my hair. "It took a bit to gain their trust, but once we did we got some good information. One of the families had three members showing magical inclinations—two in one family and one of their cousins. The other didn't have direct family members but knew of others in the village. Most of the magic we encountered wasn't magic as clear and obvious as yours, but rather skills just unusual enough to have to be magic."

"Well, it's good to know all that tedious work I'm doing with Winnie is worth something," I mutter.

"It's not that bad, is it?" Bram asks. I can hear the exhaustion creeping into his voice.

"No, not really, but it is nice to mix up all the studying with magic."

"And how are your magic lessons with Alak going?"

Bram's voice is strained. Even though he's made his peace with me being around Alak all the time, he still doesn't like it.

"I'm learning a lot about my powers and it's becoming easier and easier to do what I want with them. I can even wisp into the room without Alak's help."

I feel Bram tense. I tilt my head up and press my lips to Bram's. "I wish you could be down there with me."

"Maybe I'll come watch you sometime this week," Bram offers, kissing my nose. "Kato is chomping at the bit to practice his magic. I've given him the next couple of days off to focus on it."

"You're such a good captain," I grin.

Bram laughs. "Good? I'm the best."

His next kiss is more eager and filled with wanting. When he pulls back he sighs and starts to slide off my bed.

"You don't have to go," I say, reaching toward him.

"I wish that were so, but I'm afraid I really must go to my own bed." He stands at the foot of my bed and looks down at me. "I love you."

"I love you, too." With one last kiss, he's gone into the night, and I almost wonder if I've dreamed him.

When morning comes, I decide to ring for Kara and take a bath. She's more than eager to assist me with everything I need and even insists on helping me fix my hair and dress. When I finally exit my room, I find Alak, completely dressed for once, idling in a chair, his feet propped up on a stool. He has a half-eaten apple in one hand and a small book in the other. Felixe is curled up in a nearby chair.

"My, my. The good captain must be back today for you to be looking so prim and polished," Alak says with a low whistle.

I roll my eyes and examine today's tray of pastries. It's almost identical as past mornings. I sigh.

"Do you not like what the breakfast fairies brought you this morning, love?"

"It's all lovely, but I think I'm just tired of sweet buns and pastries. I miss eggs, to be honest," I reply, picking up a danish before setting it back down and selecting a plum from a bowl of fruit.

"I'm sure all it would take is one word from you, and we could have an entire breakfast buffet in two minutes flat," Alak replies, mouth full of apple. "On second thought, you should definitely try that. I could go for some sausages and breakfast potatoes."

Kato's door opens and he strides out into the room. It's almost odd to see him in normal, casual clothes. Alak looks up from his book.

"Hey! That's right! Someone does stay in that room!" He grins. "Welcome back, Kato."

"Thanks."

I hug him as he approaches. He plucks a sweet bun off the tray and takes a huge bite.

"Kato still likes the breakfast fairy," Alak says, his attention going back to his book.

Kato arches an eyebrow. I shake my head, rolling my eyes.

"As usual, ignore Alak," I say, waving Alak off. "Tell me, how was your trip?"

Kato purses his lips. "Like you haven't already received the rundown."

I blush. "I don't know what you mean."

"I'm pretty sure you do."

"Well, how about you tell me," Alak cuts in, rising from his chair. "No one ever tells me anything."

"There's a reason for that," I mutter, but Kato obliges, giving Alak a brief recap of events.

"And, as thanks for my help, Bram has allowed me two days off to focus on my magic," Kato concludes.

"Oh dear. That means I won't be able to play translator to you and Cadewynn," Alak says in mock disappointment. "I just hate having to do magic all day." His eyes twinkle.

"Don't worry. We'll save everything for you for another day," I reply with a wry grin and Alak narrows his eyes at me. "We probably should get going, either way."

We open the door to find Cal and Makin standing guard on either side of the doorway.

"Morning!" Makin pipes up with a grin.

"Why didn't you two come inside?" I ask, furrowing my eyebrows.

Cal and Makin exchange a quick look.

"We, uh, heard Bram was back, and well . . . ," Cal begins awkwardly. Heat rising in my cheeks.

"We just wanted to make sure we were following proper protocol should he swing by," Makin finishes with a cough.

"Right," Alak says, drawing out the word.

"You are all insufferable," I mutter, pushing past them all and leading the way to the library. They don't need to know how close they all were to being correct.

When we get to the library, Alak and Kato split off and head directly to the hidden room, but I decide to start with Cadewynn to give Kato a little time to catch up. Cal and Makin join me. Cadewynn's eyes light up when we walk in.

"Oh! You're here! I was afraid you were going to be down in the room all morning."

"Kato's back and training with Alak a bit this morning, so I figured I would stay out of their way," I explain, taking a seat while Cal and Makin lean against the entryway.

Cadewynn's face falls slightly. "Oh. I found a new entry I wanted Alak to translate. I guess it can wait until later."

"I promised him we'd make a pile," I reply with a grin.

"Oh, good!" Cadewynn says, brightening back up.

We dive into reading. I focus the first couple of hours on family trees before switching to reading through magical texts. We take a quick break for lunch, and I reach out to Kato and let him know.

Alak says you can wisp food down to us? Kato responds.

Remind Alak how well that went last time I tried.

He says it's good practice and you should try.

I sigh. *Fine. We're leaving the library now. I'll try in a few minutes.*

Once we're seated at our usual spot in the garden, I place a few of today's sandwiches and some fruit on a plate. I glance around and make sure no one is watching, even though Cal and Makin position themselves in such a way the plate isn't really visible to potential passersby. I take a deep breath and concentrate my magic.

All right. Food coming your way.

I touch the plate, focusing on sending it. I'm almost surprised when the plate vanishes.

Did you get it?

More or less.

What exactly does that mean?

It arrived, just upside down. Still edible though. Want to try to send some mead?

Gods, no.

Kato doesn't argue and I get to enjoy my lunch in peace. Halfway through, some of the king's Guard wander through the garden. They eye us but don't approach. As we leave, a group of three young men stand between us and the door, blocking our path back inside. Judging by their high-quality clothes, haughty attitudes, and Cadewynn's groan I surmise they must be sons of noblemen. Two are obviously brothers, tall and thin with matching blond hair and hazel eyes, but the third has a darker complexion and broader shoulders.

"Good afternoon, Princess," the older of the brothers says, taking a step toward us.

"It was a good afternoon," Cadewynn replies, forcing a smile. "It will begin to be better once I am back inside."

"You don't have to hide away in that library all the time, you know," the young man persists.

"I do not have to, but I rather like it. Especially since people like you seldom bother me there, Landis," Cadewynn responds curtly. "Now, if you please, I would like to go back inside."

Cal and Makin take a step forward, but Landis doesn't move. His eyes study the guards for a moment before they fall on me.

"Are these gentlemen here for you, Princess, or for your guest?"

"Didn't you hear?" I ask, raising my eyebrows in feigned shock.

Landis scowls. "Hear what?"

"I just figured with you obviously being the sons of nobility you would have heard." Landis's scowl deepens as I turn to Cadewynn. "Do you think it's truly possible they haven't heard?"

"I do believe your assertion is correct!" Cadewynn replies, her eyes going wide.

"What haven't I heard?" Landis snaps.

I look him directly in the eyes. "Apparently, you haven't heard that it's none of your business."

Landis's face goes red, his eyes flashing. I hear a stifled laugh behind me, and Landis's eyes shoot to the guards behind me.

"Something amuse you, soldier?" Landis sneers.

"No, sir," Makin replies, standing straighter, his eyes shining and the corners of his lips turned up in a suppressed grin.

"That's what I thought," Landis replies haughtily, his companions snickering.

My blood boils and my power coils, ready to strike. It takes every ounce of control I possess not to let it free.

"Pity," Cadewynn says with a shrug. "I was amused."

Landis turns his attention back to Cadewynn, leering. "If you're that easily amused, Princess, I could definitely find plenty of ways to entertain you." His eyes shift to me. "I suspect I can entertain you both."

I look over my shoulder at Cal and Makin who stand on full alert, their hands on the hilts of their swords, amusement gone.

"How important is this buffoon?" I whisper loudly, making sure Landis can hear.

"How important am I? How are you at court and have no knowledge of who I am? I am the eldest son of Duke Gillingby," he answers proudly. "Who exactly are you?"

I sigh and roll my eyes, waltzing past him without answering, which infuriates him. He grabs my arm, jerking me back. Cadewynn spins to face him, eyes flashing.

"*You* are a son of a duke. *I* am the daughter of a king. *She* is my guest and a close friend of my brother. I suggest you keep your hands to yourself or you will lose them," she hisses with a level of authority I've never heard from her.

Landis jerks back, glowering as he releases me. "You may regret that, Princess."

"I will let you know if I care," Cadewynn replies sharply, spinning on her heel and marching into the castle.

I start to follow her but pause to turn and blow a kiss toward Landis before we disappear inside. Once we're safely out of hearing range Cal lets out a low whistle.

"You two enjoy playing with fire, don't you," he whispers, his voice tinged with admiration.

"I've known since I was a child I didn't play well with others," Cadewynn replies, tossing her hair over her shoulder. "I suppose I'll have to make nice at the ball this weekend."

"What ball?" I ask.

Cadewynn waves her hand. "Oh, some ball my father has decided to throw this weekend for no real reason. He does that every so often as a way to make himself seem more approachable and loved." A worried expression crosses her face. "You're coming, aren't you?"

I laugh. "How can I have plans to come when I only found out about it ten seconds ago? Besides, I have no idea how to dance well enough for a royal ball, and I don't have a dress."

"I can help you with both of those things. Oh, please come!" she begs. "I love the dancing and the food and the general merriment, but I could use some decent company. Please? I can guarantee Bram and Ehren will be there."

"I suppose," I concede and she throws her arms around me, hugging me tightly.

"Thank you! Thank you!"

When we walk through the library door, I head to the records room with the passage with Cal and Makin while Cadewynn heads to her alcove. When we reach the records room, I turn to the guards. I reach my hand out to Cal first and he takes it. A moment later we're on the stairs. Cal's face looks weary, but he nods his thanks and starts down the stairs while I wisp back and get Makin. This time we arrive at the bottom of the stairs.

I'm used to the room being filled with my glittering, silver light, but today it's lit by fire. Kato has lit every sconce along the wall with warm, flickering flames that cast shadows down the walls. Kato stands in the center of the room, beads of sweat on his forehead as he thrusts balls of fire toward a target either he or Alak made on the far wall. He strikes with perfect accuracy.

"Your lessons look very different from my lessons," I greet him, and he turns to me grinning.

"You mean you don't shoot balls of fire at a target? Your lessons sound boring," Kato teases, sauntering over.

"What else have you been doing?" I ask.

Kato shrugs. "A lot of this. Plus some defensive magic."

I eye the target. "Can I try? I could really go for attacking something right now."

Alak nods and motions for me to step up. I take my stance in the center of the room and take a deep breath. With a flick of my wrist I summon an orb of light and throw it. It shoots across the room and lands dead center. I follow it with orb after orb, taking a step back each time. Every single one lands in the center ring of the target, most dead center. When I reach the back wall, I turn to Kato and grin.

"Gods that felt good!"

"I will pay you every marke I own if you will do that to Landis's face," Makin offers, crossing his arms.

"Whose face did you think I was picturing at the center of that target?" I reply with a smirk.

"Wait a minute. Who the hell is Landis, and why are we wanting him dead?" Kato asks, scowling.

"He's one of the nobles and a complete asshole. Astra had the displeasure of meeting him," Makin answers for me.

"Makin, careful," Cal warns.

"What? Who's going to overhear me down here?" Makin snaps, motioning around.

"Landis has it out for Makin," Cal explains to my questioning glance.

"Why?"

Makin shrugs and glances off as he replies, "I may have kissed his sister."

"He may have carried on a secret affair with his sister is more like it," Cal counters. "If it weren't for his position on Ehren's Guard, the Duke would likely have had his head."

"It wasn't like it was against her will. She pursued me," Makin mumbles.

"Was she at least pretty?" Kato interjects.

Makin looks at him and grins. "Very."

"Boys!" I shout, rolling my eyes and throwing my hands in the air with exasperation. "I should go back upstairs with Cadewynn."

"Really, love?" Alak asks, making a face. "You'd rather go upstairs and read family trees than put up with us?"

I consider him for a moment. "I suppose not."

Alak grins. "I thought as much."

"Well then, all mighty magic guru, what magic do you want me to perform now?" I mock.

"Well, we could either work on your defenses, see if you can create solid objects, or try other random bits of magic," Alak lists, ticking each suggestion off on his fingers.

"What do you mean solid objects?" I ask, intrigued.

"Well, Kato and I have been focusing almost entirely on battle magic, but being able to shoot fireballs or ice cold balls of light may not work if you're in, let's say, a sword fight," Alak explains.

"So," Kato questions, his eyes flickering with interest, "you're saying I could potentially make a sword using my flame?"

Alak nods. "Yes, but it isn't as easy as just forming your flame into the shape of the sword." He holds out his hand and a dagger appears. "This looks like a real dagger." He throws it up into the air, catches it and throws it into the target where it sticks in the stone wall. He snaps his fingers and it reappears in his palm. "It looks real but it isn't." He flicks it at Kato who throws his hands up defensively, but the dagger just goes through them without harming him at all. "It's just an illusion." Kato swears.

"Likewise, you can make a sword out of light or flame, and, while it may look threatening, it doesn't make it a usable sword in battle. It can't strike another sword. It can't block another sword. It can do damage on its own, but it doesn't work as a sword. Understand?"

We nod and Alak continues. "Now, I can only create illusions. I haven't really mastered this, so you're on your own, but I think you're both in tune enough with your magic that you can handle it. You just need to focus."

I concentrate and manage to craft a silver dagger from light. Alak walks over and examines it.

"It looks good and believable, but does it work? Try throwing it at the target."

I obey and flick the dagger. A real dagger would hit the stone wall and bounce off, but mine goes through the wall and disappears. Kato summons his own fire dagger, but it does the same. For at least an hour we try with no success, so we switch to shields. It's the same concept, but I make it work after just a few tries. My magic seems more receptive somehow. I start by creating small shields against specific attacks and move on to creating shields to block my body.

I'm working on creating a bubble shield to protect me from all angles at once, when we hear the door at the top of the stairs creak open. We all go on alert—Cal and Makin with their hands on their swords, and Kato, Alak, and I poised, ready to attack with magic. We relax, however, as Bram and Ehren come into view.

"You all look like you're ready for a fight," Ehren laughs, stepping up next to Cal.

"I'm always ready for a fight," Kato grins.

Bram makes his way over to me and greets me with a kiss. "Have you been fighting?"

"More or less. Less actually fighting, more learning how to use magic in a fight," I explain.

"Is that necessary?" Bram asks, glancing from me to Kato.

"There's a king who would likely have our heads if he knew we had magic. I think having a fighting chance might be a good thing," Kato insists, arching an eyebrow.

"Surely you aren't planning a coup against my father?" Ehren says, an edge to his voice.

"No," Kato replies, creating a fire dagger and tossing it absentmindedly into the air. "My only desire is to help you protect magic. I do not care for your father, but I will not harm him. I swear it. I would be a fool not to train with all the weapons in my arsenal."

Ehren nods approvingly. "That's one thing that makes you a good soldier."

"So, did you come down here for a purpose or just to interrupt our training?" Alak says, crossing his arms, earning sharp glares from Ehren and Bram.

"Bram couldn't stand to be away from Astra any longer and was getting downright whiny," Ehren replies, wrinkling his nose with feigned disgust.

"I was not," Bram laughs. He looks down at me. "I did miss you, and I did want to see you, though."

"Okay, fine," Ehren concedes, holding up his hands. "We're hiding from my father. He was a bit suspicious when we disappeared for three days with no real explanation. Besides we also wanted to let you all know that there will be a grand ball in four days, and you're all invited."

"Cadewynn mentioned that to me earlier. She's promised to help me find a dress and learn the court dances."

"Leave it to my sister to spread news before me," Ehren sighs dramatically. "But I'm happy you'll be there."

"I can teach you the court dances," Bram offers, his eyes twinkling. "Unless of course you'd rather have Cadewynn teach you."

"I think you know the answer to that." I grin.

"Maybe Cadewynn can teach me," Kato suggests, glancing at Ehren. "That is if you're okay with that."

Ehren shrugs. "It's up to her."

"When would we start our dance lessons?" I ask.

"How about tonight after dinner?" Ehren suggests. "In the meantime, why don't you show us a bit of whatever attack magic you've managed. I would really love to avoid my father as long as possible."

"Fine, but I suggest closing the door," Alak says. "If the king is searching, better not let his search lead to such valuable information as a hidden room."

"I'll close it," I offer, wisping away.

I quickly close the door and return downstairs. I can tell Ehren and Bram aren't too terribly thrilled about being locked below, but neither say anything. Instead, they focus on Kato who has started throwing fire at the target, changing the size of his fireballs, even turning some into daggers. When I step up and do the same with my light, Ehren mutters something to Bram about never making either of us mad. For the next hour or so, we continue practicing our magic while the others watch. It feels a little odd, but their occasional gasps make it worth it. When Kato creates a flawless sword of flame, Ehren's eyes spark with interest.

"Can your sword work against mine?" Ehren asks, stepping forward as he unsheathes his sword, balancing it in his left hand. "Care to spar?"

"Is that a good idea?" Bram intercedes, rising from where he's been leaning against the wall. "A sword alone is dangerous enough but one made of fire—"

"Don't worry," Kato cuts him off with a wave. "I'll be extra cautious."

Bram still seems less than thrilled as Ehren steps into stance across from Kato. I step out of the way and take a spot next to Bram. The first few blows of Ehren's sword strike Kato's sword like any two metal swords, but the third strike goes through the fire. Kato pulls back and refocuses, and the two begin sparring again with renewed force. I can feel Bram tense beside me as a sweep of Kato's sword slices through Ehren's sword and nearly strikes Ehren.

"Don't worry," I whisper to Bram. "Kato may be excellent at weapons and attacking, but I'm quick and efficient with shields."

Bram relaxes slightly, but he doesn't fully relax until Kato steps back from Ehren, his fire sword gone.

"I think I need a touch more practice," Kato concedes. "It takes a lot of concentration to form the sword and twice as much to use it effectively. Plus, I think my magic is drained from practicing so much today."

"I'm more than impressed," Ehren says, sheathing his sword. "Master that skill and you'll be the most deadly force among my Guard."

"That was impressive," Bram adds. His eyes narrow at Alak. "Can you do that?"

"Not even almost," Alak laughs. "But your bride-to-be can." He gestures to me.

When Bram glances at me I shrug. "I can't do it as well as Kato."

I can feel all eyes on me as I hold out my palm and create a dagger. It looks exactly like the one Bram gave me, only made of silver light. I focus and the dagger slowly grows into the shape of a sword. I adjust the weight and feel of it in my hand. I give it flip. Next, I duplicate it, a hilt in each hand. I toss both swords into the air and they vanish.

"I don't know how well it works as an actual sword, though. I'm still working on that aspect," I confess.

Makin steps forward and grips Bram's shoulder. "If you don't marry her, I will."

Bram laughs. "Unluckily for you, I am marrying her." He wraps his arm around my waist and draws me into a kiss. "And I can't wait."

CHAPTER THIRTY

I stand at one end of the stone room, nervous butterflies rising in my stomach. Of all the things I've practiced in this room, dancing shouldn't be the most nerve racking, but, somehow, it is. I've created twinkling stars all around the ceiling, draping the room in peaceful, silver light. Bram and I enjoy a few moments alone while we wait on Kato to wisp in with Cadewynn.

"It looks perfect," Bram says in my ear as he wraps his arms around me.

I turn and face him, leaning back against his grasp as I link my hands behind his neck. "You think so?"

"I do," he says softly.

His lips meet mine, warm and comforting. All the nervous butterflies vanish, replaced by ones twirling with longing and excitement.

Kato clears his throat behind me, and I pull back sheepishly, glancing his way. Cadewynn stands beside Kato, grinning.

"You're here," I say with forced cheer.

"I am, so I think we should stop kissing and get to dancing," Kato says pointedly.

"I don't know, mate. Kissing is pretty good," Alak says, popping up behind Bram. "Of course, if we're going to be kissing, I think we might need a few more people, preferably women, though I'm not terribly picky."

"Why is he here again?" Bram growls.

"Because I can do this," Alak replies, snapping his fingers. A small band of five minstrels appears in the corner, their music filling the air. "Unless, of course, you were going to dance in complete silence. In which case I will take my musicians and leave."

"You can stay," Bram sighs.

Alak grins triumphantly. "As I thought."

"It looks so magical in here," Cadewynn interjects, staring up at my stars in awe. "You should do this in the dancing hall for a ball."

"I'm pretty sure your father would not appreciate that," I laugh.

Cadewynn looks away from the stars. "That might be true right now, but one day, when he's accepted magic, you must do this."

"Okay. One day. Maybe," I agree, not bothering to voice my doubts on whether the king will ever accept magic.

"All right," Bram says, clearing his throat to draw our attention. "We have music, now let's get to dancing. I've seen you two dance before at Kriloa, so I know you are not completely helpless."

"We both know basic village dances," I confirm, "but we don't know any of the formal dances, waltzes, or anything of that sort."

Bram nods. "At least it's a starting place. We can start with a basic festival dance. They are similar to what you know. After that, we can phase into the more formal dances." He looks over at Alak. "Give us a fast paced dance."

Alak waves his hand and his musicians play a lively melody I vaguely recognize as a traditional Callenian song. Bram leads me, while Kato leads Cadewynn. Bram and Cadewynn mutter occasional instructions to Kato and I as we dance. Since all I have to do is follow Bram, I have a much easier time than Kato, but by the end of the second song, we're dancing like we do it every day.

The next dance we try is a little different and has specific footwork and steps. Cadewynn and Bram demonstrate for us first, talking us through the steps. Once it's my turn to try, it takes all of ten seconds before I'm stepping on Bram's feet.

"Sorry," I mumble.

"Just let me lead. I promise, I'll guide you straight," Bram whispers.

It works for a few more steps before I'm stepping on his feet again. After a dozen more apologies and three songs, Kato and I finally have it down. We move on to the next dance, which, thanks to Alak's song selection, is a waltz. I am incredibly out of my element, but Bram appears to be in his. He holds me close as we dance to the music. This time, it's easy to completely surrender to him and let him lead. Even Kato seems to take to waltzing faster than the other dances. I'm almost disappointed when the song ends.

"Let's do a group dance!" Cadewynn suggests eagerly.

"How can we do a group dance with only four of us?" I ask, gesturing to the other members of our small group.

"Most of them can be done with four people. As long as you have dance partners to switch with, we can manage. If we do the Fellanon, Alak can take last position to give the other two time to get in position to catch us," Cadewynn explains.

My eyebrows shoot up. "Catch? What do you mean by catch?"

Cadewynn waves me off. "Don't worry. It's easier than it sounds. How about it?"

I nod, although I still feel a bit wary. As Cadewynn and Bram walk us through the dance steps, I discover that I enjoy the group dances. The first one is slightly complicated, but repeats often, so it's not that hard to learn. The second is essentially the first one, only the steps are performed in a different order. Last, we try the Fellanon, which is a line dance. We start with our partners doing a few simple steps, then Bram grabs my waist and we twirl. As we come out of the twirl, he lifts me as I hop. When I land, it's in the arms of Kato, who is next in line. Cadewynn switches from Kato to Alak while Bram quickly goes down to the end of the line. It's fast paced, and, I must admit, my favorite. We do it twice before repeating the other dances, making sure we have everything down. It's after midnight when we finally decide to end for the night.

Alak wisps directly back to the room. Kato offers to walk Cadewynn to her room. She blushes and accepts gratefully. Bram and I are alone again. I'm relishing these stolen moments.

"I know it's rather late, but before we go to our rooms, would you care to take a walk in the garden beneath the real stars?" Bram asks, taking my hand in his.

"I would love to."

I extinguish my magical stars and wisp us into the library above. Bram leads me by the hand outside into one of the palace gardens I recognize as the one my balcony overlooks. It's perfectly peaceful, bathed in silver moonlight. For several minutes, we walk hand in hand down rows of blooming plants, not speaking. When we come to the center of the garden, Bram turns to me. Still holding my hands, he drops down to one knee, and my heart flutters in my chest.

"Astra," he begins softly. "I love you more than life itself. When you knocked me down that day in Timberborn, you altered my life forever for the better. I cannot imagine my life without you. I know that technically we are already set to wed, but I never officially asked. That needs to be rectified, so I'm asking now. Will you honor me by becoming my wife?"

Happy tears well in my eyes as I nod emphatically. "Yes! Of course!"

Bram smiles warmly as he reaches into the pocket on his Guard jacket, pulling out a ring as he stands. He slides the ring on my finger, his usually steady hands trembling.

"This ring belonged to my grandmother, and now it belongs to you."

As he releases my hand, I stretch out my fingers, watching the ring glimmer in the moonlight. It's a simple silver band with an opal stone in the center, but it's easily the most precious thing I've ever owned.

"It's beautiful," I breathe.

"I'm glad you like it."

The next moment I'm wrapped in his arms, our lips pressed together. His kiss is warm and eager. I never want it to end, but, sadly, he pulls away, although I can sense his reluctance to end the moment.

"I've missed you, Astra," Bram says, stroking the side of my face, my breath catching in my throat. "I've arranged to take most of the day off tomorrow so I can spend it with you. I can meet you around lunchtime, if that suits you."

I lean into his touch. "I would love that."

He gives me another quick kiss before taking my hand, leading me back toward the palace. As we walk, I swear I see a shadow of someone on my balcony, but when I glance up, it's empty.

CHAPTER THIRTY-ONE

I have every intention of sleeping in as long as possible, but Cadewynn has other plans. It's mid-morning when she barrels into my room, throwing my curtains open, flooding my room with light.

"I was sleeping," I moan, covering my face with a pillow.

"We have plans this morning. Time to get up!" she chides.

"I was up late last night dancing. You know. You were there." My voice is muffled through the pillow, but I know she can understand me. I pull the pillow back, scowling. "Wait. What plans?"

Cadewynn flips through the dresses in my wardrobe, pulling out a pink one.

"Put this on," she demands, tossing the dress on my bed. "Madame Reid is fitting you for a ball gown this morning, and if you don't hurry, you're going to be late."

I sit up, fighting back a yawn. "Madam who is doing what?"

Cadewynn sighs. "Madam Reid, the royal seamstress, has agreed to make you a dress for the ball. I received a note from her stating that you need to come by this morning for an official fitting. She needs accurate measurements to complete the dress in time. Now, do you need me to ring for a servant to help you dress, or are you good from here?"

"I'm good," I grumble, sitting up and sliding out of bed. "I'll be ready in just a few minutes."

"Good," Cadewynn replies primly. "I'll wait for you in the sitting room."

Cadewynn flounces out while I get dressed. My hair is a chaotic mess. The best I can do is to braid it, winding it into a bun at the nape of my neck. It's not ideal, but it's sufficient.

With a sigh, I exit my room and head into the sitting room. Cadewynn sits in an easy chair chatting with Cal and Makin.

"Ready to go?" she asks, popping up.

I nod reluctantly. I glance over at Cal and Makin as they follow us out the door.

"You boys ready for a dress fitting?"

"Oh, for sure," Makin says sarcastically. "Gonna be the highlight of my day."

Cal elbows him, but they're both grinning. Cadewynn chooses to ignore all three of us as she marches down the hallway.

"Bram is giving us the afternoon off, so we'll have time to recover," Cal adds with a wink.

When we reach the seamstress's room, Cal and Makin voluntarily wait outside while Cadewynn and I go inside. The room reminds me of the dress shop back in Timberborn, only this room is much neater and precise. In the center of the room stands a woman in her forties with shoulder-length brown hair wearing a sleek black dress.

"Good morning, Your Majesty," she says, inclining her head to Cadewynn. She looks over at me. "I suppose you are Miss Astra?"

"Yes, ma'am," I say as she studies me.

"Very well. Up on the stool."

She motions sharply to a wooden stool in the center of the room. Without questioning, I step up on it. She pulls a measuring tape out of her pocket and begins measuring me, starting with the length of my legs.

"Every eye will be on you when you walk into that ball. Everyone will be sizing you up, trying to figure you out. You must look the part you want to play, the part of power. Arms up." I lift my arms and she goes about measuring my bust. "I will create a gown so lovely, so stunning, you will awe everyone, leaving them speechless. You can wear it with confidence knowing you will be the most stunning creature in that room. Arms down." I rest my arms by my side as she measures my shoulders and neck. "Together, we will win the room."

She takes a few more measurements and scribbles them in a little black book.

"Stand straight," she instructs.

I obey. She studies me through narrow eyes, sizing me up.

"Yes. I think I can see it. I have an idea. You may go." She waves me away with her hand. "I will have your gown delivered to you the day of the ball."

"You won't need me to come in for a final fitting?" I ask, stepping down off the stool.

"Unless you are planning on changing sizes in the next couple of days, I do not see the point," she replies sharply.

Cadewynn links her arm with mine and guides me from the room. Cal and Makin lounge just outside the door, looking incredibly bored.

"Done already?" Makin asks. "That was quick."

"There wasn't much to do," I reply with a shrug.

"Are you coming to the library today?" Cadewynn asks and I shake my head.

"I don't think so. Not yet anyway." Cadewynn's face falls

and I feel a little guilty. "I just feel like getting outdoors a bit more today."

"That's fine," Cadewynn sighs. "Maybe I'll go down and watch Kato a bit today. He's with Alak again, isn't he?"

"He is, and I think he might like that. He always enjoys an audience."

I bid Cadewynn goodbye and turn to Cal and Makin.

"Well, what are your plans? We're commanded to follow you to the end of the world, so we're up for anything," Makin grins.

"Actually, I'm a little hungry. I didn't get to eat anything this morning," I confess.

Makin's eyes light up. "Have you had a chance to visit the kitchens?"

I shake my head.

"Well, then," he continues, offering me his arm, "I think it's high time you meet Cook."

I take his arm as Cal says, "Are you sure, Makin? You're not exactly her favorite person."

"I may not be, but there's no way Cook will turn Astra away. I'd be a fool not to try to get a little food at the same time."

Cal and Makin lead me through a part of the castle I've never seen. It's bustling and filled with servants dashing around. It feels alive, whereas most of the castle feels like it's on its deathbed. In my nicer dress, being escorted by two of Ehren's Guard, I'm sure I look out of place, but, for the first time since arriving in Embervein, I actually feel normal. The walkway narrows the closer we get to the kitchen, so I'm forced to release Makin's arm and walk between Makin and Cal. The kitchen is twice as busy as the halls leading to it. Servants scurry around, following the instructions of a hefty woman in the center of the kitchen. When she sees Makin enter, her eyes narrow.

"I told you to stay out of my kitchen, boy," she says, waving a wooden spoon in Makin's face.

Makin holds his hands up in surrender, ducking behind me. "I know. I know. But I'm not here today to sneak any food." He places his hands on my back and pushes me forward. "I brought you this poor, starving girl, desperately in need of nourishment."

I shoot Makin a glare before turning to face Cook.

"I'm sorry to be a bother. I was dragged directly from bed this morning and didn't get a chance to eat."

Cook's eyes assess me for a moment. "You're that girl that Captain Bramfield brought here."

It's not a question, but I answer anyway. "Yes, ma'am. My name is Astra."

She takes a deep breath and motions to a small table and stool beneath an open window. "Sit there and I'll get you a bite to eat."

I nod and weave my way to the table, navigating the chaos of the kitchen.

"I don't have many sweet buns and pastries still down here. That's what we send to your room, every morning, isn't it?" she asks, moving around some of the food on the main counter.

"Oh, um . . . That's fine," I mumble, sliding onto the stool.

Cook grins, revealing several missing teeth.

"You're craving a bit more than pastries and fruit, I take it?" I nod. "Good. It's good to see a girl who likes to really eat. You just sit there. I'll have something up for you in a moment." She turns to Makin who is trying to sneak some cheese from a nearby platter. "You, out of my kitchen!"

"We're supposed to stay by her side at all times," Makin argues, popping the cheese in his mouth with a grin.

"Fine. You take the side on her left."

Makin glances over at me, then back at Cook. "There's a wall to her left."

"Then I suppose you'll have to wait on the other side of it," Cook replies, turning her attention to the stove.

Cal snickers as Makin mutters under his breath. Makin and Cal both go outside into a little courtyard just beyond the kitchen. I look out the window and am captivated by how alive it is. People are bustling about like worker ants, arms loaded with goods to carry to other parts of the castle. A cart drives up and servants appear to unload it.

But it's not all work. In one corner a handful of children kick around a ball, laughing and playing, while a couple of small, yapping dogs nip at their heels and chase the ball. In another corner, a couple older servant boys are playing a game with dice. It's like a concentrated version of my village, and I realize with a pang I miss it.

I watch the activity in the courtyard with longing until Cook approaches me with a plate. It's piled high with eggs, scrambled with bits of meat and cheese. One forkful tells me it's the best breakfast I've ever eaten.

"This is delicious. Thank you," I say, scooping more eggs into my mouth.

Cook smiles, wiping her hands on her apron. "You're more than welcome, dear. Most people visiting the castle always want the finest meals. Not enough want good, basic food like that. You're always welcome in my kitchen."

"Well, that's entirely unfair," Makin mumbles from just outside the window.

I hide my smile and quickly clean the plate. When I offer to wash the plate, Cook shoos me from the kitchen, insisting I would be more in the way, and that her kitchen hands will happily wash it for me. When she turns her back to hand the plate off to someone, I sneak a hunk of cheese from a nearby tray and rush away before she can notice. I walk out into the courtyard and find Makin leaning against the wall outside the window with Cal a few yards away chatting with a pretty dark-haired girl carrying a pitcher.

I walk up next to Makin and hand him the cheese. "Here. For your loyal service."

Makin grins and glances over his shoulder through the window to make sure Cook isn't watching before he takes a bite.

"I swear, Astra, if you ever decide to leave Bram, I'll marry you in a heartbeat," Makin mutters, mouth full.

I laugh and nod toward Cal. "Who is Cal talking to?"

Makin swallows before answering, "Lola."

"Lola," I repeat. "Are they together?"

Makin shakes his head, laughing. "No. Cal isn't exactly interested in women."

He pops the last bit of cheese in his mouth.

"What about you? Do you have a special someone in your life?"

Makin laughs, nearly choking on his cheese. "Hardly. I'm not the settling down type, I'm afraid." He looks down at me and winks. "Though my offer to marry you will always stand."

I grin and shake my head. Makin lets out a whistle, drawing Cal's attention. When he sees me ready to go, he nods to Lola and makes his way to us.

"Did you enjoy your breakfast?" he asks.

"I did. Very much," I reply.

"Well," Makin interjects, pushing away from the wall, "what should we get up to now?"

"I'm not sure," I reply, glancing around the courtyard, "but I think I'd rather spend the day outside."

"Let's walk the palace grounds, then, shall we?" Makin suggests, offering me his arm.

I take his arm and he leads me out of the courtyard. We go around a corner and I see a group of soldiers training with their commander. The commander barks orders, the soldiers obeying without hesitation. They're younger, not yet ready for the army, but already showing skill.

"Is there anywhere we could go to train?" I ask, an idea striking me.

"Train? What kind of training?" Makin asks, raising an eyebrow.

"I think maybe sword training," I reply. "It might help me with my . . . creations."

"The upper training field should be empty today," Cal offers. "We can go there, if you like."

I nod and they lead me past other training fields filled with soldiers. We begin to make our way up a hill, and I understand why it's called the "upper" field. When we reach the top, I'm surprised at how level the ground is. The grass is green, but well-worn with patches of dirt. A stone wall about chest high surrounds the area. Racks of weapons, mostly swords, stand at one end, and targets are spread out around the edges. Some are circular targets made of colored rope and others are stuffed versions of soldiers, some complete with askew helmets and armor. Cal and Makin lead me to one of the weapons racks.

"Choose your weapon," Cal says, gesturing to my options.

I eye the swords, picking a broadsword from the center of the rack, testing it. Like most swords I've handled, it's heavy, almost too heavy for me to wield. I select another, but it's much the same.

"Try this one," Cal says, stepping forward and selecting a sword from the back. The sword is sleek and long. I take it in my hand and find it surprisingly light. I step back from the weapons rack and swish it through the air.

"I can make this work well, I think," I mutter.

"All right, then, which of us do you want to fight first?" Makin asks.

"Doesn't matter to me which of you I beat first," I reply with a cocky grin.

Makin laughs. "I'll let you start easy then, with Cal."

Cal rolls his eyes. "Fine."

Cal and I step into the center of the ring and take our places facing each other. We start slow. I block each of Cal's blows without much trouble. I'm awkward and far out of practice, but I do a decent job. Cal instructs me on my footing as we go. After a few rounds with Cal, Makin steps in and we do the same. I grow more and more comfortable with my sword and my skills sharpen. I allow my magic to flow though me, adding a certain level of grace.

"Okay," I say. "Let's actually spar."

I go up against Cal first. I let my magic seep out of me like an invisible cloud surrounding us. Cal can't sense it at all, but it's as connected to me as my own limbs. I can feel every move Cal makes and can anticipate some of his moves before he makes them. Midway in our sparring, I sense Makin approaching from behind. I spin to face him, and he takes over as Cal steps back. For the next several minutes, I switch between them. Their fighting styles are very different and keep me on my toes. Cal responds to my moves, waiting for me to strike before countering with either defense or attack. Makin is more on the offensive, making the move first and driving me to the defensive.

The faster I switch between them, the quicker I have to think. Soon, I'm fighting them both at once. I'm face to face with Cal when I sense Makin coming up behind me. I thrust

Cal back and switch my sword to my left hand, spinning to stop Makin's blow. My left hand is much weaker, but I have just enough strength to knock Makin's sword back. I toss the sword to my right hand and lunge. Surprise is still on my side, and I manage to knock Makin's sword to the ground. My victory is short lived, however, as I realize that I lost focus on Cal. That moment of distraction is all he needs. When I spin back to face him, I'm already at his sword's point. I raise my hands in surrender, dropping my sword as I draw in my magic.

I'm breathing hard, but I grin as I say, "You win."

Cal grins and lowers his sword, his own breath heavy. I hear a slow clap from behind me and turn toward the opening to the training area. Bram walks my way, grinning widely. I smile in return.

He greets me with a kiss and leans in, whispering quietly enough only I can hear, "Well, that may be one of the most arousing things I've ever seen in my life."

I'm briefly thankful my face is already bright red from the heat or I'm sure I would have blushed a deep, embarrassing crimson. With a start, I realize I probably look like a disgusting mess. Sweat has soaked my clothes, my face is red from the heat, and my hair is nothing short of chaos. I glance down at my dress, which is also covered in dirt. Bram seems to read my thoughts.

"You've never looked more beautiful."

To prove his point, he leans down and kisses me again. When he pulls back, he looks over at Cal and Makin. Makin is sheathing his sword while Cal's returning the sword I used to the rack.

"It seems you've all had a very productive morning," Bram says.

"One of the best I've had in a while," Makin replies with a grin. "You've found yourself quite the girl, Captain. I've said it once and I'll say it again—you ever decide you don't want to marry—"

Bram holds up his hand, cutting Makin off. "As much as I love your standing offer to marry my fiancé, we're quite content with our current arrangement."

Makin shrugs with a grin.

Cal strolls over. "Anything you need from us?"

Bram shakes his head. "No, you two may take the rest of the day off." He looks over at me and smiles. "I can take it from here."

"Come, Cal!" Makin cries, striding toward the gate. "The tavern is waiting!"

Cal follows him, shaking his head. "The tavern? It's not even noon yet."

Makin laughs. "Like that matters."

The two disappear down the hill, still arguing, as Bram turns his attention to me. "Are you ready for a picnic lunch?"

"Actually," I admit, "I had breakfast not all that long ago, and I'm far too hot to eat anything else right now. I hope that doesn't ruin your plans."

"Not in the slightest. I thought we might take a ride to get to our picnic location anyway. The food itself will keep until you're ready to eat."

"That sounds wonderful," I say, giving him a quick peck on the lips.

Together, we stroll over the castle grounds, busy with activity. As we walk, I let my hair down out of its messy, half-falling braid. I shake my head, my hair spilling over my shoulders.

"Is it always this busy out here?" I ask as several servants rush by.

Bram gives a half-shrug. "It's always active, but probably more so right now due to preparations for the ball and arriving guests."

I nod. "I suppose that makes sense. It just always seems quiet inside. Of course, I do tend to spend most of my time in the library."

Bram chuckles. "Yes, I would imagine that the library isn't the busiest place in the castle."

As we approach the stables, Peter rushes out to greet us.

"Good day, Captain, sir," Peter beams. "I have the horses ready that you requested. Yours is loaded with the basket the kitchen sent down."

"Thank you very much," Bram says, patting the boy on his shoulder.

The boy grins and rushes back inside the stable, returning with Solomon and Luna. I walk over to my horse and stroke her muzzle.

"Hello, Luna. Did you miss me?" I whisper. She snorts and paws at the ground. "What do you say we go for a ride?"

I mount Luna, and Bram leads me out of the castle keep into the village. We pass through the crowd before we veer off, heading toward a small forest just beyond the village. We enter the canopy of trees to greetings from twittering birds and animals scurrying through the underbrush. I close my eyes and take a deep breath. The air outside is a welcome change. I didn't realize how much I missed it.

"It's always nice to get away, as much as I love the palace," Bram says, offering me a smile.

"I love the castle, I really do. And I love reading in the library with Cadewynn and Alak, but I do miss this," I agree, motioning to the woods around us.

"I understand. Completely."

Bram leads me on a well-worn path toward the sound of running water. When I can finally see the source of the sound, I'm delighted to see a babbling brook, shallow enough to see the stones at the bottom. I dismount Luna and walk over the stream, leaving her to munch on the plush green grass. I slip off my shoes and dip my bare feet in the cool water, little fish swimming up and nibbling on my toes. I glance over at Bram to find him leaning against a tree, watching me with a beautifully sincere smile. I could happily spend every day like this.

CHAPTER THIRTY-TWO

*Y*ou're not focusing!" Alak yells as one of Kato's fireballs narrowly misses my head.

I sigh, shaking my head. "Sorry."

"We can take a break if you need," Kato offers.

"No, I can do this," I insist.

"Are you sure? Because if you get hurt, Bram will kill me, even if it's Kato's fault," Alak says. "My life is on the line, love."

"He will not kill you," I say, rolling my eyes.

"He most definitely will, and you know it," Alak counters. "I think maybe we should call it a day. Don't you two have some ball you should be getting ready for?"

"That's not for a couple more hours," I argue. "We have plenty of time."

"Maybe we should just go back to our room. There really isn't that long before the ball, and my magic is starting to feel a little low," Kato says and I sigh.

"Fine. I'll meet you in the room."

Kato wisps away, leaving me alone with Alak, which rarely happens. Normally, I at least have Cal and Makin hovering nearby, but Bram and Ehren have admitted that it's unnecessary for them to be with me when I'm training with Kato and Alak in a room nobody can find.

"You and I can practice a bit more if you want."

Alak shakes his head. "Your head isn't here, otherwise I would consider it."

"I'm just nervous about this stupid dance."

Alak smiles and cocks his head. "Why? I've seen you dance. You've practiced practically every night since you found out about the ball. You'll be amazing tonight."

"I just feel like I'm going to be on display. I'd rather hide out in my room than face all those random nobles."

Alak crosses the distance between us, his eyes locking onto mine. "Astra, you are literally one of the strongest, most amazing people on this continent. You shouldn't be intimidated by anyone, let alone some lousy nobles."

I smile. "Are you sure you don't want to come tonight?"

Alak glances away. "Bram and Ehren have made it pretty clear they don't want me there. Besides, I don't have anything appropriate to wear."

"If you did, would you want to come?"

"Not really. A fancy ball isn't really my scene." He looks back into my eyes. "We should go."

I open my mouth to argue, but he reaches out and grabs my hand, wisping us into our sitting room before I get the chance.

"That's cheating," I say, yanking my hand from his.

Alak grins. "No one ever said I play fair, love. Now, go turn into the goddess you are." He waves me off and heads to his room.

With a sigh I resign myself to my fate for the evening. I go into my room, ringing for Kara. In the corner, I notice my new dress hanging on the door of my wardrobe. It's absolutely beautiful. The main dress is made from a purple silk just a shade or two darker than my eyes, with a sheer gossamer material in a light, sparkling lavender flowing over the skirt and parts of the top. A couple pieces of coordinating jewelry are laid out on my dresser, but before I can examine them, Kara enters the room.

"Shall we start with a bath?" she suggests, going immediately to the washroom without waiting for my reply.

I step into the hot water before the tub is full, letting the water wash over me. Kara adds lots of bubbles and oils, filling the whole washroom with a beautiful, calming aroma. Kara leaves me to soak, and I lie in the tub perfectly content until the water is lukewarm. I wish I could hide in the water all night, but Kara insists I'll turn into a prune and forces me out. Instead of dressing, I put on my robe and Kara works on my hair. She winds my white locks into an extremely intricate braid wound tightly on top of my head leaving one thick piece down, curled and draped elegantly over my shoulder. She adds several sparkling pins to my braid before going to work on my face.

I've never been one to enjoy wearing any sort of makeup, so I'm hesitant to agree. Kara insists I will have to wear some or risk looking out of place. I reluctantly concede. She adds touches of color to my lips and cheeks as well as a small bit of color around my eyes.

When I slip into my dress, the silk slides smoothly, fitting perfectly to my every curve. The main part of the dress is sleeveless with a built-in bodice that pushes my breasts up. The sheer fabric is gathered over my left shoulder by an amethyst set in silver, crossing down across my chest where it is secured into a line of small diamonds just underneath my bust, leaving my other shoulder exposed. A second line of diamonds Vs down from the bust to my waist and circles around to my back, which is bare, save for a bit of the gossamer coming down from my shoulder. More of the sheer gossamer cascades down from my waist, covering the flowing skirt of the dress.

To complete my look, Kara clips a necklace around my neck made of silver links with diamonds and amethysts glistening where the links meet and presents me with a pair of sparkling silver shoes.

Kara directs me in front of the mirror, and I barely recognize myself. When the dressmaker told me all eyes would be on me, I wasn't sure I believed her. Now, I have no doubt.

"This look suits you, miss," Kara whispers. "All you have to do is wear it with pride."

I look at my maid, and she offers me an encouraging smile before she leaves. It's a few minutes before I'm ready to leave the security of my room. When I finally do, I find Alak sitting in one of the easy chairs absentmindedly knuckle rolling a coin. When he sees me, he freezes, his mouth falling open as the coin drops to the floor, forgotten entirely.

"What?" I demand nervously.

Alak chuckles as he stands, sauntering over to me. "What do you mean 'what?' Did you not look in a mirror before you came out here, love?"

I blush and look down. "My maid says it suits me. I feel . . . I don't know. Not like myself."

"I think you look extraordinarily beautiful," he says, his voice edged with something I can't quite place.

"Thank you," I say quietly, looking up into his emerald eyes.

Alak stands awkwardly for a moment before he stumbles forward and brushes his lips across mine. The kiss is brief and fleeting, over before I even have time to register it. He staggers back a step, his breath unsteady. I subconsciously lift my fingers to trace where his lips just were.

"For luck. That's all," he laughs nervously, raking his hand through his hair, glancing away. "It's a, uh, common practice in Athiedor."

I nod numbly, not sure how else to respond, my heart picking up speed.

"What's going on here?" Kato asks, strolling into the room dressed in a sleek white and gold version of his Guard uniform.

Alak jolts away from me so fast I almost think he wisped.

"I was just wishing Astra good luck tonight," Alak replies so quickly his words run together. "Have fun!" Without another word, Alak wisps into his room.

"Ready to go down?" I say, ignoring Kato's questioning gaze as butterflies twirl in my stomach.

Kato nods and offers me his arm. "Let's go see what all this fuss is about."

Before we even get to the ballroom, I can hear the lively music drifting down the hall. It does little to soothe my nerves, however. When we reach the entrance, we hand our official invitations to the man at the door so he can announce us. Kato goes in first.

"Presenting Kato Downs of Timberborn, member of His Majesty Prince Ehren's Royal Guard."

Kato struts in like it's his hundredth time doing this, striding down the long staircase to the waiting crowd below. The announcer looks at me, and I step forward, my hands trembling.

"Presenting Astra Downs of Timberborn, betrothed of Captain Bramfield of His Majesty Prince Ehren's Royal Guard."

I step out of the shadows into the glowing ballroom. My hand glides down the bannister as I float down the stairs. I hold my head high, mustering as much confidence as I can as hundreds of eyes drift to me. All my nerves disappear when I see Bram waiting for me at the base of the stairs, staring up at me in awe. I quicken my steps down the stairs and place my hand in Bram's.

"You look breathtaking," he whispers to me as he guides me through the crowd to where Ehren stands next to Cal. Makin, Kato, and several other Guard members hover nearby.

"Well, I don't think it's quite fair that Bram gets the most beautiful girl in the kingdom," Ehren teases as we approach.

"I promise to save you a dance," I reply with a grin.

"You better," Ehren laughs. "I am the prince after all."

My smile fades to a scowl as I notice an unwelcome face in the crowd behind Ehren—Landis. I'm about to look away when Landis looks directly at me, giving me a feral grin before sauntering our direction. I curse under my breath. Bram turns and follows my gaze.

"Do you know him?" Bram mutters, wrapping his arm around my waist to draw me closer to his side.

I swallow and nod. "I ran into him a few days ago with Cadewynn. I don't think he cares for me."

Landis steps up to us, eyeing me up and down. Shivers run down my spine under his penetrating gaze.

"Well, Captain," he sneers, "it looks like quite the congratulations are in order. You have bagged yourself a stunning bride. I guess that solves my question of who had the Guard escort. I didn't catch a title before her name, though, but I guess when you don't have one of your own . . ."

Bram tenses, but Ehren replies nonchalantly, "And yet you have a title and still can't seem to snag a girl. Very interesting if you ask me."

Landis's eyes flash. "I just haven't found a girl worthy of my interest."

"Yes, I'm sure that is the problem," Ehren drawls, picking at his nails in disinterest.

"Well, would you, perhaps, honor me with a dance?" Landis says, turning his attention back to me.

As I struggle to find a reason to turn him down, Bram cuts

in. "I think it's only fair I get the first dance with my soon to be wife."

"Perhaps the next dance, then?" Landis counters, flashing me a grin that turns my stomach.

"Oh, sorry, but I've claimed the second dance," Ehren says, tilting his head with mock sympathy.

"And I have the dance after that," Makin jumps in with a grin that infuriates Landis all the more.

"And I the one after that," Cal says.

A few other of Ehren's Guard, whose names I don't even know, chime in as well, and I can't hide my grin as I turn back to Landis.

"I'm so terribly sorry, but I believe my dance card is full. Perhaps I might be able to find some space for you at the next ball," I reply with a shrug.

Landis balls his hands into fists by his side and glares at us each in turn. "Perhaps."

He spins on his heel and storms away. I sigh in relief.

"Well, shall we dance?" Bram asks, offering me his hand.

It doesn't take long for me to realize I had nothing to worry about. Dancing is so much fun, and we're surrounded by so many people barely anyone notices if I misstep. Cadewynn makes her appearance three dances in and shoots me a grin across the dance hall. Despite all her complaining, Cadewynn doesn't seem to mind all the attention from the gentlemen in the crowd in the slightest. Kato also seems to be perfectly at home dancing with all the lovely young ladies flocking to him every dance.

I dance with Bram, Ehren, and the Guard as promised. Somehow, Makin makes it into the rotation twice. In between dances, I chat with Cadewynn and enjoy some of the delicious food that's been prepared. I'm standing next to one of the food tables, drinking a glass of wine and talking to Cadewynn when Kato approaches.

"Would you honor me with a dance?" Kato asks, bowing and offering his hand to Cadewynn.

Cadewynn grins, placing her hand in his. "Absolutely! I thought you'd never ask."

Kato whisks her off into the crowd, and, for the first time since entering the ballroom, I'm left standing alone. I scan the room for Bram, but I don't see him.

"Well, it looks like you just may have a dance for me after all," a cold voice says behind me, making me freeze.

Landis comes up next to me and slides his arm around my waist. I stiffen and go completely still.

"Come on. How bad could it possibly be?" he asks, his breath hot on my ear.

I swallow and try to form an excuse, but he's already forcing me out onto the dance floor. I hope for a quick dance, or one where I can switch partners, but I'm not that lucky. A slow melody begins to play and Landis jerks me close.

"I think you'll find I am a masterful dancer," he whispers, his lips touching my ear this time, making me cringe.

He holds me tightly against his body, and I want to scream. I can feel my magic swirling inside, and it takes all my power not to release it. My eyes search the dancing crowd for Bram, but I still can't find him. When the dance finally ends, I try to pull away, but Landis has a firm grip on my wrist.

"Have you seen the gardens outside the ballroom? They're lovely in the moonlight," he says, his smile sharp.

"I would rather stay inside," I say, but he's already dragging me to the nearest door.

"Come, now, don't be a spoilsport," he laughs.

"Let me go," I yell, but my pleas are lost in the cacophony of the ball.

He pulls me outside. We're alone, getting further and further from the people I love and trust. When we're a good distance from the door, he wraps his arm around me, pinning my arms to my side. We are entirely alone. I could attack him with my magic, but that would only draw unwanted attention from the king. I long for my dagger, but it's up in my room.

"You really are beautiful," he says, running a finger down my cheek. "I don't understand why you would stoop so low as to marry the captain. You could do much better."

"Oh, like you? No thanks," I sneer with more confidence than I feel, trying to pull away.

He grabs my hands so hard his fingers dig in painfully as he spins me to face him. I wince and he laughs, pulling me closer to him. I spit in his face.

"You bitch!" he shouts, wiping my salvia off his face.

I try to take the opportunity of having one of his hands off me to escape, but running in these shoes is no easy feat. He catches me and yanks me back, holding me firmer.

"I will have you," he growls and forces his lips to mine.

I struggle, fighting tears. I slam my foot down on his, which only angers him. He rears back and slaps me across the face. My cheek stings and tears break free against my will. I'm debating my next move when a fist flies out of nowhere and slams across Landis's face. He releases me, staggering back. I turn and find Alak standing behind me, his face stern and deadly. Landis looks up at Alak, face red and lip bleeding.

"Do you have any idea who I am?" he yells.

"I'm guessing you're the official court arsehole, mate," Alak replies.

Alak stretches his fingers like he often does before performing magic, and I grab his hand before he can.

"Don't," I whisper, my voice barely audible. "The king can't know. Not yet."

"I am the son and heir of Duke—" Landis begins, spitting as he yells.

Alak holds up his hand. "I don't care who ya are. I just suggest ya get back inside. Now. Or I'll deck ya again." I can't help but notice Alak's accent is stronger than usual.

Landis doesn't move and glares at Alak.

"Look, mate, either ya can stand there and we can wait for the Good Captain to come out and find out that yer out here with the love o' his life, and me, him, the prince, and her brother will take turns deckin' ya, or ya can go back inside and nurse yer wounds."

"This isn't over," Landis says, his voice heavy with anger.

"Maybe not, but it is over for tonight," Alak says with finality.

Landis weighs his words before storming away. Once he's disappeared back inside, Alak turns to me, scanning my face.

"Are you okay?" he asks, his voice shaking.

I nod. "I'm fine."

He raises a tentative hand to where Landis struck me. "Are you sure, love? He struck you mighty hard. It's likely to bruise."

I take a deep breath and raise my hand to my cheek, releasing just enough magic to cover any redness left by Landis's hand. I force a weak smile.

"See? All better."

"Where the hell is Bram?" Alak asks, anger rising in his voice.

I shake my head, glancing toward the ballroom. "I have no idea. I couldn't find him or anyone else in the crowd. There are so many people in there." I pause, looking back at Alak. "Wait. What are you doing down here?"

"I decided to see what all the fuss was about and was watching from the sidelines when I saw that creep force you outside," he confesses, his voice still tinged with anger.

"Well, I'm glad you came down. I doubt he would have done much more than kiss but still . . ." I let my voice trail off.

"You know, you could have disintegrated him like that," Alak says, snapping his fingers. "You're powerful enough."

"Perhaps, but the king is right inside, and I don't want to risk exposing my magic over someone like Landis."

Alak looks me over again. "And you're sure you're okay?"

"I am. I promise." My eyes drift back to the ballroom. "I should probably get back."

"I can go with you, if you like," Alak offers.

"I thought you didn't have anything appropriate to wear," I tease.

Alak grins. "That's when being a master of illusion comes in handy."

He waves his hand, and he's suddenly dressed in an elegant deep green, high necked tunic with gold trim and buttons. His hair is combed neatly and pulled back. He offers me his arm. I accept and he leads me back into the ballroom. A dance is beginning, so he leads me straight to the dance floor. Even with all the nights spent practicing, this is the first time I've really danced with Alak, other than the few moments in the group dances. He dances as smoothly and flawlessly as Ehren.

"Where did you learn to dance?" I ask as he spins me and draws me against himself.

"I have many hidden talents. Maybe someday I'll share more of them," he grins with a wink.

I laugh as he twirls me again, his eyes shining.

"You dance wonderfully yourself," he adds. "It seems all those nights of practicing were worth it. Other than that one incident, have you had an enjoyable time?"

"I have, actually," I reply. "It's been a lot of fun."

The music stops, and Alak leads me off the dance floor, my hand in his. No sooner are we clear of the people gathering for the next dance, then Bram rushes over to us, his jaw set as he glares at Alak.

"What are you doing here?" Bram demands, coldly. "I thought we decided you would stay in your room."

"Bram," I intercede, pulling my hand from Alak's and placing it on Bram's arm.

"You should be thankful I'm here. Where were you ten minutes ago?" Alak cuts me off, his voice hard and controlled.

Bram glances over at my expression and realizes something is wrong. "There was a small incident I had to deal with." He looks back Alak. "Why? What happened?"

"I'm fine," I insist.

"Of course you are fine. Why wouldn't you be fine?" Bram asks, fear flashing on his face.

"Landis forced me to dance with him," I say. Bram inhales sharply as I continue. "And then he forced me out into the garden."

"Did he touch you?" Bram asks, each word clipped.

"I'm fine," I say again, but Bram shakes his head.

"If he touched you—"

"He kissed her," Alak interjects and I shoot him a dirty look. "And likely would have done more had I not shown up when I did."

Bram jerks away from me, his eyes furiously searching the crowd. He finds Landis on the other side of the ballroom and starts to march away. I grab his arm.

"Please, don't make a scene," I beg. "Please."

"I already decked him," Alak says proudly, eyes sparkling.

"Fine," Bram says, but I can tell he's still seething.

I place my hand in his. "Dance with me?"

Bram takes a deep breath. I can tell he still wants to go over to Landis and make a point.

"Please?" I ask, offering him a weak smile.

"All right," he concedes, forcing a smile of his own.

We join the dancers. It's a slower dance, already half over, but I relish the moments Bram holds me close as we sway to the music.

"I love you," he whispers in my ear.

"I love you, too."

When the dance ends, he leads me off the floor to where Alak stands next to an angry Ehren.

"Do you want me to have him executed?" Ehren offers before I'm even completely off the dance floor. "Because I am sure I can find some reason to have him executed."

"No," I reply, hiding a smile. "But I think I might just end my night on this high note and head to my room."

"I will escort you," Bram offers. I nod gratefully as he turns to Ehren. "I will be back. Don't do anything reckless while I'm gone."

Ehren sighs. "Fine. I'll save all my reckless behavior for when you return."

I turn to Ehren. "Don't tell Kato. He will kill him."

Ehren nods, knowing I'm not exaggerating. "I won't."

Bram wraps his arm around my waist, leading me up the stairs and out of the ballroom, Alak trailing behind us. When we get outside our door, Alak leans against the wall, grinning.

"Thank you for what you did tonight," Bram says stiffly. "But I would appreciate a moment alone with Astra, if you please."

Alak sighs and pushes away from the wall. "Fine. I'll see you both in the morning."

Alak wisps into the room, leaving me and Bram alone. Bram reaches up and strokes my face.

"If anything had happened to you tonight," his voice breaks.

I press a comforting kiss to his lips. "I'm okay. I'm all right."

"This is the second time someone has attacked you, and I wasn't there. This is the second time I've failed you," Bram whispers, glancing away.

"No, don't think like that. You've never failed me, Bram," I say, reaching my hand up, cupping his face and turning it back to me.

He leans down and kisses me with fierceness and longing, which I gladly return. When he pulls back he seems a little more relaxed.

"You know, Landis won't see this as being over."

I nod. "I figured as much. It's a good thing I have guards with me wherever I go." I offer him a smile, but he shakes his head.

"I'm serious, Astra," Bram says firmly.

"I know. I doubt he would be brazen enough to attack me during the day, and I never leave my room in the evenings. I'll be fine," I insist.

Bram gives me a final kiss and pulls away, walking back toward the ballroom to guard Ehren. I watch him for a moment before leaving the hallway. The sitting room is dark and quiet as I cross it, heading into my bedroom. I'm still smiling as I shut the door, but I jump when I realize someone is standing on my balcony. I calm down when I realize it's only Alak.

"What are you doing in here?" I ask, approaching him.

He turns to face me, emotion written all over his face.

"Why didn't you call for Kato?" he demands, ignoring my question.

"He would have used magic," I reply.

"You don't know that."

"But I do. He would have wisped to my location immediately."

"Why didn't you summon a dagger? That would have been easy enough to explain," Alak presses.

"I . . . I didn't want to cause a scene," I fumble, glancing away.

Alak says nothing, continuing to eye me steadily. I meet his eyes and swallow.

"I panicked. Okay? Is that what you want to hear? I panicked. And I hate that. I usually have my wits about me, but, when it mattered most, I just couldn't think straight."

The feelings I've been holding inside spill out, tears streaming down my face. Alak closes the distance between us immediately and gathers me into his arms. For several minutes he just holds me as I sob into his chest. When I finally get control of my tears, I pull back slightly but remain close to him. He reaches and wipes tears off my cheeks with gentle strokes.

"There now, love," he whispers, his voice tender.

I look up into his emerald eyes and release a shaky breath. His gaze is so intense and caring. Suddenly, without fully understanding why, I raise my lips to his. He responds without hesitation, kissing me hungrily, pulling me close against his body. I feel a fire rising up inside. The kisses can't come fast enough. My magic sings, and I press closer to Alak, craving contact. I slide my arms around him, but Alak jerks back, stepping away. I gasp to catch my breath. His eyes go wide and his breathing is heavy. He runs a trembling hand down his face.

"Shite. Shite." He backs further away from me, shaking his head. "We need to forget that happened."

I take a step toward him. "Alak—"

"No," he says firmly, holding up his hands. "I need to go."

He tries to brush past me, but I move into his path, placing my hand on his chest. I can feel his racing heart beneath my fingertips.

"Wait."

He pauses, glancing down for a moment before he squeezes his eyes shut.

"Please. Let me go." His voice is lifeless and barely a whisper. "I didn't mean for that to happen. And it can never happen again."

He lifts his eyes to mine, his distress clear. I lower my hand, and he leaves without another word, shutting my door behind him. I fight every urge I have not to chase after Alak. I sit down on my bed, my heart still pounding. The longer I try to push away the thoughts of his lips on mine, the stronger my desire to go to Alak grows. Before I can change my mind, I wisp into Alak's room. Alak is sitting on the edge of his bed, his head in his hands. When I appear he looks up at me, bewildered.

"Astra . . ."

"Look, I swear I won't tell Bram, but I'm not going to forget it happened either," I say firmly. "And it changes nothing between us. It was all the emotions of the moment. Agree?"

This isn't what I came to say. This isn't why I wisped into his room. But seeing him broken like this . . . I have to say these things. I have to set things right, put everything back on course. He accepts my words without question, nodding his agreement.

"Yes. Of course." He stands slowly and approaches me, his hands shaking. "I need you to believe that I never meant for that to happen. That's not why I was in your room. I know you're with Bram, and I would never try to steal you away."

I nod slowly. "I know. And I need you to know that I love Bram, and I am going to marry him."

At least those words are true. Aren't they?

"I know. I'm happy for you, love. Really, I am. And I have no intention of getting in the way of that," Alak insists.

Something about his declaration makes my heart sink, but I'm not entirely sure why. It's the right response. Isn't it?

"All right then," I say. "Goodnight."

I wisp back into my own room, but my mind is far too awake. I won't be getting much sleep tonight.

CHAPTER THIRTY-THREE

*T*he following days fall into a simple pattern. My mornings are spent with Alak and Cadewynn in the library, researching and studying everything we can get our hands on. Most mornings Alak avoids me by spending his time studying in a neighboring alcove, claiming he needs more room to spread out. I probably shouldn't miss him, but I do. My work is frustrating but provides a decent amount of information. Cadewynn and I discover a magical family tree in a village just over a day away. Bram is less than pleased to leave me alone, but he, Ehren, and Kato are able to successfully locate several more magic users before the king.

Lunches take place inside instead of in the garden, which is overwhelmed with bugs now, anyway. Some days we go up to our room and other times we sneak food into the hidden room beneath the library.

On days Kato isn't helping Bram and Ehren locate magical families, he meets Alak mid-afternoon for his magical training. He and Alak usually go down and start without me, and I join them shortly before dinner. After dinner, which we always eat in our room, Kato and I usually go down and spar without Alak. When Bram can, he comes with us to watch, sometimes accompanied by Ehren or even Cadewynn if their schedules allow.

I'm never alone except when I'm sleeping. Cal and Makin have been made aware of what Landis did during the ball and now hover like overprotective mother hens. I don't know if it's of their own accord or at Bram's command. I have a feeling it's a bit of both. Either way, they're in the sitting room before I wake up each morning, and they only leave my side if Bram is present. Kato still has no idea what happened at the ball, and if he suspects anything is amiss, he doesn't show it.

Alak rarely appears in the sitting room unless everyone is present. Some days he even retreats to his room for his meals. Felixe appears on a regular basis, however, and often naps on the couch by the balcony.

Today, Cadewynn and I are in our alcove, and I'm practically going cross-eyed trying to interpret a poorly drawn diagram. I turn my head and pass the page to Cadewynn.

"Do you think this is a set of instructions on how to perform the spell or general information describing the spell?"

Cadewynn takes the page and holds it up, brows furrowing. "I'm not sure." She turns the page on its side. "It almost looks like an example of someone performing the spell, but it's really hard to tell."

"Makin, Cal, come here and look at this."

Makin and Cal slink in from the corridor. Makin sighs and drops his shoulders.

"Again, Astra? You know this is completely out of our element."

Cal, however, accepts the paper from Cadewynn. "I think it looks like an example of someone performing magic."

"Thank you, Cal, for your helpful input," I say, glaring at Makin as I take the paper back.

"Well, you may not be finding much clear or helpful information, but I think I've found at least one more magical family, maybe even two, in a town called Burrowbrook," Cadewynn says, sliding one of the genealogy books my direction.

"Burrowbrook?" I ask. "Where is that?"

Cadewynn shrugs. "I'm not sure. I'm afraid geography isn't my strong point."

"It's a little village about a day and a half from here," Makin says. When I shoot him a curious look he adds, "What? I can be useful. Just because I can't decipher your magical hullabaloo doesn't mean I don't know things."

"Sorry. You're right. I just didn't know you knew so much about the layout of Callenia," I say, laughing.

"Well, for your information"—Makin grins, holding his head higher—"you're right. I only knew that because it's a village near where I grew up. I'm actually not great with maps."

I throw my head back and laugh. "I figured as much."

Cal grins and shakes his head. "And here I thought you had some sort of skill beyond holding a sword."

"Pardon me," a timid voice cuts in from behind Cal.

Cal turns and steps to the side, revealing a servant boy in the hall clutching a letter. The boy's eyes dart nervously around the room.

"I'm looking for an Alak Dunne," he says, his voice barely above a whisper.

"Here!" Alak calls from the alcove across the hall.

The boy spins around as Alak approaches.

"I have a letter for you, sir," the boy says, holding out the letter.

Alak takes it from the boy with a nod. "Thank you." When the boy doesn't move Alak motions with his hand. "You may go."

The servant boy scurries away. Alak breaks the seal on the

letter, unfolding the pages. His face remains emotionless as his eyes scan the contents.

"Is it good news?" I ask hesitantly.

Alak nods, not bothering to lift his eyes from the page. When he finishes, he looks up, eyes bright. "I think we need to talk to Ehren."

"I can go get him," Cal volunteers.

I wave him off. "Not necessary. Give me a minute."

Makin narrows his eyes. "You're going to do something magic-y aren't you?"

Cal elbows Makin in the stomach as Cadewynn makes a harsh shushing noise. I ignore him, reaching out to Kato.

Alak received a letter and needs to talk to Ehren. Are you with him?

I am.

Can you meet up with us now?

Ehren is in a meeting. Hold on.

There's a moment of silence, everyone watching expectantly. After a couple of minutes Kato responds.

Ehren is still busy, but Bram says to head up to Ehren's quarters. We'll be there as soon as possible.

"Ehren is busy, but we can go on up to his room and wait," I relay.

"That is so weird how you can do that," Makin mutters under his breath.

I glance over to Alak. "Shall we go ahead and go up?"

Alak nods. "Walking or wisping?"

"Please, no wisping," Cal requests, paling slightly.

No matter how many times we wisp him, he still gets nauseous.

"I think walking would be best anyway. It will give them a little more time to finish up whatever they're doing," I say. Cal noticeably relaxes.

As we walk through the palace halls, I'm flanked on either side by Cal and Makin. I still find their escort a bit ridiculous as I doubt Landis would try anything in broad daylight, but I would rather be overly cautious than not cautious enough. Alak follows behind a couple paces. Cadewynn decides to stay in the comfort of her library, although we make it clear she's welcome. Once in Ehren's room, Alak secludes himself on the balcony while the rest of us lounge on chairs. After nearly an hour of waiting, I join Alak outside. He's leaning onto the balustrade, staring down.

"Care to share what the letter says or are you waiting for Ehren to arrive for a big reveal?" I ask as I approach.

Alak turns his head toward me, offering a weak smile. "You can read it if you wish."

"I'd settle for you explaining why you're avoiding me," I reply, leaning next to him.

"I think you know the answer to that."

"Alak, I—"

"A prince is never late," Ehren announces from behind us as he bursts into the room, throwing his arms wide.

Alak offers me a sad smile as he pushes away from the balustrade and heads back inside.

"Maybe not technically late, but gods, you took forever," I reply, striding into the room past Alak.

Ehren shrugs half-heartedly. "Duty calls." He turns to Alak, who still hovers near the balcony. "I hear you have a letter?"

Alak nods, approaching. "Yes, I was able to reach one of my relatives in Athiedor—an aunt." He unfolds the letter and passes it to Ehren who starts reading immediately.

"This is good," Ehren mumbles, then he tilts his head and adds, "Well, except for the part that I might not be welcome."

"Why wouldn't you be welcome?" I ask.

"I've told you before, I believe, that many people in Athiedor want to be their own country again," Alak explains. "You can imagine that many of them would be less than happy having a visit from the prince of the kingdom they see as controlling them unlawfully in the best of circumstances. Add in the fact that the king is openly denying magic and they are a land filled with it . . ."

"I guess that does make sense," I concede.

"Your aunt says we can visit and see the magic first hand," Ehren says, looking up from the letter.

"If you want to go, I can send her another letter, give her a heads up," Alak offers.

"Do that," Ehren says with an affirmative nod. "Let her know we will be coming as soon as possible." There's a note of urgency in his voice.

"Ehren, what's wrong?" I ask.

Ehren hesitates, then sighs, throwing his hands up. "I suppose you'll find out soon enough, though I wish I had a better solution than the obvious. My father has officially put a ban on all things magic."

"What?" I gasp.

Ehren nods grimly. "Anyone claiming to have magic or even magical heritage, or anyone suspected of trying to use magic can be, at best, imprisoned for life in the dungeons, or, at worst, executed. He's even placing a bounty on supposed magic wielders."

"I thought he didn't believe magic was back? Why kill people when he doesn't think they actually have magic?" Alak asks.

"Because even though he claims magic isn't real, he knows it is and he fears it. And that fear is driving him. He thinks he can control magic from growing stronger than him by pure force, but what he's doing is dangerous. He's turning neighbor against neighbor. People who have no magic will be dragged into this. I tried to talk him out of it, talk some sense into him. That's what I was doing, what took so long."

Bram takes a step forward. "We are also pretty sure he suspects you," he says, nodding to me. "But, of course, we won't let anything happen to you."

I swallow. "What's the plan?" I glance from Bram to Ehren. "Do you even have a plan?"

"The plan is to get you the hell out of Embervein without raising my father's suspicions, which isn't going to be easy," Ehren answers, biting his lip.

"What's not easy about it?" Alak says, taking a step closer to me, his hands in fists at his side. "We leave. Right now."

"No," Bram says firmly. "As much as that is my first inclination, we are pretty sure the king is watching you all. If we rush out of Embervein, it will only confirm that we have something to hide. He will pursue and we are all as good as dead."

"What do you want from us?" Makin asks, his eyes darting between Bram and Ehren.

Bram straightens. "You joined the Guard to protect the prince. We cannot ask you to risk your lives here."

Cal stands, holding up his hand. "That's where you're wrong, Captain. We joined the Guard to protect *and* serve." He walks over to Ehren and bends down on one knee. He pulls out his sword, placing its point to the ground, bowing his head on top of the hilt. "I am your servant, my prince, and I will serve you here within the palace walls or wherever your path may go. I will protect those you love without question. You need only say the words."

Before Ehren can respond, Makin drops down next to Cal in the same position. "The same goes for me, Your Majesty."

Ehren looks down at them, pride and affection glowing on his face.

"Please rise, both of you," he says softly. Both Guards rise, sheathing their swords. "I am truly honored that your loyalty would extend to a situation such as this. But to ask you to continue your service would be asking you to directly defy the king."

"We know, Your Majesty," Makin replies, standing tall. "And, as treasonous as it might be to say, we serve you, not the king."

Cal nods in agreement. "It's always been you alone we serve."

A flash of emotion crosses Ehren's face as his eyes meet Cal's.

"So be it," Ehren says at length. "See who else among the Guard feels the same. Those that would rather not go against the king are not required to do so. They may remain members of my Guard to protect me within castle walls, but once I am gone, they will be dismissed with honor. Those that wish to continue service will receive new orders that have yet to be decided. All should be on high alert and ready to depart at a moment's notice, but some may be required to remain here. I will not leave my sister unprotected."

"Can't Cadewynn come with us?" Kato interjects.

Ehren nods. "I will, of course, give her the option. But should she choose to stay, she will have some of my Guard."

"So, what do you need from me now?" I ask. "Just do nothing, waiting for a trap to spring?"

"I hate it, but yes," Ehren answers, his shoulders sagging. "Prepare a bag. Have everything ready to go at a moment's notice. But go about your normal schedule. Do your best not to raise any suspicion. In the meantime, I will do whatever I can to ensure that you can get away safely."

Ehren turns and addresses Alak. "Go ahead and write your aunt back. Let her know that you do plan to visit, but avoid any mention or reference to magic, in case your letter is intercepted."

Alak nods. "I can do that. Should I let her know you're coming?"

Ehren thinks for a moment before answering. "No. It's probably better that no one knows my exact destination. And since I might be less than welcome by many locals, keeping my identity secret is probably my best option. Let her know you might be traveling with friends but give no names."

"All right. I'll do that immediately."

"Give it to Cal or Makin to post when you're done. Don't trust anyone else," Ehren orders. Alak nods before wisping away.

"Speaking of destinations, Cadewynn found more evidence of magical lineage in another nearby village," I jump in. "Burrowbrook. It doesn't seem like it's too far."

Bram turns to me, shaking his head. "If you think any of us are leaving you unprotected in the castle with this turn of events to chase down potential magical families, you are insane."

"Bram, be logical," I reply, sharper than I intend. "If the king is truly out to get those with magic, it's even more dire we get to them before he does. You have to go and help them escape or prepare."

"Astra is right," Ehren says, his voice sullen.

Bram spins to face Ehren. "You cannot be serious."

"Look, Bram," Ehren says, his voice steady and commanding. "I understand entirely if you don't want to leave Astra. That's fine. You can stay here with her. I will assemble a few of my Guard to accompany me instead. I will not risk letting my father harm those people when I can save them."

Bram holds Ehren's gaze for a moment, weighing Ehren's

offer. I can see the battle in his eyes. He can choose to stay and protect me or go protect his prince.

"I'll be fine," I say, Bram turning to meet my gaze. "I have Cal and Makin. They're trained soldiers, and I have every confidence they can protect me. I also have my own magic. I can wisp now with no difficulty, so I can get out of the palace unnoticed. Go with Ehren."

Bram takes a deep breath and exhales slowly. "Fine." He turns to face Ehren. "We make quick work of this, though. No dawdling."

Ehren gives Bram a firm nod. "I swear it. We will prepare a plan tonight to have in place in case anything goes wrong, and, along the way, we will make provisions for the future."

"What do you need me to do?" Kato asks. "Remain here or accompany you?"

"Perhaps you can come with us. Your connection to Astra will help us keep in communication with the castle in case something happens on either end."

Kato nods as Bram looks back at me. Despite my assurance that I'll be fine, my body is tense, on full alert.

"Don't worry," Bram swears, wrapping me in his arms. "We will come up with a plan and we will be as quick as possible. I won't let anything happen to you. I promise." He kisses me and I relax slightly. "I can walk you to your room, if you would like."

I nod and Bram leads me toward the door.

"Astra," Ehren calls after us and I turn to him. "I will get you out of here, if it's the last thing I do."

I give him a final nod before Bram escorts me to my room.

CHAPTER THIRTY-FOUR

*T*he next couple of days are torture. I reach out to Kato multiple times, eager for any news. He, Ehren, and Bram make good time, arriving at Burrowbrook in just over a day. It doesn't take long for them to find the families they went to warn. Even when Kato tells me they are on their way back, I can't stop worrying. My stomach is twisted in knots I can't unravel.

"Careful, love," Alak says, drawing me out of my thoughts. "That poor parchment can't take much more."

I scowl in confusion, and Alak glances at my hands. Without meaning to, I've completely crumpled the piece of paper I'm using for my notes. I sigh, smoothing out the crinkled paper, thankful it didn't contain anything important.

"Sorry, I just can't seem to focus on anything today."

"Kato said they would be back this afternoon, right?" Cadewynn says, offering me a reassuring smile.

"Yes, but a lot can happen between now and then."

"All right," Alak says, shoving his chair back as he stands abruptly, holding his hand out to me. "Come on."

I look up at him, knitting my brow in confusion. "What? Where are we going?"

"We're going down to the room to practice some magic."

"I thought we agreed that wasn't a good idea," Makin cuts in with a scowl. "If anyone comes looking for you, you need to be easily found."

"We won't be long," Alak says, not taking his eyes from me, "but Astra needs to release some of her nerves. Magic is the best way for her to do that."

"Go," Cal says, earning a baffled look from Makin. "We'll keep watch up here, and if anyone comes, we'll knock three times on the door."

I rise from my chair, looking over at Cal. "You're sure?"

Cal nods. "Even I can tell you need to release some energy. When I feel stressed, I go to the sword ring. Magic is your release. So go."

I offer Cal a strained smile as I place my hand in Alak's, meeting his eyes.

"Ready, love?" Alak asks, holding my gaze.

I nod and the library fades, the secret room folding around us. I take a deep breath, casting light above us before turning to Alak.

"Okay, what now?"

Alak grins. "Now, we practice. You've come a long way with your magic, but you've really only had to perform one task at a time. Let's see how you do with multitasking."

I scowl. "Multitasking?"

"Aye, love. I pray you won't see battle, but if you do, you may have to shield from multiple angles and attack at the same time. It's best to be prepared."

I nod, licking my lips. "You're right. How can I practice that?"

"Let's start small. I'll send attacks at you from multiple

directions. They'll only be illusions, mind you, but act as if they could actually hurt you."

I nod as Alak rolls his neck. A few moments later balls of glowing orange light come charging at me from three different directions. I blast each away with my silver light.

"Good, now try to block orange lights with a sword and green lights with attack magic."

I nod and craft a sleek sword from my silver light. Alak sends several balls of colored light my way, and I block or strike each one as instructed, though it takes effort. We continue on like this for some time, the illusions getting more and more complex. Eventually, Alak turns the entire room into an obstacle course of sorts, complete with trees, rocks, animals, and more. I'm dodging multiple objects, while weaving my way around the constantly shifting landscape, focusing on warding off attacks. By the time he pulls back his illusion, I'm breathless but exhilarated.

"You did well, love." He grins, his eyes twinkling.

"That was amazing," I say, glowing. "I feel so much better."

"I figured you would. I told you to always trust me. I give good advice," Alak replies with a wink.

I laugh. "I'll keep that in mind." I pause before asking, "Can you teach me how to do that?"

Alak cocks his head. "Teach you what? Attack magic? I think you've proven pretty well you can handle that, love."

"No," I reply with a shake of my head. "Can you teach me how to weave a believable illusion?"

He considers me carefully for a moment before answering. "Perhaps. But rather, instead of you creating your own full illusion, why don't you try weaving your magic with mine? I'll create an illusion and you intertwine your magic. You support it, feel it out."

"We can do that? Combine our magic?" I ask, eyes wide.

Alak nods, somewhat hesitantly. "I believe so, love. Most any magic wielders can combine their magic to an extent. Thanks to all the practicing we've done together, your magic will recognize mine and respond to it."

"Okay," I say with an eager nod. "Let's try."

Alak nods, his emerald eyes locking with mine. He takes a deep breath, not breaking his gaze, and a forest scene appears around us.

"All right, love," he says, his voice quiet and warm. "Find my magic with yours and weave it in."

I don't look away from his eyes as I stretch my magic out. My magic senses Alak's and naturally reaches toward it. I push it forward, meeting only slight resistance before Alak's magic wraps around mine. I inhale sharply as the warmth of his magic combines with mine. I press my magic against Alak's and it responds, the illusion becoming clearer. Everything is brighter, sharper. Alak takes a step toward me, barely breathing.

"Now, add to it," he says, his voice just above a whisper.

I swallow and nod, molding a soft breeze. It whips around us, carrying the scent of home—damp trees, fresh soil, and spring flowers. Alak steps closer and takes my hands. I weave my fingers with his, not taking my eyes off his, and the illusion grows even stronger. I can feel the warmth of the sun and hear chirping birds and the rustle of the underbrush. It's a flawless illusion.

Alak and I stand, hand in hand, barely a breath apart for several moments, our hearts beating as one. I don't want it to end. I edge forward, lost in Alak's eyes. His lips part before he blinks and looks down, taking a step back as he drops my hands. The illusion around us flickers away. I shake my head, blinking as if I've just woken from a dream.

"There you go, love," he says, his voice quiet and rough. He raises his eyes back to mine, a weak smile on his lips. "Feel better?"

I nod, glancing away. "Yes. Much better. Thank you."

Alak nods, glancing off to the side. "We should probably get back upstairs, in case anyone comes looking."

Without looking at him, I nod, and we wisp back up into the alcove across from Cadewynn. Makin is the first to notice our return.

"Oh, good! You're back. That means we can go eat now," Makin says with a grin.

"Yes," Cadewynn says, sighing in a way that tells me this isn't the first time Makin's mentioned lunch.

"Can we eat outside today?" I ask as Cadewynn rises from her seat.

"Do you think that's the best idea?" Cal asks.

I shrug. "I don't really care. I only know I can't stand being locked inside another moment. I need fresh air."

The truth is, the illusion Alak and I created together has me craving more. I hope that spending some time outdoors might help push those feelings aside. Cal and Makin exchange a wary look, but Cadewynn is quick to agree with me.

"I do love the indoors, but Astra is right," Cadewynn says, linking her arm with mine as we walk down the alcove corridor. "We can't stay indoors all the time. We're like complicated houseplants, you know. We can survive inside, but we need the sun to live."

Cadewynn rings for servants and instructs them to prepare a picnic lunch for us to take in one of the smaller gardens that has a hedge maze. We weave through to the center of the maze, spreading out on a blanket. The tall hedges surrounding us keep us feeling safe and hidden as we laugh and chat, munching on sandwiches, cheese, and sliced fruit. The fresh air does us good, and it's evident it was something we all needed.

After spending an hour outside, we pack up what remains of our lunch and drift back indoors. Makin volunteers to return the leftover food to the kitchen, but Cal remains with me, Alak, and Cadewynn. We're nearly back to the library when a sharp voice calls after us, disintegrating our cheerful mood.

"Well, well, well," Landis sneers. "Look who finally left her little hidey-hole."

I spin to face him, Alak taking his place at my side. Landis is accompanied by the same two young men as before.

"What do you want, Landis?" I ask, my voice hard.

He saunters toward us, his companions hanging back, a cocky grin on his face. "Now, that's no way to treat someone who knows your little secret, is it?"

My blood runs cold. No, there's no way he can know. I school my features into confusion, but Alak tenses beside me.

"My secret?" I say, struggling to keep my voice even. "Everyone knows I'm engaged to Bram. That's no secret."

Landis laughs, but it's not a cheerful sound.

"Not that secret," he says, close enough he can lean in and whisper in my ear. "The one about your magic."

I reel back, resisting the urge to strike Landis. "What? I don't have . . . I'm not . . ."

Landis stands straighter, leering as his eyes meet mine. "I know who you are. I did some digging. Your brother isn't just your brother. He's your twin."

I shake my head. "We're close in age but—"

Landis cuts me off with a sharp wave. "Don't even pretend."

He reaches into his pocket and withdraws a letter, the seal freshly broken.

"I have proof. I suspected the truth from rumors and reached out to some people who would know. This letter," he says, holding the paper up to my eye level, "will provide more than enough evidence for the king."

Landis grins like he's just won a game, and I can't find the words I need to combat his claim. Alak takes a step toward Landis, who flinches slightly.

"Even if that were true, mate"—Alak stands at his full height, making Landis shrink back—"it doesn't make her magic."

Landis swallows and staggers back another step. "Everyone knows about the twins and their magic. It's all over the kingdom. But that doesn't even matter. We both know that the king won't actually require any evidence. All it would take is the faintest whisper of magic, and he'll throw you in the dungeon. It won't matter that you're friends with the prince."

Landis tucks the letter back into his pocket, looking at me. "Your captain is gone. Your prince is gone. Your brother is gone. There's no one left to protect you."

"Not that she needs anyone besides herself, but there's me," Alak says, taking my hand in his. "I've decked ya once before, and I'll do it again."

Landis gives Alak a feral grin. "No you won't. Because I also happen to know the path your friends are traveling and what they've been doing. You act like you're all high and mighty, but you're essentially powerless. I, on the other hand, have power. A few words from me, and your friends never make it home."

All color drains from my face at the implication of his words. Landis sees he has power over me, his grin growing. Alak's hand tightens on mine, his magic surging.

"I think that's quite enough harassing my guests," Cadewynn says sharply, stepping forward. "My brother may be gone, but I still remain. I also have power, Landis. Let's not forget that. You act out against my friends, and I will use every ounce of my influence to end you. You do realize that you just made a threat against the crown prince? That's treason, punishable by death."

Landis blanches, exchanging a wary glance with his companions.

"Come on," his friend says, pulling Landis back. "You've made your point."

Landis looks back at me and says, "Magic is evil and will destroy our kingdom. I will go to the king with what I know. I will win this game."

Landis spins on his heel and storms down the hall without another glance.

"Let's go directly to your room," Cal suggests.

"That's a good idea," Cadewynn says. "I'll have books sent up to you as soon as I return to the library."

I swallow and glance away as I nod. Cadewynn sees my distress and places a gentle hand on my arm.

"Don't worry. We'll fix this," she says.

She turns and floats down the hall toward her library as Cal ushers Alak and I to our room. Alak keeps a firm grasp on my trembling hand until we're inside our suite. Cal decides to stay outside the door to watch for any signs of trouble, leaving Alak and I alone in the sitting room. I reach out to Kato.

Landis knows we're twins and have magic. Be careful.

Are you okay, Ash? Did he hurt you?

No, but he made a threat that you, Bram, and Ehren may not make it home.

We'll be on alert.

Please, Kato, be careful. I think Landis really means to cause trouble.

I will, Ash. We're picking up our pace. We'll be home by dinner.

"Is Kato okay?" Alak asks, studying my face.

I nod, clasping my hands in front of my body. I lift my eyes to Alak and a tear breaks free.

"Hey, none of that," Alak says, crossing to me and gathering me in his arms. "They're going to be all right. It'll take more than a weasel like Landis to take down Kato, Bram, and Ehren."

I sniff and pull back, wiping my tears with the back of my hand as I turn away from Alak. "You're right. I know you're right, but this whole thing with Landis, it's my fault. I pushed him. If everything falls apart, if anyone gets hurt, it's on me."

Alak places his hands on my shoulders, turning me to face him. "Look at me, Astra."

My eyes jolt to his. He rarely uses my name when addressing me, and hearing it from his lips feels like warm caress.

"Everything is going to work out. Your brother has powerful magic, and he's learned how to wield it as a weapon and as defense. I've seen it firsthand. No matter how many men the king may send after them—if he sends any at all—your brother can handle them. And that's not even taking into account the damage Ehren and Bram can do with their swords. At the first sign of trouble, you can wisp from the castle. You can contact Kato and find him across any distance. You'll be fine."

I nod, my tears slowing. "What about you?"

"Me?" Alak asks, confusion flickering across his face as he drops his hands from my shoulders. "What about me?"

"You'll come with me, right?"

His lips part as he takes in my words.

"I can understand if you'd rather part ways after you help me find Kato," I add quickly, "but if you could—"

"Astra," Alak says, his voice rough as he takes my hands in his. "I will follow you to the end of the world."

My breath catches in my throat as I look into Alak's

emerald eyes. His eyes have a calming effect. I take a deep breath, nodding.

"Good. Good."

He releases my hands and rakes a hand through his hair. "You know, I—"

Alak's interrupted by Makin bursting through the door. Alak jerks back, putting more distance between us as Makin focuses on me.

"I heard what happened," Makin says, "and I passed the information on to the rest of the Guard. Everyone is on high alert. Don't worry, Astra, everyone will make it back safely."

I nod, but it's not what happens today that worries me. Now, I'm more concerned about the future. We've been using borrowed time, and it's about to run out.

CHAPTER THIRTY-FIVE

$\mathcal{T}$he next few hours are stressful. I'm tense and irritable. I find little to no relief until Kato's voice finally echoes through my head.

We're back. We had no issues. We'll be up soon.

I breathe a sigh of relief and relay the message to the others.

Cal smiles softly as Makin mutters "Thank the gods," and drops into a nearby chair.

The moment Bram walks through the door to our suite, I'm in his arms. He holds me tightly.

"I was so worried," I mumble against his chest.

He laughs and I look up at him in confusion.

"What's so funny?"

"The idea that you were worried about me when you were the one trapped in the castle with a fool like Landis running his mouth," Bram replies, shaking his head.

"Was anyone worried about me?" Ehren asks, his eyes twinkling as he steps forward.

Cal rolls his eyes. "I think that's a given."

"Just not enough for you to rush into my arms with

rapturous relief," Ehren replies with a wink. "Maybe next time."

Cal just shakes his head, glancing away to hide his smile.

"In all seriousness, you know what these new threats mean, don't you?" Ehren says, his face suddenly somber. "It means we will be leaving sooner rather than later. Make sure you have everything completely ready to go. I'll do what damage control I can, but, as much as I hate it, Landis does have sway. You may have to stay in your room."

I swallow and nod. "We'll be ready."

The next morning, tensions are especially high. Even Makin and Cal, who usually get along, are wearing on each other. Every noise has us jumping—Alak and I reaching for our magic and Makin and Cal reaching for their swords. I repack my bag multiple times, each time checking to make sure I have everything I need. I notice that foods good for travel have been casually added to our morning and lunch trays. Alak and I add these to our bags. Kato sticks close to Ehren and Bram.

Ehren extends an offer to Cadewynn, inviting her to come with us but, as expected, she refuses. She joins us in our suite, bringing plenty of books and texts meant to be distractions, but they're only reminders of what looms over us.

I stare at an old piece of text, reading the same few words over at least a dozen times, but nothing is sticking. I'm about to give up when Kato's voice echoes in my head.

It's time to go.

Now? Right now?

Yes. You and Alak get your bags and wisp directly into the stables. Your horses should be ready. Bram will meet you there.

What about Cal and Makin?

Tell them Plan One is a go. That's it. Just those words. "Plan One is a go." They'll know what it means.

And you?

I'm staying next to Ehren in case he needs to be wisped away. But don't worry about me. I'll be fine. We'll meet up with you at a rendezvous point. Now, GO!

"What is it?" Cadewynn asks, studying my face. "It's Kato, isn't it? What did he say?"

"It's time to go," I say standing.

Alak jumps up. "Go where?"

"You and I get our bags and wisp to the stables. Bram will meet us there." I turn to Cal and Makin. "Plan One is a go."

Cal and Makin exchange nervous looks.

"That means we part ways for now," Cal says, inclining his head. "Hopefully, we will see you again soon, but just in case, it has been an honor to serve with you."

My stomach swirls with nerves but I nod my appreciation. Cal and Makin turn on their heels and head off. I turn and look at Alak but before we can leave to get our bags, Cadewynn stops me.

"I have something for you before you go," she says. She reaches down and grabs a small black book. "This book has records I think you will find useful. I've written down anything I think you might need, including some of the more prevalent twin prophecies."

I take the book and flip it open. "Thank you," I reply, tears in my eyes.

She nods. "I was hoping to be able to add a few more things, but it is what it is. I only filled in the first few pages," she says softly. "The rest is for you to fill. You wanted to be a historian for your village. Now you can record magical history for someone in the future to read."

I envelop her in a hug. "Thank you so much, Winnie."

"Astra," Alak says urgently. "We need to go."

I rush to my room and add the journal to my bag. For a

moment, I stand there staring at the room I've come to call home the past couple of weeks. I'm going to miss it.

"You ready?" Alak asks from the doorway.

I nod and cross over to him. I hold out my hand but he pauses, looking me in the eye.

"We're going to be okay," he says, placing his hand in mine. "We're going to be okay."

I nod and wisp us into the stables. We appear just a couple feet away from a very startled stable boy. Peter stares at us wide-eyed, mouth gaping for a moment before he finally finds his words.

"Miss Astra! Captain Bramfield told me you should appear soon, but I didn't quite think it would happen like that!"

"Are our horses ready?" I ask, eager to change the subject.

Peter nods. "Yes, ma'am. Right over here."

He leads us to Luna and Fawn who stand next to Solomon, all saddled and ready to go. Solomon is even fully equipped with Bram's bag. I look around for Twilight or Ehren's horse but they're nowhere to be seen. I swallow and try to push down the fear rising in my chest. I'm fastening my bag to Luna when familiar footsteps enter the barn. I spin around and run into Bram's arms. He catches me and gives me a quick kiss.

"What's happening?" I ask breathlessly.

"Alak," he says, looking past me and ignoring my question. "Head out of town. Go straight out on your own. You will find more answers a little way down the road."

Alak nods and mounts Fawn. He's gone before I can question what Bram's said.

"We are going for a picnic in the forest," he says, trying to sound at ease but I can hear the tension in his voice.

"A picnic?" I ask in disbelief as he leads me to Luna.

He nods. "Yes, a picnic."

We mount our horses and take the exact same path we took

over a week earlier when we went on our previous picnic. I'm confused, but Bram is trying very hard to act normal. He even waves and nods at villagers as we pass. It's not until we're well into the forest Bram lets his façade drop. He slows and lets out a long breath.

"Bram, what is going on?" I ask, my voice strained.

"We are on our way to a safe house. We will meet up with everyone else there."

"But they're safe? Everyone is safe?"

Bram doesn't answer.

"Bram," I press. "Is everyone okay?"

He glances over me. "Yes."

I relax a little, but something about the way he's avoiding my eyes still has me concerned. "What aren't you saying?" I ask, heart pounding.

Bram sighs. "They are all safe. While everything was going according to plan when we left, there are many components to consider. Everyone has different parts of the plan to complete. I can't be sure what happened after we left, but if everything continues to go smoothly, we will all be fine. Alak is taking the main road. It should look like he is on his own. The king's men believe Alak was already planning on leaving to visit family and have been expecting him to leave. They should just assume he is on his way. Outside of town, he will meet up with Makin, who will guide him to the rendezvous point."

"And, according to any witnesses, you and I are headed out for a picnic in the woods?" I clarify and Bram nods. "And Ehren, Kato, and Cal?"

"Ehren can't just up and leave. His father is watching him very closely. I don't know all the details, but the king is taking definitive action against magic. Ehren is trying to talk him down and will wait until the very last second to leave. Knowing how stubborn Ehren is, it's more than likely Kato will have to wisp him out. Cal, too, since they're together."

I nod and we fall into silence. I try reaching out to Kato, but I just get a clipped response.

I'm fine but busy.

Nothing else. My nerves are wound so tightly that every snap of a twig has me jumping. I'm a swirl of emotions. My hands grip the reins so tightly they hurt, but I can't seem to let go. We ride for hours, and the sun is starting to set when we arrive at our destination, which I don't even see until we're upon it.

There's a little cottage woven into the woods. Its walls are made of wood and vines climb the outside, blending it perfectly with the surrounding trees. We approach the cottage and Bram hops off Solomon, tying him to a post outside the house. As I follow suit, a little old woman hobbles out of the home.

"Alexander," she says affectionately, stretching her hand toward Bram in greeting.

"Mistress Kellan," Bram says with an equal level of affection as he takes her hand and gives it a kiss.

The woman turns to me. "You must be Astra."

"Yes, ma'am," I say, offering her a small smile.

"Well, come in. Come in," she says, motioning us inside.

We follow her into her little cottage and find a cozy one room area. It's a little hot and stuffy, partially due to the hot weather outside and partially due to the fire crackling in the fireplace. A delicious smell fills the air.

"I only received your message a short while ago, but I've started preparing a bit of soup," Mistress Kellan says with a nod to a cast iron pot sitting over the fire. "It's not much, I'm afraid, but it will fill your bellies."

She eases down onto a rocking chair near the fire.

"Thank you," Bram says. "I'm sure it will be more than enough."

I figure by the time the soup is ready, I'll be hungry, but when the time comes, my stomach is still tied in too many nervous knots to eat anything. I manage a few sips of the onion soup, but that's all I can get down, despite Bram's prompting. When we hear horses approaching outside, Bram goes on high alert.

"Stay there," he orders sharply, standing and drawing his sword. There's a knock on the door and Bram opens it slowly. When Alak and Makin's faces appear, he relaxes. Felixe is perched on Alak's shoulder.

"Thank the gods!" I cry, jumping up and rushing to them.

I throw my arms around Alak, who freezes, not sure how to respond. I release him and turn to Makin, doing the same. Makin returns my embrace.

"You know, I am a member of the prince's Guard," Makin chuckles as I pull away. "I'm trained for these situations."

"I know," I sigh, "but I hate not knowing where everyone is."

Makin nods. "Understandable. I don't care for it either." He turns to Bram. "Any word from the palace?"

Bram shakes his head. "But I don't expect to hear anything for a while yet. Ehren, Cal, and Kato are taking the most indirect route."

"Come in and have some soup," Mistress Kellan says, drawing their attention.

Makin and Alak each take a bowl of soup and sit down on the floor with me and Bram. Now that I know Alak and Makin are okay, I'm able to at least finish my bowl. Once we're done with dinner we settle down on the floor for the night. Felixe curls up in a little ball at Alak's feet. It's still a little early but, if the plan goes as it should, we'll leave first thing in the morning.

I know it isn't exactly proper, but I set my bed close to Bram. Tonight, I need the comfort of his presence. No one says anything or even gives me a second glance as I lie down next to him, and he wraps his arms around me.

"We're going to be fine," Bram whispers into my hair. "All of us."

I snuggle closer to him in response and slowly drift off to sleep.

CHAPTER THIRTY-SIX

I'm awoken by a chill a few hours later. I sit up and turn to see a figure in a purple hooded cloak behind me. Before she even lowers the hood, I know who it is. It's me.

"You're going to make it," she says.

"How can you know that?" I ask.

"Because I do. Because you do."

"I don't think I've ever been this worried or terrified in my life," I admit.

"You know, you have great power. You have no need to fear. You are no longer hiding your power from the king. You can use it, uninhibited."

I shake my head. "He's still hunting us. I don't want to draw unwanted attention."

The other me nods her head. "That is wise, but when confronted, do not fear your power." She pauses, then adds, "They're here. And they need you."

I jolt awake to the sound of someone pounding on the cottage door. I glance over at Bram to find he's already on his feet, hand on his sword. Makin isn't far behind. I stand slowly and take a step toward Alak, who stands nearby, magic twirling around his fingers. Someone bangs on the door again, rattling the lock.

"Anyone in there?" a familiar voice yells.

"Kato!" I gasp as Bram strides to the door, unlocking it and throwing the door open.

Kato staggers through the door, supporting an unconscious Ehren. Cal limps in behind them, his uniform tattered, torn, and covered in blood and dirt. Bram rushes to support Ehren from the other side.

"What happened?" Bram demands, helping Kato ease Ehren onto the floor.

In the light from the dying fire, I can see that Ehren's right leg is soaked with an uncomfortable amount of blood. I stand to the side with Alak, watching with swelling panic.

"We were attacked," Kato answers. "I wisped us out as planned, but soldiers ambushed us along our planned route."

"If it weren't for Kato, there's no way we would have gotten away," Cal says weakly. His eyes dart to Ehren, flooded with panic. "Will he . . . is he going to live?"

"He will if I have anything to say about it," Bram says, tearing away what remains of Ehren's pant leg.

Ehren shifts and moans but doesn't wake. The leg has been tied with what looks like a scrap from Cal's Guard coat. Bram removes the makeshift bandage, and bile rises in my throat at the sight of the raw, bloodied flesh, the bone gleaming crimson in the firelight.

"Shit, this is bad," Bram mutters as Makin swears.

"You have to save him," Cal pleads. "He can't die because I failed to protect him."

"It's not your fault, Cal," Kato insists. "We were seriously outnumbered."

Cal shakes his head and glances away.

"He lost a lot of blood. You shouldn't have let him ride like this," Bram says, shaking his head.

"I told him the same," Cal mutters, traces of terror shimmering in his eyes. "But he kept insisting. He gave a direct order. I didn't—"

"We didn't have a choice," Kato cuts in. "I had to use my magic to ward off the soldiers and more were on the way. I wisped us as far as I could, horses and all, but without knowing the exact location, I couldn't get us any closer to the rendezvous point. We had no idea if more soldiers would appear. We had to keep moving. I could have tried wisping us at least a little farther, but wisping three horses and two others by myself the first time drained too much of my magic to try again."

"No one blames you," I whisper and Cal nods.

"You saved us."

Ehren moans again as Bram cleans the wound with water that Mistress Kellan fetched while I focused on Kato and Cal. Cal inhales sharply and looks away from Ehren, his face tense with distress.

"We have to stop this bleeding," Bram says, his voice controlled but edged with fear.

Alak takes a step closer to me, whispering in my ear, "You might be able to heal him."

I turn my head toward him, eyes wide. "I have no idea how to do that."

Alak holds my gaze for a moment. "You have the power. You healed yourself in the garden when Landis struck you."

"That was nothing compared to this!" I whisper, my eyes darting back to Ehren.

"I think you can do it," Alak insists as Ehren moans again. "You have to try."

I shake my head. "Can't you Syphon my power and do it?"

"No. I mean, I could try, but you would have a better

chance of being successful. It's your magic, so it responds to you in a way it never will to me. Stolen magic seldom works as well for things like this."

I glance at Ehren. His chest is barely moving, his breathing almost nonexistent. His face is pale, too pale. He's fading quickly. It's a miracle he's lasted this long. If I don't do something he's not going to make it.

"No, no, no. Don't you die on me!" Bram yells, his voice breaking. "Come on, Ehren! Fight!"

Cal swallows and exchanges a terrified look with Makin, both their eyes filled with something close to anguish. I glance back at Alak. He watches me with a steady gaze. Before I can talk myself out of it, I kneel next to Ehren, Alak easing down behind me. I call my magic, though I have no idea what I'm doing. I close my eyes and take a deep breath. I can feel the cool power coursing through my veins. The magic pools in my hands, and I open my eyes to find them glowing. I hesitantly reach toward Ehren's leg and wrap my magic around his wound.

He inhales sharply and lets out a moan. I flinch but continue. I don't fight my magic. I tell it what I want and let it work. Closing my eyes allows me to see clearly through my magic. I sense more than see the parts of Ehren's leg that are torn and broken. The damage is worse than I thought. I slowly weave the pieces back together, cleaning away the dirt and other foreign material with nothing more than my magic. I feel the process draining me, but I don't stop, not until Ehren's breath evens out.

I open my eyes to find Bram watching me in wonder. I glance at Ehren's leg. A jagged, swollen red line seals the flesh back together. It will scar I'm sure, but at least Ehren is out of danger.

"I am not sure if it is completely healed, but you have cured the worst of it," Bram breathes, studying the wound carefully. He looks back up at me. "You saved his life, Astra."

I smile. Exhaustion washes over me, and I fall back. Alak is close enough behind me that he supports me without anyone noticing how drained I am.

"You did it," he whispers in my ear. I smile softly, looking up at Kato who's hovering nervously.

Are you okay? I ask him.

Kato looks at me, and I can see the weariness in his eyes.

I'm fine. Minor wounds. My magic protected me. Ehren took the brunt of the attack. Kato's eyes shift to Cal sitting behind me. *Cal took a hit to his leg as well. He's been acting like it was nothing, but I can tell he's in pain.*

I turn to Cal. "Let me see your leg."

Cal's mouth falls open, and he hesitates before answering, "I'm fine."

"No, you're not. Please let me help you."

"Show her your leg. That is an order," Bram commands.

Cal slowly peels back his pant leg and reveals a decent gash on his left shin. It's not nearly as bad as Ehren's but it's still a significant cut. I look up at him and shake my head.

"That's no small wound, Cal. This can easily become infected, and you could have lost that leg."

"It was nothing compared to Ehren's wound," Cal says quietly. "I didn't want to distract from him. I don't matter as much."

Before he can protest, I summon my magic and silver tendrils stretch from my fingers and wrap his leg. He tries to hide his pain but inhales sharply as soon as my magic touches his skin. His wound is much less complicated to heal but it drains what little energy I have left. Whatever concentration I'm not using on the healing process I rally to keep from collapsing. When I finish, I slump back, Alak catching me. I close my eyes and take a shuddering breath.

"Astra!" Bram cries, scrambling from Ehren's side to mine.

His strong arms take me from Alak. I force my eyes open and look up into Bram's face. Everything is out of focus. I close them again, shaking my head. I try to sit up, but I simply don't have the strength.

"Will she be okay?" Cal's voice asks, rich with guilt.

"She'll be fine," Alak replies.

"What are you doing?" Bram growls as Alak takes my hand in his.

Alak doesn't answer but links his fingers with mine. I feel a rush of magic, gasping as it fills me. It's different from my own magic. My own magic is cool and liquid, like a starlit winter night. This magic is full of bright sparks and warmth like a bonfire on spring day. I feel a pulse rush through me as my energy returns just enough that I can open my eyes. I look over at Alak, my hand still in his, realizing with a start his own magic is draining too quickly. I jerk my hand away and offer him a smile.

"I'm fine." My voice is weak and hoarse, hardly convincing.

Alak offers me a small smile as he leans back on his palms, his magic obviously weak.

"You didn't have to do that," I mutter. "How did you do that?"

Alak gives a small laugh. "Magic."

Bram's focus is on me. "Are you sure you are okay?"

I sit up. My head is pounding, but I feel stronger. "I'm good. Alak somehow shared his magic and refilled mine a bit."

Bram glances over to Alak who looks like he could fall asleep at any moment. "Thank you."

Alak shrugs him off. "It was nothing. Her magic would have replenished soon. I just helped her get there faster." He glances around at everyone. "We should probably all get to sleep, eh? King's men after us and all?"

Bram nods, clearing his throat. "Alak is right. We really need to get some sleep. If we can, we need to be on the road as soon as possible in the morning to put as much distance between us and the king as possible."

Kato and Cal go out and unload their supplies. After a few minutes we're all settled back down. Exhaustion takes over, and I'm soon fast asleep.

I WAKE the next morning to bustling around me. I sit up, rubbing my eyes. The door is open. Kato and Makin are outside packing the horses. I glance around the room and see Ehren standing with Bram in the opposite corner of the room. A rush of relief sweeps through me when I see Ehren's color has returned. In fact, he looks perfectly healthy, and I would never guess that hours ago he was on the brink of death. Bram is scowling more than usual, and Ehren looks exasperated as they argue in low voices. They stop when they notice me heading their direction.

"Good morning, Astra," Bram, says, greeting me with a quick kiss on the cheek.

"Are we leaving now?" I ask, glancing toward the horses.

"Yes," Ehren says firmly. "As soon as the horses are ready, we'll leave."

Bram shakes his head. "You are still healing. We should give you more time to recover. You almost died."

"I'm fine. From what I understand, Astra saw to that," Ehren insists, motioning to me.

Bram looks down at me, and I can read the question in his eyes.

"I may not have healed him completely, but he should be fine to travel."

By the way Bram sighs, I have a feeling he was hoping I would side with him.

"Fine," Bram concedes, turning back to Ehren, "but if your leg starts to act up, you inform me immediately. Understand?"

Ehren grins. "I thought the prince was the one who gave orders."

Bram sighs in the exhausted way he reserves for Ehren. "I am going to go help Kato and Makin. We should be able to leave shortly."

Once he's gone, Ehren turns to me. "It seems I owe you my life."

"It was nothing," I mumble, looking down at my hands.

Ehren places his finger under my chin and tilts my face up so my eyes meet his. His cool sea-green eyes are steady and calm.

"That was not nothing. You literally saved my life. I am indebted to you."

"I couldn't let you die, Ehren."

He smiles, his eyes twinkling. "Well, naturally, a world without me wouldn't be worth living in."

I laugh and shake my head. "Exactly."

He holds my gaze a moment longer before kissing my cheek lightly. "I will never forget it, Astra. You are an amazing person, and I am glad, for many reasons, that you're a part of my life. I've had very few people in my life I trust as much as you, and very few of them would risk what you did for me."

Color rises in my cheeks as I glance away. "It was nothing. Really."

He smiles. "Never underestimate your power. I know I never will. Thank you."

He walks away without another word, and I turn to find

Alak standing not far behind me. Felixe is perched on his shoulder nibbling some fruit.

"How are you feeling this morning?" Alak asks, scanning my face.

"Honestly, I feel pretty normal. How are you?"

"Right as rain, love," he grins.

"How *did* you share your magic with me last night? I thought Syphons could only take magic."

"Usually, that's the case," Alak says with a shrug. "But I'm not a full-blooded Syphon. I have my own magic, so I was able to reverse the process. At least, with you. I'm not sure if it would work for anyone. Maybe it's because my magic recognized yours from training together. I really don't know how I knew it would work, but I just felt it would."

"Well, however it worked, thank you."

"It really wasn't anything. You needed the magic more than I did." I don't say anything and he shrugs again. "Look, love, it really wasn't a big deal. You weren't in any immediate danger. You were just a little weak from using so much magic to heal, so I just gave you a little boost."

"Well, regardless, I truly appreciate it."

Alak starts to turn away then pauses. "You should eat something. Your body needs it after using so much magic."

I nod in agreement and go over where Cal sits near a tray of fruit and bread. He grins at me, tossing me an apple. I thank him and take a bite.

"How's your leg?" I ask, nodding to his wounded leg.

He stands up. "Like new!" His face grows serious. "I would have been fine if you hadn't healed it. I could have at least waited until you recovered from healing Ehren."

"I'm still adjusting to my power, but it's my choice to use it. I chose to heal you, and I have no regrets," I say, offering him a smile.

"Thank you, not just for me, but for healing Ehren. I know you were unsure and I . . ." His eyes shift past me and focus on where Ehren stands outside with the horses. He swallows and turns back to me. "Ehren can be so stubborn sometimes. He almost died. I don't know what I would . . . He can't die. I—we all need him. Everything falls apart without him. He's our only hope to fix everything."

I offer Cal a reassuring smile. "Don't worry, I'll keep my eye on him. I'm pretty sure Bram isn't going to let Ehren out of his sight for a while, either."

Cal gives me a grateful nod. I excuse myself and join Kato by the horses to make sure my things are ready to go. I'm whispering to Luna when Kato comes up next to me.

"We're officially outlaws," he says with a grin.

I laugh. "Are you supposed to be happy about being an outlaw? Because it sounds like a bad thing."

Kato's grin widens. "I guess it depends on who you ask. Besides, I want to be on the side that doesn't oppress magic, don't you?"

"Since I have magic, I think that's a pretty obvious answer." I glance over to where Bram and Ehren stand near Solomon. "Did you really wisp three people and three horses? That's an insane amount of magic."

Kato nods. "It wasn't easy. It took a lot of focus and concentration. Honestly, I barely did it. It was quite exhausting. I wish I could have gotten us closer. If I had, you might have had an easier job healing Ehren, which, by the way, was an impressive feat on its own. I didn't know you were able to heal."

"I didn't know either. Alak thought I could, so I had to try."

"Good thing you did, Ash. You saved Ehren's life."

"So everyone keeps saying."

"Everyone ready to go?" Bram calls.

We nod, mounting our horses, and follow Bram as he rides into the surrounding forest.

"What exactly is the plan from here?" I ask as we pick up a steady pace.

"We're headed for Athiedor, taking the least traveled path. Basically, we're going on an adventure," Ehren replies with a grin. He glances over his shoulder at me. "Are you ready for an adventure, Astra?"

A smile plays on my lips. "I suppose I don't have a choice, so I might as well embrace the idea."

Ehren grins and turns back around. "Excellent attitude."

I grin as we follow Bram into the sunrise. Adventure or not, here we come.

Part Four:

Outlaws

CHAPTER THIRTY-SEVEN

The life of an outlaw is far less exciting than it sounded when Kato first presented the idea. We spend every moment tense, expecting the king's soldiers to find us and drag us back to the castle at any time, but we manage to stay one step ahead. We spend two days traveling through the woods. The trees provide decent protection from the increasingly burning sun but trap us in a muggy, bug infested atmosphere. The only real advantage is the flowing stream we follow. It's a constant water source, and the cool water offers refreshing breaks from the heat.

Breaks themselves are few and far between, however. Even when we stop at night, it's only for a few hours, and those hours are spent more tossing and turning than actually sleeping.

On the third day, we abandon our little stream and the cover of trees in favor of wide-open land, traveling directly under the blazing rays of the sun. I'm so used to the protection of shade I don't even realize the effect the sun is having on my fair complexion until the day ends and my skin is red and raw. Luckily, Healer Heora provided a healing aloe salve that helps, so I'm not entirely miserable. On the second day of traveling exposed to the elements, Alak gently reminds me I can use magic to create protection from the sun. Naturally, I snap at him although I'm inwardly grateful.

By the fourth day, we're running low on food. We all managed to gather bits and scraps and store it for our journey, but it isn't much. Without the stream for water, our supply is running low. We're tense and irritable beyond compare.

Every time we stop, I can feel the gazes of Makin, Alak, Ehren, Bram, and Cal, sure they're wondering if all this trouble is worth it. I feel guilty. I feel like this whole situation is largely my fault. I begin slowly distancing myself from the group, physically and emotionally. I don't talk or join in on any conversations as we ride unless directly addressed, and even then I answer only as much as necessary before falling silent again. When we stop at night, I make my bed at the farthest outside ring of our group. Bram, of course, always stays near me. I can tell he notices something is wrong, but he lets me be. At least, he lets me be after I snap at him the first couple of times.

We may have all escaped the king, but the longer we travel, I wonder if we can survive each other.

On our fifth day of travel, the terrain changes as we approach the Marbourne Mountains, supposed neutral territory between Callenia and Ascaria. The land gathers into rolling hills and uneven land, but the horses don't seem to mind the change. We as their riders, however, aren't having as easy of a time with it. The constant shifting over the rocky, uneven ground is creating blisters in areas I didn't know could blister.

It's almost a relief when the rain starts. It's the coolest it's been in days and the rain gives us water to drink. After a couple, hours, though, the rain gets old. I'm tired of being wet and uncomfortable.

The foot of the mountains is a welcome sight. We don't

have to travel long before we find a little pocket cave in the mountainside that serves as a perfect place to camp for the night. There's a dip in the cave at one end that serves as a stable for the horses. They munch at the green grass and bushes growing around the edge of the cave. We make ourselves comfortable in the larger portion. Kato uses his magic to create a roaring fire before rushing a warm wind over us all, drying us completely.

We haven't been resting long when several rabbits burst from some nearby brush. Bram, who's standing at the edge of the cave, is quick and sends a dagger at one while Makin gets another. I manage to call my magic quickly enough to summon a silver dagger, snagging a third rabbit. Grinning, Kato and Cal volunteer to skin the rabbits and soon all three are roasting on a spit over the fire.

As the rabbits roast, Bram takes watch, leaning against the outer edge of the cave, staring out into the falling darkness through the pouring rain. Cal, Makin, Kato, and Ehren pull out decks of cards and huddle together, playing and laughing. Alak stands over them watching and grinning while Felixe chases a bug near his feet. I sink down at the opposite end, as far away from everyone possible, and stare into the crackling flames. The only person who seems to notice is Alak, who eventually makes his way over and settles down next to me.

"Those flames are downright interesting," he teases, glancing sideways at me.

I attempt to force a smile, but it doesn't quite take. Alak cocks his head and meets my eyes.

"What's been bothering you, love?" he asks, softly.

I shake my head and glance away. "Nothing."

"It's not nothing. I can feel it."

I sigh and glance at the others. "No one would be here,

hiding from the rain in a forgotten cave, literally on the run for their life, if it weren't for me. I've doomed us all."

"Love, that simply isn't true."

"I think you know it is."

"Not one of us is here by force. Not a one," Alak says firmly. "We have all chosen to be here. Not just because of you and you alone, but because of what you stand for. But even if it were because of you, that would be a worthy enough cause. You're important, Astra."

"Maybe," I mutter. "But Ehren wouldn't have been forced to flee Embervein with Cal and Makin if he hadn't brought me to Embervein, right under his father's nose. And Bram, he puts himself at risk just being near me. Even you would be better off without me."

Alak reaches over and takes my hand. "I choose to be here by your side. Would it be easier for me to be off on my own? In some ways, yes. I've become an expert at living alone and dodging danger. I've done it most of my life. It's what I know best. But if you think for one second that I would leave your side for even the slightest security for my own self, you're not nearly as smart as I thought. I choose you, love."

He glances over to the others playing their card game. "Even they're not here by force. I wasn't there, but from the story I heard, Ehren and Bram actively sought you and your brother out. Isn't that correct?" I nod and he continues. "Ehren risked his father's wrath to travel all the way to Timberborn, not just to meet you, but to save your lives. And even when that mission was complete, he didn't just leave. He and Bram took you to one of the best Healers they could find. Even then, they could have left you. They could have continued on their way. But they chose to stay in contact. Bram, gods bless him, had already fallen in love with you. Ehren had grown to love you in a different way. They both willingly chose to stay in your life.

They knew the risks and accepted them. Up front. No questions asked. They knew where that path would most likely lead, and they started on it willingly."

I avoid Alak's eyes, blinking back tears. "Makin and Cal had no part of that. They're just here as part of their loyalty to Ehren."

Alak huffs. "Wrong again, love. When we were on our way to meet you at that lovely little cottage, Makin told me he and Cal volunteered to go on this part of the journey to stay near you and protect you. Ehren has his Guard spread out on multiple assignments across the continent and beyond. Any of them could have ended up here. Cal and Makin could be in completely different locations, where they would be safer, but they, like the rest of us, willingly chose this path."

I look back at Alak, tears brimming in my eyes, ready to spill. "Why?"

"Because you and magic are worth it."

"Magic, yes. That I can understand. But why come with me? Why not send me off on my own and fight for magic without me?"

Alak laughs and Bram, for the first time, glances our way, his eyes narrowing at Alak.

"Have you not been listening to me? You are amazing and worth fighting for. Simply put. You want me to elaborate? Fine. You have a power inside you that can change the world. It has already changed the world and will continue to do so. Kato has a similar power. That kind of power is worth supporting. It's worth following. It's worth protecting. And if that was all there was to it, that would be enough for most people. But, for me, that's not the case."

Alak reaches over and cradles both my hands in his. He looks deep in my eyes and offers me a small smile. "Your real power isn't magic. You have one of the kindest souls in this world. And all of us have witnessed it. We saw it just a few days ago, when you risked draining your power to heal not just Ehren but also Cal. And that kindness, that gentleness, is your real strength. I have a feeling any one of us will follow you to the end of world, not just me."

I swallow as a trembling smile forces its way onto my lips. "Thanks, Alak. I needed that."

Alak releases my hands and gives me a little nudge with his shoulder. "You know, there's something else you can do that might make you feel better."

I roll my eyes. "If you suggest releasing magic . . ."

I let my voice trail off. Alak hasn't said many words to me the past few days, but most of those words involved him reminding me to use my magic.

He throws his hands up in defense. "I'm just saying that your power is growing. A lot. With your magic increasing at the rate it is, you need to release some, or it will affect you in many ways. Affecting your mood is one. Having too much magic putting pressure on you can make you depressed."

"What about Kato? He seems fine," I say, nodding over to where Kato laughs, having won another hand of cards.

"Kato has been releasing magic on a regular basis. Not just by drying us all off and creating that fire, but in dozens of little things throughout the day. Things I've been trying to get you to do, like deflecting bugs and the sun."

"Fine," I sigh.

I glance around, trying to find some way to use my magic. In the distance I hear a wolf howl. His call is echoed by a dozen more. I can only imagine that the scent of three roasting rabbits smells more than appetizing to wolves and fighting wolves away from my dinner isn't something I want on my agenda. I focus and reach into my magic. I wave my hand and craft a shield along the outside of the cave. It helps keep out the rain while blocking our scents from wolves or any other creatures that might find us delicious. It also hides us from eyes that may look our way. There's just the slightest hint of a shimmer as the shield goes up. The only people who notice are Bram, who still stands at the edge of the cave, and Alak. Bram glances at me, arching an eyebrow.

"A shield," I mouth.

Bram smiles. He noticeably relaxes, sensing we're a little safer.

"You feel better now, don't you?" Alak grins, giving me another nudge.

"Yes," I mumble, attempting to hide a smile but failing.

Bram, feeling less on alert now that my shield is in place, saunters over and settles down on my other side, placing his arm behind me and drawing me against him. Alak rises and goes back over to the others, giving me one last encouraging wink over his shoulder before focusing his attention on the card game.

"You okay?" Bram whispers, kissing the top of my head.

I smile and nod. "I am now."

When the rabbits are ready, we dive in. We all know we should save some of the meat for another meal, but we're too hungry to plan for the future. We clean the rabbits to the bone, Felixe happily gnawing on those bones. As we settle down to sleep, the rain starts to let up a little. I take my usual spot next to Bram and Felixe curls up next to me, earning a quick scolding from Alak. The warmth of the fire combined with my full belly make me drift off quickly.

I'm not sure how long I've been asleep when I awaken to something crossing my shield. I shift and raise up just enough to look around. Everyone is fast asleep, save for Kato, who's missing. I carefully pull away from Bram and step outside the cave. The rain has stopped, but the ground is slippery and muddy. I glance around and see Kato perched up on a ledge not far away. When he sees me, he smiles and waves his hand over the spot next him, instantly drying the area with a red glow. I climb up and settle beside him.

He looks up at the sky. The clouds have started to clear, revealing patches of sparkling stars. He takes a deep breath, releasing it slowly.

"It's no roof in Timberborn, but it's not a bad view," he says, turning his head to me.

I give a short laugh. "Yeah, I guess it's not too bad."

"That's some impressive magic down there," Kato says, nodding toward the shield around the cave.

"Alak was on me about needing to use my magic, so I created a shield to appease him," I mumble with a shrug.

"Well, it's good. Alak certainly understands a decent amount about magic. He's not exactly what I envisioned when we set out looking for a teacher, but he's done a good job."

"Yeah, I think we were lucky to find him. We were lucky to find everyone down there."

"Hm? Yeah. Maybe," Kato says with a noncommittal shrug, staring off into the distance.

I raise my eyebrows. "What's with that reaction?"

"Oh, nothing. I just . . ." He looks back at me. "Do you feel like maybe they're holding us back?"

"Holding us back how? They've done nothing but support us and help us." I frown.

Kato shakes his head. "I know. But other than Alak, none of them have magic. They don't understand us. Not really. They can support us all they can, but their support has limits. We might be better on our own."

"So, what are you saying? You want to abandon our friends, after all they've done for us?"

"No," he says quickly. "No, not at all. I'm so grateful for

their friendship, but as long as they're around we're going to be concerned about taking care of them and defending them and vice versa. On our own, we can focus on us and our needs, and they can do the same."

"I'm not leaving them," I say firmly.

"I'm not really suggesting we need to right now. Just maybe at some point in the future."

"I love Bram," I whisper. "I don't think I'll ever want to leave him behind, even momentarily."

Kato grins at me. "Fine. You're just a hopeless romantic."

I smile but a yawn creeps onto my lips. I snap my hand over my mouth. Kato laughs

"You should go back to bed," Kato says, nudging me with his shoulder.

"I can stay a little longer. Unless, of course, you want to be alone."

"You can stay as long as you want. You're always welcome by my side."

I lean against Kato and we stare up at the stars together. At some point, I drift off to sleep, but when I wake up, I'm back in the cave, snuggled safely between Bram and Felixe.

CHAPTER THIRTY-EIGHT

The next few days follow the same rhythm as the ones before, only this time we have the threat of bandits from the mountains hanging over us. Neutral territory is apparently code for "criminals welcome." With no soldiers or guards patrolling the area, there is no real law, often allowing the bandits to get away with robberies sans consequences. The first day of travel, we jump at every sound.

We stick near the base of the mountains as much as possible, but our path eventually twists into the mountains themselves, which means braving the infamous Hellmouth Pass. As we approach the opening of the pass, Ehren slows his horse to a stop, glancing around nervously.

"Everyone stay on guard. This is the worst pass for bandits as well as bounty hunters. Since there is likely some sort of bounty being offered by the king, we are at exceptional risk if the news has reached this area," Ehren explains uneasily.

"Can you create some sort of illusion like you did when we were attacked on the way to Embervein?" Bram asks Alak.

Alak chews on his lip for a minute as he considers his options.

"I can, but I couldn't maintain a spell that complicated and complex for the entire length of the pass. I could create an illusion where we would technically be seen, but whoever sees us wouldn't care." Bram furrows his brow in confusion. "Essentially, we can pass through unnoticed. We wouldn't be invisible, but they wouldn't pay any attention to us or have any desire to inspect us closer or rob us."

"And you can do that for the entire pass?" Ehren asks.

Alak hesitates for a moment before replying, "I can."

I study him for a moment. "No, you can't. Not without draining your magic completely."

He dodges my gaze. "I can still do it."

I reach out my hand to him, allowing tendrils of silver lights to dance around my fingers. "Take some of my magic."

Alak looks up at me. "I have a better idea. We can combine our magic. I'll create the foundation of the spell, and you weave in your magic to support the spell and keep it lasting and strong. Like when we created the illusion of the forest in the library room."

A rock crashes nearby and Ehren jerks his focus from us to look around, his hand on his sword. "However you do it, do it soon."

"Okay, just let me know what to do," I say.

Alak grins and holds out his hand, palm up. He stretches his fingers and a soft glow rises and spreads around us. My skin prickles as the magic settles over me. Once we're all blanketed by his spell, Alak looks over at me.

"Now, reach your magic out and find mine. Just like before, your magic should seek mine."

I close my eyes and lift my hands, focusing and finding my magic. Alak's magic calls to mine. I twist my fingers and weave my magic into his. My magic intertwines with Alak's as if they were always meant to be one, the warmth from his magic flowing through mine. I open my eyes and grin.

"Is it working?" Ehren asks, glancing from me to Alak.

"Yes, I think it is," Alak murmurs, his expression unreadable.

"I'd really love more than a 'think' right now," Ehren says sternly, eyeing the rocky cliffs above us.

"It's working," I say.

Kato nods as well. "I can sense it all around us."

"All right, then. Let's do this!" Ehren says, urging his horse forward into the pass.

Even with the magic hovering around us, we're all anxious and tense as we make our way through. There are a few times when we think we spot people in the shadows, but no one bothers us. Our magic is working. With Alak and I sharing the weight of the spell, I don't feel my magic draining, but I can't help but glance toward Alak to make sure he's the same. I have no idea how deep his magic goes. It takes a couple hours to cross the pass but even after we are done, Alak insists on keeping up the illusion to protect against other bandits we may stumble across. After a few hours, I start to notice his shoulders drooping and his breathing grows rougher. By the time we decide to stop for the night, I can see the strain on his face, and I'm feeling a drain on my magic as well.

"How much longer until we're out of danger from bandits?" I ask Ehren as he unhooks his bedroll from his horse.

"A few hours travel tomorrow and then we should be able to leave the mountains and cross into Athiedor." He glances up at me, knitting his eyebrows together. "Why?" He searches my face. "Is your magic draining?"

I shake my head. "Not my magic." My eyes dart to where

Alak sits on the ground, leaning against a rock, eyes closed and breath ragged.

Ehren gives an understanding nod.

"Alak, I think we can let the illusion drop while we sleep," Ehren suggests casually, straightening his bedroll. "The darkness should be enough cover. We just won't make a fire tonight."

"I can keep it up," he insists, opening his eyes and lifting his head.

"We'll need it more tomorrow in the daylight. Save your magic tonight," Ehren says, his voice ringing with authority.

Alak shifts his eyes to me and I give him a nod. I feel the magic relax and slowly fade away. I unpack my own things and settle down next to Bram. Kato glances around and flips his hand, creating a shimmering black dome of smoky shadows around us.

"You protect us during the day, I'll take night," he says with a grin.

Everyone else seems perfectly content with the arrangement but something about the dark cloud unsettles me. Curiously, I reach out and touch it with my magic. Kato's magic is hot and the coolness of my magic hisses and jerks back. If Kato feels anything he doesn't react. I ignore the rising feeling of unease my magic had against his and settle down, snuggling up with Bram and falling asleep.

The next morning, we're up and on the road before dawn has even settled in the sky. We're all eager to leave the mountains behind. When Alak and I knit our magic together, it's almost automatic, my magic seeking his out with little guidance from me. I expect Alak to start to wane again after a couple of hours, but he doesn't. In fact, the longer we travel, the stronger he seems to get. I get stronger as well.

The sensation starts off subtle, like the warmth from the

sun, breaking through the clouds on a cool day. Then it grows, feeling like the joy of seeing a friend on a special occasion. It becomes the excitement of racing down a hill as carefree as a child without a burden in the world. I glance over at Bram to see if he's feeling the increasing levels of happiness I am, but his face is focused and firm, like always. A glance at Ehren shows the same look of concentration. Kato, however, is glowing, a smile playing on his lips. He sits lighter in his saddle and his shoulders are relaxed. Cal and Makin are chatting casually and seem at ease, but they're not as relaxed.

"It's magic," Alak whispers, pulling his horse up next to mine.

I look over at him, and his eyes are bright and full of life. I open my mouth to ask what he means but somehow, I understand. There's more magic in the air here and the closer we get to Athiedor—the closer we get to the source—the stronger it grows. Just like the woods outside Wickbriar, the air is beginning to purr with magic, and that magic calls to my own. It connects to my heart like a string, pulling and tugging me closer and closer, and I willingly follow that path.

As we begin our downward spiral, finally leaving the mountains, the pull is almost overwhelming. Even once Alak and I are no longer spinning our illusion, I can't help but keep sending my magic out into the air to feel the full effects of the magical energy. Ehren suggests we stop and eat what little lunch we have, but Alak, Kato, and I are quick to disagree. Judging by the furrowed brows of our four companions, they don't understand our reasoning in the slightest, but we don't care.

The second we step onto Athiedor soil, I know. The magic ripples through the air. I gasp, overwhelmed by its welcoming warmth. A bubble of joy bursts inside my chest, and I can't help but laugh. I glance over at Kato and Alak. Both are grinning so wide I can't imagine their smiles any bigger. Everything about us seems to glow, inside and out. Even Felixe has extra energy, dashing around, yapping excitedly, popping from the ground to Luna to Fawn. Ehren is eyeing us like we're insane. Bram and Cal have the decency to look concerned, whereas Makin is watching us with unabashed amusement. When Kato creates a little fire fox to run alongside Felixe, and Alak starts laughing for no apparent reason, Ehren snaps.

"What the hell is wrong with you three?" he demands, eyes wide.

I throw back my head and laugh, which does nothing to allay his concerns. I twirl my fingers and send a flutter of glowing silver butterflies his way.

"Magic," I whisper reverently.

"What?" Ehren asks, arching an eyebrow.

"There's raw magic in the air, mate," Alak says, throwing his arms into the air, sending a flock of birds spiraling into the sky. He looks directly at Ehren and grins wildly. "Can't you feel it?"

Ehren shakes his head, still eyeing us like we're insane.

I turn to Bram. "You can't feel it either, can you?"

Bram smiles softly at me. "No, I can't feel the magic, but I can see it in you."

"Gods above," Alak says, rolling his eyes as Kato yells, "No kissing!"

I ignore them both.

The longer we're on Athiedor soil, the more I grow accustomed to the feeling of the magic. It still feels warm inside my heart, but I don't feel quite as giddy. After an hour or two of travel, we make our way onto the first real road we've seen since starting our journey.

"Is it safe to be back on a road?" Makin asks warily.

Ehren nods. "We have to get on one eventually. This road

should be as secure as any. Just make sure that you don't address me by my titles. Or Bram for that matter. No one can suspect who we are."

Makin nods uneasily. "Okay. I'll admit, I'll have a little difficulty calling you Ehren."

Even as he says it, I can hear how awkward Ehren's name sounds coming from his lips. Unlike the rest of us, he's never addressed Ehren so informally.

"It might not be a bad idea to call us by different names than usual, just in case there are people looking for us," Bram suggests.

"What else would we call you?" Kato asks.

"You can always call me by my actual first name," Bram suggests, eyes glinting.

"Alexander?" I ask. "I'm not sure. I know it's your name but somehow it doesn't really suit you."

Bram laughs. "How about Xander?"

"Hmm . . ." I cock my head and study him while he chuckles. "I suppose. It could work."

"What about you? What do you want us to call you?" Cal asks, nodding to Ehren.

"Oh, let's see," Ehren muses. "It's not often one gets to pick a new name."

"What's your middle name? You have more than one, right? Pick one of them," I suggest.

Ehren looks at me, mouth gaping in mock disappointment. "How is it that we're friends and you don't even know my full name? For shame, Astra. For shame!"

I laugh. "I'm terribly sorry. You must forgive me."

"I'll forgive you. This time," Ehren says, winking at me. "But it's not a bad idea. And yes, I do have two middle names, Daniel and Andrewe."

"My vote is on Andrewe," Kato says.

"Mine, too," Makin agrees. "Andrewe. I can remember that."

"All right then. Andrewe it is!"

"Now, do we all get new names or just the important people," Alak inquires, grinning.

I send out a flick of magic and nick his ear.

"Hey!" he laughs, twisting in his saddle to face me.

I school my features into feigned innocence. "What?"

"You hit me!" Alak says, his eyes glittering.

"I'm all the way over here! I can't reach that far," I reply, shrugging him off with a mischievous grin.

"I know what your magic feels like, love." Something about his tone makes my breath catch. Bram seems to notice and shifts on his horse, his eyes narrowing at Alak.

I clear my throat. "So what's the plan now that we're in Athiedor?"

"Well," Ehren replies, "this road is bound to lead some-where. I say we follow it and figure out our exact location. Once we know where we are, we know which way to go."

We all nod. It's a good plan, or as good as any we could come up with. So for the next few hours we follow the road. After four days traveling through mountains, the new land-scape is a welcome sight. Rich, emerald-green hills topple and turn over each other, sprinkled with bright flowers. Occasion-ally, we see herds of sheep grazing and bleating. Eventually, we see the makings of a village in the distance. As we approach, a stone wall appears on the side of the road, guiding us.

This village is unlike any other I've seen. The buildings, made of smooth stones, are scattered around in no obvious pattern. Goats and sheep roam the village freely while children play carelessly in the street. The entire atmosphere is warm and happy.

"We should see if there's an inn," Bram suggests and Ehren nods.

"Eh, let me do the talking," Alak interjects, earning a sharp look from Ehren. "Your accents will stand out here, and we want to blend in."

"Fine," Ehren concedes, waving Alak ahead. "Work your magic."

Alak hops down off his horse and approaches a brawny man guiding a goat.

"Evenin', good sir!" Alak calls out, raising his hand in greeting, his accent thick and rich.

"Evenin', lad! What can I do fer ya?" the man replies, taking off his brown cap and wiping the sweat from his brow.

"Me and my companions are searching fer a place to lie our heads. Pray tell, is there any lodging nearby?"

"Aye, lad, there is. Just head that way, to yer left," the man replies, motioning. "You'll see it. She can't be missed."

Alak thanks the man and mounts his horse, leading the way. It doesn't take us long to find the pub, The Barefoot Maid, with rooms to rent. We tie our horses in front and head inside. It's warm and inviting in every way. In the corner a small band plays lively music with a fiddle, banjo, and tin whistles, harmonizing as they sing along. Everyone near the band seems to be tapping along in time, either with a bouncing foot, the tapping of a mug, or clapping. The center of the room is cleared for dancers. We take a nearby seat and Alak looks around, grinning, his eyes more alive than I've ever seen them.

"What can I do ya for?" a pretty young red-haired barmaid asks, approaching the table.

"Tell me, love," Alak says, leaning in. "Have ya any stew? We've been travlin' many long days and need somethin' hearty to fill our bellies."

"Aye! Best stew this side of the Fenwick, if ya ask me!"

"Bowls all 'round, then!" Alak replies with a laugh. "And ale for us each. Best ya got!"

"Aye! I'll have that up fer ya in a moment!" The barmaid whisks away to fill our order, and I turn my focus to those dancing. They look so happy and free.

"Just you wait," Alak whispers, leaning forward. "Before the night is over, that dance floor will be filled."

And he's right. By the time we've eaten our dinner—an absolutely delicious stew with large chunks of meat and thick potatoes served with white bread—the dance floor is full of people laughing, dancing, and singing. My own foot is tapping along as I gulp down my second pint of ale. Alak leaps out of his seat and offers his hand to me.

"Come dance with me, love," he grins. "I can tell you're dying to!"

I shake my head, laughing. "No, no, no! I'm not dancing."

"Aye, ya are, love!" Alak laughs, grabbing my hand and pulling me to my feet.

Bram glares at him, but Alak doesn't care and, quite frankly, neither do I. The dance floor is crowded but we find a place. The dancing is fast paced and lively, and soon I'm swirling and laughing. Alak leads, but it hardly matters. There seem to be no wrong steps as long we never stop.

Everyone else in the pub is clapping along as we twirl and bounce. A barmaid weaves between us with mugs of ale, and we drink as we dance. I can't stop smiling and Alak's eyes shine. It's freeing and wonderful. I don't even know how long we dance and drink. Time doesn't exist. There's just me, Alak, and the music. My heart is light and my cheeks are warm. I'm perfectly happy and want to dance forever. But eventually exhaustion and the countless pints of ale catch up with me, and I'm staggering more than dancing. When I stumble and nearly crash to the ground, Alak catches me, laughing.

"All right, love," he yells over the music. "Time to take a break!"

"No!" I argue, trying unsuccessfully to stay on the dance floor.

The world is starting to spin, and I want to spin with it. When I try to twirl, I only stumble. Alak scoops me into his arms, laughing. As he carries me, I bob my head to the music. Once we're away from the crowd, Bram rushes to us.

"I can take her," he says stiffly, his eyes flashing.

"I got her, mate," Alak says with a wink.

I can't see what Bram does next because Ehren pushes between us, holding his hands up toward Bram.

"Not here," Ehren says, barely audible above the music and merriment. "Go make sure the horses are good for the night. Makin, go with him. Go. Now." Bram disappears and Ehren turns to Alak. "You need to secure us rooms."

"Fine," Alak sighs. "But what should I do with her?"

"I'll watch over her," Ehren replies. "Now go get us some rooms."

Alak sets me on my unsteady feet, and I stumble into Ehren who wraps his arm around me. I look up at him and sigh. He shakes his head at me smiling.

"How much did you drink while you were out there?"

"I have no idea," I slur, smiling.

I hiccup and burst into uncontrollable giggles. Ehren grins, his eyes twinkling.

"I won't lie, I rather like this side of you," he laughs. I grin, hiccuping again.

Alak returns, dangling a key. "We're all in one room."

"One room?" Ehren asks, raising his eyebrows.

"Aye," Alak grins. "Welcome to Athiedor!"

Alak leads the way up the stairs, and we find our room. It's one long space with ten wooden beds lined up against one wall with tables bearing candles between them. There's little else in the room. Ehren leads me to the nearest bed, and I crash onto it, face down.

"Mmmm, bed," I mutter burying my face in the blankets.

Alak's rich laugh fills the room. "You're pissed, love!"

"Who sleeps where?" Kato asks, clearing his throat and glancing to the other beds.

"Any bed is as good as the next, I guess," Cal replies with a shrug. He glances at me. "Though perhaps the person the most wasted shouldn't be closest to the door."

"Fine, I'll move," I mumble, rising from the bed.

I stumble forward and this time it's Kato who catches me. He leads me to the third bed where I happily collapse again. I'm curled up nice and comfortable when Bram and Makin join us. Bram glances toward me, and I smile up at him. He's still seething. Without warning, he punches Alak square on the mouth.

"Whoa! What the hell!" Makin yells, jumping back as Alak tumbles toward him.

"Look at her!" Bram yells at Alak, who's lifting his hand to wipe blood from his lip. "She's wasted!"

"She's fine," Alak says, waving Bram off and pushing past him, heading toward a bed.

"Hell she is!" Bram roars.

"Bram! Settle down!" Ehren commands, but Bram ignores him and grabs Alak's shoulder.

"Feck off, mate!" Alak says, yanking out of his grip.

The next thing I know, Bram is tackling Alak, and the two are brawling on the floor.

"You bastard!" Bram growls as he pummels Alak. "You've gotten her completely wasted."

Alak shoots harmless sparks into Bram's eyes. When Bram

jerks back reflexively, Alak takes the opportunity to slam his fist across Bram's face.

"Hey! Stop it!" Ehren yells, trying to grab Bram and pull him off Alak. "Stop!"

Alak wisps and he's standing two beds away. His eyes flash angrily and magic twirls his fingers. Bram jumps up, his own lip bleeding now. He looks ready to charge across the room when I sit up.

"Stop!"

Bram glances toward me, breathing hard.

"Just stop! Alak didn't make me do anything I didn't want to do." My head starts swimming, and I lie back down, staring up at the ceiling. "Just shut up and go to sleep."

I close my eyes, but hear Ehren say, "She's right. Let's get in bed."

I hear shuffling around me as everyone makes themselves comfortable. I feel a warm kiss on my forehead.

"I love you," Bram whispers. Then, judging by the creaking of the bed next to me, Bram lies down.

It doesn't take long at all before I'm fast asleep, dreaming of dancing and ale and bright, emerald eyes.

CHAPTER THIRTY-NINE

*I*f you could all be much quieter, I would greatly appreciate it," I grumble, my eyes closed against the harsh light that dares shine through the window.

"We're not being loud," Cal counters.

I open one eye and squint at him. "My pounding head disagrees."

"Maybe don't drink so much next time," Kato says, grinning.

I groan and close my eyes. "I hate you."

"Do not."

"I've been there many times," Makin says sympathetically. "It's no fun."

Bram settles next to me on my bed and brushes hair out of my face. "I'm sorry you feel so bad."

The door is thrown open, banging into the wall. I curse, wincing, and Kato laughs. I make a rude gesture in his direction.

"Well, we're all paid up and set for the morning! There's fresh sausages, bacon, beans, bubble and squeak, and fried eggs downstairs at a reasonable price if anyone is in the mood to eat," Alak says.

"What the hell is bubble and squeak?" Makin muses while I jerk up and pause, waiting for the room to still before I mumble, "How the hell are you so cheery this morning? You drank at least as much as I did."

Alak grins. "I'm from Athiedor, love. We're born with a mug of ale in our hand. Trust me, what you need is a nice, greasy breakfast, and you'll feel all better."

I groan again, easing to my feet. "Maybe you're right."

Kato cocks his head, looking me over. "You look a little green."

"I feel a little green."

Once downstairs, I settle at the nearest table and lay my head down, cradled in my arms. Bram sits next to me and rubs my back. A few moments later, Alak plops down across from me, pushing a plate piled high with food toward me. I force myself up and stare at the plate. I start by tentatively taking a bite of a fried egg. I'm afraid it's going to come right back up. When it stays down, I dig into the mound of vegetables and potatoes.

"This is delicious," I mumble, shoving more food in my mouth.

I glance down the table and see that everyone has similar plates. Cal is poking at his potatoes like he expects them to spring up and attack him.

"Dontcha like your bubble and squeak?" Alak asks Cal, his mouth full.

"I don't even know," Cal says, looking up, bewildered. "What is it?"

"It's vegetables. It won't bite you," Alak replies, scooping more food into his mouth.

Someone slaps a mug full of swishing greenish liquid in

front of me, and I look up to see a hefty bartender looking down at me.

"Drink that, love," he says in an accent so thick I can barely understand him. "T'will clear yer head."

I mumble my thanks as he shuffles off. I take a sniff and rear back, gagging. Alak grimaces.

"Aye, it won't taste the best going down, but I can guarantee it will do the trick," Alak says, giving me a sympathetic smile.

One sip of the sludge and it almost comes right back up, but by some miracle I manage to get it down. Somehow, between that drink, a cup of black, bitter coffee, and the greasy, filling breakfast, I'm on my feet with a clear head after a few minutes. I accompany Bram to get the horses. There was no official stable, but he made sure they were tied near a trough filled with water and had plenty to eat. I fall into step beside him as we approach the pub with the horses in tow.

"I'm sorry about last night," I say quietly.

"You didn't do anything," Bram says, waving me off. "It was all Alak."

"We both know it wasn't. I got a little carried away, but I was having a lot of fun."

Bram looks down. "I just wish you could have that kind of fun with me."

I stop him, placing my hand on his arm. "I have plenty of fun with you. I love you."

He brushes his lips quickly across mine. "I love you, too." We start walking again and he confesses, "I guess I had more to drink than I care to admit and jealousy got the better of me. I'm sorry."

We stop outside the inn, and he looks down at me. I reach up and brush his wounded lip. He winces, but I let my magic flow out, healing him. He lifts his fingers tentatively to his lip and smiles.

"You should have left it as a reminder for me not to be such an idiot next time."

I laugh but before I can reply, the pub door is thrown open and the others saunter out.

"The barkeep says that we need to continue on this road to get to Killhorn. We'll go straight on through Gillskeep and then follow the left fork," Alak says as we mount our horses. "After that, straight on to Brackenborough."

"How many days?" Kato asks as we start off down the road.

"Three at most," Alak replies with a shrug.

Our journey is mostly uneventful. Every moment we travel, I fall more and more in love with the countryside. I can't entirely tell if it's because I love the lush green landscape, or if it's the effect of magic, but either way, it's the most enjoyable road we've traveled so far. I don't even mind when the rain starts, though I am happy when we stumble into another little pub called The Freckled Hen. This barkeep is young and wirey with a scruffy red beard.

"Evenin'," he calls out as we enter. "Take a seat anywhere."

The pub is mostly empty. There are two fiddlers in the corner, and I find my head already bobbing in time. Alak looks over at me, grinning.

"You gonna join me on the dance floor again, love?"

"Absolutely not!" I laugh.

"Come on! You know you had a blast last night. Don't even try to deny it."

"I did have fun, but tonight I'll just watch and listen."

Alak shrugs but doesn't push the issue further.

As the dance floor fills with villagers driven in by the now pouring rain, I hold my resolve, remaining in my seat, stuffing my face with potatoes and mutton. Alak, however, downs his plate of food and quickly finds a pretty girl to dance with.

I feel a slight pang of jealousy that he has a different partner, but seeing him laugh and dance is enjoyable enough. I limit myself to only one pint of ale tonight, unwilling to risk another headache in the morning. After an hour of watching everyone else dance, I request that we get a room and head upstairs. Like the night before, we get a room with multiple beds. This room only has six beds to our seven people.

"Alak is the only one still downstairs, so I say he gets the floor," Bram states matter-of-factly.

The rest of us begrudgingly agree, and we begin to settle down for the night. When Alak finally makes his way upstairs, singing loudly and off-key, he doesn't mind sleeping on the floor at all.

The next morning we wake to find the rain has only gotten worse.

"We could stay another night," Cal suggests with a shrug, staring out the window.

"I'd really rather not stay in one place too long until we reach our destination," Ehren says, shaking his head.

"I was afraid you'd say that," Makin mumbles under his breath.

"I can create a bit of cover from the rain with my magic," I offer.

Bram shakes his head. "I don't like that. Someone could see."

"We're in the land of magic, mate," Alak counters. "No one here cares."

"I'd rather not take that chance."

"It's not your chance to take, mate."

"Hey!" I cut in before they come to blows again. "I'll use magic once we're out of town and on the road, but I won't use it when others are around." I glance between Alak and Bram. "Everyone happy with that?"

"Works for me!" Makin calls from the other end of the room. "You know, just in case anyone cares."

"Works for me, too," Kato says with a nod.

Bram throws his hands up. "Fine. Let's just get on the road."

Even with my magic protecting us from the rain most of the time, the day is still miserable. The roads are muddy and hard to travel, and the air is thick and muggy. The rain is pouring so hard we can barely see a few feet in front of us. By the time we trudge into a small village mid-afternoon, we're all more than ready to stop for the day. We don't see an inn, but we do find a little pub. We stumble inside, rain-soaked and ready for food. We huddle around a small table and order potato and leek soup. When it's brought over, Alak asks our server if there's an inn in town where we might stay.

"Naw, no inn," he says, "but there are many townsfolk always willing ta rent a room or two."

"Thank ya," Alak replies. "If ya wouldn't mind directin' us, we would greatly appreciate it."

The man gives us a few names and directions to their houses. We linger for a while at the pub, not wanting to make ourselves unwelcome guests any earlier than need be, but eventually we slosh back out into the rain and hunt down places to stay. The villagers are very friendly, and anyone that has a room is more than willing to share it. Unfortunately, no one has room for us all, so we're forced to split between three houses. Makin, Alak, and Kato end up at the house of a cheery older couple who usher them inside to two spare rooms. Bram, Ehren, and Cal end up at the butcher's, staying in a spare room he has above his shop. I end up at a separate house, the home of a kindly older woman by the name of Cara O'Connell. Bram is less than happy about leaving me on my own, but we have little choice. I'm actually a little relieved.

"Now, you take off those wet clothes while I draw ya a bath," Ms. O'Connell insists despite my objections.

When I finally surrender and sink into the tub, it's a relief. The water itself is cool, but I use just a trickle of magic to warm it. I relax for a moment before finally washing away the filth from the road. When I dress and come out into the living area, Ms. O'Connell greets me with a smile.

"Come, dear," she says, beckoning me to take a seat near her on the other side of a small tea table. "Have a cuppa?"

"I would love tea," I say gratefully, taking a seat.

She pours me a cup and slides it my way. "I can imagine that after traveling with so many young men, it must be a wee bit o' relief to take a break from them."

I smile as I sip my tea. "I love them all dearly but, yes, it is a welcome break."

"Good. I don't get all too many visitors, meself, so I hope ya don't mind if I keep ya a bit, chattin?"

"Not in the slightest," I admit. "It's been awhile since I've been able to just relax and chat."

Ms. O'Connell smiles. "Do ya have a good friend back home that ya used ta chat with?"

I smile and tell her all about Mara. I share our adventures, and she chimes in with adventures of her own. We go through the entire pot of tea, and I'm a little sad when it's empty. She directs me to my room. It's small, no more than a few feet wide in any direction, but cozy. I settle on the small bed and snuggle beneath a homemade quilt. The pattering of rain on the roof quickly puts me to sleep.

The next morning, I'm awakened by the smell of eggs and sausage. My stomach grumbles in response and I rise quickly. When I enter the main room of the house, I find Ms. O'Connell heaping mounds of eggs mixed with bits of sausage and leeks onto a plate.

"Mornin'!" she greets me, smiling. "Please, have a seat!"

I ease myself into the chair and eagerly eye my plate before I take a bite.

"This is delicious. Thank you very much," I say, scooping more into my mouth.

I'm nearly halfway through my plate when there's a knock on the door. Ms. O'Connell excuses herself and answers.

"Good morning, Ma'am," I hear Bram's voice say. "We met briefly last night. My name is Xander."

"Aye, I remember ya," she answers. "The betrothed of my young guest. Please, come in and have a bite ta eat."

She leads Bram to a chair beside me, and he sits, offering me a greeting nod. Ms. O'Connell sets a plate in front of him and begins piling on eggs.

"Thank you, but I don't need to eat," Bram says, holding up his hand.

"Nonsense," Ms. O'Connell chides. "Young men always have room for more food. And if ya don't help clear up these eggs, I'm afraid I'll have ta toss them and they'll go ta waste."

She winks at me and I smile. Bram gives her a grateful nod and scoops up eggs. We quickly clean our plates and then rise, giving Ms. O'Connell our thanks.

"I hope yer stay was pleasant?" she asks, as she guides us to the door.

"Yes, ma'am. I'm most grateful for the chance to stay here."

"I was most honored ta have ya. Please, travel safely."

Bram and I stroll through the damp village to where the others wait with the horses. Alak is chatting nearby with a beautiful local girl. He laughs and leans in toward her.

"Who's Alak talking to?"

"I think she's the pub owner's daughter. He's confirming directions to his aunt's village," Bram answers. The girl laughs, reaching out and touching Alak's arm while he grins at her. Bram frowns. "At least, that's what he's supposed to be doing."

I force my gaze away from Alak and focus on mounting Luna.

Are you okay?

I'm fine. Why?

You just seem . . . off this morning. Did you sleep well?

Yes. Did you?

Yes.

Kato goes silent for a moment. I think he's done, but he asks one more time: *Are you sure you're okay?*

"I'm fine!"

I don't realize I've spoken out loud until I notice the concerned look on Bram's face. I feel heat rise in my cheeks as I wave it off mumbling, "Kato's bugging me."

I glance over at Alak. He's still standing next to the girl, but he's looking at me, a strange expression on his face. He suddenly remembers the girl and glances at her, smiling. After a few more words, he waves to her and makes his way to us. I purposefully look away.

"Are we good to continue the way we were going?" Ehren asks as Alak mounts Fawn.

"Aye," Alak replies. "We should be there by the end of the day."

It doesn't rain, but the sky is still overcast, thick heavy clouds looming above us. The roads are muddy and make travel difficult. The closer we get to our destination the more and more sheep we start to see. At one point, a whole flock comes into the road, and it takes several minutes for us to wade through them. When we finally approach Brackenborough, I notice a little forest not far off from the village. The closer we get, the more the trees call to me. I have to force myself to stay on the road.

The village itself isn't much. There are a few buildings in a circular cluster with everything else spread out. We slow as we enter the main square. Alak hops off his horse and approaches three older men sitting on a bench outside a pub puffing on pipes. When they speak, their accents are so thick I can barely understand a word they say. Alak doesn't seem to have any issues. In fact, as he talks to the men, his accent grows thicker.

"We're almost there," Alak says, walking back to us. He doesn't get back on his horse, but instead leads Fawn. We follow Alak as he winds between houses and leads us to the edge of the village. Here, the houses are farther apart with wide stretching yards surrounded by short stone walls. Alak stops in front of one of the stone houses.

This house looks like most of the others. It's tall and cylindrical, reaching up three stories. The yard is plush and green with a pebbled path leading up to the stone structure. A handful of young children play in the front yard, kicking a ball back and forth while a middle-aged woman with red hair hangs laundry on a line extending from the house.

"Saran!" the woman cries out as the ball goes flying past her, barely missing her head. She turns, hands on her hips, and frowns at the children. They've stopped playing, and a little red-headed boy is staring at her, grimacing.

"Sorry, mum!" the little boy calls out.

A soft smile breaks out on her lips. "Just be careful."

The boy grins, rushing past his mother to get the ball. "I will!"

The woman starts to turn back to her laundry, but she glimpses us out of the corner of her eye. She turns to face us, scowling.

"May I help you?" she asks, her voice cool and wary. Her eyes slide to Alak, who's grinning. She drops the shirt she's holding, and her hand flies to her heart. "Alak?"

Alak waltzes down the path toward her. "The one and only! I take it you got my letter?"

The woman covers the distance between them and pulls Alak into a hug. "I did. You said you had friends possibly coming with you . . ." Her voice trails off as she eyes our traveling party. "I must admit, I wasn't expecting quite so many people."

Alak pulls out of the hug. "Oh, you don't have to worry about housing them. Many of them prefer sleeping in a barn or outdoors, anyway. Especially that tall, scowling one with brown hair."

I hide my smile as Bram mumbles, "He's dead."

The woman gives a light laugh. "I'm sure." She turns back toward us. "Well, are you going to sit on your horses all day, or are you going to come down and introduce yourselves?"

Alak grins as we dismount.

I stumble forward, leading Luna. "I'm sorry, ma'am." I dip my head in greeting. "My name is Astra."

Kato strides up next to me, "And I'm her brother, Kato."

The woman inclines her head. "It's a pleasure to meet you. Alak mentioned the two of you in his letter." By the shine in her eyes, I suspect Alak likely told her we were twins. I glance at Alak, and he pointedly glances away, biting back a smile. "My name is Shannon Murphy, Alak's aunt." Her eyes once again slide to the others.

"I'm Xander," Bram says, looping his arm around my waist. "Astra is my fiancé."

Something about his announcement interests Alak's aunt and her eyebrow quirks up.

"And I'm Andrewe," Ehren adds in awkwardly, his name sounding odd. I try my best not to react.

A strange, mistrustful expression crosses Shannon's face. "Your accent sounds very . . . proper," she scowls, glancing over at Alak, her jaw set. Alak opens his mouth but doesn't say anything.

"He's a family friend of ours," I cut in quickly. "He grew up as a servant to a noble family, so he was taught to speak properly."

Her eyes narrow, but she doesn't question me. Instead, she addresses Cal and Makin. "And who are you? More servants of nobles?"

"No, ma'am," Cal replies swiftly, taking a step forward. "My name is Callon Browen. I'm a soldier for my village."

"And I'm Makin Parelli," Makin adds quickly.

"All right then," Alak's aunt nods, turning to her son. "Saran, why don't you show these travelers where to put their horses, then show them inside."

"Yes, mum!" Saran says with a grin.

He motions for us to follow and we comply. He leads us around the back of the house to a small farmyard, complete with a goat pen, roaming chickens, and a barn for horses. Saran helps us get our horses situated and leads us back inside.

The inside of the house is cozy. The bottom floor is essentially one large room that serves as kitchen, dining area, and sitting area, all furnished with hand-carved wooden furniture. In the far corner stone stairs wind up to the other levels. Saran, having obeyed his mother's orders, runs back outside to be with his friends. We stand awkwardly in the center of the room for a moment before Alak finally speaks.

"Well, we made it," he says weakly. "And can we all just take a moment to appreciate how good Astra is at lying in the moment?" He smirks gesturing to me. I roll my eyes, biting back my grin.

"But what do we do now that we're here?" Bram says. "Stand in your aunt's house waiting to be found out?"

"We do what we came here to do. What we were planning

before we had to run," I reply, stepping forward. "We find magic. See how Athiedor was affected and see if magic is stronger here." I pause, then add, "But I can already tell you it's most definitely stronger here."

Kato nods. "A lot stronger." He stretches out his arm and opens his hand, a flame flickering on his palm. "I barely even have to concentrate to use my power."

"Careful," Bram admonishes him. "Don't use magic so freely. We don't know who might see."

"Magic is always welcome here," a voice booms from behind us, causing us to spin around, Kato immediately extinguishing his flame.

A tall figure with broad shoulders stands in the doorway, silhouetted by the sun behind him. He steps into the room, his features becoming visible. He has sharp green eyes and fiery red hair that's cut short. He looks over to Alak, grinning.

"Long time no see, cousin."

Alak matches his grin and strides across the room, clapping the new arrival's shoulder in greeting.

"Niall! It's good to see you! It's been so long!"

Niall grins. "You're no longer the little runt that stayed here all those years ago. You still look like you're up to no good, though."

Alak's eyes glint. "Some things will never change."

Niall looks past Alak to where we stand. "So who are your friends? Are they all magic users?"

"Naw, only two of them, plus myself, can wield magic. The others are friends."

"Greetings. Welcome to my family home. I am Niall," Niall greets us, smiling.

We quickly introduce ourselves, Niall nodding politely as we each give our names.

"Do you have magic?" I ask tentatively.

Niall grins. It's the same, mischievous grin I've seen many times on Alak's face. "I do."

Suddenly, the room goes completely dark. We're engulfed entirely in shadow. Someone near me gasps, and I hear at least two others swear. The air around me bites as the magic falls on my skin. My magic rises up defensively in response. I let it. I release my light, and my body begins to glow silver. Slowly, I extend it out through the shadows, reaching for Niall, the source of the darkness. As my light reflects on his face, I see the awe. His jaw is dropped and his eyes wide, blinking fast, trying to take me in. I grin slyly, then pulse my light out, forcing his shadows away. The room is naturally lit by the sun again and my glowing has ceased, but the wonder in Niall's eyes has yet to fade. Alak stands next to his cousin, eyes glistening, not even attempting to hold back his grin. There's also a little pride shining in Alak's eyes.

"I—I've never seen anyone be able to fight off my darkness like that," Niall stutters, shaking his head. "You must be extraordinarily powerful."

"That's putting it lightly." Alak chuckles.

Niall looks from Alak to me to Kato. "So you three all have magic. You"—he points at Kato—"control fire. And you"—he nods to me—"have whatever that silver light is. Starlight, maybe?" He turns and faces Alak, crossing his arms. "What can you do?"

Alak waves his hand and suddenly we're outside. Or, at least it looks like we're outside in a forest complete with mossy trees and twittering birds.

Niall looks around, nodding his head. "Not bad."

Alak scowls as the illusion fades. "Not bad? That's a top-class illusion right there."

"So," Kato cuts in, his eyes and voice eager. "Does everyone here have magic?"

"Most," Niall replies with a shrug. "You'll find people with no magic, but almost everyone here in Brackenborough has some level." He glances at Cal, Makin, Ehren, and Bram. "People like you are few and far between in these parts."

Alak's aunt pushes into the room, an empty laundry basket on her hip. She glances around at us before storing her basket and returning, her hands on her hips.

"Well, I suppose we should figure out what to do with you all," she says with a scowl.

"Please, ma'am," Ehren says, stepping forward. "We mean no inconvenience. We understand you may not have room or food for us all, and some of us are more than happy to stay at the village inn if there is one."

"Nonsense," she says, waving Ehren off. "You're friends of my nephew and therefore as good as family. We will find places for you all."

"Some of them can stay with me," Niall offers.

"You have your own house?" Alak asks, shocked.

"Naturally! A man of twenty-three can't live at home forever. Besides, I don't think my bride-to-be would be all too happy to be brought to this house on our wedding night," Niall grins, waggling his eyebrows.

"You're to be married?"

Niall's grin widens. "Indeed. To Caitlyn Murray."

Alak's eyes go wide. "I remember Caitlyn! She was a pretty girl!"

"And a more beautiful woman."

Alak's aunt clears her throat. "Yes, you could house a couple of them at least. That would help me find space for the rest here."

"I'll take all the magic users," Niall says.

"Actually," Bram says, stepping forward as he slides his

hand around my waist, drawing me to his side. "If possible, we would like to be in the same house."

Niall's eyes narrow where Bram's hand grips my waist before his gaze slides up to our faces. "You two are together?"

Bram nods firmly and I answer, "Yes, Xander and I are set to be married in just a few weeks."

"Hm. Well, that's . . . interesting," Niall muses.

"Perhaps it would be best to split the two of you up for propriety reasons," Niall's mother interrupts. "There are many in town who do not look kindly upon certain activities before marriage."

I feel the heat rise in my cheeks. "I haven't . . . I mean, we've never . . ." I look up at Bram whose face has gone nearly as red as mine.

"I can assure you, we have never engaged in any of those activities," Bram says sternly.

"You better not have," Kato mutters under his breath, narrowing his eyes.

Shannon waves us off. "Regardless, being in different houses would stop any rumors from spreading."

I glance over to Kato who gives me a slight shrug of his shoulders. "All right, then. We want to make it as easy on you as possible."

Shannon gives us a grateful nod. "Though you are all welcome here for any meals. As much as I love my son, cooking was never a skill he mastered."

"Can't cook worth anything, eh, cousin?" Alak teases, elbowing Niall.

"Right. Like you can?"

"Actually, I am an excellent cook," Alak says, crossing his arms.

"Fine. You're in charge of breakfast," Niall says, but Alak doesn't back down.

"No problem."

Shannon gives me a sympathetic glance. "You must be tired of all the masculinity."

I give a light laugh. "You have no idea."

"Would you mind helping me inside to prepare everything we need for such a large dinner party? My daughter should be home soon, and she will help us. While we prep, we can talk about more womanly things," Shannon offers with a smile.

"Yes, I would like that very much."

CHAPTER FORTY

a pleasant silence falls over the house after Niall and Alak usher the rest of the group off to do whatever they feel the need to do. I fall into a steady rhythm peeling potatoes with Alak's aunt while she hums quietly.

"What should I call you?" I ask after a few minutes.

She smiles gently. "Since you're a close friend of Alak, why doncha just call me Aunt Shannon, as does he."

I nod, trying out her name. "Aunt Shannon. I can do that." I glance at the growing pile of peeled potatoes. "What exactly are we making?"

"I think colcannon potatoes would serve our purposes well tonight," she says, focusing on her work. "We'll need a lot to feed all these mouths. You keep peeling potatoes while I get cabbage on to boil."

"I hope we haven't caused you any inconvenience," I mumble, fumbling with the small knife I'm using to peel.

Aunt Shannon shrugs. "A minor inconvenience, perhaps, but nothing we cannot handle." She glances over at my hands struggling to peel the potato. "You didn't have to peel many potatoes where you lived, did you?"

I blush slightly as I reply, "No. Am I doing it all wrong? I've peeled many apples and other fruits but not many potatoes."

"No, you're doing okay, but it could be better. Perhaps if you use your magic it would be easier."

I furrow my brow, looking up from the half-peeled potato in my hand. "Magic?"

Aunt Shannon nods. "Aye, my dear. Your magic."

I stare down at the potato. "How?" I whisper.

Aunt Shannon's eyebrow quirks up. "How? I thought you knew magic? Alak implied in his letter that you were quite powerful."

"I—I do . . . It's just relatively new. I'm not great with smaller magic."

"Well, all magic is essentially the same. So whatever you do, just focus." She holds out a potato in the palm of her left hand and slowly twirls the fingers of her right hand above the potato. "Concentrate." The peel slowly begins to cut away from the potato, almost like an invisible knife. When the peeling is complete, she looks up at me. "You try."

I look down at the half-naked potato in my hand. I take a deep breath and mimic her movements, visualizing what I want. I almost jump as the peel starts unraveling.

"Excellent," Aunt Shannon says, smiling. "Now, let's finish these potatoes."

As we peel we chat a little. Shannon shares a few stories of Alak when he was a boy, and I laugh, chiming in with some of my own childhood stories. We're almost done peeling potatoes when a pretty girl with waist-length red hair, my age or perhaps slightly younger, enters the house. Her green eyes fall on me, and her eyebrows rise in confusion.

"Ah! Kayleigh!" Aunt Shannon greets her. "Come, meet our guest, Astra!"

Kayleigh makes her way over, still eyeing me.

"Hello, I'm Kayleigh," she says slowly.

"I'm Astra. I'm a friend of your cousin, Alak."

"Alak . . . oh!" Her eyes go bright. "Alak! I haven't seen him in forever!" She gives a light laugh. "He was so much trouble!"

"He still is," I laugh.

"Come, help us with these potatoes. Alak brought a whole group of people for dinner," Aunt Shannon says.

"How do you know Alak?" Kayleigh, asks, walking over to us and grabbing a knife and potato. "Are you two involved?"

I choke on air as I stutter out, "Oh! No! Not at all. We're just—we're just friends!"

"Oh," she replies quietly, not looking entirely convinced. "I just assumed." She nods to the ring on my hand.

"Astra is engaged to another member of their party. A Xander was it?" Kayleigh's mother asks, a hint of disapproval in her voice.

I nod. "Yes, Xander and I are betrothed."

"And this Xander is a friend of Alak?" Kayleigh asks.

I pause. "Yes. They aren't terribly close but close enough, I suppose."

"And what brings you to our door?"

"No need to be rude, Kayleigh."

"No, it's not rude," I say. "We have come to see if magic is stronger here in Athiedor than in other places."

Kayleigh nods her head slowly, her eyes studying my face. "And what do you think so far?"

"Magic is so alive here," I breathe, unable to keep my eyes from shining. "I can feel it everywhere in everything. I don't know how to explain it, but I feel connected to the land here."

Kayleigh grins. "I know exactly what you mean. You need

to go to the Lushwater Woods. That's where magic is the strongest."

"Is that close?" I ask.

Kayleigh nods. "It doesn't take more than about fifteen to twenty minutes to get there on foot. We can go after dinner, if you like."

I nod eagerly. "I would like that very much. Thank you."

With Kayleigh helping us, it doesn't take long for us to finish prepping all the potatoes. Aunt Shannon sets the cabbage aside and adds the potatoes to boil in the remaining cabbage water while she goes about chopping up some green onions. Kayleigh and I get to work making soda bread while her mother finishes up the other parts of dinner. I'm covered in flour when everyone else tumbles back indoors, laughing and joking with each other.

"Did you have a good time?" I ask, a slight pang of jealousy at being left out, although I appreciated my time in the kitchen.

Kato grins at me. "We did!"

"Niall challenged us to a bow shooting contest," Makin adds, also grinning.

I look at Niall and grimace. "You didn't bet money, did you?"

The set expression on Niall's face is answer enough.

"Niall is quite good with a bow," Kayleigh jumps in. "He hasn't met anyone who can best him."

"He has now," Kato grins, eyeing the pretty girl for the first time. Kayleigh notices his gaze and blushes, dipping her head.

"Kato, meet my cousin Kayleigh," Alak says with a smile.

"Pleased to meet you," Kayleigh mumbles.

"Likewise, I promise you," Kato says with a wink.

I clear my throat. "Anyway, is that all you boys did? Play with weapons for money?"

Ehren shrugs. "More or less. Though the rest of us knew better than to bet against Kato."

"I feel like I was conned," Niall grumbles.

"I'm sorry. My brother can be like that sometimes. I'll tell you what, I'll challenge you later, and you can win some of your money back." I give a soft smile, but my eyes flicker wickedly.

Cal glances away quickly, while Makin turns to hide his grin. Ehren's hand flies to cover his mouth, but he tries to act casual as if he's scratching the stubble on his chin. Kato bursts out laughing and Alak grins. Bram is the only one who manages to steel his face into a casual, serious look.

Niall studies them all for a moment before slowly replying, "Sure. Why not?"

"Your funeral, mate," Alak says, clapping his cousin on the back.

Aunt Shannon insists Kayleigh and I go chat with the others while she finishes up dinner and we oblige. Makin, Cal, and Kato play cards while the rest of us watch. A few minutes before dinner is ready, a tall, broad shouldered man with dark green eyes and reddish-brown hair and beard strolls into the room. His eyes flit to us then to Shannon, who is placing food on serving dishes.

"Callum. You're home. Do you remember Alak, my sister Fiona's son?" Shannon says hurriedly. Callum nods, scowling at us. "Remember, I told you he might come back to visit?"

"I didn't realize that would mean bringing a caravan into my house," Callum grumbles, but then a smile spreads across his face. "However, now that you are all here, you are welcome."

I relax, not even realizing I'd tensed up. Bram, whose arm is around me, relaxes a bit as well.

"Kayleigh, would you mind calling Saran and Molly for dinner?"

Kayleigh nods and jumps up, heading outside to fetch her brother and sister while Shannon brings plates over to the table. I rise from my seat and help her. She offers me a grateful smile. A few minutes later we're all seated around the table. We pile our plates high with colcannon potatoes, which are apparently potatoes mixed with onions, milk, cabbage, and a lot of butter, as well as mutton chops and soda bread. There's ale for us and milk for the younger two. When we've finished, I feel full and very satisfied. I rest my head on Bram's shoulder.

"That meal was very good, thank you," I mumble.

Aunt Shannon nods her head. "You're very welcome."

"If you think that was good," Kayleigh adds, "just wait a few days until the Festival of Aoibhinn." She pronounces the name "ay-veen" in a tongue that sounds ancient.

"What's the Festival of Aoibhinn?" I ask, cocking my head.

Kayleigh's eyes go wide, as do the eyes of most of our other hosts. "It's the festival of the goddess Aoibhinn, the giver of magic! It's one of the greatest celebrations! You'll love it!"

"It sounds like fun," Kato says. "I love a good festival."

"Why don't you all go and get out of my way so I can clean this all up," Shannon declares, rising.

I rise with her. "I can help."

"Nonsense. You helped prepare the meal. And you are my guest. Please, go and enjoy our little village."

Kayleigh hops up from the table. "We can take you to Lush-water Woods, now, if you like."

"Yes, that sounds good," I reply.

Everyone else slowly rises, stretching.

"Is it a long walk?" Makin asks. "Because I was hoping to check out the local, uh, pub before it gets too late in the day."

Niall laughs. "It's not a far walk but the pub is closer. The woods will appeal more to the magic wielders, so the pub may be a better fit for you, anyway."

"I'll join you at the pub," Ehren says. "I can use a drink."

Bram knits his eyebrows. "Maybe that's not the best—"

"I'm in, too," Cal cuts Bram off.

"They'll be fine," I whisper in Bram's ear, then add for everyone to hear, "Why don't you go with them?"

Bram turns to me. "Are you sure?"

"I'm sure. I'll meet up with you later." I kiss him lightly and brush my hand on his stubbly cheek. "Now, go."

Bram leaves with the others, glancing over his shoulder before he goes out the door.

"Clingy a bit," Niall mutters.

"You have no idea," Alak replies, rolling his eyes.

"So, these woods?" I say, my cheeks turning slightly pink.

Kayleigh and Niall are eager to show us the woods and walk quickly. As promised, it doesn't take long to reach them. Everything hums with magic. It courses through the air, and my magic reaches out, singing. I close my eyes, tilting my head back as I inhale deeply.

"Isn't it wonderful?" Kayleigh asks, breathless.

I open my eyes and nod. "I feel like I could fly."

"With your magic," Alak interjects, "you probably could."

"Your magic is powerful?" Kayleigh asks, arching her eyebrows.

"Incredibly," Niall answers. "She dispelled my darkness with little effort."

Kayleigh's eyes widen. "Really? That is impressive."

"What magic can you do?" I ask casually and Kayleigh shrugs.

"My magic is very basic. I can move things without touching them," she replies. She reaches out her hand and a small pebble from the ground floats up to her. "It's not much but it's useful."

"I think it's amazing," Kato says, offering her a smile.

Kayleigh blushes. "Thank you."

Niall watches the two of them interact with interest.

"I hear water," I say, glancing away from Kayleigh and Kato.

"Yes, that's the Lushwater Crick," Niall says.

"Its water is known to have magical properties," Kayleigh adds.

They lead us through the trees to a glittering, shallow river tumbling over a bed of colorful rocks. We step onto a bridge made of twisting branches and vines covered in blooming pink flowers. I look down into the crystal water as it glistens and gleams in the evening sunlight. I swear I hear a song rising up from the water. My lips part and I take a step closer.

"Beware the Water Nymphs," Kayleigh warns, grabbing my arm.

"Water Nymphs?" I ask, looking over at her, my eyes sparkling.

Kayleigh nods. "The water may be mostly shallow, but they'll still draw you in and drown you."

"Come now, we're not all bad," a silvery voice floats over the air. I glance back at the water and see a translucent figure standing in the center of the creek. She's female with long, knee length hair. Her entire body, which is entirely unclothed, is made of water.

Kayleigh purses her lips. "Maybe not all bad, but you're deceitful."

The Water Nymph pouts. "And I thought we were friends."

"Hardly. We just aren't enemies," Niall laughs.

"Well, I can see when I'm not wanted," the Nymph sneers, splashing back into nothing but river water.

I blink my eyes quickly, sure that I can no longer trust them. I'm still staring at where the Nymph disappeared when I hear Alak say, "Hey! Felixe!" I spin around and see Felixe on Alak's shoulder, flicking his tail in Alak's face.

"You have a Fae Fox?" Kayleigh cries, clapping her hands. "Can I pet him?"

Alak grins. "It's up to him but he's usually pretty open to pampering."

Kayleigh reaches out her hand to Felixe. He gives her a couple quick sniffs and barks defensively. She tries to pat his head, and he growls before snapping from Alak's shoulder to mine.

"That's . . . unusual," Alak scowls.

"What's the matter, boy?" I ask, scratching Felixe between his ears. Felixe yaps again.

Niall's eyes glance curiously at the Fae Fox now on my shoulder.

"Wait, whose Fae Fox is he?" Niall asks.

"Mine," Alak replies hesitantly.

Felixe seems to find that the best moment to lick my cheek. I giggle and wipe it off. Felixe then pops back over to Alak, eyes narrowed at Kayleigh.

"But, if he's your familiar—" Niall begins but Alak cuts him off.

"We should probably head back. We've been traveling a lot the past few days and rest sounds really good right now."

Niall glances from Alak to me and then shrugs. "So be it."

They lead us back through the woods, Felixe bounding along beside us most of the way. When we get back to the house, we find that Bram has already returned from the pub. Bram helps me gather my things to take to Niall's home.

"I don't like the idea of you sleeping in a different house," Bram mutters, brushing my cheek with his fingers as we stand by the stone gate.

I lean into his touch. "I slept in a different house last night."

"I didn't like that, either. But I really don't like this arrangement since it seems more long-term."

"You just don't like the fact that Alak is staying in the same house," I say, giving Bram a knowing look.

Bram chuckles. "I can't deny that it bothers me."

I cock my head. "You worry too much."

"Perhaps," he offers me a smile. "It's only because I love you so much."

He leans in and presses his lips against mine, and I receive the kiss eagerly. When he draws away I want to pull him back to me, but, instead, I just touch his lips with the tips of my fingers. He gently grasps my hand and presses it more firmly to his mouth, kissing my fingers each individually. My heart flutters.

"Goodnight, Astra," he says, his voice rough.

"Goodnight."

I leave him leaning against the gate, and his gaze doesn't leave me until we've gone around a curve and out of sight. Niall leads us up to a stone house that looks like a smaller version of his parents'. It too has a small green yard surrounded by a small stone wall. Niall's house, however, is only two stories tall.

"It's not much," he says, ushering us inside. "But it's home. There are two rooms upstairs, mine and a spare. I'm afraid, as the home is relatively new, that the only furnishing in the spare room is a cot with a blanket, but it should be suitable."

"We can definitely make do," Alak says, dropping his bag on the ground. He turns to me. "Why don't you take the room and Kato and I can bunk out here."

I nod. "That sounds fine."

Niall grins. "Let me show you to your room, then."

He leads me upstairs to a wooden door. He throws the door open, revealing a small, cozy space. As promised, the only thing in the room is a small cot in the corner, a red blanket folded on top. At least there's a big window looking down into the street below.

"Thank you. This works fine."

He opens his mouth to say something and then shuts it, shaking his head.

"What?" I press, though my instincts tell me I shouldn't have.

He pauses then finally says, "Why is that you, someone who possesses strong and unusual magic, is engaged to someone who possesses not an inkling of magic?"

I frown. "Because I love him. Br—Xander," I begin, barely catching my mistake in time, "has been there for me in ways no one has. He even saved my life."

Niall nods, considering my words. "All right, love." I've grown used to being called "love" by Alak but the term coming from Niall's lips sounds wrong. "Have a good night. We'll see ya in the mornin'."

I feel a little uneasy, but I dress for bed and settle on my cot, pushing my discomfort aside in favor of sleep.

CHAPTER FORTY-ONE

I'm not surprised in the slightest when I wake up and find my other self standing in the room, looking out the window.

"Not a bad view," she muses before turning to me. "What do you think of Athiedor?"

"I like it," I reply, sitting up on my cot. "I like it a lot. There's so much magic."

She smiles. "I thought you might, but you must be wary of a place so magical. It can stir up feelings of power that you may not be accustomed to."

"What do you mean?"

"Sometimes," she explains slowly. "When magic comes too easily, when it's right at your fingertips, it's easy to surrender to desires of power."

I shake my head. "I would never do that."

"Perhaps," she replies with a nod. "Others might, though, and sometimes, we must be strong for them." She smiles and walks toward me. "Now, sleep. You have busy days ahead. And remember, always conserve a little of your magic. You never know when you'll need it."

Then, with a gentle touch of her fingers to my forehead, I fall back asleep.

The next morning, I wake up to the smell of sausage and eggs. I stretch and take a moment to recognize my surroundings. I dress quickly and head downstairs where I find Alak, wearing an apron but no shirt, cooking sausage and eggs over the fire. I arch an eyebrow at Alak and he grins as I approach.

"Mornin', love! Care for some fried eggs and sausage?" he asks, holding out a plate bearing both.

I narrow my eyes at the offered plate. "Is it safe to eat?"

"Is it safe to eat?" Alak yells, his eyes glinting. "Of course, love! Would I ever lead you wrong?"

"Hmmm . . . ," I consider, tapping a finger on my chin.

Alak huffs at me and tosses an eggshell at my face. I squeal and manage to knock it out of the air right before it hits me.

"Fine, I'll try them, but if I die, you have to explain it to Bram and Kato." I take the plate and glance around. "Where is Kato, anyway?"

Alak shrugs, turning his attention back to the eggs he's cooking. "He and Niall were both up and gone when I got up. I borrowed these eggs and sausages from my aunt."

"Curious," I mumble, taking a bite of my breakfast. "Hey! This is good!"

I take a second bite and Alak laughs. "You constantly underestimate me, love."

I look up at him. He's staring at me with his intense emerald eyes. For a moment, they steal my breath. Kato and Niall returning are my salvation, and I break Alak's gaze as they enter the house.

"Hey, Ash! You're up!" Kato says, grinning. He approaches

us and eyes the fried eggs and sausage Alak is placing on a platter. "Who made breakfast?"

"I promised everyone breakfast, so I made breakfast," Alak replies. "Now eat up."

Kato sits down, arms crossed, and watches me for a moment. "What?" I demand, my mouth full of food.

"I'm just watching to make sure you don't drop dead from Alak's cooking before I eat anything," Kato says, eyes sparkling mischievously.

Alak throws another eggshell at Kato, and this time his strike is successful.

"Hey!" Kato laughs, brushing the eggshell from his cheek and shoulder.

"I'm offended none of you think I can cook," Alak grins. "So I will continue to throw eggshells at all you non-believers."

Alak slides his eyes to Niall who throws his hands up in surrender. "I have no doubts about your breakfast. I can already tell it's far better than anything I could do."

Kato takes a plate and sits next to me at the table. "So, Alak hit you with an eggshell, too, huh."

"Nope," I reply, taking another bite. "I was quicker than you. I blocked it."

We finish up our breakfast and head out. A beautiful young woman with strawberry blond hair is rushing our way. Niall strides to her, sweeping her into his arms and kissing her. When they're done with their greeting, Niall turns to us, grinning.

"Alak, you remember Caitlyn, right?" Niall asks, his hand around Caitlyn's waist.

Alak lets out a low whistle. "You truly have grown into a beautiful woman, Cait."

Caitlyn's eyes go wide. "Alak? You mean, little Alak, your cousin?"

Niall chuckles. "The one and the same."

Caitlyn looks at Alak, her face glowing. "I haven't seen you since we were young children! I never imagined we would cross paths again!"

Alak gives her a slight bow. "And yet, here we are."

She grins, looking over at me and Kato. "Are these your friends?" She raises her eyebrows excitedly. "Perhaps a betrothed of your own?"

Kato bursts out laughing while I vigorously shake my head. Alak sighs dramatically, throwing his arm around my shoulders. My heart skips a beat.

"Unfortunately, I'm just too much man for Astra."

"Yeah, that's the reason," I scoff, shrugging out from under his arm.

"My sister's actually engaged to another friend of ours, Xander, who is staying down the road," Kato cuts in with a grin. He then inclines his head and adds, "My name is Kato."

"Such a pleasure to meet you both! And terribly sorry for the confusion." She turns to Niall. "I was just coming to walk with you to work this morning, unless you have other duties."

"We're fine," Kato waves them off. "Go do whatever you need."

Niall gives us a parting nod, and they head one way while we head the other. It's a beautiful, warm morning and the walk to Alak's aunt's house is pleasant and almost too short. When we enter the yard, we're almost knocked over by Molly and Saran rushing out.

"Sorry, Cousin Alak," Saran calls over his shoulder, not bothering to slow down.

Alak chuckles as we walk into the house. Shannon and Kayleigh are clearing away what remains of breakfast, and the others lounge around the table.

"Do ya dears need any breakfast or was Alak able to provide something edible for you?" Shannon asks.

"Alak made you breakfast?" Ehren asks, rising from his seat with the others. "And no one died?"

"I am an excellent cook!" Alak says, throwing his hands into the air dramatically.

I laugh. "It actually was quite good."

Alak's frustration turns to smugness. "It was quite good, wasn't it, love?"

"What are your plans for the day?" Kayleigh asks, approaching us.

I shrug. "I don't know that we really have any plans. I'd love to go back to the woods today, if no one minds."

"If you'd like to take a picnic, I can pack a few things for you," Shannon offers and we accept.

"Well, I unfortunately have to be at work today, or I would join you." Kayleigh sighs as her mother busies herself packing us food for lunch.

"What is it you do?" I ask.

"I work with a seamstress." Kayleigh perks up a bit. "You should come by, Astra! We can fit you for a new dress for the Festival of Aoibhinn!"

"I don't need a new dress," I protest, shaking my head.

"A young lady always needs a new dress," Kayleigh insists. "Please?"

"Okay, maybe, but I don't really have much money, so—"

"I'll pay for it," Bram cuts in, waving his hand.

"You don't have to."

He tilts his head and smiles gently. "I know. I want to."

"Great!" Kayleigh says. "Just come by anytime today or even tomorrow morning and we'll get you fitted."

With that, she rushes out the door. A few moments later, Alak's aunt presents us with lunch and we're on our way. I

don't even have to question which way to go—my heart knows.
When we enter the forest, I can't help but spin and skip. Felixe
appears and hops along with me. When we reach the river, I
turn to Bram, smiling so wide my face hurts.

"Isn't it beautiful here?" I ask.

He smiles, his eyes on me. "My view is extraordinary."

I blush as Ehren rolls his eyes. "You can surely do better
than that. Have you learned nothing by my side?"

Bram glares at Ehren, who settles down next to the water.

"Well, what are we going to do now that we're here?"
Makin asks, skipping a stone across the creek's surface.

I shrug. "I wouldn't mind practicing some magic. It's so
easy here." As I speak I mindlessly swirl a twist of silver light in
the air.

"Why don't you and Kato battle, and the rest of us will bet
on the outcomes?" Ehren suggests with a grin.

"I don't think—" Bram starts but Kato cuts him off.

"I'm down for that."

"Fine," I agree with a smug smile. "But I want a cut when I
win."

Kato and I start with a dagger throwing contest. It's close,
but I win. Cal and Alak grin while Makin and Ehren pay up.
With the bow and arrow, we tie, our arrows literally landing on
top of each other, no matter how many times we try. For the
third competition, we decide on a sword fight. Kato's fire
sword is well crafted with a dragon hilt. My silver light sword
is sleek with a twisting handle. The first blows are matched
evenly, but sword training has never been my strongpoint. It is
Kato's specialty, however. I dodge and block blow after blow,
even instigating a few strikes of my own, but in the end, Kato
wins.

"You failed me, Astra," Ehren moans, passing coins to
Makin.

"Sorry," I say, still trying to catch my breath. "I need some more practice with my sword. Perhaps you'll spar with me?"

Ehren arches his eyebrows. "Me?" he asks, drawing out the word as he splays his fingers across his chest. "You wish to spar with me?"

I nod, grinning. "Unless you're afraid I'll beat you?"

Ehren jumps to his feet and saunters toward me, his eyes glowing. "You do realize I have trained with and under some of the top swordsmen Callenia has to offer?"

"Is that supposed to impress me or intimidate me or . . ." I let my voice trail off.

Makin bites back a laugh and Bram grins. Ehren runs his tongue across his teeth, smiling wickedly. He whips his sword out in one smooth motion.

"Your magic against my steel," Ehren declares, balancing his sword in his left hand and taking his stance as I take mine.

Ehren strikes first, and I block it easily. After his first few blows, I can tell he's holding back, so I dive in full force, pushing him to show his skill. The magic around me in the air sings and links with my own magic. Just like when I sparred with Makin and Cal, I can feel and sense every move Ehren makes. He nearly gets me several times, but what I lack in sword skills, I make up for with fleetness. For several blows, I dodge him before charging, my own blows coming fast and hard. Ehren swings somewhat wildly, and I duck under his blade, twirling behind him. He spins and we're face to face again. Our feet move quickly across the uneven forest floor, neither of us missing a step. I step up onto a fallen tree, barely dodging Ehren's blade. I leap forward and my blade crashes down on his. He's not prepared to defend from that angle and he nearly drops the sword. I take advantage of his weakened position to strike his blade again, from the bottom, and his sword goes spinning through the air. I leap up and snatch it, twirling to face a flabbergasted Ehren. He stands there, hand still held out, his mouth open and eyes wide. My heart is pounding as I grin.

"Some prince," Makin mumbles, passing coins to Cal.

"You . . . you beat me," Ehren fumbles. "You actually beat me!"

He stares at me in wonder as I offer him his sword. He takes it and slides it into his sheath, shaking his head.

"I blame you," Ehren says, turning to face Bram who is beaming with pride. "You clearly didn't push me hard enough."

"Yes, I'm sure that was the problem," Alak scoffs.

"Did you bet for or against me?" I ask Alak and he turns red.

"I, uh, well . . ."

"He lost to me," Bram grins, flipping a marke coin in the air while Alak glares at him.

"Trust me, love, that's the last time I will ever bet against you."

"Well, I'm starving," Kato says, putting his hands on his stomach. "How about we eat?"

We all agree and dig into the sandwiches and fruit Aunt Shannon provided for us. She also included a bottle of ale, which we pass around. When I finish my food, I lay on my back, arms crossed behind my head, and stare up into the trees at the blue sky shining behind the treetops while birds flutter from branch to branch. I close my eyes and can feel myself drifting off to sleep when I hear a slow and beautiful song. I open my eyes and jerk up. I look over at the water and see two Water Nymphs standing in the water. Everyone's eyes seem to be locked on them. Bram, Cal, Makin, and Ehren are slowly drifting toward them. I send a stream of silver light shooting through the Nymphs and they shriek, cursing as they disappear into the water. The others shake their heads and glance at me.

"Water Nymphs," I say with a shrug.

"I think I like this forest a little less now," Makin mumbles, glancing at the trees like he expects them to attack next.

"Why weren't you affected?" Bram asks, easing back down on the ground next to me.

"I think they were targeting you four since you don't have any natural magical resistance."

"Maybe we should take that as a sign that we need to head back into town," Ehren says, glancing tentatively at the water.

"Why don't you all head back. I would like to spend a few moments alone with Astra," Bram says, taking my hand in his.

"Alone time in a magical wood. Oh, to be young and in love," Makin sighs, placing his hand over his heart.

Cal laughs and pushes Makin away from us. "Let's leave them alone."

"You two, don't do anything I wouldn't do," Ehren says with an over exaggerated wink.

Kato rolls his eyes and adds, "Don't do half the stuff he would do, either."

"I feel like I should be offended by that, but I can't deny you have a valid point." Ehren chuckles.

Alak doesn't say anything. He just meets my eyes and gives me a tight smile before he saunters off with the others. When we're alone, Bram turns to me and presses his lips against mine. He slowly lowers me down onto the ground as we kiss. He pulls back and looks down at me.

"I love you so much, Astra," he whispers, his voice raw.

I reach up and brush hair out of his eyes. "I love you, too."

He stands and offers me his hand. When I take it, he pulls me to my feet, leading me to the bridge. He leans on the vine railing and stares down into the water. I lay my head against his arm and inhale deeply in contentment. He looks down at me, his brown eyes shining.

"You love it here, don't you?" he asks quietly.

I nod. "I really do. It's odd, but I feel more at home here than I did in Timberborn."

"Do you think it is because of all the magic everywhere?" Bram asks, placing his hand over mine and lacing his fingers with mine.

I look around at the sparkling, glowing forest around me and a smile creeps onto my lips. "Maybe. I think that's part of it. It's also just so beautiful here."

I look back at Bram and his eyes seem sad. I reach up and stroke his face. "What's wrong?"

He glances away. "Nothing. I just hate the thought of having to take you away from here eventually."

"Hey," I whisper, gently turning his face back to mine. "I will always be happy anywhere you are."

He smiles, but it doesn't quite reach his eyes. "Are you sure?"

I stretch up on my tiptoes and kiss his cheek. "Definitely."

He leans in and kisses me, fiercely. When he releases me he lets out a long sigh. "We should probably catch up with the others."

I sigh, nodding in agreement. Hand in hand, we walk back to the house. When we get there, Ehren hands me a thick letter.

"This came for you while we were gone." Ehren's eyes are dark and serious, his mouth a tight line.

I take it from him. "What is it?"

Ehren nods to the letter. "That's my sister's handwriting."

"Oh," I mutter. I glance toward Aunt Shannon. "I think I may take it outside to read better."

We shuffle out into the yard, and I take a seat on the stone wall, opening the letter. Ehren watches me nervously. Inside is a second letter. I glance at it at first but focus on what Cadewynn has written.

My Dear Astra,

I hope you are faring well. I believe this letter will arrive more safely if I address it to you rather than any of your traveling companions. My days in the library seem longer without my friends, but then again, the books have always been loyal friends themselves. My studies continue to confirm everything we knew and expected. Thus, I expect you will find your time spent most profitably.

Things here in the capital have become increasingly more intense since your departure. Those few who seem to have exceptional or unusual talents are being rounded up by the hundreds. Many have been disposed of without trial or even proof. Times grow more and more grim. I'm hoping you will be able to aid soon.

Shortly after your departure, you received a letter from your friend in Timberborn. I have included it in my own letter. I am sure you will find very important details hidden inside.

Best wishes on your travels,
Winnie

"What does it say?" Ehren asks as my eyes lift from the page.

"Not much," I say with a shrug, passing the letter to Ehren. "She also did pass on this letter from Mara." I open the second letter and find a third one hidden inside.

"How many letters did she send you?" Alak laughs.

"Maybe this is what she means by 'important details hidden inside,'" I muse. I turn over the letter and see that it's addressed to Ehren. I hold it out to him. "This one is for you."

Ehren takes it, puzzled, handing back Cadewynn's letter. He opens his letter, scanning the page for a moment before his eyes go wide.

"What is it?" Bram asks.

"It's from the Order of Naskein. They received my inquiry and have formally invited us to visit at our earliest convenience."

"The Order of Naskein?" Kato asks. "Who are they?"

"They're a magical order that live on the Isle of Naskein off the shores of Portia. Technically, they're part of the nation of Portia, but they govern themselves. They're essentially a religious order that revolves around magic," Alak explains and all eyes turn to him.

"And," Ehren adds, "if they're willing to join us in our fight for magic, they could prove powerful allies against my father."

"Aren't they pacifists?" I ask. "How could they help?"

"They are pacifists, but they are well-trusted. We could easily gain more allies—allies with armies—with their support. Plus, they have unlimited magical resources that could also aid us," Ehren replies.

"Should we leave immediately?" Makin asks.

Ehren shakes his head slowly. "I think we should stay here at least through the festival. Perhaps we can leave a day or so after."

"Speaking of the festival," I say, "I should probably go meet up with Kayleigh and let her make my dress."

"And we," Makin adds, "should go to the pub."

"It's barely past midday," I say and Makin grins.

"It doesn't matter what time of day it is, there's always gossip a-plenty at the pub or tavern or anywhere you can get a good pint."

"So that's why you go every chance you get? For the gossip?" I ask skeptically.

Cal coughs. "He also likes to drink and gamble."

Makin clicks his tongue. "I support businesses. That is very important."

Cal rolls his eyes. "Whatever."

"Well," Makin says. "Are we going or not?"

With a shrug we all trudge into town. Ehren, Cal, Makin, and Kato head to the pub while Bram, Alak, and I try to find where Kayleigh might be. There aren't many businesses, so it doesn't take long to find the seamstress Kayleigh works for. It's a small back room in the woman's house. Kayleigh greets us with a bright smile.

"I'm so glad you came by! I already have a traditional design in my head, I just need to get your measurements, so it shouldn't take long," Kayleigh says, ushering me inside while shooing Bram and Alak away. "You boys can wait outside."

Kayleigh flutters around me in a nervous fluster. She checks each measurement multiple times before scribbling it down.

"This will only be my third solo dress," Kayleigh explains, twisting her tape measure in her hands. "It has to be perfect, not just so you look amazing, but so I can prove my skill."

I offer her a smile. "I'm sure it will be perfect."

CHAPTER FORTY-TWO

*W*hen I finish with Kayleigh, I find Bram and Alak waiting outside, leaning at opposite ends of a stone wall, backs facing each other.

"You know, you could probably be farther apart if you went to opposite ends of the road instead of just the wall," I tease as I approach them.

Bram scowls toward Alak, who grins in response. "I suggested such, love, but we couldn't decide which of us should be farther away from you, so we settled on the wall."

"I don't understand why you came with us in the first place," Bram mutters, glaring at Alak.

"I wanted to see my cousin. Besides," Alak replies with a shrug, "I don't have any interest in the pub at this hour."

"Why not? It seems like you'd be happy to go to the pub any time of the day or night," I say as we walk aimlessly down the street.

Alak looks down at his feet. "This time of day it's mostly gambling. I don't care for gambling in general much anymore beyond casual friendly wagers like in the woods earlier."

Bram clenches a fist at his side and looks straight ahead.

"Oh," I reply lamely. "Well, what shall we do then to pass the time between now and dinner?"

"What did your letter from your friend say? Any interesting details you want to share?" Alak says, lifting his head and smiling.

"I forgot about my letter from Mara!" I cry, reaching into my pocket and pulling out the letter.

We settle on a little portion of a stone wall bordering the main road and I read. The first half of her letter is typical of what I expect from Mara. She goes on and on about how lucky I am to have all the services of a palace. She asks about Kato and Ehren and requests information about any other handsome guards. She congratulates me on my engagement and begs that I send her details of when the wedding is to take place so she can attend. The second half of her letter is more disheartening. She speaks of the king's soldiers coming into town, looking for magic. She writes of homes and businesses destroyed and of trust betrayed, families divided, and neighbor turning against neighbor.

"What's wrong, love?" Alak asks, concern edging his voice.

I relay the last part of Mara's message and Bram swears. "We knew it would get bad, but this is escalating quicker than we anticipated."

"What can we do?" I ask, my voice quiet.

Bram lets out a long sigh. "I really don't know. Just what we're already doing, I suppose—stay alive, keep Ehren alive, and find more allies."

I open my mouth to say something, but Alak shakes his head ever so slightly and nods down the road. I turn and see Niall striding toward us accompanied by Caitlyn, two other young men, and a stunning woman our age I haven't seen before. He grins, walking up to us.

"You three look like you're up to no good," Niall says.

"Always," Alak grins.

"Who are your friends?" I ask, glancing at his three companions. One of the young men is shorter with broad shoulders, short reddish-brown hair, and thick eyebrows hovering over brown eyes set on a square face. The girl has the same reddish-brown hair but paired with sharp green eyes and pretty, feminine features and a sleek, curvy body. The other young man is tall and lean with strawberry blond hair and narrow features.

"This is Fionn," Niall says, slapping the blond on the back, "and that chap is Ian and his sister Aine."

"Awn-ye?" I reply, trying out the strange name on my tongue. The girl nods and I add, "It's a lovely name."

"It's very traditional in these parts," she says, her accent thick and rich.

"Don't you have work to do?" Alak asks and Niall shrugs.

"We all got off a little early today. We were headed to the pub. Care to join us?"

"Please, say that you will," Aine says, addressing Alak, gazing at him through her long eyelashes.

Alak doesn't miss Aine's attention, and his lips turn up in a flirtatious smirk. "Well, how can a man resist an invitation from such a pretty girl."

I don't care for the way Aine continues to eye Alak, or the way he returns her gaze.

"Or," I suggest, "I believe Niall challenged me to a shooting contest that we have yet to complete. Perhaps now would be a good time to see who is the better shot?" I raise my eyebrows in challenge and Niall laughs.

"Of course," Niall says, dipping his head. "I would never back away from a challenge. I just need to fetch my bow from my house. Then, perhaps into the woods?"

I give a short nod. "That sounds good."

As we make our way to Niall's house, Niall and Caitlyn take the lead, while Aine walks alongside Alak right behind them. Bram and I take up the rear, walking hand in hand behind Ian and Fionn, who keep giving us distasteful glances over their shoulders. Alak doesn't seem to notice, completely enraptured with whatever Aine is saying. Bram senses my uneasiness and gives my hand a gentle squeeze. I look up at him. He offers me a smile, but I can see concern in his eyes. I force my own smile, and he quickly brushes a kiss on my temple. I look away from him just in time to catch Fionn's eyes narrow before he drops back, coming up alongside me.

"Niall tells me ye have strong magic," Fionn says, his accent thick.

I nod. "I do. Or at least I believe I do. I'm still discovering it. Do you have magic?"

"Of course," he replies curtly. "My skill set is mostly in spells and potions. Most people have to use specific spell books to find the ingredients and steps. I don't need all that."

"Spells? That's interesting. I don't know much about spells or potions," I admit.

Fionn's eyes narrow, studying my face as we walk. I feel Bram tense.

"It does seem ye have much ta learn about magic," Fionn says slowly. "Perhaps, we kin teach ye a thing or two."

I manage a smile. "That's what I'm hoping."

I look up and am relieved to see that we've arrived at Niall's house. Fionn steps back over to Ian and the two whisper to one another in low voices. I don't miss the fact that they both glance my way more than once. Bram turns and places himself between me and Fionn and Ian, his back to them. He leans in and kisses my cheek.

"I don't trust them," Bram whispers as he lifts his lips. He keeps his face close to mine and studies my face, worry shining in his eyes. I reach my hand up and stroke his cheek.

"Don't worry. I think we'll be fine. They're just wary of strangers, I think," I reply, keeping my voice low.

"I'm ready to go!" Niall calls from behind us, holding up his bow, arrows strapped to his back.

"Shall we wisp to the woods?" Aine asks, lightly. Then her eyes shift to Bram and she gives us a sympathetic look. "Oh, but I forgot we have a non-magic wielder amongst us. Pity."

"I can wisp us both," I reply tersely.

Aine smiles like a snake. "Well, then. Shall we?"

Niall grins, amused by our interaction. "Meet by the bridge."

Niall spins, vanishing. The others follow suit immediately, save for Alak who lingers just a moment, his eyes linking with mine right before he vanishes. I take a deep breath and focus, taking both of Bram's hands in mine before we wisp through the air and reappear surrounded by trees.

"Well, it seems you are capable of wisping two people," Aine says with feigned disinterest as she examines her nails. Her eyes dart up and focus on Bram as a catlike grin spreads across her face. "How lucky for you to be engaged to someone who can assist you with magic where you would otherwise fail."

I hear Bram inhale sharply and look up at his face to find his eyes set and cold. His hand tightens on mine.

"Now, now, Aine," Ian chides, his eyes shining gleefully. "No need to be rude."

I force a laugh. "It's actually a relief to be able to use my magic for two." Her eyebrows quirk up as I continue, "After all, with the intense amount of power I have coursing through me, I need every reason and excuse to use magic, or it builds up to an unbearable point. I'm sure you understand."

Aine's expression turns cold, but I see Alak's hand fly to his mouth to cover his smile, his eyes laughing. Fionn and Ian seem less amused.

"I suppose I know what you mean," Aine says stiffly, tossing her hair over her shoulder.

Niall clears his throat. "We came to shoot arrows, not each other."

"Do you have a target? Or are we just shooting at trees?" I ask, glancing around.

Alak smiles and twists his hand, a target appearing nearby on a large tree. "Does that suffice?"

Niall grins. "Works for me."

"Are we placing bets?" I ask casually.

Niall shrugs, his grin growing. "Do you care to place a bet?"

"I really wouldn't, mate," Alak warns, his voice quiet.

"I bet a marke-and-a-half in favor of Niall," Fionn says, his dark eyes sizing me up.

"I'll also bet on Niall," Ian adds, crossing his arms.

Niall laughs. "No one wins if everyone bets on me."

"I'll bet on Astra," Bram says quickly.

"Naturally, you would want to take the side of your betrothed," Caitlyn says softly. "So I will take the side of mine."

Alak takes a step forward. "How about we make it a bit more interesting, since all of you foolishly seem set on Niall?"

Ian huffs. "It's not foolish when it's a simple girl going up against the strongest marksman in the village."

"Perhaps," Alak replies with a nod, "but I still like my odds. If you're so confident in my dear cousin's skill, let's set the ante a bit higher. If Niall wins, Xander and I will give each of you ten markes—five from each of us. But if Astra wins, each of you gives Xander and I five markes each, making our cut a total of twenty markes apiece."

Alak grins, his eyes glinting mischievously as he looks from face to face.

The others consider his bet for a moment, glancing from me to Niall.

"That's a lot of markes," Caitlyn says hesitantly.

Alak shrugs. "If you don't feel confident in Niall's skill then I underst—"

"Deal," Fionn grunts.

Alak grins and they shake on it.

Niall shifts his shoulders and stands a good distance from the tree. He pulls an arrow from his quiver and places it on the string, but Aine holds up her hand before he can shoot.

"Wait," she says, her eyes narrowing at Alak. "I don't trust your target of illusion when you have so much to gain from it."

She stretches out her long pale fingers and slowly moves them in a circle. It takes me a moment to realize she's tracing Alak's target, carving it deeper into the tree with conjured metal spikes. When she's done, she smiles at Alak, who gives an approving nod before snapping his target away, leaving hers behind.

"Satisfied, Aine?" Niall asks. She nods smugly, crossing her arms.

Niall resumes his position, considering the target. He takes a deep breath and the arrow flies straight. It lands inside the center ring but hits just to the right of dead center. A second arrow flies, landing slightly to the left of dead center, but his third arrow hits the mark. He lowers his bow and takes a step back, grinning.

"Your turn," he says, motioning me forward. "I suppose you'll need to borrow my bow?"

I shake my head, smiling. "That won't be necessary."

I hold out my hand and a sleek, silver bow appears, a quiver of silver arrows strapped on my back. Niall's eyes go wide.

"It doesn't seem fair that you use magic," he mumbles.

"Don't worry. I won't use magic to win the bet, just skill. I only need magic to create the bow and arrows." I hold the bow out to him. "Would you like to see how it compares to yours?"

He takes it from me and weighs it in his hand. His eyes widen. "This is a fine bow."

"But will it help her cheat?" Aine asks sharply, glaring at me.

Niall considers the bow for a moment then asks for an arrow. After he's examined everything he shakes his head. "There's no magic in these. She'll have to win on skill."

I give him a grateful nod as he returns my weapon. I step into place and eye my target. I pull the arrow back to my lips, take a deep breath, and release. My arrow meets Niall's center arrow point to point. Before anyone can react my second arrow is in the air, splitting Niall's arrow as it lands. My third arrow also strikes dead center. I lower my bow, grinning.

"Well, mates," Alak crows, holding out his hand. "Pay up!"

"We were tricked!" Fionn yells, his face red. "She clearly had magical arrows and bow! She just masked it somehow."

I give him a pitying look, which angers him further.

"If you want our markes, she must use a real bow and real arrows," Fionn insists, crossing his arms.

"Fine," I concede.

I wave my hand, clearing my arrows from the target. I hold out my hand and Niall places his bow in my palm. His bow is heavier than mine, but it's not much different than ones I've used before. I take three arrows and take my first shot. Arrow after arrow flies free and lands almost in the exact places my previous arrows hit.

"Do you need her to go again, or are you satisfied?" Alak grins as I hand Niall back his bow.

"I still think she used magic somehow," Fionn growls.

"Where did you learn to shoot like that?" Ian asks, eyeing me with equal suspicion.

"My brother."

"And her brother is also exceptionally skilled," Niall offers. He glances over at Alak who is still grinning triumphantly. "I suppose I was warned."

Alak lifts his hands in surrender. "Fine, fine, fine. We'll let you out of the bet this time. Not because she didn't win by skill alone, because she most certainly did, but because I feel sorry for you."

"No," Ian says firmly. "I won't keep my money on pity."

Aine glances at her brother, her eyes narrowing. "Do you even have that much money to throw at them? Don't let your pride make you foolish."

"I honestly don't even want your money," Alak says, his eyes clouding. "I don't make bets that big anymore. I haven't in years." He glances fleetingly at Bram. It's a movement so slight I wouldn't have caught it if I wasn't watching Alak closely. "I was more set on proving a point than anything."

"And what would that point be?" Aine asks sharply, eyes flashing.

Alak's grin returns. "That I always know best."

For the next couple of hours, we stay in the woods. Everyone seems interested in what else I can do with my magic, so I have a bit of fun showing them the different weapons I've practiced making as well as a few other basic tricks. Eventually, we head back to Aunt Shannon's house. Caitlyn stays for dinner but the others end up wandering back to their homes, promising to meet us later at the pub. I insist on helping out in the kitchen and we prepare boiled ham and cabbage. I don't care much for the smell of cooking cabbage but, I must admit, the taste has grown on me. Kato and the others show up just in time for dinner.

Dinner is lively. The village has started full preparations for the upcoming festival, and everyone seems to have tidbits of news. Kayleigh gushes about my dress, her eyes glowing. Niall shamefully admits how I bested him in the forest.

"Who's up for a trip to the pub?" Niall asks as I help clear the table.

"I'm always up for a trip to the pub," Makin says, rising.

I shoot Makin a judgy look. "Weren't you at the pub most of the day?"

"It wasn't like I was drinking all day," Makin replies defensively. "I was mostly enjoying the good company of newfound friends. And the money from their wallets."

"So you spent your day gambling at the pub."

"He and Kato wiped the floor with many of the locals," Cal says, smiling.

"Man's got to make a living," Makin says with a shrug.

Bram shakes his head at Makin, but Makin only grins.

"Well, I'm going to the pub," Niall says, pushing up from the table.

As Niall walks toward the door, the others follow him. Kayleigh and I volunteer to stay behind and clean up. Bram acts like he wants to stay as well, but I promise him I'll meet him shortly. When everything is cleaned up, Kayleigh and I sit and have a cup of tea and chat before heading to the pub. By the time we get there, night is starting to fall. Kayleigh sees one of her friends a little further up the road and rushes over to meet her. I start to head inside, but I pause when I hear a familiar voice hidden just out of sight outside the pub.

"But who is stronger?" Fionn is asking.

Something about the way he asks unnerves me, and I'm ready to rush away into the pub when another familiar voice answers him.

"I'm not sure. I think we're pretty much equals." Kato's voice makes me freeze.

I creep over to the corner and peer around it just enough to make out Fionn, Ian, Niall, and Kato sitting on the ground outside the pub, leaning against the outer stone wall. They appear to be passing some sort of pipe from person to person as they chat. I quickly pull back around the corner before they can spot me, but I don't walk away. I press my body against the cool stone building, my heart pounding as I listen.

"There's no denying she's extremely powerful," Niall's voice says. "She'd make a strong ally."

"She's not against magic. Or using magic. She uses it all the time," Kato replies.

"But what's her reason for using it?" Ian asks. "Is she using it to make herself more powerful and more controlled, or is she wasting it on those pathetic non-magic users you spend time with?"

My blood boils at his flippant tone, and I clench my fists at my side.

"They're good people," Kato says.

"No one's saying they aren't, mate," Niall says. "But they're holding you back. They're holding your sister back."

"I can't believe she's actually engaged to a *nildraiocht*," Fionn spits.

"A what?" Kato asks.

"A rude Yallik term for someone without magic," Niall explains.

"It's disgustin'," Fionn adds, his voice filled with hatred. My fists clench tighter.

"Oh. Xander's not a bad man. He's honorable enough," Kato says passively.

"He may be. And if your sister didn't have the power she does, he might be a good match. But can you honestly say you wouldn't rather have your sister be with someone who also has magic?" Niall asks.

Before Kato can answer Ian adds, "Aye. If she marries a magic wielder she could create a powerful magical dynasty through her children."

"My sister isn't a breeding mare for magic," Kato says, his voice hot and threatening. I smile.

"Whoa, mate," Niall says. "No one is suggesting that. We're just saying that a magical match would be better for her and any future family she may have. There's a war brewing between magic and non-magic. Do you really want nieces and nephews that can't defend themselves?"

I expect Kato to defend me again, but he's silent. My heart sinks.

"Besides," Niall continues, "that fiancé of hers makes her weak."

This makes Kato laugh. "Astra is hardly weak."

"All right, imagine this, mate," Ian cuts in. "You're in a battle to the death. Two shots are fired. One at yer sister and one at her beau. Who is she going to use her magic to defend?"

Kato is silent again.

"You see, mate?" Niall asks, his voice low and serious. "If you can't break her free from those friends of yours that can't protect themselves, she's going to continue putting herself at risk. Those friends may make good allies now, but unless they can defend themselves against magic, they'll only weigh you down. A grand divide between magic and non-magic is coming. You both need to make sure you're on the right side."

My stomach twists into knots, my head spinning. I hear them shifting and I scurry away. I have no desire to be caught eavesdropping. I rush inside and bump into someone trying to exit. I look up into Alak's emerald eyes.

"Hey there, love. Mighty eager to rush into my arms." His

grin fades and he furrows his brow as he studies my face. He pulls me to the side out of the way of the door, his hand resting on my arm. "What's wrong?"

I shake my head. I'm not quite sure how to put into words what I just overheard. "Nothing. I'm fine."

"Astra, you're not fine," Alak presses. "What's wrong?"

I glance away and spot Bram through the crowd. "There's Bram. I should get over there before he sees us together. You know he hates that."

I pull away from Alak and weave through the crowd toward Bram. Alak calls after me, and I can feel his eyes boring into my back. I refuse to turn and look, forcing a smile on my face as I focus on Bram. And I do so the rest of the night.

CHAPTER FORTY-THREE

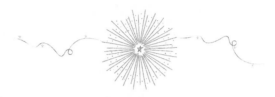

$\mathcal{T}$he conversation I overheard weighs heavily on me the next couple of days, but I don't say anything to anyone. I don't want Kato to know I was eavesdropping, though I really wish he would bring it up with me. I hate not knowing what his true feelings are. It's the first time I've ever had a concern and not shared it with him. It feels like some sort of betrayal. I'm not sure where Alak would stand on the issue. After all, it was his cousin initiating the conversation. He's admitted to me before his sense of self-preservation is strong. I definitely don't want to tell Bram or Ehren. They have enough on their plates to worry about without me adding additional concerns that probably mean nothing. So I worry about it for them, all while forcing a smile on my face good enough to fool them all.

We spend our days switching between helping out around Alak's aunt's house and spending time in the woods. Using magic always seems to lift my spirits. Bram and I find several moments to ourselves, and I can sense him starting to relax, even if I'm secretly tense.

The evenings after dinner are spent at the pub. There's always music and dancing, which never ceases to be fun. Even Bram has learned some of the dances and can lead me just as well as Alak or one of the more practiced villagers. We drink ale and everyone laughs and sings and dances for hours.

The only thing I don't like about our days are Niall's friends, particularly Aine. She always seems to be glaring at me and plotting, a feline smile on her lips. Anytime she's near Alak, she feels the need to touch him. Constantly. Every time she touches him, she watches me for my reaction. I try my best to pretend I don't notice, that I don't care, but the truth is, I don't trust her, and I don't like her using my friend as a pawn in whatever game she's playing. Alak seems oblivious to it all. He gravitates toward their group at every occasion, which makes sense. It is his home, and these are his people in every way.

When the morning of the Festival of Aoibhinn finally arrives, the air is thick with excitement. Kayleigh is giggling and twirling, promising to meet me mid-afternoon with my dress. Even Niall seems almost giddy. By noon, we're all caught up in the enthusiasm. When Kayleigh brings me my dress, her face is glowing.

"I really hope you like it," she says as she hands me the folds of sage green fabric.

I smile. "I'm sure I'll love it."

Kato, Alak, Niall, and I get ready at Niall's house. Of course, there's not much for the men to do to get ready. It's mostly for my benefit. When I slip into Kayleigh's dress, I love it immediately. The fabric is soft and feels like air. The short sleeves hang off my shoulders and swoop down into a scooped neckline. A corset type piece of brown leather fits over the waist of my dress, pushing my breasts up and slimming my waist, lacing up the back. The bottom is a flowing, wispy skirt I can't help but twirl. When I go to tighten the corset, I can't quite lace it tight enough or successfully tie it. I decide to go ahead and fix my hair and then see if Kato can help me finish the lacing. I pull my hair out of my face, twisting it into a loop and pinning it securely, leaving the rest of my hair down. I try one more time to lace my dress, but after a couple frustrating minutes, I finally give up and head downstairs to look for Kato. When I get downstairs, it's not Kato I find, however. It's a shirt-less Alak.

"Hello, love." Alak grins, cocking his head. "I must say, that is a beautiful masterpiece."

"Kayleigh did make a lovely dress," I agree, smoothing my hands over the fabric.

"My cousin did create a nice dress, but you're the thing that makes it a beautiful masterpiece," Alak says, his eyes glinting.

I'm used to Alak's joking, but something about his expression seems more sincere than usual. I brush it off, rolling my eyes.

"Have you seen Kato? I need his help with something."

"He already left," Alak says, pulling a shirt out of his nearby bag. "Maybe I can help you."

"So he's not coming back?" I ask with a frown.

"I don't think so. Not for a while anyway." Alak studies my face, his expression puzzled. "What do you need?"

"I just . . . I need help lacing my dress," I finally get out, reaching my hands back and tugging on the laces.

"Oh," Alak says, awkwardly glancing away. "I mean, I could do that. If you want." He looks back up at me, and my heart skips a beat.

"I don't see that I have much choice."

Alak drops his shirt back on his bag and walks toward me. I turn around and pull my hair over my shoulder out of his way.

"Just tighten them a little and then tie it," I instruct, motioning at the laces.

I feel his hand at the base of my waist as he grabs the laces and gives a slight tug.

"That's not too tight is it?" he mumbles. He's close enough I can feel his warm breath on my neck. It's not too tight at all, but somehow I'm finding it a little harder to breathe.

"No, that's perfect," I manage. "Just tie it in a bow, so it looks nice."

I feel a little more tugging as Alak ties the laces and works them into a bow. He stands back a step, surveying his work. I look over my shoulder at him.

"Is it tied?"

"The bow is lopsided." He steps forward and unties the laces, reworking the bow before I can object. "There," he whispers, his lips barely a breath from my ear, his hands still resting on my lower back.

I take an unsteady breath and turn my head slightly, my eyes meeting his. His face is mere inches from mine. My eyes unwittingly flick to his mouth, and his lips part in response. For a moment I forget how to breathe as he shifts slightly closer.

"Do you need me to wish you luck, love?" Alak says, his voice low.

My heart skips a beat, my mind whirling at the implication of his words. "Perha—"

"What are you doing?" Bram's voice cuts across the room, dripping with venom.

I'm not sure who jerks away faster—me or Alak. Alak throws his hands up, looking truly terrified of Bram for once.

"I was helping her out at her request," Alak says quickly.

Bram's nostrils flare and his eyes flash.

"He was," I insist. "I needed help tying my dress."

"You couldn't have waited for me?" Bram asks, his voice cold. "And he couldn't at least put on a shirt?"

"I didn't know you were coming," I reply, taking a step

toward Bram. "And I've seen Alak shirtless dozens of times. Sometimes, I'm more surprised to find him fully clothed."

Bram scowls. Alak leans toward me and mutters, "I don't think you're helping, love."

I quickly cover the space between me and Bram and press my lips to his. I stand on my toes and whisper in his ear. "If it would make you feel better, you can take your shirt off, too. I think I might like that very much."

A slight flush appears on Bram's cheeks as a smile plays on his lips. I pull back and look up into his eyes. He wraps his arms around me and whispers, "Maybe later."

He lowers his lips to mine and kisses me intensely.

"There's an empty room right up those stairs if you need it," Alak says, finally pulling on his shirt.

Bram glares at him, but just shakes his head, turning to me. "Shall we go?"

I nod and we leave Alak behind, making our way to the festival. Bram laces his fingers with mine and pulls me close.

"You do look beautiful tonight," Bram says quietly as we walk.

"Thank you," I reply, smiling. I pause then ask, "Will you ever trust Alak?"

Bram walks quietly for a moment before replying, "Not with you."

I look up at him, eyebrows raised. "What do you mean?"

Bram releases a long sigh and runs his thumb over my hand. "Alak has proven himself overall trustworthy and reliable, but I love you, Astra. I love you more than anyone or anything. I just simply cannot—" He takes a deep breath. "I just don't feel like I can trust him with you. I see the way he looks at you and I . . ."

I squeeze his hand. "I love *you*, Bram."

He glances down at me and smiles. "I love you, too."

The lively fiddle music calls to us, drawing us into the

center of the village. It's still a couple hours from dusk, but there's already a crowd gathering. We pause at the edge trying to sort out what to do when Kayleigh rushes toward us.

"You look amazing in your dress!" she cries, pulling me away from Bram and spinning me.

I laugh. "I love it!"

"Now, remember, if anyone even slightly comments on your dress—" she starts.

"I'll tell them you made it," I finish for her.

"You're the best, Astra!" she grins. "I hope you're sticking around for a while."

"I hope so, too," I reply, realizing that I truly mean it.

"Now, stay alert and make sure you see the best of everything tonight!" Kayleigh says, guiding us through the crowd. "Oh! Look! A storyteller!" she cries, pulling me toward an older lady surrounded by a small group, mostly composed of children.

"Aren't storytellers for children?" I whisper, eyeing the young crowd.

"You're never too old for a good story." Kayleigh smiles as I take a spot standing behind the seated children. She's about to settle beside me when she sees someone she knows beckoning to her from the crowd. She apologizes and runs off to meet them, promising to catch up with me later.

"While you listen to your story, I'll go get us something to eat," Bram whispers, kissing my cheek and disappearing into the crowd.

"Who wants to hear the story of Aoibhinn?" the storyteller asks, smiling down at the children. The children all cry eagerly in unison. "All right then," she says, holding out her hands, blue sparkles rising from her palms and forming shapes. "Let's begin.

"Once, many, many years ago, before we even started

515

counting the days, there was a young woman who became pregnant with a special child. The gods and goddesses of old looked down and blessed the child with a taste of their power to see what a mere human would do with it. When the babe was born, her mother named her Aoibhinn, for she was the most beautiful child she had ever seen. But it was more than her beauty that people found striking, for she emitted a strong energy. At first, they laughed, telling themselves it was ridiculous to be afraid of an infant. But that infant became a small child and that child grew and with her, so did her power."

The storyteller's magic shifts into the form of a small girl bent over a path of flowers while other blurred figures watch.

"People would watch in fear as she manipulated the world around her and healed broken plants with little more than touch. They began to plot a way to contain her and control her power, for, as men often do, they let their fear drive them."

The magic twists into a new scene—a dozen figures constructing a tower.

"So they built a tower from the strongest rocks they could find. They built it stretching into the clouds. There was but one small window they covered with bars through which they could pass her food, but they covered it with a curtain so she would have no light. And when the tower was the perfect prison, they threw the girl in and left a guard always stationed at the base."

Several of the children whisper as the magic twirls into the sad form of a little girl locked in the tower with the guard below. Little by little the scene shifts, the girl aging as the story continues.

"Days turned to weeks and weeks to months and months to years. She received one piece of stale bread and some water every day, but nothing more. No one ever spoke to her or showed any care or concern for her in the slightest. And so her power dimmed as her hope dimmed, and she became a shadow of whom she had been and whom she was supposed to be. She began to fade away, hidden from the world, until one day, when she was on the verge of womanhood, she heard a voice besides her own."

The girl, now a young woman, presses her hands against the wall by the covered window while a guard stands below, his face turned upward.

"The voice was that of a young man sent to guard her tower. He sang a ballad of a battle, and she listened, hanging on every word. When he finished and fell silent she called to him, asking him to sing more. At first he froze, silent in fear. But when she pleaded again, he could hear the hopelessness and desperation in her voice. So he sang her song after song, and told her tale after tale. Every day he returned, taking extra posts so that he could share with her the secrets of the world beyond her tower.

"One day, when he came to guard the tower, she called down to him, asking him if there were other maidens locked in other towers. He reluctantly told her that she was the only one he knew that was trapped in such a way. It was then that he shared with her the secret of her power. Then, and only then, did she remember. She searched within her soul until she found that small trace of power that had hidden itself away in her. She pulled at it, and it grew until it burst from her, filling the dark tower with light. She tore the bars from the window and threw away the curtain. She stepped through the window but did not fall. She walked on air, like invisible stairs, down to face the young man who had saved her."

The children gasp and scoot closer to the storyteller as the image shifts. I smile, finding myself leaning in, caught up in the storyteller's every word.

"Upon viewing her for the first time, the young guard fell on his face at her feet, begging forgiveness and mercy, for not only was he startled by her overwhelming beauty, but also felt the immense power emanating from her. She begged him to rise, and he looked up into her eyes and saw nothing but kindness and gentleness. She asked him to lead her to the village, and so he did. He expected her to exact revenge on those that had locked her away, but she did not. Instead, she forgave them without hesitation. She walked through the village, reaching out her healing hand to anyone who needed it. She healed the sick with a touch from her fingertips, and by placing her hand on the ground, it burst forth full, healthy crops. Water was made clean and families were fed. And when everyone in her town had benefited from her magic, she moved on, traveling the countryside, caring for any and all she met."

The storyteller's magic flourishes in broad stokes as scene after scene plays out, depicting the beauty of Aoibhinn's deeds.

"There was no one too low or too poor to benefit from her magic. Everyone she touched was left with a small kernel of their own magic. Some of them went on to use the magic as she did—for kindness. Others used their power for evil. No matter how long she walked the earth, Aoibhinn only ever used her magic for good. Though the years passed, her body ceased to age, her power making her immortal. She walked until there was nowhere left to walk, no place left entirely untouched by her good deeds.

"It was then that the gods and goddesses of old smiled down on her. They offered her their hands, beckoning her to join them in the heavens as the goddess of magic. She accepted their offer and took her place at their sides to watch over magic from the heavens. Even now, when you look up in the sky, you can see her form, looking down from the stars."

As the story finishes, the storyteller throws the last image made from her sparkling magic above our heads, creating a picture of the night sky, the constellation of Aoibhinn shining slightly brighter than the rest of the stars.

"Tell it again!" a little girl pleads from the front row.

The storyteller chuckles. "I am sure I will tell the story many times before the night is over, but perhaps let's tell a different tale, shall we?"

A few children express their disappointment, but most of them cheer, excited for more stories.

"You remind me of her," Alak's voice says in my ear, making me jump.

I turn to face him, smiling. "Who? The storyteller?"

Alak laughs. "No. Aoibhinn. You remind me of her."

"How?" I ask.

"You really need to ask?" Alak says, his voice a little rougher than usual. I realize suddenly how close we're standing, and I take a half step back. "You're filled with the same overwhelming power, unlike anything anyone has ever known, at least in our lifetimes. And with it, you have stunning, incredible beauty to match your kindness and grace. How could you not remind me of her?"

I expect him to laugh, but there's no laughter in his eyes, just gentleness and a little of . . . something else. Something that makes my breath catch and my heart beat faster.

"I found us some food," Bram's voice says. I look up to see him approaching, some sort of fried dough in his hands, his eyes narrowed at Alak. He hands me a piece and I take a bite.

"This is really good," I say, quickly following my first bite with a second.

"There's lots of good food here," Alak says. "I can show you—"

"We're good," Bram cuts him short.

"Suit yourself," Alak mumbles with a shrug before disappearing into the crowd.

My eyes follow him and I feel Bram watching me. "I wonder where the music is coming from."

Bram relaxes a bit. "I saw several small bands playing further down the road. Are you in the mood for dancing?"

I grin. "I'm always in the mood for dancing."

It doesn't take long for us to find a group of dancing couples. Soon we've joined them, and I'm laughing and twirling. I take turns dancing with Makin, Kato, Cal, and Ehren throughout the night, taking occasional breaks for food and ale. I try looking for Alak, but he must be in a different part of the crowd. Finally, after hours of dancing, I spot Alak, Aine draped around him as they dance. I feel a surge of hate toward her, and I'm so focused on them I miss a step, causing Ehren, my current dance partner, to stumble.

"Sorry," I mumble as Ehren pulls me to the side.

"Are you all right?" he asks, his brow furrowed with concern.

"Yes," I reply, forcing a smile. "I think all the ale is just catching up with me a little."

"Let's take a break," Ehren says, leading me out of the crowd.

I take a seat atop one of the stone walls while Ehren offers to find some food to settle the ale and locate Bram. I'm enjoying watching everyone dance when Niall and his friends approach, Alak with them. I notice with a sinking feeling Aine has her arm linked through Alak's, her fingers tracing along his arm.

"How are you enjoying the festival?" Niall asks, grinning.

"I'm enjoying it very much," I reply with a soft smile.

"My favorite part is the food," Fionn admits, his eyes watching me.

"The food is excellent."

"Come with us, and we can show you some of the best food carts," Caitlyn says, extending her hand.

I start to protest, but the next thing I know, I'm being dragged into the crowd, handed treat after treat, washing bites down with different flavored ales and ciders. At some point Bram catches up with us, which I imagine doesn't please them at all, though they more or less ignore him. Eventually, Bram and I manage to break away from their group and return to dancing. We're in the middle of a dance when I start to feel lightheaded. The world tilts, and I stagger back a little. Bram steadies me.

"Are you okay?" Bram asks, holding me tighter against his body.

I rest my head against his chest. "I don't know. I think I've had too much to drink. And I'm a little tired. It must be midnight by now."

Bram nods and leads me away from the dancers. "If you're ready to go, I can walk you back to Niall's house."

I give Bram a sleepy nod. We wander through the crowd toward Niall's house. The more we walk, the more exhaustion creeps over me, causing me to lean more heavily on Bram. A headache presses against my temples, making my head swim. When we get to the house, Bram stares down at me, worry written all over his face.

"You look a little pale."

"You would think that I would have learned my lesson the last time I had this much ale," I say weakly, attempting a smile.

He returns the smile, leaning down and brushing a kiss across my lips before I turn and start inside. I pause. The idea of being alone in the house of someone I don't really trust seems like a bad idea when I'm feeling this off. I turn back to Bram.

"Do you want to come in with me?"

Bram's lips part as he studies me. I realize how that probably sounded to him, but at this moment I don't care. I don't feel well, and I really don't want to be alone. Bram traces a finger down my face, and I close my eyes, leaning into his caress. When I open my eyes, he's staring intently into them.

"Astra," he says softly, drawing me to him. "I won't lie, I want nothing more than to come inside. I've missed you being close to me the past few nights. But tonight, I don't think it would be the best idea."

I consider arguing, telling him I just want him near and nothing more, but instead, I shake my head. I'm just too tired.

"It's fine. I understand." I offer him a smile. "I'll see you in the morning."

"Wait," Bram says, and he pulls me in for a long, passionate kiss. One that makes me want to reconsider just letting Bram go. He pulls back and smiles down at me. "Goodnight."

I'm still smiling when I get upstairs. I consider undressing, but my head is pounding now and something deeper feels unsettled. I feel a surge of pain and I gasp. Something isn't right. I feel hot all over and beads of sweat start to form on my head.

"Go to the river," a voice whispers inside me. "Go to the river."

I remember with a start that Kayleigh had mentioned that the river had magical properties, so maybe it can help with whatever was happening to me now. Maybe it was just the ale, and I need to sleep it off, but it feels like more. It feels like it runs deeper. Either way, a trip to the magical woods can't hurt.

I attempt to wisp, but the second I do, a sharp pain shoots through my body. I have no choice but to stumble downstairs and through town. My feet feel heavy and I struggle to lift them. Every part of my body aches. The world keeps tilting and swaying, but I manage to make my way into the woods to the edge of the river. I crouch down, scooping the cool water to my lips. After just a couple sips, I begin to feel slightly settled. The pounding in my head becomes a little more bearable. One last sip and I stand shakily to my feet.

"Astra, what are you doing out here?"

I spin as Alak approaches through the trees.

"I just needed some fresh air," I say weakly. "What are you doing here?"

"I was heading home and saw you go off alone. I followed you to make sure you were okay, love." Alak studies me for a moment, his forehead creasing. "You don't look like you're feeling well."

I wave him off. "I'm fine. Shouldn't you get back to the festival? I'm sure Aine is looking for you."

He looks even more confused. "Aine?"

"Yes," I slur, taking an uneven step toward him. "You two have been all over each other the past couple of days. I figured you two would want to be a little extra close tonight."

"There's nothing going on between me and Aine. I wouldn't trust that snake as far as I could throw her," Alak scowls. "My heart belongs to someone else."

It's my turn to look confused. "But she's always touching you and everything."

"And it's been driving me insane. I asked her to stop but she keeps 'forgetting.'" Alak eyes me, closing the distance between us. "Why would it matter to you anyway?" he asks, bitterness edging his voice. "You have Bram. Or did I miss something? Is there a reason why I shouldn't show open interest in someone?"

"I just . . . I don't trust her," I manage. It's becoming increasingly difficult to put words together. "And you're my friend and I . . . I care about you."

I look down and shake my head. I look back up and Alak is closer, inches away.

"You do still love Bram, don't you?" Alak says, his voice quiet but hard.

"Yes." My voice is barely a whisper.

"Have you ended things with Bram?"

"No."

"Are you—" He breaks off, and I look up at him. His eyes meet mine. "Are you still going to marry him?"

I open my mouth but no words come out. His expression shifts, his lips parting as his eyes search my face.

"Are you going to marry Bram?" he repeats, his voice breathless, almost hopeful.

"I don't . . . I'm not . . ." I struggle to find the words.

My brain isn't thinking clearly. Everything is fuzzy and disjointed. Alak reaches out and takes my hand, but his touch burns. I jerk away, gasping sharply as pain ricochets through my body and I collapse to the ground. Alak drops down next to me.

"What's wrong?" he asks, his voice tinged with fear.

"I don't know," I moan, leaning forward wrapping my arms around my stomach. "Everything hurts. I thought the water would help but—" I break off with a scream as more pain ripples through my body.

Alak's hand grabs mine again. This time he jerks back with a gasp.

"Your magic," he says, his voice hoarse, distressed. "Somebody has put a spell on it. Your magic has been poisoned."

I look up at him, my eyes wide with terror. "What does that mean? Can it kill me?"

"I don't know. It depends on what spell was used." His voice sounds panicked. "I can help draw it away, out of you."

"No, you—" I scream again. The pain is more intense. I feel like I'm burning from the inside out.

"Astra, just hang on," Alak pleads, his voice trembling. "I need you. Do you understand? I *need* you. Please, just hang on."

He pulls me up against his chest and wraps his arms around me firmly. I feel his magic against my skin. At first it burns. Whatever spell is affecting my own magic fights against his. He gasps in pain. I try to pull away, but he holds me too firmly. I feel the spell being siphoned away, but it's a struggle for both of us. Pain courses through me, consuming me until the world goes black.

CHAPTER FORTY-FOUR

*E*arth. That's what I smell. Wet soil and fresh grass. Even before I open my eyes, I know I must be outside. We must be on the road, camping still. Strong arms are wrapped around me. I snuggle closer to the warm body behind me.

But wait. We're not on the road anymore. I shouldn't be asleep outside. I slowly open my eyes and a blurry patch of grass comes into view. I blink a couple of times, sure I'm seeing something wrong. But no. In front of my eyes is plush green grass, glistening with morning dew. The memories from last night crash into my brain. Flashes of dancing followed by exhaustion. Running to the forest to drink water. I remember panic. Terror. I remember—

"Alak!" I cry, sitting up, making my head pound.

I twist and look at the person whose arms hold me. Alak lies on the ground behind me, far too still. For a moment, I'm afraid he's dead, but then he shifts ever so slightly, a groan escaping his lips. I nearly collapse with relief.

"Alak," I whisper, reaching my hand out to brush red locks from his face.

He blinks up at me, confusion washing over him. "Astra? What—" I see everything click into place. His eyes go wide as he forces himself into a sitting position, wincing. "Your magic. Can you access it?"

I hold out my hand. With little effort, I create my simple silver orb of light. Nothing hurts and nothing holds me back. A smile breaks onto my lips.

"I'm fine," I whisper, relief washing over me. I look up at Alak. "What about you? Are you okay?"

Alak smiles softly as blue and gold butterflies swarm around us. "It seems my magic is fine. I'm a little weak, but as long as I don't have to use a big burst of magic anytime soon, I'll be okay."

Alak locks his gaze on my face as a breeze blows loose strands of hair across my face. He traces his thumb across my lips as he brushes the hair away. My stomach flips and my pulse quickens. I reach up and place my hand on his hand. He smiles, weaving his fingers with mine as he drops his hand.

"Astra, I've never been so terrified in my life. I was so afraid I was going to lose you. Do you have any idea how much losing you would destroy me?" His voice breaks and he looks away, his grip on my hand tightening.

I reach my free hand up and cup my palm on his cheek, turning his face back to mine. "I'm okay," I say quietly.

His eyes meet mine and he turns his face, kissing my palm. I swallow and slowly lean toward him, my heart racing. Our lips are barely an inch apart when it strikes me that it's daylight. I gasp and jerk back, jumping to my feet. Alak looks up at me, eyebrows etched in confusion.

"It's morning," I say, my voice uneven.

"Wha—oh. *Oh.*" Alak registers what I've said and he jumps to his feet. "Shite."

"Do you think anyone has noticed we're missing?" I ask, wrapping my arms around myself.

"I don't know, but we need to go back immediately before anyone can. Hopefully, with everything that happened last night, everyone is still sleeping and hasn't looked for either of us yet." He holds out his hand toward me. "Wisp with me?"

I nervously take his hand and the forest fades as Niall's house appears. The house is vacant, everyone presumably at Aunt Shannon's house. We quickly change before we wisp out of the house to join the others. We make our way down the path to the door, putting several feet between us. If we were hoping for our entrance to go unnoticed, we lucked out. Every single person, including Niall, is up and seated around the table, eating breakfast. As we enter the room every pair of eyes falls on us.

"Where were you this morning, mate?" Niall asks Alak, his mouth full. "I missed having breakfast served in my own humble house."

"I, uh, I went out for a morning walk," Alak says, raking a hand through his hair as he glances off to the side. "After all the ale last night I needed to clear my head."

Niall nods sympathetically. "Been there."

I look over at Bram and smile, but he's glaring at me with lethal focus, his eyes dark and cold. Ehren seems oblivious to Bram's terse reaction and scoots closer to Cal, motioning for me to sit between him and Bram. I squeeze in, but Bram refuses to look at me.

"Good morning," I whisper tentatively.

"Is it?" Bram asks sharply, his hand clenching into a fist on the table.

I lean closer to him. "Bram, what's wrong?"

"I think you know."

"I really don't. Please, can we talk?"

Bram abruptly stands up from the table and marches outside. Alak's eyes dart from Bram to me, his concern evident. I bite my lip as I scurry to my feet and trip after Bram. Kato reaches out to me as I dash outside, following Bram toward the back of the yard.

Ash, everything okay?

I don't know, Kato. I'm sure it's fine. I just need a moment with him.

Okay. Let me know if you need me.

Always.

Bram doesn't stop until we're at the furthest point of the yard, behind the stables and other farm animals. He stands, his back to me. I catch up to him and place my hand on his shoulder.

"Bram what—"

I drop off as he spins to face me, my hand falling from his shoulder. His face is red with fury, pain sharp in his eyes.

"I saw you," he spits.

"Saw me? Saw me where? What are you talking about?"

"Last night, I went back to the house to make sure you were okay, but you weren't there."

"You went in my room?" I ask, feeling violated somehow. It must show on my face because Bram shakes his head quickly.

"No. I knocked, but you didn't answer. I was leaving when Kato arrived. He went in to check on you, but you weren't there. He suggested maybe you went for a walk in the woods. He tried reaching out to you, but you didn't respond. I was worried, so I went to the woods and . . ." Bram pauses, clenching both fists by his side and gritting his teeth. "And I found you. Asleep. With Alak."

My eyes go wide, and I reach my hand toward Bram. "No.

No, Bram I—"

"You what?" he yells, jerking away from my touch, more red flooding his face. I swear I see tears brimming in his eyes. "Were you or were you not with Alak last night after I left you?"

I struggle to meet his eyes. "Yes, but—"

"But nothing," he says, his voice shaking. "I had no idea that when I turned you down last night it would mean you running into Alak's arms. I thought you were better than that. I knew I couldn't trust him, but I thought I could at least trust you. I guess I was wrong."

His words sting. He starts to walk away, but I grab his arm and yank him back, seething.

"I almost died last night," I yell.

His mouth drops open, concern replacing some of the fury in his eyes. "What? What do you mean you almost died?"

"I mean," I snap, "that I almost died. At least that's what it felt like, and Alak very possibly saved my life."

Bram's shoulders fall as he takes a step toward me, but I jerk back. Regret flashes across his face.

"Astra, I had no idea."

"I know." My anger is barely controlled as I meet his eyes, jaw set. "Because you decided to jump to conclusions instead of just asking me."

"I am sorry. I am so sorry. Alak makes me so insanely jealous. He brings out a side of me that I hate. I think I had too much to drink last night, and I'm still not thinking clearly this morning." He reaches out and takes my hands in his. I don't pull away, though I'm tempted. "Tell me what happened. I'm listening now."

I glare at him, debating on whether I want to tell him. I see the earnest anguish in his face, and a touch of my fury fades.

"Someone poisoned my magic. I've never experienced pain

like that before. I remembered that the water from the river had some magical properties, so I stumbled into the forest last night, hoping I could drink the water and fix whatever was wrong. Alak was on his way back to Niall's house when he saw me leaving. He was concerned, so he followed me. The pain overwhelmed me, but he was able to syphon away the spell at great risk to himself. The power it took drained us both, making us black out."

Bram closes his eyes and lets out a long breath. "That's why you were together like that." He opens his eyes and looks deeply into mine. "I am so sorry. Can you forgive me?"

I hesitate and glance away. I want to forgive him. I really do. But something has broken between us. I would be a fool to ignore that.

"Astra?"

I look back up at him. "It really hurts that you would think I would rush off and sleep with Alak just like that."

"I know. I know. I told you I am sorry. So incredibly sorry." He pauses, glancing away for a moment before continuing. "But can you really blame me?"

I yank my hands from his, staring at him in disbelief. "What? I told you I was poisoned!"

"Last night, yes. But last night wasn't the first time I suspected something going on between you two."

I back away shaking my head. "I don't believe this." Even as I say the words, guilt swirls inside me knowing he's not entirely wrong. I don't know what is happening between me and Alak, but we have undeniably had our moments. And a piece of me wants more of those moments.

Bram drags his hand down his face. "This is not coming out right at all."

"I would say not," I snap with a sharp nod.

"Look," he says, stepping toward me and taking my hands

back into his own. "Our engagement was set up suddenly, as a cover before a king who would be happy to see you dead. I didn't expect you to hold to that, but you agreed a few minutes later in your room to go through with it. You agreed to marry me."

I nod. "Yes, I did."

"And then I formally asked you to marry me when we were walking in the garden. You said yes. I gave you my family ring."

I swallow, becoming very aware of the ring on my finger. "Yes."

"But the question remains, do you still want to marry me?" He searches my face. "Our wedding would only be a couple weeks away if we had stayed in Embervein. I would marry you tomorrow, today even. Are you willing to do the same?"

"Bram," I whisper, "I love you."

He looks down at me, sadness filling his eyes. "And I love you, but I am starting to think that maybe I love you more than you love me."

"Bram . . . ," I say, my voice breaking.

He squeezes my hands. "If we could marry tomorrow, would you marry me?"

I take a deep breath, my head spinning, but before I can answer, we hear a scream coming from the direction of the house. Bram jolts to an alert position, his hand flying to the sword hanging loosely at his side.

The house is under attack! It's the king's soldiers!

"The king!" I gasp. "His soldiers found us!"

Without another second of hesitation, Bram and I race back to the house. Dozens of soldiers in black uniforms are swarming the yard. Ehren, Kato, Makin, Cal, and Alak stand back-to-back in the center of the swarm, weapons drawn, Alak twirling magic at his fingertips. Kayleigh stands in the doorway of the house huddled with rest of her family, save for Niall who stands sneering next to the man who appears to be the commander in charge of the soldiers. Niall's friends stand not far behind him, lethal grins on their faces. Bram pushes me down as we hide behind the corner of the house.

"Why Niall?" Alak hisses.

"The king has promised that, in exchange for his son and his soldiers, he will allow our area to openly practice magic with no penalty," Niall answers. "It was an easy decision. You can join us, you know. You are a member of my family."

"Never!" Alak snarls.

"I wouldn't trust the word of my father," Ehren says, his voice even and controlled.

"And I should trust you?" Niall sneers. "After you've been lying to me and my family? Not even telling us your real name, or remotely who you were? Creating a lame cover story about being a servant for nobles. Why should I trust anything you have to say?"

"I apologize—"

"The time for apologies is over!" Niall yells. "Now, where are your other friends? Your captain and that girl?"

Bram reaches back and touches my arm. "You need to get out of here while you can. Wisp."

I scowl at him. "If you think I'm going to bail on everyone else, you have another thing coming."

"Astra, please, get out of here. I can't protect you against all those soldiers," Bram pleads.

"It's a good thing you won't have to, then, isn't it?"

I stand up and charge into the soldiers, magic swirling at my fingertips. Bram swears, yelling after me. I ignore him, forming my magic into lethal twin blades, one in each hand. I slice into the crowd, striking a stunned soldier down with each blow.

"Get her!" their commander bellows and more soldiers rush

toward me.

"Shit," Bram swears, leaping into action behind me.

With the attention on me, Ehren and the others rush into the crowd, striking down soldiers.

"Do not let the prince get away," the commander roars. "The king wants him alive!"

Chaos erupts over the yard. Swords clang as we fight fiercely, but we're severely outnumbered. It doesn't help our chances when Niall and his friends start to use their magic against us. Niall's darkness pours out, but it's controlled, targeting our group, leaving the soldiers free to see. I trade my swords for swirling lights that chase down his shadows, absorbing into the bodies of soldiers they strike, stopping their hearts. Niall narrows his eyes at me and says something to Ian next to him.

Aine doesn't miss her opportunity to attack. She leaps forward, shooting metal spikes my way. They narrowly miss as I dodge, diving into her attack, throwing up a shield. I shoot silver lightning from my palms. It strikes her directly in her chest, knocking her unconscious. Ian screams, reaching for his sister. When he looks up at me, his eyes are gleaming with hate. But I don't have time to focus on him. I'm under attack by multiple soldiers at once. I summon my swords back, and it's all I can do to block their blows. I thrust one sword through the neck of one soldier and watch in horror as his eyes go wide and he falls back, dead, blood staining the ground. I don't have time for what I did to wash over me. Not yet. I strike again and again, nearly missing blows made against me as I strike down more soldiers.

I look up at Alak not far away. His magic does little good in a battle other than the occasional strike of power. Judging by the glazed, vacant expressions on the soldiers nearest him, he's managing to weave some sort of illusion. But I know he's weak and can't hold up that much longer. I shoot out silver lightning and take down several soldiers and leap closer to Alak.

"We have to get out of here," I gasp, barely warding off an attack. I glance around. The person Alak is closest to right now is Bram. "We need to wisp but I can't take everyone. Can you get—"

Alak nods, following my gaze. "I've got him. Meet at the bridge."

As Alak sends out a trail of magic, clearing a path to Bram, I reach out to Kato.

We need to get out of here. NOW.

You need to go. I'll meet you.

No, you grab Makin. He's closest to you. Wisp to the bridge. I'll grab Ehren and Cal.

I'm not leaving you.

KATO! We don't have time to argue. Grab Makin and I will meet you.

He glares at me across the yard but fights his way toward Makin, setting everyone and everything in his path on fire. I hear the commander roar with anger as Alak grabs Bram's arm and they disappear. A few moments later, Kato and Makin flash away. It's just me, Ehren, and Cal. Infuriated by allowing the others to get away, the remaining soldiers, along with the magic wielders, narrow in on us. Their strikes are coming fast, and I can barely keep up with them. Ehren and Cal are together, fighting side-by-side. I throw a shield around them, protecting them from magical attacks.

"DO NOT LET THE PRINCE ESCAPE!" the commander bellows.

Time is running out. I reach deep into my magic and swirl it around me like a tornado, lifting myself in the air. I feel my power course through, controlling me. My eyes flash as I send out a surge of magic, shaking the ground with such force the entire army drops. I don't hesitate, immediately sending out a second strike of lightning. The men scream as my magic hits them. I throw another wave of magic hissing over the soldiers, silver smoke covering the ground like a rising fog, smoking tendrils rising up and wrapping around each individual person.

As I lower to the ground, the silver fog twirling around my knees, my magic coils around my captives, squeezing, tightening, restraining, suffocating. I'm pretty sure they're dying, my magic slowly draining their life-force. Niall and his friends manage to fight my magic, but only barely. I ignore the carnage around me, focusing on getting Cal and Ehren out of here. I cover the distance between us, moving swiftly through the twirling magic coating the ground amidst the screams of dying soldiers. Cal and Ehren stare at me in silent shock as I grab them each by their arms and we spin into oblivion.

When our feet land on the forest floor, my heart is still racing. Kato and Bram are pacing but freeze, staring at us when we appear. Alak sits on the ground, his side bleeding. Makin grips a bleeding arm. Cal and Ehren stumble away from me, their eyes wide.

"Your eyes," Cal chokes. "They were completely silver."

"What?" Kato asks, rushing to my side and staring into my eyes.

Ehren nods when I shoot him a questioning look. "Your eyes looked a lot like Kato's when they had flames in them, only with your light instead. They were pure silver."

"What happened back there?" Bram asks, his eyes cautiously examining me. "We heard screaming all the way out here."

"Astra took care of the soldiers," Cal says, his face ashen.

"What do you mean?" Bram scowls. "How?"

Something snaps a twig nearby and we all jump.

"We need to stop talking and get the hell away from here,"

Alak says, wincing as he stands.

"Niall and his friends are down now, but they won't be for long. If they wisp to us they'll strike to kill," I say.

"Where do we even go?" Makin asks. "We don't have any of our supplies or our horses."

"I hate to say it but we have to leave everything if we want to get out of here alive," I say, casting an apologetic glance to Bram. "Even our horses."

"She's right," Ehren says.

"I know a place not far from here that would still put a safe enough distance between us and our pursuers. I remember it well enough I think I can guide us if we wisp." Alak looks from me to Kato. "I will need help, though. Removing the poisoning spell from Astra took a lot of my energy, and I wasn't fully recovered before this battle. I'm almost completely drained now."

Kato's eyes flash. "What poisoning spell?"

"Later. I'll tell you later. Right now we need to focus," I say, turning my attention to Alak.

"Weave your magic with mine like we did before," he says to me. "Kato, just reach out your magic and combine it with mine and Astra's. Then, I should have enough support to wisp us all."

"What do we need to do?" Ehren asks, stepping closer to Alak.

"Just link hands. We all need to be touching," Alak answers.

We step into a circle, grabbing hands. I close my eyes and my magic easily finds what little remains of Alak's, and we intertwine our magic together, Kato's joining us. At first, our magic fights his, but eventually it gives. The next thing I know, we're drifting into nothingness, ripped from the glade, going to gods know where.

CHAPTER FORTY-FIVE

*W*e're on a hillside. About a mile in the distance we can see a small village, but we're not on a road and there's no road in sight. There are also no trees or any way to hide beyond tall grass, not that anyone is anywhere nearby to see us. My heart still races and my magic still tingles at my fingertips, yearning to be used, despite exhaustion creeping over me.

"You're hurt," I say, turning to Alak. "I can heal you."

Alak shakes his head, backing away, wincing. "Heal Makin first. Then, if you have enough magic left, maybe you can heal me."

I turn to Makin, reaching my hand toward him. "Let me see your arm."

Makin doesn't even argue, but steps forward right away. His right sleeve is completely soaked with blood, his face very pale. He winces as he lifts his own blood covered hand from his wound, reaching his arm toward me. I gently pull up his sleeve and see a deep slash gushing blood on his forearm. I wrap my cool fingers around his arm, ignoring the fact that my pale fingers are now covered in hot, crimson blood. He gasps as I close my eyes and focus my magic. Like when I healed Ehren's leg, I can somehow see everything in my mind as I slowly close the wound. The healing magic is undeniably more draining than my attack magic, and I can feel the effects as I pull my hands back. I struggle to keep my weakness masked.

Makin looks down at his arm. It's still caked in blood with a thin line that will more than likely scar, but the worst of the wound is gone. He looks up at me, appreciation shining in his eyes.

"Thank you," he whispers.

I nod and turn to Alak. He's eased down on the ground behind me, his legs stretched out in front of him, leaning away from his wounded side. I kneel down next to him and lift his shirt. His wound isn't quite as bad, but it still shouldn't go unchecked. I reach out my fingertips and gently place them on the cut, barely touching the skin. Alak grabs my hand, pulling it away.

"Don't," he says. I look up and he's staring at me intently. "Give yourself time to refill your magic. I don't have enough magic to help you this time."

"I'm fine," I protest and start to reach toward his side again, but his grip on my hand tightens.

"I can sense your magic. Don't."

"Listen to him, Ash," Kato says gently but firmly from behind me.

I sigh and start to pull my hand back. He releases my hand and lies back on the grass. Before he can notice, I quickly extend my hand again. This time the magic is already flowing from my fingertips. He lets out a hiss as my cool magic twists over the cut. I hear him protest, but my eyes are already closed, stitching the skin back together. When I'm finished, I'm glad

I'm sitting. My head is pounding and I feel dizzy. My magic is deeply drained now. Alak sits up and twists to look at his side.

"Damn it, Astra," he growls. He looks at me, and I smile weakly, everything shifting out of focus for a moment.

"You know, with that accent, 'Thank you' sounded a lot like 'Damn it.' You should work on your enunciation."

A slow smile spreads on his lips as he shakes his head, running his hand through his hair. "Thank you."

Bram clears his throat, commanding our attention to him. He's watching me and Alak steadily. I know I should stand, but I don't quite have the strength. Instead, I shift my position slightly away from Alak so we aren't as close.

"What did you mean earlier when you said Astra had been poisoned?" Kato cuts in.

"Oh, right," Alak murmurs. "Someone created a spell that poisoned Astra's magic."

"What does that mean? Is she still at risk?" Kato asks, sharply.

Alak shakes his head. "I siphoned the spell away, and I don't think there are any lingering effects. None I can sense anyway, and her magic is obviously fine." He gestures to his freshly healed side.

"If you hadn't siphoned the spell, would she have died?" Ehren asks softly.

"It's very possible," Alak replies in a low, serious tone. "She was . . . she was in a lot of pain. It was a very powerful spell. If Astra was any less powerful than she is, she would have likely died before I found her."

Kato curses. "It had to be Fionn," he spits. "Fionn was always bragging about the spells he could create."

"What matters now is moving forward," Ehren says sternly. He takes a deep breath as he straightens his shoulders, the leader in him coming through.

"What's the plan?" Bram asks, straightening to attention.

"First, we must establish our current location." Ehren faces Alak. "Where are we?"

"Well," Alak replies, easing to his feet. "Assuming we are indeed at the location I intended, which, by all appearances we are, we should be just outside the town of Fairfellow, roughly a couple days travel from the border of the Athiedor region."

Ehren nods. "All right. We need to confirm our location, and then we can create a plan to get to Portia and the Isle of Naskein. Will we be able to wisp that far?"

Alak shakes his head. "The greater the distance the harder it is and the higher the risk something could go wrong. The only reason we were able to come this far is because I spent a lot of time in this area a few years ago, so I have clear memories of the landscape. But even then, it was still risky. I wouldn't have tried it if we hadn't been desperate. We might be able to wisp across borders to escape detection into various countries, but I wouldn't count on wisping as Plan A."

"Okay," Ehren says, considering Alak's words. "So, that means we will be traveling entirely on foot. We need to pool our resources. Unfortunately, we had to leave almost everything behind. Let's inventory what we have and what we need."

We empty our pockets and any pouches we might have on us. Between the seven of us we have a handful of markes and a golden ring belonging to Ehren as well as his signet ring. My fingers twist the ring on my own hand, but I can't bring myself to remove it and no one says anything. We also have at least one weapon each.

"We will need water skeins unless we want to die from the heat," Ehren says at length. "We can hunt for our food. Alak and Makin, you both need new shirts. Mud covered travelers won't draw much attention but blood in that amount will. Everything else can wait until later."

"Are you suggesting that we actually go into that village and purchase those things?" Bram asks slowly.

Ehren nods. "We don't have much choice. Alak, can you help Kato find his way around the village? Make sure you know for sure where we are and get the supplies we need?"

Bram eyes Alak as he leans closer to Ehren. "Are you sure you want to send them? I would be more than happy to—"

Ehren stops Bram, holding up his hand. "No. It must be them. We need two people who are least likely to stand out or be recognized. Alak knows the town and has the accent and look of most of Athiedor. He's the obvious choice. My father could easily have people in this town keeping an eye out for us. You, Cal, and Makin have been part of my Guard for too long. Anyone even remotely familiar with my Guard would be likely to place you. Kato, while a member of my Guard, is a newer face so he's less likely to be recognized as quickly. Honestly, if Astra wasn't weak right now, I would send her and Alak."

I push myself up from the ground, rising on shaky legs. "I can still go."

"No," Alak, Bram, and Ehren all say at once. A sharp look from Ehren and the other two back down.

"Even I can see you need to rest, Astra. As soon as we have what we need, we need to get on the road. We can't do that if you are too weak to walk," Ehren says firmly. I nod.

"We need to do something about your shirt, though," Ehren addresses Alak, his eyes focusing on the blood stain at Alak's side. Before anyone can make a suggestion, Ehren is pulling his shirt over his head, revealing a tan, lean yet muscled torso. "Here, take my shirt."

Ehren holds his shirt out to Alak, and Alak reaches for it. Ehren's face narrows into a puzzled expression, his eyes on

Alak's wrist. I realize with a start that Alak's magic is so drained he can't maintain the illusion that usually conceals his scars. Alak realizes it, too, grabbing the shirt quickly while looking purposefully away from Ehren's prying gaze, shame and guilt flashing in his eyes.

"You'll need to wipe away some of the blood from your skin before you put the new shirt on," I point out, drawing the unwanted attention away from Ehren's eyes on Alak.

"Right," Alak mumbles as he pulls his blood soaked shirt off, using it to wipe away the blood before slipping Ehren's shirt over his head. It's a good fit.

"All right," Ehren says. "Be quick and efficient. Get what we need and get out."

Kato nods with the obedience of a well-trained soldier, but Alak's agreeing nod is a little more casual. They turn and walk toward the village. I notice Alak's hands hanging awkwardly at his sides as he tries to hide the scars normally hidden by magic.

"Alak, wait a moment," I say, hurrying toward him.

He pauses and turns to me, cocking his head in curiosity. "I'll be right back, love."

My eyes meet his and his eyebrows arch in confusion for a moment.

"Take a little magic with you, for safety," I say quietly, tracing my fingertips discreetly along the lines of scars on his wrist.

His eyes go wide as my magic whispers across his skin, hiding the scars. It's a small bit of magic, one that would normally be very little effort but, as drained as I am now, I feel like someone punched me hard in my gut. I stagger backward slightly.

"You didn't need to do that," Alak whispers, his voice hoarse, but I can see the gratitude shining in his eyes.

"And yet, I did it anyway." I smile.

He offers me a slight nod of thanks before turning and joining Kato. As they get further away, I turn back to the others. Bram is watching me stiffly while Ehren merely looks curious.

"What do we do now?" I ask Ehren.

"For now, we just need to lay low and rest," Ehren replies, sitting on the ground. The rest of us follow suit. I hesitantly take a seat next to Bram. He tenses slightly but then relaxes, slipping his arm around me, pulling me closer. With a sigh, I rest my head against his shoulder and drift off to sleep almost immediately.

I'm awakened later by movement. I open my eyes and look up to see Bram's face at an odd angle above mine. I realize after a moment that he's carrying me. Bram glances down and smiles.

"You are awake," he says quietly.

He pauses to set me on my feet. The others are slightly ahead of us, but they stop, looking back.

"Are you good?" he asks, studying my face. I nod and we begin walking. He takes my hand.

"How long was I asleep?"

"A few hours. We actually tried waking you, but you were out cold. Alak"—Bram says his name sharply—"insisted you needed to rest to restore your magic. For once, I agreed with him."

"How long have we been walking?"

"About three hours."

"Have you carried me the whole time?"

He glances down at me, a half-smile on his lips. "Are you suggesting that I might be too weak to carry you for three hours?"

"No, I—"

He laughs and, I must admit, after the tense morning, it's a wonderful sound. "I carried you most of the way but Ehren also carried you, as did Kato."

I glance toward Ehren. I'm almost disappointed he's found a new shirt.

"I guess the trip into the village was successful?"

Bram nods. "Yes. Alak and your brother were able to get a few water skeins with the markes we had, and we still have some left over. They also got a couple shirts, though judging by Alak's evasiveness, markes were not used toward those items." Alak's back is toward me, but I swear he smiles.

It doesn't take long before I start to feel hungry, remembering I never even got a bite of breakfast. But we have no food and nothing growing nearby to eat. So I suffer in silence. By the time night is falling, I'm starving, and I'm not the only one. We're all irritable and hungry. We're on the lookout for some sort of animal to eat. When Felixe appears, he nearly gets daggered. Shortly after, I hear birds above me. They're too high up for a dagger or sword, so I summon my bow and arrows. I've never had to shoot a bird from this distance before. I miss on my first try, but my second shot brings one down. Kato also manages to bring down a bird with a fire arrow before the rest of the flock scatters. The birds aren't big, but they're better than nothing.

As we settle down for the night, thunder rumbles overhead, threatening rain. Ehren volunteers to take first watch, and Cal insists on helping him. Bram lies down on a soft patch of grass and I hover hesitantly nearby. On any of our previous journeys, I always spent my nights next to Bram, but now everything between us feels uncertain. He senses my hesitation, raising up slightly to look my way.

"Are you ready to get some sleep or are you rested enough from your nap earlier?" he asks, smiling.

I return his smile. "I could use the sleep."

Bram motions to the spot next to him. "Then let us get some sleep. I have a feeling we have a lot more walking in the days ahead."

With a small sigh of relief, I take my place next to him. As I settle down next to Bram, I can feel Alak's eyes on me, but I ignore him and snuggle into Bram's embrace.

CHAPTER FORTY-SIX

$\mathcal{T}$raveling with little food or water and no real protection against the elements is exhausting and frustrating. Most days we manage to scrounge up some sort of food, whether it's wild onions, bitter berries, or some sort of animal, but there are some days we have to survive with empty stomachs.

We do our best to avoid villages and any well-traveled roads. This means taking the long way over somewhat rough terrain. It means no replenishing our supplies, not that we have the money to do so anyway. All we have are a couple of marke coins and our rings.

The days bleed into each other and we lose track of time. I'm tired and soul-weary. I know it's been at least twelve days, maybe longer. Ehren has stepped into the role of commander, managing to keep us going, but we're all ready for this journey to be over, taking it out on each other. Even Cal snaps at us all. Alak has stopped joking.

In fact, Alak rarely speaks. Whenever I look toward him, his eyes are almost always on me. Bram hovers near me at almost all times, tense and overprotective. At this point, I've debated the pros and cons of stabbing him for some gods-damned space. Our nerves are all rubbed raw, and we're on the brink of falling apart.

That's when we finally reach the sea region.

Only a small portion of Callenia actually touches the sea. Those seaports are often heavily guarded and watched. The village of Brineshore is no exception. Brineshore serves as the main port for travel and commerce to and from the island kingdom of Portia. This means that it's crawling with soldiers even on days when they aren't searching for a runaway prince. Since it's been around two weeks since our last escape, we're sure that the king will have extra soldiers posted at every border and in every city by now.

For the past day we've been hiding in the marshes just outside the city, studying the movements of the guards posted at the city walls, crafting a plan. Bram suggests trying a smaller city or crossing into one of our allied neighboring countries with their own seaports, but Ehren insists on using Brineshore.

"We need to keep our journey over water as short as possi-ble. This is the closest port," Ehren says firmly. "Any other port means a longer journey over water, which puts us at higher risk of being discovered. If we're discovered on a boat, there will be no quick escape."

Bram shakes his head. "I understand what you are saying, but if we are discovered before we can even get on a boat, what good is that?"

"We fought our way out of Brackenborough and can fight our way out here too, if needed. But we won't need to. Our plan will work," Ehren insists.

"It's a good plan," I jump in. "It *will* work."

"Time to start trusting me, mate," Alak says, forced levity in his voice.

Bram glares at Alak. "I just think we should at least wait a few more days and weigh all our options."

"Enough arguing. It's time for action. This is the plan and we are sticking to it." Ehren's voice is authoritative and unforgiving.

Bram clenches his jaw but doesn't argue further. He bows and murmurs bitterly, "As you command, Your Majesty."

Ehren's shoulders go slack, his face falling. He opens his mouth then closes it, turning away.

"We're heading down in a few minutes, so prepare yourselves however you need," Ehren says, his voice even, his back still to us as he walks several yards away.

With a quick glare at Bram, I leave the others and go over to stand next to Ehren. I stand close enough that my arm brushes against his. He leans toward me as I follow his gaze to the city not far away.

"You're making the right decision," I say, my voice just above a whisper. "We've got this. We're going to be fine."

Ehren pulls his eyes away from Brineshore to look down at me, drawing an unsteady breath. "I was trained all my life to make decisions, but the moments when I have to make ones like this where people's lives—my friends' lives—are on the line, I feel so unsure." He glances briefly back at Bram before shaking his head and looking back at the cityscape. "It doesn't help when the person I trust the most disagrees with me."

"Bram is tired and frustrated and hungry. That's enough to make anyone irritable and disagreeable," I point out.

Ehren manages a small laugh. "I think we've all reached that point." His face grows serious again. "Which is why I'm wondering if he's right. Is my own exhaustion clouding my judgement? Do I just want to get this over with? Am I making a reckless decision?"

"Hey, look at me," I command gently. Ehren turns his sea-green eyes to mine. "You can never be sure how a decision will turn out until it's been made and followed through. Every day we spend in Callenia is another day we risk being discovered by your father's soldiers. You aren't wrong in wanting to get to Portia and Naskein as soon as we can. Alak's magic is strong. Combined with mine it's even stronger. We can weave a believable illusion and hold it as long as we need. Kato will have his arsenal of magic ready to use if we're attacked. We can do this."

I bump him playfully, my fingers brushing his. He smiles weakly. "All right then. Let's do this."

Ehren turns around and faces the rest of our group. We're a sad bunch to look at at. We're ragged and dirty. All the men have stubbly beards on their faces and their hair is an unruly mess. Even Cal's short hair has noticeably grown. There's no doubt we've been vagabond outlaws for weeks. But Ehren straightens his shoulders and stands like a proud general before a strong army. And then he says two words, and two words alone, but they're backed by enough confidence and power they're enough.

"Let's go."

Without any hesitation, Alak stretches out his fingers and weaves his magic. I can't see it, but I feel it caress my skin. I look over at the others as they hold out their hands and arms, marveling as the illusion takes hold.

"Holy shit," Makin murmurs as Ehren and Bram start to completely disappear. "It's working."

I look over at Kato, although he doesn't look like himself anymore. He's still young, but now he has paler skin with light brown hair and a matching beard. His amethyst eyes flicker into a pale blue. Cal and Makin's appearances are the next to change. Cal now has a head full of brown hair and paler skin, appearing slightly younger. Makin takes on a similar look, but with an added beard, looking older. Side by side, Makin, Cal, and Kato look like brothers, which is ultimately our goal.

Next, Alak changes my appearance. My skin darkens to a golden brown and my hair, which I can see in the long braid draped over my shoulder, turns a golden blond. I can't see my eyes, but I assume they're now brown, making my appearance mimic a typical Portian woman. Alak tweaks his own facial features before changing his bright red hair to jet black and shaping a slim black beard along his chin. He keeps his emerald eyes.

"How do I look?" he asks with a wink.

"You look like an idiot, but no magic can change that," Bram's voice says from beside me and I jump.

"You look like a different person. We all do," I answer. I stretch out my hands. "Now it's my turn."

I weave my magic into Alak's. I don't add or alter anything, I just support it. With an illusion this intricate, it's important it not slip in the slightest. There's no way he can maintain it on his own for an extended period of time. With my magic woven in, however, we should be able to hold the illusion without any issues.

We proceed slowly toward Brineshore. My heart races, but I try not to show how terrified I really am. Even though we don't look anything like ourselves, we can't afford to raise any suspicions. Our plan is simple and straightforward. I know it can work. Beyond just altering our appearances, we've lowered our traveling party from seven to five by making the two most easily recognizable members invisible. We've also decided to split into two groups, staying close but trying not to interact. Using false identities we've created, we need to sell one of Ehren's rings to pay for passage into Portia. It will work. It has to work.

Brineshore is a walled city. As expected, we find guards at

the entrance gate, scrutinizing anyone who passes in or out. We join the line of people shuffling through the gate. I can't see Bram and Ehren, but I can sense them with my magic. They fill the apparent empty space between our two groups. Having them stay close to the group helps to reduce the number of people they might accidentally bump into. The merchants in front of us step up and the guards inspect their cart loaded with caged chickens and crates of eggs. The guards look bored as they wave the merchants into the city. As we slowly move forward toward the guards, Alak slips his arm around my waist, pulling me to his side.

"Just because you can't see me, doesn't mean I can't see you," Bram growls, but Alak just grins.

"Stop it," I whisper as we step up the guard station.

"Names and purpose for visiting Brineshore," one of the guards drawls.

"Fenrik Lowry. Just taking my new bride back home after showing her a bit of our kingdom," Alak says, his accent dropped.

I give the guard a shy smile as his eyes fall on me. "New bride, eh? And what is your bride's name?"

"Rivianorra," Alak answers for me.

The guard raises an eyebrow. "Is she a mute?"

Alak laughs. "If only!" The guard behind the one interrogating us twitches his lips up into a smile. "But, alas, she does only speak Portian. Her Callenian is not so good."

The guard eyes me for a moment and then nods, waving us through the gate. Once we're safely inside, I let out the breath I've been holding the last couple minutes. Bram goes through with us, but I can sense Ehren hovering near Cal as they wait to pass inspection. I want to wait for them, but we've decided it's not best to linger. We move inside the city, daring not to go too far, lest the illusion fail. Alak pauses at a vendor's nearby cart, examining the goods. I keep my eye on the gate, pretending to glance around nervously at the crowd in general. When I see Kato, Makin, and Cal enter the city I give Alak a light nudge.

The next stage of the plan is in motion. Alak and I wind our way through the crowd, Bram close behind. Kato's group travels at a slower pace, keeping us in their view as they travel along the outskirts of the crowd. We'll need to get off the busy streets soon, but first we need money for passage to Portia. Alak and I search the shops until we find a place that will buy jewelry. He slips into the shop to haggle alone while I lean against the outside wall of the building, Bram beside me. Across the wide street, Kato, Makin, and Cal pause at a booth filled with food, pretending to consider a purchase.

"You have to admit, so far it's working," I mutter under my breath so only Bram can hear.

"So far. Let's hope it stays that way. How are you holding up?"

"I'm fine so far. I've barely used any of my energy. Right now, Alak is bearing the main weight, but if he starts to fade, I'll pick up the slack."

"You can tell?"

I nod slightly. "My magic is literally intertwined with his. Right now, I am as much aware of it as he is."

Bram falls silent, and I really wish I could see his face. I can sense him still beside me and feel his hand brush against mine. I can't hide my smile.

"I love you," he whispers.

Before I can respond, Alak charges into the street.

"Did they buy it?" I ask, pushing away from the wall.

Alak nods. "They sure did. I haggled best I could, but I feel they swindled us a bit. It should be enough for passage, though."

"Let's hope so," I mutter.

Now we move onto the third stage: booking passage and leaving Callenia. Ships travel between the two countries on a regular basis, so we hope to get on one today. We make our way to the nearest shipyard and start our search for a ship taking passengers. We're lucky enough to be able to purchase five tickets on a ferry leaving within the hour. Alak and I discreetly pass three tickets to Kato, who sits with his "brothers" on a bench near the port. According to the ticket master, the boat will begin boarding thirty minutes before the ship is ready to leave. After that, it's roughly an hour ride across the water.

As we wait to board, a slow drizzle starts. Most people duck under cover, but we stay out in the open. It's a relief to be out of the crowd, and in the heat of the day, it's a bit refreshing. By the time we're able to board, we're all soaked. Most people head below deck to avoid the rain, but we take seats along the top deck. My stomach twists in knots as we wait for the ferry to start moving. When it does finally pull away into the water, I can feel Alak's magic starting to strain. I twist more of my magic with his, and he shoots me a grateful look.

A fog has settled over the water, making it difficult to see the land of Portia as we approach. It gives an overall ominous feeling that doesn't help my nerves in the slightest. I try not to glance toward the others, but it's difficult. Kato is casually conversing with another passenger. He's a natural at this. I stand and lean on the rail, staring down into the water.

"You okay, love?" Alak asks, leaning next to me.

I nod. "I'm fine." I look over at him. "You okay?"

"Thanks to you," Alak says quietly, bumping his shoulder against mine, smiling. He scoots closer, his pinky brushing mine.

"Still here," Bram says from directly behind us, making us both jump.

"You gotta stop that, mate," Alak mutters, not bothering to

turn, but he slides his hand away from mine. I fight the urge to move closer to him.

When the land settles into a clear view through the fog, we can make out people and specific buildings. My nerves rise even higher. I feel sick. The ferry jerks as it comes into port. I clench my hands at my side and try to steady my breathing as we walk to the exit ramp, the others a couple groups behind us in line.

"Shite," Alak whispers, looking ahead to the base of the ramp.

I try to stand on my tiptoes to see over the crowd to no avail. "What is it?"

"They have a Zaodillo," Alak replies, his face paling.

"A what?"

But then the crowd shifts and I see it. It's not a very large animal, maybe three feet long and one foot high. It has a short, stumpy body armored with green scales, with four stumpy legs and short pointed ears. Its wide black eyes search over each passenger leaving the ferry while its long green snout sniffs wildly. The worst part is that it's not just Portian authorities scanning passengers, but several of the king's soldiers.

"Zaodillos can literally sniff out magic," Alak explains, his voice tight. "They're clearly expecting someone to try to use magic to sneak through. If we try to go past that, we'll most definitely be found out."

Even as he says it, I can see the creature excitedly sniffing and glancing our way. With as much magic as we're currently using, I'm sure he can sense it already. I press tighter against Alak.

"What can we do?" I whisper.

"We have to wisp," Alak says, shaking his head. "We don't have a choice."

"But won't that creature sense it?"

"Most definitely. We'll have to wisp as far away as possible. But we have to make sure it's still a place we can see."

I glance around, trying not to look suspicious. My heart hammers against my ribcage as the line to exit moves forward. I settle my gaze on the city beyond the port. Most of the buildings are tall with flat roofs.

"What about that roof, over there? The red one?" I ask, leaning against Alak and motioning toward the building with a quick nod. It's close enough I can easily visualize wisping there, but far enough it shouldn't be one of the first places they look.

Alak glances over and nods. "I think that could work."

"I'll let Kato know."

Kato, they have a weird creature at the bottom of the ramp that sniffs out magic. We have to wisp to that building over there. The one with the red roof. Can you handle wisping all four of you that far?

I was wondering what that thing was. But yes, I can handle that.

I reach my hand back and grab Bram's hand and place my other hand in Alak's. Then, we wisp. We reappear on the red clay roof along with Kato, Cal, Makin, and Ehren. Using the wisping magic must have weakened the illusion magic because everyone looks normal. We hear shouting from the city below, so we drop down and slink to the edge of the roof, peering down at the chaos.

More soldiers, both Portian and Callenian, are pouring from every corner. The Zaodillo is going crazy, sniffing wildly and trying to run up the ramp. Even the other passengers are looking around as the guards storm the ship.

"Shit," Makin murmurs. "That was close."

"Too close," Ehren agrees. He glances around the roof. "We need to get out of here. We're too exposed."

I look down the street. Most the roofs are relatively flat with plenty of covering.

"We split up. Wisp from roof to roof until we're far enough away. Then we can meet down on the street," I suggest.

"That sounds like a good plan," Ehren agrees with a nod.

"I can handle wisping Bram and Ehren. Kato, can you take Makin?"

Kato glances at Makin and shrugs. "Sure."

"And can you take Cal?" I ask, turning to Alak. "Or is your magic too drained?"

"I can handle a couple wisps, but not too many with someone else in tow," Alak says, shaking his head.

"I'll take Cal and Makin," Kato sighs.

I link hands with Ehren and Bram. "Let's do this."

We pop from roof to roof, not lingering for more than a second or two each time. We just need enough time to assess our location and find the next safe spot to wisp. Each time as we wisp, I glance around and try to locate Kato and Alak as they wisp. Alak is noticeably slowing down and falling behind, his magic weaker than ours. As I wisp to another rooftop, I pause, searching the street below for a place we can hide. I spot a dark alleyway not far away.

Kato, see that alley?

Kato appears on the roof across the street from me, pausing and glancing my way.

Which alley?

I point down a few houses. *Right over there.*

Kato looks down and over to where I'm pointing and gives me a thumbs up. I turn, glancing to Alak a couple rooftops behind me. I wave my hand to get his attention. I'm afraid he's going to wisp away, but he looks up and makes eye contact. He wisps and reappears at my side, the exhaustion clear on his face.

"We're going to go down to that alley over there. It should give us enough cover," I inform him, gesturing to the alley that Kato, Makin, and Cal have already disappeared into.

"Affirmative," Alak mumbles, a little breathless.

"Hey, are you okay? Can you wisp there on your own?" I ask, knitting my eyebrows.

He nods slowly. "I can handle one more wisp, but then I probably will need to rest some."

I offer my hand to him. "I can wisp you down there if you need."

Alak glances over at Bram and Ehren, who are standing slightly behind me. He considers my hand for a moment before shaking his head.

"Naw, love. I'll be fine on my own." He pauses, then adds with a wink, "Just be ready to catch me."

I roll my eyes and take Ehren and Bram's hands. We wisp down into the alley and find ourselves facing Kato, Makin, and Cal. Cal looks ill, immediately drawing Ehren's attention as I look around for Alak. He's nowhere to be found. I scowl.

"Where's Alak? Did he know we were coming down here?" Kato asks, stepping toward us.

"He knows," I reply nodding. "I think he was weaker than he was letting on. That illusion magic he was using earlier was no small feat."

I'm ready to wisp and find him when he flickers into view a few yards behind Kato. He lets out a quiet moan as he drops to his knees. I rush over.

"Alak! Are you okay?"

When I reach him, I drop to my knees in front of him. I place my hands on his face and lift his head so his eyes meet mine. He's weary, but a smile plays on his lips.

"Careful, love," he whispers weakly. "Your lover boy is

watching." He gives a slight nod to Bram, standing behind me with the others.

"Eh, don't worry about him," I whisper with a shrug. "He'll live. Can you stand?"

Alak nods and tries to rise, but it's a struggle. I stand and offer him my hand. He looks at it for a moment before hesitantly placing his hand in mine. I pull him to his feet, and he leans heavily on me as we make our way back to the others. Bram eyes Alak with distaste as we approach.

"Here," Kato says, holding his hand out to Alak. "Take a little of my magic. I have some to spare."

Alak shoots Kato a puzzled look but accepts his hand. He gives a slight gasp and winces as he absorbs Kato's magic, but when he pulls away, he's not quite as pale and stands on his own.

"So what now?" I ask, looking at Ehren.

"Well," Ehren answers, standing a little straighter, "I'm sure that there are already people scouring the city for us since we disappeared at the port. Thankfully, they don't know for sure that it was us. Either way, it's best that we get out of the city as soon as we can."

"I agree," Kato says. "But I think we also need some supplies. It's been a couple days since we've had a decent meal. We need food."

The hunger pang in my stomach has me nodding in agreement

"We don't really have the money for food," Ehren replies, looking down.

"Look, mate," Alak says. "I know you didn't want us stealing our way across Callenia because you didn't want us taking from your people, but we're not in Callenia anymore. We're in Portia. These aren't your people. They aren't your responsibility."

"Portia is still an ally," Ehren argues, shaking his head firmly.

"An ally that is currently helping to hunt you down," Alak points out.

Ehren grits his teeth. "That's beside the point—"

"Actually," I cut in, "Alak has some valid points."

Ehren looks at me, shock on his face. "What?"

"Alak has valid points," I repeat. "Alak and I have used a good bit of magic. We need food and rest to fully recover. With us being hunted down still, even though we've crossed into Portia, we need to be at the top of our game, at full-strength."

Ehren's face falls as he looks away. I take a step toward him.

"I know you don't like the idea of us taking anything without paying, but in our current circumstance it may be our only option. If it makes you feel better, we can always come back and repay everyone when times aren't as difficult."

Ehren sighs and runs a hand through his hair. "Fine. But this is a temporary, one-time solution. I'd rather not repeat it."

"Understandable," I reply softly. He offers me a small, weak smile before turning to Alak.

"I know from experience you're the best thief amongst us and also the least recognizable. Do you have enough strength back to head into the market?"

Alak nods. "Thanks to Kato, I'm good."

"Are you fine going alone?" Ehren asks.

"I work faster alone."

Alak starts sauntering to the end of the alley, but Ehren calls after him. "Remember to keep a low profile, getting only what is necessary, and be quick."

Alak glances at Ehren over his shoulder, grinning. "I got it, mate."

After Alak disappears, I settle on the ground, leaning against the closest wall. Bram eases down beside me.

"Are you okay?" he asks gently, taking my hand.

I nod. "I'm just a little tired. Using so much magic wore me out. Not as much as Alak, but it still had its effect."

Bram lets go of my hand and reaches his arm around me, pulling me close. I rest my head on his shoulder as he murmurs, "There you go. Just relax."

He kisses the top of my head, and I drift off to sleep.

CHAPTER FORTY-SEVEN

*Y*ou're a little traitor, you know that?" Alak's voice wakes me up.

I slowly open my eyes and blink up at Alak in confusion. I startle when something warm and fuzzy brushes against my hand. I glance down and find Felixe curled up in my lap.

"Hey, buddy," I whisper, scratching his ears. He snuggles into a tighter ball. I look up at Alak, grinning. "He just likes me better."

Alak holds up a shiny red apple. "It almost makes me want to keep this for myself."

I narrow my eyes at him. "You wouldn't dare."

Alak surveys me for a moment before tossing me the apple. I catch it with one hand.

"Your lover boy over there would probably kill me if I didn't." He nods down the alley where Bram stands talking to Ehren over a piece of paper while eating an apple of his own. "I'm not ready to die over an apple. Not today anyway." He grins and I laugh.

The apple doesn't take long to devour, but it does little to assuage my hunger. I offer Felixe the core and he perks up, eagerly munching on it, making little grumbly noises.

"See," Alak says as he takes a seat on the wall next to me. "That's why he likes you. You buy his love with food."

I grin. "Whatever it takes."

My stomach grumbles and Alak's face falls.

"I tried to get more food, but the market was crawling with Portian and Callenian soldiers. I had to be discreet, and it's hard to get food for seven people while avoiding detection."

I offer him a smile, placing my hand over his. "It's okay. We all understand." I glance back down the alley at the others and notice Ehren is now scowling at the paper. "What are they looking at?"

"I found a lovely wanted poster," Alak answers, leaning his head back against the wall and closing his eyes. "The king has placed a reward on our heads."

My eyes go wide. "What?"

Alak opens one eye and looks at me. "A reward. 20,000 markes for Ehren, 10,000 for your captain, and 5,000 for each of the rest of us."

I jump to my feet, Felixe falling to the ground with a huff. I rush over to the others, and Ehren hands me the poster before I even ask. Across the top reads the word "WANTED." Dead center is a perfect sketch of Ehren, likely drawn from one of the many portraits in the palace. His face is the largest with smaller versions of our faces in a circle around him. Bram's sketch is the next most accurate, followed by fairly accurate depictions of Cal and Makin. Alak, Kato, and I are the least accurate, but still look enough like us to make me uneasy. Underneath each picture are details including our names and how much reward money we are each worth. Ehren and Bram are requested to be brought in alive, but the rest of us are marked as "wanted dead or alive." I swallow and shake my head.

"Yeah, this is definitely an unwanted development," Ehren mumbles, taking the poster back. "It was bad enough when guards and soldiers were searching for us, but with money like this on our heads, we're goners."

"No, we'll be fine," I say and everyone turns to look at me.

"This is bad, Ash," Kato says, shaking his head. "We need to split up."

"No, we're strongest together," I insist.

I see something flicker in Kato's eyes. I know what he's thinking. He thinks the non-magic users are weakening us. I need to prove him wrong.

"What do you suggest?" Ehren asks.

"We do exactly what we always planned," I reply. "We leave this city, cross Portia, and get to the Isle of Naskein. We've made it this far, and we can make it the rest of the way. We just need to be more cautious. The further we get from the port, the less trouble we're likely to have."

Ehren studies me for a moment and then nods slowly. "You're right. We've always been wanted. Now, we might have more people looking for us, but we've always been at risk. We stay here tonight and leave first thing in the morning. Tonight, under the cover of darkness, we can scout out possible routes to escape the city, but we'll probably have to use the main exit gate, using an illusion."

"I can handle an illusion," Alak says from directly behind me, making me jump. I didn't realize he was so close. "Let's just hope they don't have any other Zaodillos at the exit gate."

"Scouting will help us determine what sort of magic tracers they have in place," Ehren states matter-of-factly. "Are you willing to be on the scouting team tonight to help check for magic?"

Alak nods. "I can definitely do that."

"Good. Good." Ehren looks at the rest of us then asks, "Who else wants to scout?"

"I'll head up the mission," Bram offers, stepping forward.

"No," Ehren replies, shaking his head. "You and I are too high profile. Even in the dark, it's too risky."

"I'll go," I say, looking Ehren in the eye. "People are less likely to suspect women, so even if I'm caught, I can probably get away without any trouble. If all else fails, I have my magic and can wisp at a moment's notice."

Bram shakes his head adamantly. "We need someone with Guard experience."

"I'll go, too, then," Cal jumps in. "I've done recon work before, so I know what to look for."

Bram opens his mouth to argue some more but Ehren cuts him off. "Good. As soon as it gets dark, you three will move out. Until then, we wait here."

The next few hours are exceptionally tense. Ehren paces up and down the alley, occasionally peering around the corner to make sure no one is nearby even though Makin has taken up residence at the end of the alley as guard. Kato is playing guard on one of the neighboring roofs, crouching low and watching anyone approaching from a different angle. Alak, Bram, Cal, and I wait, passing the time in nervous silence. I can tell Bram is less than happy about me going on this mission without him, but I don't care. As dusk starts to fall, I stand, wringing my hands as a nervous pit grows in my stomach.

"Hey," Bram whispers, closing his hands over mine. "You don't have to do this. Cal is trained for this. His eyes will likely be enough. Alak is taking care of the magical aspects. You don't need to go."

I smile weakly. "I'll be fine. I'm actually a little excited."

His eyebrow quirks up. "Excited?"

I nod. "Yes. I've never really been very useful. I like the idea of helping out."

"What do you mean you haven't been useful? You have been incredibly useful! You fought off all those soldiers in Athiedor and got Cal and Ehren to safety. I still don't know the whole story of what happened there, but you put Ehren and Cal in awe. You have also wisped us multiple times. And that's not even mentioning the times you have used your magic to shield us or help Alak hold up illusions. Compared to you, *I* am starting to feel useless."

I blush slightly and glance away. "Maybe. But I can still be useful here." I look back up at Bram. "It would be selfish to not try to help out when I can."

A smile plays on Bram's lips as he draws me closer. "Can I be a little selfish and admit I don't want you to go because I want you here with me?"

My blush deepens at the intense look shining in his eyes.

"I also don't like the fact I won't be there to defend you if something does go wrong," he says, his smile faltering.

"She'll be fine, mate," Alak cuts in, approaching us.

"I don't recall asking your opinion," Bram snaps. "Or inviting you into our conversation."

Alak shrugs. "I'm just pointing out that Astra is more powerful than you, and you would be more likely to get in her way than help her."

Bram's eyes flash as he releases my hands and leaps toward Alak who jumps back. Despite Alak's quick reflexes, Bram still grabs Alak by his shirt with both fists and throws him against the nearest wall with a thud.

"Hey!" Ehren reprimands sharply from further down the alley, raising his voice just enough to get Bram's attention.

Bram turns his head toward Ehren, but he doesn't release

Alak. Alak tenses, his jaw set, but doesn't struggle in Bram's grasp.

"We are supposed to be keeping a low profile. Throwing people up against walls and yelling at or attacking them is not a great idea, no matter how much they might deserve it," Ehren hisses firmly.

"Fine," Bram concedes, releasing Alak with a jerk that slams him into the wall again.

Alak scowls and rubs the back of his head where it hit the wall. He looks back up at Bram and mutters, "The truth hurts sometimes," before sauntering down the alley toward the exit.

Bram clenches his hands at his side, still seething. I pull Bram away and look up into his eyes.

"Hey, calm down. I'll be fine."

Bram releases a long breath. "I know. It just—I hate that he's right. You don't need me."

His shoulders sag as he looks away from me. I place my hand on his cheek and direct his gaze back to me.

"I need you." I lift my lips to his. He forces a smile.

"All right," Ehren's voice echoes down the alley. "You should get going." I step back toward Ehren along with Alak and Cal for our last-minute instructions. "They'll close the gate after night falls, so you'll want to get there a little before and see how they're operating. After it gets dark enough, you should be able to get closer to the gate and check for any magical properties or extra defense. Gather as much information as you can, but don't do anything stupid. If anything starts to go wrong, get out immediately. Everyone understand?"

Ehren looks to each of us and we nod. He takes a deep breath and gives us a nod of his own. "All right. Good luck." His eyes meet Cal's as he adds, "And be careful. I need you back alive and well."

The nervous feeling returns as Alak, Cal, and I exit the

alley and into the street. We decide we have more of a chance of not being noticed or recognized if we split up. Alak goes off on his own, but I try to stick reasonably close to Cal so I can get to him quickly in case we need to wisp away. The streets aren't as busy as they were earlier in the day, but plenty of people still bustle about. We don't look suspicious or out of place, but there are enough people that it feels like a bit of a risk.

One by one we arrive at the exit gate right before nightfall. Portian guards stand by, their stern eyes examining everyone approaching the gate. As far as I can see, there's no extreme security measures, but Cal's the expert. My job is to look for any possible escape route should things go awry.

It doesn't take me long to find the best path to approach the gate with the least amount of interaction. Cal ducks out of my view behind a building to get a better look at the guards' operation. I'm not sure if Alak is hidden behind a building or if he's simply made himself invisible. Either way, he's nowhere to be seen.

Once it's officially night, the guards close the gate. They leave behind one sentry to let in or out any latecomers, but the rest head off into the darkness. The sentry pulls out a deck of cards and starts playing some sort of one-person game. Cal sneaks up behind me.

"Hey," he whispers in my ear, making me jump. "Sorry, didn't mean to frighten you."

I look at him and his eyes are twinkling.

"Hey," I whisper. "What do you need?"

"I just need you to play lookout while I get a better look at the gate itself. I have a pretty good idea of the security they have set up, but I need to get a little closer." He pauses and looks like he wants to ask something else but shakes it off.

"What else do you need me to do?"

He hesitates but finally says, "If I can get close enough to touch the gate, I can actually test out the security, but in order for that to happen I need a distraction." Cal watches my reaction for a moment before adding, "But if you're not comfortable with that—"

"No, I can do it," I say, putting as much confidence into my voice as I can, despite the fact that my stomach is turning and twisting at the mere thought.

"Are you sure?" he asks, searching my face. "Because if you're even slightly unsure, it might be—"

"I can do it," I cut him off, my voice strong.

"Okay," he says slowly. "Just draw his attention away long enough for me to get between him and the gate for a minute or two. He's not right up against it, but if you can get him to move a little further away, that would be best."

I nod. "All right. I got it. Draw him away and hold his attention until you're clear. I can do that."

"All right. Give me just a minute to get closer and into position before you go."

Cal slips off into the darkness. The seconds tick by, my heart pounding with each one. Cal shifts into the shadows near the gate and gives me a thumbs up. So far the guard hasn't looked up from his card game, so there's no way he's seen Cal.

I look down at my ragged appearance. Unless I'm going to play the part of a vagabond beggar, I need to change my look. My magic doesn't naturally lean toward illusion, but I've woven my magic together enough with Alak's that the memory of illusion magic isn't too difficult to access.

I start by changing my clothes. Instead of the worn and filthy dress I've been wearing since Athiedor, I'm now wearing a dark blue dress with a high neckline and quarter-length sleeves with a dark pink sash wrapped around my waist and looped over one shoulder. I also add a head scarf in the dark pink color to help hide my features a little better and change the color of my hair that's still peeking through to a golden blond. I take a deep breath and push aside my fear and the nerves. I don't know many words of the Portian language but, thankfully, one of the words I do know is "help," so that's what I cry as I stumble into the road.

The sentry's eyes shoot up from his card game and look right at me. My pulse quickens as I fall to the ground, panting and yelling "help" over and over, forcing tears to run down my cheeks. I look directly at the guard as he scrambles from his station toward me. Cal doesn't waste any time and immediately leaves the shadows to get closer to the gate. Alak takes advantage of my distraction to approach the gate as well.

The sentry drops to my side and begins talking rapidly in Portian. My brain scrambles to interpret the words, but I simply don't know enough about the language. I manage to start weeping while I work my illusion a little more, creating a fake wound on my ankle. I grab at the wound, the man's eyes shifting to the fabricated blood. His eyes go wide, and he rattles off more words I can't understand. He starts to turn back toward his station, presumably to get some sort of bandage for my wound, but I cry out and he looks back at me. I manage to recall a few more Portian words.

"Man!" I gasp in broken Portian. "Help!" I point back the way I came, completely opposite from where Cal and Alak are now. The man quickly follows my motioning, his eyes darting like crazy.

"Help!" I cry again.

The man stands, saying several words I don't know, but I understand the motion he's making well enough. He wants me to stay put. He takes off running a little way down the road, looking left and right. He ducks into the shadows, and I take the opportunity to glance at Cal and Alak. Alak has disappeared back into the shadows. Cal looks almost done as well. I look back down the road and see the sentry reemerging, still searching for my imaginary attacker. I gasp and point just past the man, and he spins, jerking his head around. I look back at Cal and find he's slinking into the shadows. The man's attention is still elsewhere so, while he's distracted, I take a deep breath and wisp into the shadows. I hear the man's confused yells as I stumble through the darkness and find Cal.

"Did you get what you need?" I whisper, my heart still pounding.

He grins. "I did."

I glance toward the road where I can hear the sentry's hurried footsteps approaching.

"We should wisp. Otherwise, that guy will probably see us."

"Let's go," Cal says with a nod.

I hesitate, not wanting to leave Alak behind, but I have to make a decision. I reach out and touch Cal's arm, and we wisp back to the alley. When we reappear, there are four pairs of nervous eyes on us. Bram visibly relaxes while Ehren lets out a sigh of relief. I turn and glance all around.

"Has Alak come back yet?" I ask, even though I can clearly see he's not present.

Ehren shakes his head. "Were you not together?"

"Not when we wisped," I say, turning to Cal. "I need to go back and let him know we left."

"No," Bram says quickly, grabbing my arm.

I jerk away. "We just left him. I have to make sure he knows."

"With that sentry looking around, it's too risky. You have no idea where he'll be," Cal says.

"He has magic," Kato says. "He'll be fine. If he's not back in a minute or two, I'll go after him."

I shake my head. "You don't know where to go." Guilt

swells in my chest. I shouldn't have left without him. "I need to go back. I need to—"

"Everyone back safely?" Alak says, appearing behind me.

I spin and throw my arms around him. "Thank the gods you're okay."

Alak's face turns from shock to smugness. "Well, of course I'm all right, love," he chuckles, returning my embrace. "I'm the best there is."

"Astra was just a little concerned that we wisped away without letting you know we were leaving," Cal says as I pull back from Alak.

"Ah. I figured you two had left, but I waited a moment to make sure that you didn't reappear and to make sure that the guard didn't call for any sort of backup."

"That was actually a smart move," Cal replies with a nod.

"Wait, there was a guard looking for you?" Bram cuts in.

I nod. "Well, not for me, exactly. But a woman. I created an illusion for myself so I wouldn't be recognizable. Cal and Alak needed a diversion."

Bram's eyes flash but Ehren nods, clearly impressed.

"So, did you get the information we need?" Ehren asks before Bram can say anything.

Cal nods and steps forward first. "It's a standard gate. Nothing special from what I could see. Plenty of access points to approach, too, so we can get pretty close without being noticed. Before they closed it for the night they only had four guards on duty—two watching those coming in and two more watching those leaving."

"I agree. There are plenty of ways to get there without taking the main road if we don't want to," I add.

Ehren nods, pleased. "Alak, what did you find out? Any magical hindrances?"

"No magical animals," Alak answers. "At least, there

weren't any today, but the gate is warded. These guys didn't waste any time implementing magic."

"What does that mean for us?" Ehren asks.

"Not much. It just means we can't wisp past the gate, but we should be able to pass through the gate under an illusion."

"There's nothing in the warding that would undo an illusion?"

Alak shakes his head. "Not that I could sense, and I was able to get right up on the gate and feel the magic. Unless they change it or update it before morning, we should be fine."

"Okay, that's good. That's all good information," Ehren muses. He looks back at Cal, "What sort of documentation was needed to leave the city? Anything?"

"Not that I saw. Of course, by the time we arrived they were mostly done for the day and not many people were leaving. They were basically watching for anyone who is wanted. They actually had several wanted fliers near the gate, including ours. I think they were also asking for general names, but it didn't look like they were keeping any records unless the person acted suspicious."

"Good," Ehren says, standing straight and tall. "We will leave first thing in the morning. Alak, you will weave an illusion with Astra supporting as needed."

Alak nods and I say, "I can definitely do that."

"What happens if there are more wards tomorrow? Wards that destroy our solution?" Makin asks.

"Then," Ehren replies, "we fight our way out and wisp as soon as we can. If they still only have four guards, they won't be any match for us."

"And if they have more?" Bram asks coldly. "Perhaps we should stake out the gate a day or two and make sure that we have an exact count."

Ehren shakes his head. "No. The longer we stay in this city, the more we risk being found. We can't live in this alley forever. We make our move tomorrow morning as soon as the gate opens. I also think we should all be able to understand and speak a few basic Portian phrases. I will try to be the one to speak when addressed, since I have formal training in Portian, but it's likely we will have to give at least our names. I also believe that our best bet in getting out unnoticed will be to look and sound like typical Portians. If we don't understand the questions being asked, we will stand out and blow our cover. I won't pretend I speak perfect Portian, but I can teach you all a few phrases."

"That's not a bad idea," I say with a nod.

Ehren nods and releases a long breath. "Okay, let's start with the basics."

Ehren launches into a quick language lesson, each of us repeating word after word and phrase after phrase until we feel we have enough down to pass. I can tell Ehren is still stressed, but it's getting late.

"Well, I guess that will do for now," Ehren concedes after an hour or two. "I suggest you all get a good night's sleep."

Ehren walks away from us and settles down on the ground at the back of the alley. We glance awkwardly at each other before Makin finally speaks up.

"I'll take first watch."

"And I'll take second," Kato adds. "Wake me up in a couple hours.

Makin nods and goes to the end of the alley and the rest of us join Ehren and settle on the ground. I can feel Bram's eyes on my back as I lay near him, but I don't turn to look or move any closer. Tonight I just need sleep and not the guilt I know I'll feel if I look at him. I can deal with him tomorrow.

CHAPTER FORTY-EIGHT

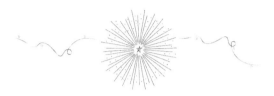

$\mathscr{T}$he sun hasn't even risen when Ehren wakes us.
Judging by the completely exhausted look on his
face he got little to no sleep. We blink at him, rubbing sleep
from our eyes, but slowly rise. We practice our nearly learned
Portian phrases, working on our accents. Ehren still seems a
little hesitant, but he's overall pleased with our progress and
more relaxed than last night. Once we have our accents down,
Alak goes to work on creating our illusion.

To go along with Ehren's idea, we will all be Portian travelers. No one will be invisible this time since that illusion is
harder to maintain and may be easily detected if they start
using magical tracers. By the time Alak is done, we all have
variations of golden blond and dirty blond hair with tan skin
and brown eyes, all wearing typical Portian clothing. Bram is
furious when he discovers Alak made him into a woman.

"You change me to a man, RIGHT NOW!" Bram yells, his
face red with fury. He tries to grab Alak, but Alak wisps away
laughing.

Makin and Ehren are laughing so hard they're crying, and

Cal and Kato are shaking with laughter. I try to hide my laugh and smile behind my hand but am utterly unsuccessful.

"I think it's an excellent look for you, mate!" Alak laughs, dodging another one of Bram's blows.

"Bram, relax!" Ehren chokes, managing to gain enough control to speak before breaking into laughter again.

"Relax?!" Bram yells. "Relax? Do you see what that bastard did to me? I'm going to kill him!"

"Actually, it's not a bad idea," I say, and Bram spins to face me, eyebrows arched.

"Not you, too! I thought at least you'd be on my side."

"Well, if the guards are looking for a group of six males and one female, you being female may just be the trick."

Bram's jaw drops. "You've got to be joking! Tell me you're joking."

"I hate to say it, but she's right," Ehren says, wiping the tears from his cheeks as he struggles to regain his composure. "It does give us a slight advantage."

"See, that's what I had planned all along," Alak grins, his eyes sparkling with mischief.

Bram clenches his fists at his side. "I will kill you later for this."

Alak's grin only widens. "Not in that dress."

Bram lunges for Alak, but Ehren steps between them.

"Let's get going," Ehren says, his voice stern and serious, but his eyes are still laughing.

We trudge through town toward the gate, traveling the indirect routes Cal and I mapped out last night. Thankfully, there isn't much of a crowd waiting to leave the city. My magic is woven with Alak's, so our illusion is strong. We even have bags to make our cover as travelers seem more legitimate. With help from my magic, our bags are physical objects and not just illusions, so if anyone touches or bumps into them they'll seem real.

When it's our turn, we step up to the gate cautiously. Bram's still seething, but does his best to play the part. Ehren steps up as planned and gives a brief reason for our travel. All we have to do is confirm our names. Then we go through the gate. As we cross under the gate's arch, I can feel the tingle of magic from the warding. I hold my breath, expecting it strip away or affect our illusion, but our magic holds firm. As we walk down the road away from the city, we hold the illusion until we're alone, which is about an hour later after the people that crossed the gate behind us go a different way. Now we just have to cross the entire Island of Portia on foot. According to Ehren it will take at least a week unless we wisp occasionally.

Our journey starts out slow. The energy from the food we ate yesterday has worn off and the air is muggy and gray. We manage to find some berries along the road, but they do little to assuage our hunger. By the end of the day we reach a town. We stay outside the town, however, when recon done by Kato and Alak reveal that the wanted posters are everywhere, though they don't see any soldiers. This seems to be the pattern for the next couple towns as well, but the farther we get from the port city, the less we see of the posters until they're finally gone. At that point, we can actually earn some money by going into the towns and don't have to rely on hunting, foraging, or stealing.

Even though magic has returned here as well, Alak still draws a regular crowd with his magic tricks. He definitely has a charismatic personality that draws a lot of coins. He uses a little illusion magic to change up his appearance just to be safe. The rest of us tend to hang back in groups of two to avoid being seen together.

Makin has proven to be a master gambler. He hits up all the taverns and enters every game he can. The games he loses, Kato wins. They're careful not to be too brazen and always stop before the pot gets too big. Thanks to them, we get to eat again. Between them and Alak, we manage to pool enough money for new clothes, so we don't look quite as ragged.

It takes us eight days to cross Portia. When we reach the port city of Arkney, we enter with no issues using a similar illusion to the one we used last time (except this time Bram is male), but there's a dark sense of foreboding. I feel like there's a heavy, evil presence in the town and I can't shake it. I glance at the others but, if they notice, they don't show it. Ehren does, however, notice my scowl.

"What's wrong," Ehren murmurs, coming up next to me.

"I don't know for sure," I reply, my scowl deepening. "Something just feels . . . off. But I don't know why, and I have no idea what to do about it."

"Stay alert," Ehren says a touch louder so everyone can hear without drawing attention.

The farther into the city we walk, the stronger the feeling grows. I try to chalk it up to the weather. It's a gray, dreary morning. Anyone would feel some trepidation with weather like this. I glance around and everyone else seems to be going about their regular day. I take a deep breath and try to concentrate on what we need to do. The sooner we can leave this port city behind and get within the walls of the Order of Naskein, the better.

Despite my unease, we decide to split up to cover more ground. Alak, Kato, and Makin go down to the harbor to see if they can find any boats going to the Isle while the rest of us hunt down some food. Our last couple of stops proved fairly profitable and, for the first time, we may actually have enough money for a decent meal as well as passage to Naskein. It's already midday and several vendors are frying up fish for purchase. We find some particularly delicious smelling options and take a seat at one of the many outdoor tables. The entire time I can't shake the feeling that someone is watching us.

"Oh, that looks amazing," Kato says, as he and the others return from their mission. He reaches for my piece, but I bat his hand away.

"We got you your own," I say to him, pointing to the basket of fried fish in the center of our table.

"You always go for the violent option," Kato whines, rubbing his hand dramatically before taking a seat next to me and grabbing his own piece.

"So," Ehren says, swallowing his fish. "Were you able to find passage to Naskein?"

Makin nods, his mouth full. He tries to swallow and answer, but Alak jumps in first.

"There's a supply boat heading out tomorrow morning. They said they would give us passage at no charge," Alak says, examining a piece of fish before taking a bite.

"A supply boat?" Ehren asks, raising an eyebrow.

"Yes," Makin says, having swallowed his fish. "Apparently not many boats go to and from Naskein. It's a religious order and they prefer their privacy. The ship's captain even made it clear that we may not be accepted once we get across the channel. Apparently, they rarely let outsiders in."

"It's a good thing they invited us," Ehren mumbles.

"What are we going to do if they have changed their minds?" Bram asks. "When they extended their invitation you were requesting entry as the crown prince in good standing. Now that your father has a bounty on your head, do you think they will allow us entry?"

Ehren sighs. "I considered that, but I'm really hoping they'll still accept us. After all, we are on the side of magic and they've always been a sanctuary for magic, even when we thought it was dead and gone. I doubt they would change now."

Something catches my attention out of the corner of my eye. I swear someone a couple tables over is staring directly at us, but when I look over, no one is watching. I shake my head at myself and turn my attention back to my food.

Astra, is something wrong?

I just thought I saw someone watching us. I think I'm just tense and ready for this adventure to be over.

Are you sure? If you think there's something to worry about . . .

Kato glances around, trying to look casual, but he catches Ehren's attention. Ehren glances over at me and leans toward the center of the table, closer to me.

"Do you sense something?" he asks, his voice low.

I shake my head. "I don't know. I just feel really uneasy. The sooner we get to Naskein, the better."

Ehren leans back in his chair and nods. "We should get off the streets. Since we can't leave until tomorrow, we should find an inn as soon as we can and lie low until morning."

Bram nods. "I agree. As soon as we're done here, we will see what we can find."

We all go quiet, focusing on our food. Despite the fact I haven't had a decent meal in weeks, I can't really eat. My stomach is twisting with apprehension. We're almost done when a stranger approaches our table. He has short, dark hair and dark eyes. I tense but Ehren greets him casually.

"Good afternoon," Ehren says cheerily in perfect Portian.

I focus on breathing, trying to act normal. As far as this guy knows, we're just normal Portians out for a meal together. I force a smile, but the man's face is like stone.

"Can we help you?" Ehren asks when the man doesn't say anything.

There's movement behind the man and all around us as several people start rising from their seats. My heart starts beating fast. Something isn't right. The man seems to sense my discomfort and his lips turn up into a smile.

"Yes," the man says in Callenian. "There is something you can do for me, Prince Ehren."

Ehren's eyes go wide as Bram's hand drifts to his sword subtly, but he doesn't pull it. Not yet. Ehren schools his features into confusion.

"I'm sorry, but I believe you have me confused for someone else," Ehren replies, still speaking Portian.

The man laughs. "I think not."

Before any of us can react, the man pulls his hand to his face and blows a strange sparkling powder over us all. The second it touches us, the spell creating our illusion is shattered. We're exposed.

Bram jumps to his feet, sword drawn. The rest of us are on our feet moments later.

"Now, now," the man sneers. "I wouldn't do that if I were you. I think you'll find it best to surrender."

He gestures around, and I see that we're surrounded. Most of the crowd around us are his men in disguise. We're severely outnumbered. I glance at Bram and Ehren, but they don't look worried. Their faces are like steel, betraying no emotion, but I can see the calculated look in their eyes. Ehren's looking for an escape while Bram's looking for the best place to attack. I take a deep breath. We've made it this far. We have to make it the rest of the way.

"Sorry," Ehren replies coldly. "But surrender isn't something I like to do."

The man laughs. "Well, I think you'd better start considering it. You and the captain are wanted alive, but all these others"—the man gestures to the rest of us—"are wanted dead or alive. My men will have no problem killing them. And even though you're to be brought in alive, that doesn't guarantee we won't rough you up a bit."

The man smiles wickedly and several of the men around us chuckle. These are mercenaries. They don't answer to anyone but themselves. I hold my head higher and make direct eye contact with the man. I'm pleased to find it unsettles him.

Get ready, Kato.

Careful, Astra. This guy isn't playing.

I know. Neither will we.

"You might be making a mistake," I say evenly. Bram's eyes slide to me and he scowls.

"Excuse me?" the man spits.

"I'm just saying, you're about to make a mistake. You may want to reconsider."

The man considers me for a moment before he throws his head back, laughing. He turns slightly toward his men, still keeping one eye on us and yells, "You hear that, men? This girl thinks we're in over our heads." The men roar with laughter as he turns back to face us, lethal amusement twinkling in his eyes. "I'll take my chances."

"Fine. What happens next is on you," I say with a shrug.

I quickly summon a flash of light and cast it over the mercenaries surrounding us. It's bright enough that they all turn away, shielding their eyes.

"Run!" I yell, leading the way.

No one hesitates as we dash from the table. The men don't take long to recover, and they're quickly in pursuit. Kato throws fireballs over his shoulder and manages to take out two of them, but we're still outnumbered.

"Get to the port!" Ehren yells. "Everyone get to the docks!"

I'm not quite sure what his plan is, but we follow it. We split up, staying in sight of each other but not within reach. It's harder for them to catch us all if we're not together. I slam an orb of light into one man's chest, throwing him back into another man behind him, clearing a path between me and the docks. A man leaps in front of me, cutting me off. I dodge him and jump up onto a chair and then a table. Another man leaps in front of me, sneering. I jump as high as I can off the table and throw my light in front of me, creating stepping stones in midair under each foot. I easily soar over the man's head and land several feet behind him. I hear an explosion and look over to see smoke curling from a place where Kato just struck down several of our pursuers.

The mercenaries start dropping back as we approach the water. Once we get there, we'll be trapped, and they know it. They're already forming a circle, herding us back together. I head toward an area where I can access the water directly, but I don't stop at the water's edge. Instead, I summon my magic and begin crafting a bridge made of solid silver light. It's only a few feet wide, but it's quickly stretching out over the water, snaking toward Naskein. I jump off the shore and onto the light. It holds firm beneath my feet and I keep running. The others follow behind me, racing onto the bridge without hesitation. Soon, everyone except Kato has joined me. Kato freezes at the edge of the water and turns back toward the mercenaries, throwing up a wall of flames, completely blocking them from us.

Hurry, Kato! I can only sustain so much of the bridge at a time! I need you on the end before I start to retract it!

I know. I'll be fine. Go ahead and start retracting it, just leave enough space for me. I'll wisp to you.

I take a deep breath and slowly draw the end of the bridge toward me. It's several yards from connecting with the shore when Kato drops his fire wall, wisping from the shore to the end, already running full force.

Maintaining the bridge is difficult. I have to keep it

perfectly permanent, or we'll slip through to gods know what in the water. It doesn't help my concentration when an arrow whizzes past my face.

"Shit!" Makin cries. "They're shooting at us!"

"Kato!" Ehren yells. "Can you—"

"I'm on it!" Kato cuts him off, shooting fireballs back toward the shore.

"They're still shooting!" Cal yells as another arrow lands near my feet.

"Just keep running!" Ehren yells. "Get out of range!"

We're over halfway to the isle when I start feeling a drain on my magic. It's exhausting trying to run and hold my magic at the same time. I've never run this much in my life. My legs are aching and my heart is pounding. The closer I get to the wall surrounding the Isle of Naskein, the harder it is to maintain my magic. The wall is seriously warded, and it's fighting against my magic. I stumble as the bridge beneath my feet starts to soften.

"No, no, no!" I mutter under my breath.

I send another surge of magic, but it stings this close to the warding. I feel something wrap into my magic, filling all the places where it is weak. It's Alak. I look over my shoulder and shoot him a grateful look.

"Shit!" Makin yells. "Shit! Shit! Shit!"

I'm about to ask what's happening now when Ehren yells, "They have boats! Hurry!"

Somehow, we manage to pick up speed, racing toward the front gate of the wall. Then, as if being pursued by mercenaries wasn't enough, I see the front gate of the Isle slowly begin to rise. My heart pounds even harder, which I didn't think possible. Are they going to let us in? Or are they opening the gate to fire at us? Will they see us as an attack?

The gate continues creeping up, revealing a group of about a dozen people standing directly inside, all wearing floor-length ivory robes with gold around the edges. At their head is a man with a long gray beard, his gaze fixed on us. They don't seem to be advancing or ready to attack. Instead, they stand calmly, hands folded in front of their bodies, watching us approach.

We get closer and closer, but we don't slow down until we stumble from the bridge onto the short dock in front of the gate. I step to the side, concentrating what little I have left of my magic on maintaining the bridge until everyone has stepped off. Ehren walks directly up to the man standing at the front and bows slightly from the waist.

"I am Prince Ehren from Callenia," Ehren gasps, but the man holds up his hand, silencing Ehren.

"We know who you are, Your Majesty. Please, come inside as our honored guests," the man says, smiling gently. He steps aside slightly, gesturing us in with his hand. "Welcome to the Order of Naskein."

We don't hesitate. We immediately dash inside, the gate crashing down behind us.

CHAPTER FORTY-NINE

$\mathcal{I}$t takes a moment for us to register that we're safe. I look around at our new surroundings and find an amazingly peaceful scene. We're in a courtyard with stone paths and a foundation at the center. In between the pathways are flower beds with bright, colorful flowers and plants.

"I am Master Arcanis. I hope that you will make yourselves at home while you are staying with us here at the Order," the man says. "We understand you've had a perilous and exhausting journey. Acolyte Aura will guide you to your rooms and allow you to freshen up. We can meet with you later at your leisure. Please know that you will be safe as long as you remain within our borders."

A young woman wearing her hair in a long black braid positioned directly on top of her head steps forward from the crowd behind the man. She bows to us.

"If you will please follow me I will show you to your room," she says, speaking Callenian with a sharp accent.

We follow her down the path out of the courtyard into a second courtyard. This courtyard seems to be filled mostly with herbs and other practical plants. Our guide notices me glancing around.

"This is the courtyard where our Healers live and practice," she explains, gesturing around.

"Are there many courtyards?" I ask.

Acolyte Aura nods. "Yes. The entire isle is set up in hexagonal courtyards similar to a beehive. Each courtyard has its own purpose. Some are for relaxing or specific recreational activities. Others are for living or practicing magic. Everything and everyone here has a purpose."

"And it all revolves around magic?" Kato asks, his eyes shining with interest.

"Yes. It is the responsibility of the Order of Naskein to protect and honor all things magical."

We leave the second courtyard and pass into another. Despite that it's mid-afternoon, this courtyard is dark. In the center of the courtyard is an obsidian statue of a man with a long cape.

"This is the Courtyard of Velios, the god of shadows. This is where those who are gifted with shadow magic practice their craft," Aura explains.

Kato's eyes lock on a nearby acolyte, weaving shadows through the air. "Do you have courtyards for every kind of magic? Like fire magic?"

"Of course," Aura replies with a wave of her hand. "There's an entire courtyard for just elemental magic. After you've had a chance to rest and meet with Master Arcanis, we'll make sure you receive a full tour." She glances at me. "We also have a rather impressive library. Every single magical work or any text referencing magic has a copy or original in our library."

My eyes brighten. "That's amazing! I can't wait to have a look."

We weave through several more courtyards and finally get

to one that she announces is the courtyard containing living quarters for non-magical acolytes and guests.

"Wait," Cal says as we climb stairs to reach an upper level of one of the housing units. "There are people here who don't actually practice magic?"

Aura nods. "Yes. There are many in the service of the Order who wish to protect and preserve magic who do not have magical skills. It has always been this way."

Aura leads us down a hallway on the second floor that is open on one side to look down on the courtyard with doors lining the other side. She stops outside a door marked with an ancient symbol.

"This will be your room. I assume you are all fine sharing?" She glances around our group for our response, but she acts as if she already knows the answer before Ehren replies.

"Yes, we would actually prefer to stay together."

She gives one quick nod. "Very well. The room next door has been made into a temporary washroom for you. There is a tub for each of you already prepared with dividers between each for privacy. For any further bathing needs, you are welcome to use the hot springs in Courtyard Nine or the washroom on the first floor. Inside on your beds you will find a complimentary change of clothes. When you are ready, someone will be back to direct you to a meeting with Master Arcanis. Any questions?"

We all stare are her for a moment, blinking, before she smiles and says, "I will leave you to it then. I am sure we will meet again."

She gives a quick bow before wisping away. We stand for a moment looking at the space where she stood, slowly processing everything.

"Well, I'm tired and need a bath," Alak says, striding

forward and placing his hand on the door handle to our room. "Let's go inside, shall we?"

We step inside the room. It's simple but welcoming. The floor is made of ivory and gold hexagon tiles with a high ceiling stretching above us. A gold and ivory rug runs from the door to the opposite wall, which bears three tall, lean windows with ivory curtains. There are seven four-poster beds along the walls, four on the left side and three on the right. Each one is equipped with ivory curtains that are tied back with golden ropes. At the foot of each bed is a trunk for storage. In the corner of the room on the wall with only three beds is a wooden changing screen. Along the walls between each bed, tapestries hang depicting different forms of magic.

"It's nice," Makin muses with a nod as he strides to the last bed along the right wall. Cal follows him, selecting the center bed.

I walk over to the second to last bed along the left wall and find a pile of clothes on top of the trunk. I pick it up and find a simple floor length white dress made from linen. I glance over to see Bram at the bed to my left examining the clothes left for him. It's a basic white shirt with white pants, also linen.

"How do they know which bed each of us would choose?" he mutters.

"I'm assuming they have a Seer, or multiple Seers, here. They knew a lot of details," I reply.

"That is very likely," Ehren says, examining the clothes laid out for him at the foot of the bed he selected, one down from Cal. "I imagine they have almost every type of magic represented here."

We gather our clothes and head next door. As promised, seven tubs have been prepared for us, each separated from the others by divider screens much like the one in the corner of our room. I take the one in the farthest corner which feels the most secluded and private. Once I slip behind the screen, I find a little table with a fluffy white towel, sponge, and soap. I awkwardly undress and slide into the water. It's cool but, after the hot day, it's welcome. I hurry to scrub the weeks of dirt from my skin and hair. I wrap the towel around my body before I've even completely exited the tub. I dry hurriedly and dress. I consider using magic to dry my hair, but after all the magic I had to use to maintain the bridge, I still feel a little weak. I glance back at the tub, now filled with filthy water, and wonder what to do with it when I notice that a small note has been left beneath the towel. I pick it up and read the script-like writing.

Please do not fret about the water. Someone will be along shortly to dispose of it. You may also leave any garments you wish to have washed and they will be taken care of and returned to you.

I smile and make my way back through the room to the door. I blush slightly at the thought that it's mere screens between me and the naked bodies of my traveling companions. I hurry my steps and quickly leave the bathing room, rushing back to our bedroom. Alak sits on the trunk at the end of the bed to the right of the one I've selected. Naturally, he's only wearing his pants. His hair is also still wet, leaving me to believe his magic is also a little weak. When I enter the room, he grins at me.

"This place is pretty amazing, isn't it?"

I nod, running my fingers through my damp hair. "It really is. I can't wait for the full tour."

"The full tour?" Alak laughs, arching an eyebrow. "You mean you can't wait to see the library."

"Guilty." I grin. I glance at the shirt lying beside him. "Aren't you going to put that on?"

"Sorry, love," he says, his mischievous grin playing on his lips. "I forgot how hot and bothered you get when you see me without my shirt."

I shake my head at him as he winks.

"Alak," I say, my voice unsteady as I take a step toward him. His eyes meet mine and my heart races. "Yes, love?"

"I—"

The door opens and Alak jumps, grabbing the shirt. He relaxes slightly and slips the shirt over his head when Makin enters the room. Makin glances from Alak to me and shrugs. A few minutes later everyone has joined us, ready to go. All conversation and thoughts of Alak are driven from my mind.

"I wonder how we're supposed to let them know we're ready," Ehren says.

No sooner has he spoken then there's a knock on the door.

"That's just creepy," Makin mumbles and I have to agree.

Bram opens the door to find a boy no more than twelve years old outside. He glances at us nervously.

"My name is Acolyte Chase," he says with a slight bow. "Master Arcanis has asked me to take you to the meeting room."

"Lead away," Ehren says, gesturing out the door.

The boy moves quickly, weaving in and out of courtyards. He anxiously glances at us over his shoulder every few steps until we reach what they call the center courtyard. This is the only courtyard we've seen so far with any sort of ceiling, although this domed ceiling is made of glass, so it still feels like it's outside. In the center of the room, Master Arcanis stands along with a few other individuals who eye us curiously with stern faces.

"I assume you're finding your accommodations satisfactory," he says as we approach.

"Yes, thank you," says Ehren. "We are extremely grateful."

"We won't keep you long," Master Arcanis continues. "We just want to introduce ourselves. I am Master Arcanis. I am the Head Mage here on the Isle of Naskein. If you have any major concerns, please do not hesitate to find me. It is my duty to conduct positive relations with everyone outside the Order while maintaining the Order from within."

He then goes on to introduce the other Masters with him, beginning with a tall, stern faced woman named Master Heilen, their Head Healer, and ending with Master Divonos, a shorter man with a neatly trimmed brown beard who oversees the more religious aspects of the order.

Once all the Masters have been introduced, Master Arcanis adds, "Of course, beneath each Master are many apprentices and mages of varying degrees along with hundreds of acolytes, all working in their own specialized areas. Even those without magical abilities are welcome to serve in our ranks. It is by working together as a united force we are able to operate while still preserving and serving magic."

"It is an honor and pleasure to meet you all," Ehren says, diplomacy ringing in his voice. "With magic so long forgotten beyond these walls, I believe it is crucial for those of us unfamiliar with magic to maintain partnerships with those such as your Order that have studied magic and have experience dealing directly with it."

Master Arcanis nods. "Indeed. And we here also believe that it is our allies outside the wall that help to make us strong."

"After all," Master Divonos adds. "The gods and goddesses of old did not contain their magic to only themselves, but shared it with the world."

The other Masters nod and mumble something under their breath that sounds like some sort of prayer.

"Elisabet," Master Arcanis calls.

A girl about sixteen years old with two long red braids

rushes forward from where she's been observing along the edges of the room.

"Yes, Master?" she says with a slight bow.

"Please, if you don't mind, give our guests an official tour of the grounds."

She nods and leads us through the maze of hexagons. We see every corner of the Isle. It takes a few hours and it's a little overwhelming. Elisabet smiles constantly and continually reassures us that soon we will have everything memorized and be able to navigate on our own. She points out that most of the acolytes and others staying in the hive, as they call it, often use magic if they have it, to wisp from place to place to save time winding through the courtyards.

By the time we are done with our tour, it's time for dinner. Elisabet leads us back to a courtyard lined with wooden tables and bench seats. Each table has several bowls and trays down the center with plates and cups at each seat. We take our place as directed at the end of one of the tables. Master Divonos rises and says a prayer in a language I don't quite recognize before we begin eating. The food is simple but delicious. The fruits and vegetables have been grown and tended right on the Isle. The main course is fish, caught and prepared here as well. The only thing that doesn't come from this Isle is the wine which, an acolyte seated nearby nervously informs us, comes from the mainland of Portia.

After dinner we're invited to attend various activities, but we all decline. Our beds call our names. When I finally make my way to my bed, I collapse on top of the covers, not even bothering to undress or close my curtains. I almost instantly fall asleep.

CHAPTER FIFTY

I open my eyes but don't immediately rush from my bed. Instead, I snuggle beneath the covers, enjoying a few more cozy moments. We've been in Naskein for four days now, and I've fallen into a comfortable yet hectic schedule. I spend most of my morning in the library with Pria, a woman not many years older than I am with long black hair and brown eyes who serves as the apprentice for Master Viden, the Master of Magical Knowledge and Histories. She's very helpful but is almost overly eager. She has stacks and stacks of things ready for me each morning before I arrive. I wonder if she ever sleeps.

While I'm in the library, the others are off fulfilling whatever duties are necessary for the day. For Ehren that means a lot of diplomatic meetings with the different Masters, trying to gain respect and knowledge. Once or twice, Ehren has actually ended up in the library with me. Bram, Makin, and Cal follow Ehren wherever he goes, though guards are unnecessary within these walls. Alak and Kato usually end up in the courtyards dedicated to their particular magical skills, learning the basic knowledge and history behind their forms of magic.

Midday is one of the few times we're all guaranteed to be together. Everyone filters through the courtyard meant for dining over a period of a couple hours to eat lunch every day, and we make a point to eat at the same time. After lunch, however, we're all sent off to learn our different forms of magic in a practical from.

Kato has taken up training under an apprentice by the name of Cendis, and I'm under an apprentice named Tes. Neither have anywhere near our level of power, but they do have years of training. They help us understand the source of our power and work through the best ways to channel it. Most of what they show us is similar to what Alak taught us, but they build on that foundation and apply their knowledge and skills directly to our forms of magic. It's thoroughly exhausting, but we're both already showing increased skill and control.

Alak works with an apprentice named Rune. Rune is just a few years older than Alak but has a younger sister who always seems to be on the sidelines watching. Alak is eager to show off and impress her, and I can't help but wonder if he's actually learning anything, even though he swears he's come a long way.

Even Bram, Makin, Cal, and Ehren study magic in the afternoons. Master Vigos, the Master of Spells, was quick to set them up with various apprentices to learn the basics of spell work and potions.

"One does not need to have natural magic to be able to use spell work," he told us all on the first day. "It does help if there is a magical bloodline, but even the most basic human can manage it, especially in a land flowing with magic."

"So anyone can actually wield magic?" Kato had asked, his eyes wide.

"Yes and no. Many of those born without natural magic flowing in their veins will never be able to move beyond repeated words and mixtures and will rely heavily on magical or enchanted ingredients. It takes a lot of study, concentration, and practice, but almost anyone who has the desire can learn to have some skill, even if it's minute. Some will eventually be able to conjure basic spells without the use of materials, though that is rare. More commonly, those born without magic can learn to enchant objects and draw from their magic, though that does take years, sometimes decades, of practice unless there is an inherent skill."

Intrigued by his offer, they couldn't turn him down. From their descriptions of their classes, it's slow, frustrating work laying the foundations of spell work, but Ehren is especially eager about the prospect of magic. While Bram, Makin, and Cal all seem to enjoy learning spell work, Ehren is the one that has truly taken to it, even studying books in his bed at night while the rest of us sleep or staying behind in the library to study until a Guard, usually Cal, drags him back to the room for proper rest.

In the evenings we sit together for dinner. By that time of the day, we're all typically worn out from our schedules. We barely speak and just shovel food into our mouths. After dinner we tend to wander back to our room and crash. Last night, however, Bram and I spent a few hours lying in one of the courtyards, staring up at the stars. Being up so late last night is one reason I'm not ready to get out of bed quite yet.

I snuggle down under the covers a little more and close my eyes. I wonder what will happen if I don't show up in the library today. Will Pria care to notice?

"Morning, love! Are you ever going to get out of that bed?" Alak's voice cuts into my pleasant near-sleep.

He can't see me because my curtains are completely closed, but I can make out his silhouette through the curtains. I groan and pull the covers over my head. He chuckles.

"Now, come on. This place isn't worth hiding from. Unless

you and your beloved captain were doing more than just looking at stars last night, and you're just too physically drained. What exactly did keep you up so late, love?" I hear strained amusement in his voice.

"Go away, Alak," I grumble, my voice muffled by the blanket.

"Fine, but if I go away then you won't have any breakfast."

I pop my head up from beneath the blanket. "What? What do you mean?"

"I mean," Alak replies. "That as of right now breakfast is officially ended for the day, so, if you're hungry, you're at my mercy since I managed to snag just a bit of food."

I struggle to free myself from the blanket as I scramble from my bed, throwing the curtain wide. I jump out of bed, wearing only my basic white nightgown.

"What do you mean breakfast is already over? It's not really that late, is it?" I cry desperately.

Alak grins. "Aye, it is. But lucky for you, I brought you this." He holds out a wooden plate bearing a few slices of fruit, an apple, a slice of buttered toast, and kippers.

"Shit!" I yell as I grab my dress from the trunk at the foot of my bed and dash behind the screen to get dressed. "Apprentice Pria probably already has a massive stack of things for me to go through. If I don't get there right now, I'll never get through them!"

I jerk my nightgown over my head and pull on my daily clothes. Today's white dress has a simple golden sash across the waist.

"She sounds like quite the slave driver," Alak says nonchalantly from the other side of the screen. "Are you going to eat this food? If not, I will." I hear him crunch the apple, and I pop out from behind the screen.

"Of course I'll take the breakfast if you don't eat it all first."

Alak offers me the partially eaten apple, and I glare at him, snatching the plate from his other hand. I sit down on the trunk at the end of the nearest bed, taking a bite of the fruit. I'm not entirely sure what it is, but it's sweet and citrusy. I poke at the kippers as I chew on my second slice of fruit.

"I don't understand the appeal of fish for breakfast," Alak muses, watching me poke the kippers. "I mean, who really wants to start the day with fish breath?"

"I agree, but I guess when you live on an island, you get used to eating fish all the time," I reply, shoving the rest of the fruit in my mouth.

"Ah, yes. Gotta love the permanent fish breath," Alak grins.

"Doesn't Felixe like the kippers?" I ask, my mouth full of toast.

"He most certainly does."

Alak gives a low whistle and Felixe appears next to me. He places his two front paws on my leg and leans forward, sniffing my food. He looks up at me with his big blue eyes and blinks. I laugh.

"Even if I loved these stupid fish, I don't think I could resist those eyes." I slide the kippers off the plate in front of Felixe, who scoops them up in his mouth, hopping down to the floor to eat them. Alak grins down at his familiar.

"Felixe has managed to manipulate me out of my food many times with those eyes."

I shove the rest of the food into my mouth and stand, wiping crumbs away. I quickly run my fingers through my hair and pray it isn't a complete disaster.

Alak seems to read my thoughts and says, "You look lovely as always, love." His eyes glint mischievously as he adds. "Even when your hair looks like a sheep that got caught in a tornado."

"Ugh!" I yell as I try to weave my tangled hair into a half-decent braid. "Don't you have somewhere else you need to be?"

Alak shrugs. "Probably." He pauses, tossing the rest of the apple down to Felixe before shoving his hands into his pockets and glancing away, staring toward one of the tapestries on the wall. "May I ask you a question?"

His voice sounds anxious. I pause in braiding my hair for a moment and look at him in concern.

"What? Is something wrong?"

He glances back at me and laughs nervously. "No need to look so worried, love. I was just wondering if you and your captain are actually going to follow through on your proposed marriage."

He looks down at his shoes while I sigh and finish my braid. "Is that all? Can we talk about this later? Or, perhaps, never?"

I try to brush past him to get to my shoes at the foot of my bed, but he places his hand on my arm. When I turn to face him, his face is serious as his eyes lock onto mine.

"I'd like an honest answer this time instead of you avoiding the question again. Let's call it a birthday present. After all, you two were supposed to have a summer wedding. And it's summer. We're at the home of a magical order with no shortage of religious leaders to perform a ceremony. I understand you've been busy, but I have to wonder—do you still intend to marry him?"

His eyes search my face and my heart leaps into my throat. I jerk away from him and rush to my shoes.

"I don't have time for this," I mumble, shoving my feet into my boots and using a bit of magic to lace them up. I look back up at Alak and his eyes are still boring into me. "Why do you need to know?"

He smiles sadly. "I just do, love." His voice is barely a whisper and something about the intensity of his tone sends shivers down my spine.

I shake my head. "If Bram knew you were asking—"

"Oh, I'm well aware," Alak says bitterly. "He's punched me in my face more than once you know. You've witnessed our brawls. I'm almost positive he wants to punch my lights out every time I even glance your way. And I can't say that I blame him. Not really. But my question still stands: are you going to marry him?"

I turn away from Alak. "I can't talk about this right now. I'm already late enough as it is."

"Astra," he says firmly. I'm not used to him using my actual name and I freeze. "Please, just yes or no. That's all I need. A simple yes or no. I don't need a date or an invitation to the wedding. I just want to know—I need to know. Yes or no?"

I take a deep breath and slowly turn back around. Alak stands perfectly straight, his hands clenched at his sides, his expression heavy. Something in me breaks looking into his eyes.

"If I have to say right now at this very moment?" I glance away so I don't have to see his reaction as I say, "I don't know why I shouldn't still marry him."

I look back at Alak to find his eyes closed. He nods his head. "All right, love. That's all I needed to know." He opens his eyes and forces a smile, but sadness and disappointment are written all over his face.

Devastation rocks through me. I've played this conversation over in my head a million times, knowing it was coming. This wasn't how it was supposed to go.

"But I'm not saying I'll marry him for sure anytime soon, if it happens at all," I add quickly, taking a step toward Alak. "Everything is so unsure right now and I—"

Alak holds up his hand and takes a step back. "No. Don't do that. You know why I'm asking. Don't pretend you don't. Please, don't give me false hope, Astra. If you actually cancel your engagement, let me know. But don't backtrack. You want to marry him, so be it. I wish you all the happiness in the world.

I wish you long and glorious lives together. I really do. He deserves you more than I ever will. He's the better match, magic or no." He stops and swallows; everything about his tense movement and forced smile creates an ache in my chest. "Now, if you'll excuse me, I just remembered there is somewhere I need to be."

I can tell he's about to wisp, so I quickly call out to him. "Alak," I say, catching him just in time. He looks up at me. I struggle to find the words, but nothing comes. I can't find the way to voice what I feel, what I want. Instead, I settle on, "Thanks for breakfast."

His smile is weak as he nods and disappears. I wait a moment, fighting down my own emotions, before I follow his lead and wisp directly into the library. Pria looks up at me from behind a pile of books.

"Ah, I see you finally decided to show up," she murmurs, glancing back down at the book she was reading. "I've prepared you several texts to look through that I believe you might find beneficial."

Without looking up from her book she gestures to the massive stack of books and texts. The stack is far larger than anything she's provided me the last couple of days. I have a sneaking suspicion that she's been adding to the pile every few minutes that I was late. I suppress a groan and thank her, settling into a nearby seat as I grab the top text.

Today, I am basically doing the same work I'd been doing with Cadewynn back in Embervein. I'm searching through texts finding mentions of magical sources, animals, and other elements that would be beneficial to our war in favor of magic. Only it's less work here to locate the texts I need. This library has been built and organized around magic, so it's much easier to find the pertinent information. As I search, I scribble my findings in a journal, occasionally drawing maps or diagrams.

It's tedious work, but in the past four days I've made more progress than I ever made in Embervein.

I'm determined to stay on course and not fall behind despite my late start, so I'm writing faster than usual. My hand keeps cramping, and I have to stop every few minutes to stretch my fingers. Pria pretends not to notice, but I catch her occasional smug smile. I'm starting on my second page of notes when a young boy about nine years old appears a few feet away, causing me to jump. Pria finally looks up.

"What is it Matthew?" she asks curtly.

"I have a message for Mistress Astra," he says breathlessly. Pria nods to him and he turns to me. "Master Arcanis has requested your immediate presence in the center courtyard."

Once he's delivered his message, he wisps away. I glance at Pria and she shrugs. Without another moment of hesitation, I wisp. Master Arcanis is in the center of the courtyard with Ehren, Bram, Makin, and Cal. Ehren's face is knit into deep concern and Bram is standing a little too straight. Alak and Kato haven't arrived yet. I quickly cross to the others.

"What's going on?" I ask, glancing from Ehren to Bram.

"It may be best to wait until everyone is here," Master Arcanis says evenly, his presence somehow calming.

I nod. A few feet away a pillar of fire appears, the flames unfolding and sinking into the ground, revealing Kato. Of all the things he's learned, his fire wisping is probably the thing he loves the most and the thing I find the most annoying. He grins at me, but his grin quickly turns to a frown when he sees the seriousness on our faces. Alak pops up directly behind me. I purposely avoid looking at him.

"Good," Master Arcanis says slowly. "Now that you are all here, I will share the latest development. It seems that the Callenian armada is docked off the coast of the mainland and is requesting that we turn you all over immediately."

He says it so calmly I'm almost positive I heard him incorrectly. "What?"

"My father has sent his armada to fetch us," Ehren adds, bitterness stinging in his voice.

"Is the armada a significant threat?" Kato asks, scowling.

"Our armada isn't the largest since we only have a small amount of land along the sea, but it does have a decent amount of force behind it."

I look at Master Arcanis. "What does this mean for us?"

"For now, it changes nothing. The Prime Minister of Portia is requesting a presence with us to discuss our options, but we will not relinquish you to the king of Callenia. We have always protected magic and any positive alliances with magic. King Betron is clearly anti-magic, and we are unwilling to support his cause. Our alliance is with you, Prince."

Ehren inclines his head to Master Arcanis. "And we are grateful for that."

"You are welcome to stay here as long as you wish, under our protection. While we do typically adhere to the laws and wishes of our mother country, we have our own rights. We have always served as a sanctuary for magic. Our walls have never been breached and, while we promote peace and neutrality, many of our members are trained in battle magic, though I must stress that is the last resort. We always strive for a peaceful resolution first and foremost. We have no desire for war or violence of any kind. You will be safe here, but we ask you follow those guidelines. If you desire to leave, we have methods we can use to get you far away discretely. Methods that most people beyond our walls are completely unaware of." Master Arcanis steps back. "I will allow you a moment to discuss this amongst yourselves."

Once he's at the other end of the room, Ehren turns to us,

his shoulders straight. "What are your thoughts?" he asks, looking at us each in turn.

"I think we should stay here for now," Bram says. "We have good footing here. The king can't reach us." Makin and Cal nod in agreement but Kato shakes his head.

"We need to fight," Kato says firmly. "We can't keep running."

"But if we choose to fight we lose any protection we have here," Makin says. "My vote is that we stay. At least for now. See what more we can learn. We can always change our minds later."

Ehren nods. "I'm afraid I agree."

Kato throws his hands in the air. "Of course you do!" he yells. "It's because you're weak, and you don't have magic. If you had magic you would actually have a fighting chance."

"Kato," I cut in. "I have magic, and I'm inclined to agree with them. There are vast resources here. We can use those to our advantage."

Kato shakes his head. "It would follow that you would choose the weaker side."

"What does that mean?" I snap.

"It means that as long as you're linked to him"—Kato spits back, thrusting his thumb toward Bram—"you'll always be too weak to fight like you need to."

Kato reaches his hand for me. "Come with me, Astra. You know we were meant for more than castle politics. Our power is too great to be controlled and manipulated by kings and princes or Prime Ministers and Masters. Together, you and I are the greatest power ever known. The world should answer to us, not the other way around. We need to stop running and cowering in fear. It's time to take action."

I shake my head, tears in my eyes. "No, Kato. No. Not this

way. We have friends and allies." I gesture to everyone around us.

"We don't need those allies!" Kato yells, his voice echoing. He turns in frustration and stalks several yards away before spinning back to face me, his features set and firm, anger etched on every bit of his face. "They're weak and as good as no allies at all. Even those with magic are unwilling to use it until pushed. We deserve allies of power, allies of might who aren't afraid of using their magic to the offensive. But those allies won't come to us if we're burdened down with loyalty to a country who doesn't even want us."

"Friendships and loyalty aren't burdens, Kato. Please, don't do this," I beg. "Just stay and we can work together to find a plan that benefits us all."

He laughs cruelly. "Anything you don't need is a burden if you continue to carry it around. We don't need them. Come with me, Astra."

Some of the Order members that have been hovering near the edges of the courtyard with Master Arcanis take a few steps toward Kato and he sneers, motioning with his hands to surround himself with a circle of flames. The Order jump back as the flames roar to life.

"Come with me, and we can bring magic out of the shadows and to greatness," Kato says once again, parting the flames directly in front of him so I can see him clearly. "We are the only twins in our kingdom. We are different. We are better. We are stronger. Read your prophecies, and you'll see we were meant for greatness. Come with me."

He reaches his hand out, taking a step toward me. I shake my head, taking a step back. "No, Kato. I can't go with you. My place is in Callenia, by Ehren's side, fighting for magic from within. I know this with all surety. I don't need a prophecy for that."

"No!" Kato yells and his flames shoot higher. Everyone except Ehren, Bram, and Alak scurry further away. Even Makin and Cal take a few nervous steps back.

"No," Kato repeats, regaining a sense of composure. "Our place has always been to be side-by-side. We've never really been apart."

"Then stay," I say, my voice breaking. "You once swore to me that you would never abandon me. If you leave right now, that's exactly what you'll be doing—abandoning me." I take a step toward him as I see the pain flicker on his face. "Don't leave me, Kato. You're right. We are meant to be side-by-side, but not the way you're suggesting right now. We need to do this the right way."

Kato's eyes flash with flickering flames. "And why are you so sure your way is the right way?"

"I don't know. Not for sure. But your way incites violence and domination. It's too risky. Too many good people could get hurt. Let's try for a peaceful solution first."

For a moment it looks as if he's considering my words, but then he shakes his head. "No. If I've learned anything here it's that the only way to ensure our victory, to allow magic to truly regain its full power, is by a show of force." Shadows cross his eyes. "If you're not with me, Astra, you're against me. The line is being drawn, and you have to pick your side. One last chance. Will you come with me?"

He reaches his hand out again. I take a shuddering breath, glancing over my shoulder at Bram and Ehren. Bram's eyes meet mine and I can see him pleading with me to stay, but to be careful. Ehren's face is stern, showing no emotion, but he also looks at me and gives the slightest shake of his head. I turn back to Kato.

"I can't," I say, a tear sliding free.

Kato's flames shoot so high they reach the domed ceiling above as he roars, "How dare you choose them over me?"

"You're the one making me choose!" I scream back at him, my own voice reverberating around the hall.

My magic rolls out and swirls around me in silver tendrils, colder than ice. They snap at the air like living, writhing creatures that answer only to me. I snap my wrist and shoot a full blast of icy light toward him, but he closes his shield of fire and my light turns into a hiss of steam. He responds by shooting fireballs at me, but I block each one effortlessly, shooting a snaking tendril toward him. He blocks me again. I explode my power in his direction, engulfing him in a dome of silver light. He builds up his own power and his flames press against the cage.

With each strike my energy wanes and a physical pain stabs my chest. His flames free him from my hold, the ground shaking with the blast. He looks past me and shoots fire toward where Bram and Ehren stand. I'm barely able to throw up a shield to protect them before he shifts his attack to the few members of the Order who remain in the room. I shield them as well and send another attack directly at Kato. He blocks it again with a sneer.

"I don't want to hurt you, Astra!"

"Likewise," I yell back, but I shoot lightning toward him.

He blocks my strike and retaliates. I try to block his attack, but a small flame sneaks past my shield, burning my neck and cheek. I hiss, snapping a hand up to my neck. Kato's eyes go wide. I can tell he wasn't expecting any of his flames to actually make it through my shields. Out of the corner of my eye, I see Bram make a movement toward me, but I hold up my other hand, stopping him.

"Stop this Kato. Stop now and all will be forgiven." Ehren's voice is firm and unshaken.

Kato laughs. "You have nothing to offer to me." His gaze shifts to me. "I don't want to leave without you, Astra, but this is your last chance. Come."

"I will never join you when you're like this," I say weakly, barely audible above the roar of his flames.

Kato takes a deep breath. I can tell he's about to wisp away, lost to me, but there's a movement to my right.

"Wait!" Alak cries out. "I'll go with you."

My eyes snap to him. He looks at me apologetically, his expression heavy, as he strides forward toward Kato.

"I know I'm not Astra, but I do have magic. And you're right. There's no place for magic in the shadows. Let me join you," Alak insists.

Kato considers him and then nods, a wry smile forming on his lips. "At least one of you has sense."

"Alak, no!" My voice breaks as I stumble forward. "Please, don't leave me!"

He doesn't even glance at me as he takes his place at Kato's side.

"I knew you couldn't be trusted," Bram snaps, his voice cold. "Once a traitor, always a traitor."

Tears stream down my cheeks. My voice is quiet as I plead with Alak. "No, please, Alak. I can't lose both of you in one day. Don't go. I . . . I need you."

Alak slowly lifts his eyes to meet mine. My heart beats a steady rhythm as his lips part. I wait to hear him speak, but he remains silent. He takes a half-step toward me but stops, shaking his head.

"Alak?"

My voice is quiet, but I know Alak hears me. In two smooth strides he closes the distance between us and stares down at me, his hand gently wiping away tears from my uninjured cheek. I struggle to read everything written in his expression, but I can't decipher between the many emotions pulsing in his eyes.

He leans in and his lips brush my ear as he whispers, "Trust me, love."

He glances over my shoulder toward Bram and Ehren, saying loudly enough for them to overhear, "One last kiss?"

I nod, struggling to wrap my head around his words. He hesitates only for a moment before he presses his lips to mine, one arm looped around my waist, holding me firmly against his body. Bram yells something from behind me, but I can't focus on his words. This kiss is fierce and all-consuming, unlike any I've ever experienced before. It sets every bit of me on fire while numbing my senses at the same time. It fills something inside me, my magic singing.

When he pulls away, I gasp, catching my breath, and look up into his eyes. He releases me with a jolt that makes me stumble back, and he resumes his place at Kato's side, refusing to meet my eyes. I feel empty, as if a piece of me has been stolen. I have to fight my urge to run after Alak and pull him away from Kato, back to me.

Kato's eyes gleam with the knowledge he has something I want, and he seems to derive some sort of power from my weakness. Alak looks at me one last time, his face unreadable.

"We could have been great, love," he says, his voice uncharacteristically void of emotion. "But you've made your choice."

His name catches in my throat. I give Kato one more look of desperation, but he only shakes his head in disappointment, a cruel smile on his lips as they vanish in a circle of flames, leaving behind nothing but twirling curls of smoke. I stare at the place where they stood seconds before, dropping to my knees. I feel as if all the air has been sucked from my lungs, and I gasp, struggling to find a breath that refuses to come. My heart aches, and it's a pain like I've never experienced. It's as if the entire world is pushing down on me at one time. I lean over and press my forehead against the ground and weep. I'm broken, shattered. I feel a hand on my back.

"Astra," Bram says, voice calm and steady. "You need to see a Healer."

I can't move though. I barely have a desire to live. I feel as if my heart has literally been ripped from my body. There's another strong hand on my arm, and Ehren pulls me upright. I crash into his chest, weeping, and he holds me tight.

"I will find a way to make this right, Astra," Ehren whispers in my ear. "I swear to you."

He scoops me up and passes me to Bram, who cradles me against his chest.

"I will take you to the Healers," Bram says quietly. "We will get you fixed up."

I shake my head and look away. No Healer can truly heal what part of me is most wounded. There is no Healer with strong enough magic.

EPILOGUE

*I*t's been six days since Kato left. Since then, I've been staying in the healing rooms. My burns were easy enough to heal, leaving behind only hints of scarring on my neck and along my left jawline. My strength, however, has yet to return. The Healers say I have no will to live, and they're right. How am I supposed to live with only half my soul? I know I should leave my bed. I know I have responsibilities, especially now that Kato is out there planning gods know what. But I'm hurt in a way I don't know how to heal.

Bram comes to visit me multiple times a day. Sometimes he talks. Sometimes he just sits there, holding me. Sometimes he weeps. I never say anything back to him, and I rarely even look at him or acknowledge his presence. I just can't right now.

Ehren comes at least twice a day. He never enters my room but stands at the doorway watching me. We often stare at each other for several minutes, neither of us speaking, before he turns and leaves.

I know they're both eager to move on, to take the next steps toward uniting magic, heading off Kato's plans, and developing a plan to evade the king's armada. They're waiting on me. That should be enough motivation for me to at least attempt to get up. But somehow, it's not.

I'm too broken, and I don't know how to put the pieces back together.

I turn on my side and stare at the same wall I've been staring at for six days. The wall I may stare at for the rest of my days, however long that may be. I hear a sound behind me, and I assume that Bram must be back for one of his useless visits or perhaps a Healer come to tempt me with medicine or food. When I hear a sharp bark my eyes go wide and I sit up, shifting to look at the chair next to my bed. It's Felixe. He spins in a little circle, yapping happily. I feel a slight smile on my lips—a foreign feeling of late—and I reach my hand weakly to him. He presses his head against my palm and makes a purr-like grumble. He pulls away and barks again before dipping his head down and grabbing a small scroll in his teeth. He inclines his head toward me with a grumbling growl, and I hesitantly take the scroll, unrolling it. The familiar scrawl makes my heart stop and my breath catch.

My Most Beloved Astra,

Please, do not throw this away. Read every word of this. I have much to explain.

I am so sorry I followed your brother. I knew he was going to leave and that you wouldn't be able to stop him. His power has been growing, as has his greed. I saw it and I did nothing. I feel it is my fault for several reasons that he got out of control. So I left with him. I felt there was nothing left for me to do by your side and that I would only be in your way. Here, I will do my best to guide Kato back to you, back to reason.

I know that you and Kato can communicate with one

another across every distance, but I doubt Kato will be so willing now. If my plan works, Felixe should be able to go between us, carrying messages as we need. Consider me your eyes and ears. I will let you know that your brother is still alive and well. I will also share with you his plans as he reveals them to me, if you so wish it. Perhaps, for the first time in my life, I can actually be useful. I've failed miserably to save those I love before, but now is my chance for redemption.

I am sorry I did not write to you immediately. Your brother was wary of me. He knows how much I care for you. I don't think that final kiss helped to ease his mind. I have had to wait and find just the right moment when I knew I could contact you without raising suspicion. I had truly hoped that he would change his mind and go back to you, but he has yet to see sense.

I am not your enemy. I am your ally, and I always will be. Please, never doubt that. I will always choose you. If you need me, simply call out with your heart to Felixe, and I believe he will find you. I will try to communicate with you as much as possible. I won't deny that I miss you already. Hopefully, I can come back to you soon.

Continue to practice your magic. You don't need me or anyone else anymore to instruct you. You surpassed a need for me long ago, and there is only so much you can learn from books. Kato is strong, and when you see him again—for you will face him again—you must be able to stand against him.

You are stronger than this. You will survive this. You are not alone. Even though I will not physically be by your side, I am with you. Always.

Forever your servant,
Alak

I read the note over at least a dozen times. Every time I read it, I gain a little strength. Hope warms the parts of me that have gone cold. Breathing is easier.

Finally, I rise. I scoop Felixe up, and he perches on my shoulder, licking my scars. I stride from my healing room and into the main room where the Healers are working. Their surprised eyes shoot to me. I open my mouth to ask where I might find Bram when Ehren walks in. His eyes go to my face and his lips part before turning up into a smile. When his eyes slide to Felixe on my shoulder, his eyebrow arches.

"I have news," I say, holding out the scroll.

Ehren reads it, brow furrowed. When he's done his eyes meet mine.

"We have work to do," he says. "Are you up to it?"

I nod. Ehren studies me for a moment.

"Good."

When I walk out the healing room door, I know I'm not the same girl that was carried in six days ago. Ehren knows it, too. And it's a good thing. Because the girl I was before could never survive the war I know is coming.

ACKNOWLEDGMENTS

Ah, yes. The acknowledgments. This is the part of the book where the author is supposed to bare their soul and thank everyone who helped their book come about. My problem? I don't even know where to begin. I am so fortunate to have many people in my life who have supported my journey, even before I knew that I had started a journey at all.

My mom has always been one of my biggest supporters. Even before I could really read and write, she was encouraging my love of books. She never let me think I couldn't be a writer. She always encouraged me to follow my dreams.

Other countless members of my family have also supported me throughout the years. Aunts and uncles, cousins, my brother, grandparents, and anyone in-between. Without them cheering me on across the years, I'm not sure I would be here today.

I also feel like I can't leave this page until I thank my friends. Despite my introverted nature, yes, I do have friends, and those friends have supported me in a way like no one else. Even as early as elementary school, I had friends encouraging my writing. Of course, back then I only wrote rambling stories, but they loved them anyway.

In high school my support team gathered more members. Not only did I gain more friends who eagerly cheered me on, but I had teachers who helped me grow. I will forever be grateful to my high school English teachers, Mrs. Wynn and Miss Herdklodtz, for helping me cultivate and sharpen my writing skills.

The last two people I need to thank before I can wrap up this rambling platitude are my husband and my friend Lana.

My husband has been by my side throughout my entire writing journey, encouraging me at every step. He read the earliest drafts and helped me make my story better. He also used his artistic skills to bring my characters to life and create the art that appears on the back cover of my print book. Without his help, this book may have never left my first draft.

Lana was the one who really helped me make the book what it is. She read early drafts and helped me find plot holes and mistakes. She fell in love with the characters and hated others. She gave my writing life in a way I couldn't. She made me believe that I could finish the series and create a world that people would love. Without her and her support, there's a good chance you wouldn't be reading this book today. Honestly, she deserves at least a dozen pages of acknowledgments, but I think my brain is running out of the words I would need to do them justice.

And I guess that's everyone. Well, not everyone. I suppose I can always think of more people to thank. My editor, Andi, who helped make my words better and my story flow. My supporters on social media who cheered me on. You, the reader, who made it this far. There's always someone more to thank, I suppose, but for now, I'm taking my bow until the next book is in your hands. Thank you.

CONTENT WARNING INFORMATION

A few places throughout the book reference abuse by parental figures. The main character, Astra, is threatened and attacked by a man in Chapters Seven and Eight, though she escapes both times and gains the upper hand in each situation. (Chapter Eight is the more descriptive and violent of the interactions.) She also has a brief encounter with unwanted attention and confrontation in Chapter Thirty-Two but it is resolved quickly in her favor.

Chapter Twenty-Five has brief mentions of suicide. One character is mentioned in a story from the past and another tells of their attempted suicide and shows their scars. Both attempts and acts of suicide happen off-page and are not described in detail in this book.

This story also contains mentions of alcohol and gambling.